The Wrong Sister

The Wrong Sister

CLAIRE DOUGLAS

MICHAEL JOSEPH

MICHAEL JOSEPH ·

UK | USA | Canada | Ireland | Australia
India | New Zealand | South Africa

Michael Joseph is part of the Penguin Random House group of companies
whose addresses can be found at global.penguinrandomhouse.com.

Penguin
Random House
UK

First published 2024
001

Copyright © Little Bear Artists Ltd., 2024

The moral right of the author has been asserted

Set in 13.75/16.25pt Garamond MT Std
Typeset by Jouve (UK), Milton Keynes
Printed and bound in Great Britain by Clays Ltd, Elcograf S.p.A.

The authorized representative in the EEA is Penguin Random House Ireland,
Morrison Chambers, 32 Nassau Street, Dublin D02 YH68

A CIP catalogue record for this book is available from the British Library

HARDBACK ISBN: 978–1–405–95759–5
TRADE PAPERBACK ISBN: 978–1–405–95760–1

www.greenpenguin.co.uk

For my family

I've been watching you for a while now. I see you come and go from that grey-brick house with the broken aerial on the roof and the tiles that have gone mossy. You're always in such a hurry, always rushing, rushing, rushing, in your own little world. You stand out with your red hair that sometimes shines like polished copper, but mostly looks as dull and uninteresting as you. I bet you don't appreciate your life, do you? Or your handsome husband or your house with the rose bush in the front garden that I've watched bloom and die? I bet you're too busy thinking about what you haven't got and taking for granted what you have.

That's where I come in. Oh, I'm going to make you wish you'd cherished everything in your life. Treasured it.

Because I'm about to take it all away.

PART ONE

I

TASHA

At the sound of a car I rush to the bay window that over-looks the street, but it's not them. I stare with dismay at the overcast sky. Everything always looks so much nicer in the sunshine but today the modest cottages opposite are in shadow, making them seem dingy. I wonder what Kyle will think of the village. There is a graffito on the wall around the corner, definitely not a Banksy, and the man who likes to camp out in the entrance to the local park is shouting obscenities. There are the lakes, of course, on the edge of the village, which are a tourist attraction in the summer, and the centre of Chew Norton is awash with beautiful listed buildings, cobbled pavements, expensive boutiques and a gastro pub, but the streets surrounding it, where we live, would once have been the workers' cottages. We do have beautiful views of a large pond and the Mendip Hills from the rear, even if they are shrouded in mist at this time of year.

I resist the urge to dust the windowsill again. Instead I shake the cat's hairs off the cushion on the armchair.

'Tasha?' I hear Aaron behind me and turn to see him standing in the middle of the room with a mug in each

3

hand, still wearing his work overalls that smell of turps. 'Relax. You'd think it was royalty coming to stay.'

'Hardly.' I take one of the mugs. It's too-strong coffee. You'd think, after we've been together for nearly eighteen years, he'd remember that I like it weak and milky.

'Alice has been here loads of times.'

Yes, but Kyle hasn't, I think, but don't say. Aaron will only take the piss out of me for wanting to impress Alice's relatively new husband. There's nothing pretentious about Aaron. He never tries to be something he isn't, which is admirable but also, on occasion, frustrating.

'Just because she hasn't lived in Chew Norton for nearly twenty years, she still grew up here,' he says, as though I've somehow forgotten. 'It's not like your childhood home was any bigger than this one.' He plonks himself down on the sofa, and I try not to wince at the indents he's making in my freshly plumped cushions. Our childhood home was the old vicarage, next to the Gothic graveyard I always loved and where Alice and I used to play between the old, decrepit headstones. The house was twice the size of this one, but I don't say it, or how her and Kyle's impressive detached home in London is at least three times bigger than ours. 'I don't get why you're so jittery about it. This was your idea.'

'It was Alice's, actually.'

'You didn't have to say yes.' He slurps his coffee. I can't face mine and put the mug on the coffee-table. My feelings oscillate between dread at them arriving and excitement about seeing them.

'Don't you want to spend a week in their fancy Venetian apartment overlooking the Grand Canal?' I tease.

'Ah, well, now, I didn't say that, did I?' He crosses his ankles like he's settled in for the afternoon. No concept of time, his mother, Viv, always chuckles, as though it's something to be proud of. Yet the longer we've been together, the less funny it is. 'Who wouldn't want a slice of your sister's lifestyle? And we've never been to Italy.'

A few months ago I was offloading to Alice on the phone about how Aaron and I have never had any time to ourselves since our twin girls, Elsie and Flossie, were born and how our wedding anniversary was coming up and, as usual, we had nothing planned, when she suggested we stay for a week in her and Kyle's holiday apartment in Venice. Aaron had jumped at the chance, not least because we only need to pay for our flights and my husband likes a bargain.

And I found myself thinking that, yes, I could be the type of person who whiles away hours in bijou canal-side cafés, quaffing cocktails, or wandering carefree and child-free through high-ceilinged galleries marvelling at the sculptures. I pictured myself and Aaron, tanned and relaxed, kissing on the Rialto Bridge, the years peeled back to reveal the people we were when we fell in love as teenagers: rebellious, fun and besotted with each other. But even though the thought of walking in Alice and Kyle's glamorous footsteps for a week massively appealed, now that it's time to go I'm having doubts. For one thing I've never left our nearly three-year-old twins for longer than a night. And another, I just can't imagine Alice and Kyle living our provincial life for a week. Will they judge us, snigger to each other as they slide between our bobbled sheets? No. I'm being unfair. Despite my sister's success and wealth, she's still the same Alice.

'Although,' Aaron casts an eye around the room and nods approvingly, 'the place scrubs up all right, doesn't it?'

It does. Our house has never looked as tidy. At least, not since we've had Elsie and Flossie. Even so, I glance around with a critical eye – with Alice's eyes – at the internal doors that need repainting, the wooden floor that could do with oiling, the grubby fingerprints on the pale grey walls and the rug that's been clawed by our cream Persian rescue cat, Princess Sofia.

I assess Aaron sitting there in his dirty overalls. 'Are you going to jump into the shower before they get here?' Aaron has been at work this morning at the local garage where he's been a mechanic for the last fifteen years. He has a streak of oil on his cheek and his fingernails are filthy.

'Fine. But I'm not standing on ceremony for them – I don't care how much money they have.' He gets up and stretches his long legs before downing the remainder of his coffee.

Aaron and I met when we were seventeen. He was doing his apprenticeship and I was at a college in Bristol learning Teeline shorthand and how to touch-type. Alice, only thirteen months older than me, was about to go off to university. The first one in our family to do so. *The only one.* And Oxford no less. Aaron has never been particularly impressed with Alice's high IQ or wealth. He's never felt less than good enough and I admire him for that. I just wish I felt the same.

6

He opens his mouth to say something else when we hear the slam of a car door and we turn automatically towards the window. Alice is stepping out of the passenger side of a bright orange sports car, looking stunning in a low-cut jumpsuit, her red hair lying in perfect waves around her shoulders.

Aaron emits a low whistle as he moves to the window. At first I think he's whistling at Alice – who is, after all, a glamorized version of myself – and I'm just about to tell him off for being a sexist pig, when he says, 'Fuck me, it's a McLaren!'

I have no idea what that is but it looks expensive, not that I've ever cared less about cars as long as they get me from A to B. I notice it has only two seats. Nice and impractical when you've come to look after two children. Good job I got Alice insured on my old Honda. Before I can react, Aaron has dumped his mug on the windowsill and is hot-footing it out of the front door. He looks comical in his overalls, which are slightly too short for his six-foot-two-inch frame. I watch, rooted to the spot, as he hugs Alice, and then Kyle is emerging from the driver's side.

I first met Kyle just over four years ago. Alice had introduced him to me and Aaron over sushi in some swanky Covent Garden restaurant. He was like a Greek god. A Greek god in trendy jeans and an expensive Tom Ford shirt (I only knew it was Tom Ford because Aaron had asked him where he'd bought it). Three months later Alice married him in a Las Vegas ceremony while on holiday, without any of her friends or family in attendance – Mum has never quite forgiven her.

7

I watch from the window as Aaron gets behind the wheel, Kyle leaning in to show him the gadgets. I can't help but cringe at this excessive token of wealth on our unpretentious street. What will the neighbours think?

I take a deep breath and leave the room just in time to see Alice tripping into the hallway in heels. 'There you are!' she exclaims, pulling me into her arms and engulfing me in a cloud of perfume. Then she stands back, holding me at arms' length, assessing me, and I immediately feel underdressed in my old Nine Inch Nails T-shirt and ripped jeans. 'You look great. It's been too long.' It's been at least six months.

I want to say, 'Well, if you didn't spend all your time gallivanting around the globe,' but I won't as it would sound churlish and I don't want to ruin this moment. Despite our differences, Alice and I have always been close. Less so since Kyle came on the scene, but that's only because their lives are so busy we don't get the chance to spend much time together. 'It's great to see you. I love your jumpsuit,' I say instead.

'Bella Freud,' she replies, and I nod and pretend I know who she's talking about. She follows me down the hall-way to the kitchen at the back of the house and sits at the wooden table, which is encrusted with dried paint courtesy of the twins. The kitchen is long but quite narrow, with just enough space for a dining table against one wall. Near the patio doors we've managed to squeeze in a two-seater sofa next to the twins' toy chest, but it's already covered with Princess Sofia's fur despite my hoovering it earlier.

'Tea?'

'Oh, yes, please. I'm parched. So, where's Elsie Else and the Flossmeister? I'm desperate to see them.' She's always got special names for everyone, as though we're DJs or in a metal band. I was the Tashatron for years.

I click the kettle on. 'Aaron's mum, Viv, took them to the park this morning.' I don't say it was so I could thoroughly clean the house. 'They'll be back in a bit.'

'I bet they've grown loads.' Alice has always been great with them although she's adamant she doesn't want any of her own. 'I've missed the little munchkins. I've brought them a gift.' Alice's gifts are always too expensive, purchased at posh little Hampstead boutiques, then handed over in fancy gift bags and trussed up in tissue paper. 'Kyle will bring them in from the car.'

I make her a strong cup of tea and place it on the table in front of her.

'So,' she says, as I pull out the chair opposite and sit down. 'Are you excited? We were at the apartment last week and it's such a lovely time of year to go. Quieter than August, but the weather still warm . . . mostly! And the views. So romantic.'

Alice and Kyle bought the apartment last year, their first holiday home. Initially I was surprised they bought in Venice as Alice always said she'd love a second home in Cornwall, until she explained Venice was special to them as that was where Kyle proposed.

'Yes, of course . . .'

Alice must hear the apprehension in my voice because she says, 'I know this is the first time you've left the girls

9

but Kyle and I will take excellent care of them. And we have Viv down the road if there are any problems. Which,' she reaches out and brushes my fingers, 'there won't be!' The implication being that if Alice can hold down a job as a biochemist at a top biotech firm she can look after two little girls. 'You need this, you and Aaron. I know it's not been easy, especially when the twins were babies . . .'

'Don't get me started on the terrible twos.' I laugh to hide my anxiety. Something I'm good at. It had been hard, those early months juggling two babies. Aaron couldn't afford to take more than a fortnight of paternity leave but Viv was a godsend, coming over every day to help me. I don't know how I would have coped without her, especially with Mum so far away. For financial reasons I had to return to work when the girls turned one even though I didn't really want to but, in hindsight, my receptionist role at the dental surgery has been good for me. Viv looked after the girls until recently when they started at a lovely little nursery within walking distance and I could extend my hours to five mornings a week. It finally feels like we're emerging through the all-consuming fug of those early years.

'I've put the schedule on the fridge,' I say. 'What time nursery starts, what time to pick them up. I've left some of their favourite meals in the freezer . . .' I trail off at the look on my sister's face. 'What?'

'Stop worrying. I won't let them out of my sight.'

My eyes well up and it's there, suspended in the air

between us, always unvoiced but ever present. Our Family Tragedy. I blink away the tears, embarrassed. 'You promise?' I say, my voice sounding small.

Alice squeezes my hand. 'On my life.'

I believe her and my anxiety ebbs a little. I know really that the twins will be safe with Alice. She's the only person who truly understands. I often wonder if the real reason my sister has never wanted children of her own is Holly.

Just then Aaron strides into the kitchen closely followed by Kyle, who's clutching two pink gift bags, still talking about cars and mileage and top speeds. Alice releases my hand as Kyle squeezes in on the bench seat next to her and she smiles up at him as he tenderly reaches for her thigh under the table. They are always touching. Even in public their fingers find each other, or they sit so close their legs are pressed together. 'You can tell they haven't been married long,' Aaron had said, the last time we stayed with them, back in March, and there had been bitterness in his tone, something accusatory, and I'd instigated sex that night as a way of proving to myself, and him, that things between us hadn't gone stale. That we could still be spontaneous and sexy.

Will they still be so touchy-feely when they've been married as long as Aaron and I have? Probably.

Kyle catches my eye and jumps up from the table, remembering his manners. 'Tasha. So lovely to see you again.' He crosses the room to give me a brotherly hug. God, he smells good. Then he steps back. 'Love this location. Chew Valley is such a stunning area. All the green space, the beautiful lakes, and the river, of course. It's nice to be back.'

He's never been to stay with us before. 'Do you know this area then?'

'Yes, a bit. I had a girlfriend who was from Chew Magna. A long time ago. We were at Bristol Uni and used to come to Chew Norton sometimes.' Chew Magna is only a few miles away.

I realize there is still so much I don't know about Kyle. I'm not sure what else to say so I ask him if he wants a coffee.

'I'd love one, thanks. Black, no sugar.'

Aaron is leaning against the doorframe, watching us with an amused expression. I catch his eye and he raises one of his dark brows. 'Right, well, I'd better jump in the shower. I still haven't finished packing.'

'Typical man,' quips Alice. 'Always leaving things until the last minute.'

Aaron grins and flicks her a finger in response. She pokes her tongue out at him and rolls her eyes at me in mock exasperation as he leaves the room.

Just then Viv bustles through the back door, all cheery hellos, her short white hair windswept. She ushers Elsie and Flossie into the kitchen where they kick off their wellies and run to me, burying their faces in my legs, while bashfully glancing up at Alice and Kyle.

'Hello, my gorgeous girls,' says Alice, jumping up from the table, clearly delighted to see the nieces she adores. Kyle hands the gift bags to his wife. Elsie, always the braver one, twirls a copper curl around her finger and moves away from me first. She's lured onto her aunt's lap by the gift – a floppy cloth bunny in a pretty dress. After a few seconds Flossie does the same. Within minutes they're acting like they only saw their aunt and uncle yesterday. Flossie is sitting on Kyle's lap and, with her mop of fair hair and big blue eyes, she's just how I imagine Holly would have turned out. A dark feeling settles inside me as I watch them, and I can't push it away. It's the spectre of my baby sister and what happened to her. It's always in the back of my mind. Aaron knew about Holly, of course, even before we started going out. The Holly Harper case had been all over the national news at the time, and sporadically since. A few years ago, after Dad died and just before I got pregnant with the twins, my mum could no longer cope with being branded tragic Jeanette Harper and moved to a rural village in France.

'Do you want me to stay a bit, duck?' asks Viv. She's standing by the back door, already looking surplus to requirements.

'Thanks, Viv, I think it's all okay, but I've given Alice your number in case there are any problems.'

'Not that there will be,' Alice says, looking up and smiling, but I notice the determined set of her chin at the suggestion she might not be able to cope. Alice never fails. At anything.

As we're leaving the house, two hours later, Aaron dragging the suitcases to the taxi and me trying not to cry at the thought of being away from my daughters for a week, I notice the drawing on the pavement outside our front gate. A small asterisk in blue chalk.

I don't think much of it, putting it down to kids or workmen. It's not until later that I realize its significance.

If only it had occurred to me before.

Because if it had, I might have been able to save them.

2

It's dark by the time we arrive in Venice. We've already argued twice, thanks to Aaron's insistence that he knows where we're going – he's never visited Venice in his life – and then proceeding to lead us down one narrow, winding street after another. There's a damp smell of canal water in the air, and all I can see is a phalanx of buildings with flaky walls in shades of ochre, mustard and salmon, with green shutters and little balconies containing drying washing. It's a lot dingier and more oppressive than I'd imagined, and as I trudge up and down steps after Aaron, lugging my suitcase behind me, I wish I was at home, snuggled up on the sofa with the twins and the cat, watching *Peppa Pig*. This is so not me. I've never had the urge to travel, to see the world. I'm a homebody. I still live in the same village I grew up in. I hate crowds and too much noise. Being here has reinforced what I've always known, deep down. I'm not adventurous or exciting. I'm not Alice.

'Not far now,' Aaron calls over his shoulder. He has sweat patches under his T-shirt and, despite the late hour, it's humid, even in mid-October, and my jeans are sticking to my legs. I can tell he's trying to remain positive by making me think he has the faintest fucking idea of where we're going.

I stop to take a deep breath. My mouth feels like the bottom of a parrot's cage and the strap of my bag is digging into my shoulder. 'Wait. I need a rest.'

He spins around to face me, his phone in his hand, the little blue dot flashing on Google Maps. 'It's just down there, according to this.' A gaggle of youths moves around us, chattering away in Italian. I can tell Aaron's pissed off too but he won't want to show it or admit that we're lost. That's not his way. He is, mostly, a very patient person but he never likes to admit he's wrong.

'You said that before.'

'It's a bit further than I thought. But come on, Tash, we're nearly there.'

I hadn't fully comprehended how many canals and winding streets there would be, or how the taxi could only take us so far before dumping us in a car park. We should have got a water taxi but Aaron said they were too expensive. 'I wish I hadn't packed so much stuff.'

Aaron steps towards me. 'Look, it's just around the corner. I promise.' He smiles reassuringly at me. 'St Mark's Square isn't far.' I don't have the heart to tell him I'm not feeling this at all, and that Venice so far isn't anything like I thought it would be.

He holds out his hand and I remember why I'd agreed to this in the first place. I promised myself I'd try to be more adventurous, to make an effort to recapture some of our lost passion and spontaneity. We haven't had sex for months. We're always either too exhausted, or one – sometimes both – of the twins decides to crawl into our bed in the middle of the night and neither of us has the

16

energy to send her back to her own room. We need to reconnect, to see one another as more than just a parent to our children, to spend quality time together.

I take his hand and we walk along in silence, Aaron slightly ahead, leading me through the throngs of people taking selfies on one of the bridges. And then, finally, the streets get more interesting with little shops and restaurants. I can smell pizza and carbonara and my stomach growls. We haven't had dinner yet and it's nearly nine o'clock.

At last the street opens into a huge, bustling square, lined with grandiose buildings, and I stop in awe. Straight ahead is the most stunning of them all: domed roofs, ornately decorated with mouldings and other carvings that Alice would know the name of but I have no clue. It's lit up in golds and creams against the black sky.

'This is it! St Mark's Square. That's the basilica. Isn't it beautiful?' Aaron isn't really into travelling either, but there is something endearing about him having done his homework, and I realize he's trying.

'It's breathtaking,' I reply, meaning it. And suddenly I forget about my blisters and my sore shoulder, and that I only managed to grab a mini tube of Pringles on the plane, and I take in the scene before me, basking in the warm heat of the night, the smell of food, the clinking of glasses and the joyous cries of the children in front of us chasing the pigeons. We stand and stare at it for a while, our fingers interlinked.

'Alice and Kyle's apartment is just around the corner from here. In a palazzo apparently,' he says, looking down at his phone.

I've seen photos, of course. Alice proudly showed them to me after she and Kyle had purchased it. But now that I'm here I'm beginning to grasp just how magnificent the apartment will be and a flame of excitement flares inside me.

I follow Aaron through the square, past the pigeons and the clusters of people taking photos, past the man playing the accordion and the artists offering their paintings. The lights from the surrounding buildings reflect onto the warm pavement. I'm desperate to get there now. I follow Aaron as we wander down a cobbled side-street that is pretty but quiet. And then we're at a set of wrought-iron gates that fronts what looks like a palazzo with Roman pillars and steps leading up to a huge front door.

'Wow. Is this it?'

'According to the map.' Aaron pockets his phone and pushes open the gates with a creak, making a joke about the need for oiling. We wander into the front garden as if we've stumbled into an alternate universe, marvelling at the fountain and the twinkling lights dotting the curved slabs, like rose-coloured cats' eyes. We haul our suitcases up the steps and I take out the set of keys Alice gave me to open the heavy front door.

'Fuck me,' Aaron exclaims, as we step into the huge atrium with marble flooring. The ceiling is painted in strokes of blues and apricots with fat-cheeked babies draped in fabric and floating on clouds. I stand open-mouthed. The cool air hits us as soon as we get inside and a huge vase of white blooms sits on the table filling the atrium with a sweet scent. 'And this is just the communal hallway.'

I laugh. 'It's a bloody palace.' In front of us is a sweeping staircase; Alice and Kyle's apartment is on the first floor.

'Is there a lift?'

I look around for one but all I can see is marble and pillars, silk wallpaper and intricate mouldings. 'Doesn't look like it.'

There are only three doors on the first floor and Alice and Kyle's apartment is number two. I'm brimming with anticipation as I turn the handle and we step inside.

We are greeted with huge windows overlooking the Grand Canal and a domed roof, which, Aaron announces, as though he's reading a guide book, is the Basilica della Salute. Two large white sofas are strategically placed to make the most of the views. (Trust my sister to go for white. I can't even wear a white top without spilling something down it.) A highly polished oval table takes up most of the dining room, which leads into a quaint corner kitchen with cream units and brass handles. Aaron grabs my hand and we wander into the bedroom. The bed is a four-poster with – I silently laugh to myself – silk sheets in dusky pink! Of course. I'd expect nothing less.

'Look, there's even a terrace,' Aaron cries, dropping my hand and sprinting over to the large French windows. The key is in the lock and he turns it and throws them open. 'Oh, my God. Babe. This is just . . . I have no fucking words . . .'

Babe. He hasn't often called me that since the twins were born.

A lump forms in my throat. I feel like I'm in some glamorous film. I can't speak as I follow him onto the wooden decking just in time to see a gondola sail by. A tear slides down my cheek and at the same time I start laughing.

'Are you okay?' Aaron asks softly, placing an arm around my shoulders and pulling me towards him.

I can only nod as I lean into him, and we stand there, inhaling the night air, gazing at the stars punctuating the velvet sky, hearing the water lapping gently at the banks of the canal.

We have sex that night, of course. This place is built for it. And it's not the rushed 'Quick, let's hurry before the kids walk in' kind of sex but the kind we'd had in our early twenties, before stress, demanding jobs, sleepless nights and the pressures of life got in the way. As soon as we arrive back in the apartment after dinner we head straight for the bedroom. And as Aaron climbs naked on top of me I'm shocked when an image floats through my mind of Kyle making love to Alice on this very bed.

The next morning we wake up to rain but it does nothing to dampen our excitement. While Aaron's in the shower I decide to unpack. I throw open the enormous ward-robes. One section is obviously Kyle's – I can smell his scent. The other, much larger, section is my sister's. We've never really had the same taste in clothes – I'm more of a

T-shirt-and-jeans kind of a woman – but I run my hands along the expensive fabrics: floaty silk, frothy chiffon and soft cotton. Reluctantly I turn back to the bed to take my denim dress from my suitcase but it feels stiff and ugly in my hands. And it occurs to me that as I'm living Alice's life for a week, why not dress like her too? She wouldn't mind. Alice is nothing but generous and always has been, even when we were kids. She'd happily let me have the extra biscuit or the last packet of crisps. When she went on a school trip to Amsterdam she brought home a cuddly Miffy for me that she'd paid for out of her own pocket money.

I hesitate. Is it weird to wear Alice's clothes? I look down at the denim dress, which, compared to Alice's finery, looks out of place in this stunning apartment. Sisters share each other's clothes all the time, I reason. I drop my dress back into the suitcase and rummage through Alice's clothes, pulling out a navy-blue and white floaty cotton dress. Alice is about an inch taller than me, and slimmer, with more of a waist (thanks to not spending nine months carrying twins), but even so the dress goes on like a dream. I twirl in front of the full-length mirror, marvelling at how the cut makes my boobs look bigger and my stomach flatter. With our long red hair and green eyes, we could pass for twins, which Alice is always wistful about. Mum told her once that her pregnancy with Alice was a vanishing-twin one. 'I basically ate my sibling,' Alice joked, when she recounted the conversation to me and, despite the flippant remark, I know she wonders what might have been. Selfishly I'm glad Alice's 'twin' didn't survive. I doubt the two of us would have been so close. Maybe Mum wouldn't have gone on to have me. But then I think of Holly and know that's not true.

I'm interrupted from my thoughts by Aaron exiting the bathroom, a towel around his waist. 'Wow,' he says, when he spots me. 'I've not seen that dress before. Is it new? It looks expensive.'

'It's Alice's,' I say.

He frowns. 'That explains it then. Won't she mind . . . ?'

'Course not. Come on,' I say, reaching into one of Alice's drawers and taking out a cashmere cardigan in the softest marshmallow pink. I can't resist picking up one of Alice's handbags, too: a pale ivory Gucci. After all, my beaten-up old rucksack wouldn't go with this outfit. 'Hurry up and get dressed. We've got exploring to do.'

I feel like a different person in Alice's clothes. I'm even wearing a pair of strappy sandals that I found in a shoe-box at the bottom of the wardrobe. I usually stick to black and, when I'm not in my ugly navy-blue dental-receptionist scrubs, I'm always in jeans. But I feel lighter in Alice's clothes. Happier, playful somehow, as though the colours and the frivolousness of them are seeping into my skin, injecting me with joy. I never knew clothes could do that.

It's stopped raining and the sun has come out, glinting off the surface of the canal. Aaron grabs my hand, and we head to a pavement café with views of the Rialto Bridge for brunch. It's heaving but a waiter in formal attire appears and ushers us to a table for two. A constant stream of people drifts by and the waiting staff have to dodge in and out of them, plates held high, as they dart from the café's building to the seating section. I take out my mobile from Alice's designer bag.

'Stop looking at your phone,' Aaron chides, noticing. 'The girls are fine. Your sister can cope, stop worrying and my mum is –'

'Down the road. I know! I just haven't heard anything from Alice this morning, that's all.' She'd texted me last night to ask if we'd arrived safely and to say the girls were in bed.

'We're an hour ahead, remember.'

'And you can talk. I saw you looking at your phone earlier.'

He sits back in his chair, grinning. He looks more relaxed than I've seen him lately. Aaron's always been laid back but I've noticed a tension in him that he tries to hide from me but sometimes comes out when he's overly snappy with Elsie and Flossie. He works hard at the garage, which he loves – he's tinkered with cars since he was a teenager – but it's a physical job and he often comes home shattered. 'I was just checking the football scores. Bristol Rovers played yesterday.' He grins. 'Now order something.' He thrusts the menu at me and I reluctantly put down the phone to take it. 'And no talking about the kids. They're fine.' I wonder what we *will* talk about then.

I don't notice the man at first. I'm too busy perusing the menu and the area is so busy, but when I look up he's standing outside the restaurant, one leg bent, his foot resting against the flaking render and he's staring straight at me. At first I feel flattered – he's probably in his early thirties, good-looking in the rough kind of way I've always found attractive, with a tattoo of a skull poking out of the arm of his T-shirt – until I notice the expression on his face. It's intense. Unfriendly. His gaze moves to Aaron and then back to me. He's smoking a cigarette and, although our eyes meet, he doesn't look away. I drop my gaze to my lap.

When I look up again he's staring at Aaron, who is oblivious, head in the menu. And then the man turns his attention back to me, mouthing something slowly, deliberately. I can't make out what it is. I turn behind me, thinking maybe he knows the people sitting at the next table, but they are chatting and laughing, paying him no attention. Unease settles over me.

My husband, blissfully unaware of my discomfort, is suggesting dishes from the menu. 'What about tomato and mozzarella bruschetta?' he says. 'Or ham and olives? I know you don't like those big green ones, though . . .' When I don't answer he lowers his menu. 'Tash?'

'Don't look now but there's a man over there, standing by the wall. And he keeps staring.'

Aaron narrows his hazel eyes and is just about to turn his head.

'I said *don't look*,' I hiss. 'He just mouthed something to me.'

'Ignore him. I doubt he's talking to you. Why would he?' His attention is once again focused on the menu.

Why indeed? I glance down at my dress – at Alice's dress. 'Maybe he fancies me,' I joke.

Aaron throws his head back and laughs. Too loudly.

'All right, it's not that funny.'

'Sorry.' He concentrates on pulling himself together. 'Of course he fancies you. You're stunning.' His eyes crinkle.

'That's better. But you don't have to sound sarcastic.'

He rests the menu on the table. 'You know I fancy you. Didn't last night prove that? And this morning?'

'Oh, stop. It doesn't take much for a man to want to have sex.'

He looks hurt and is about to open his mouth to say more when we're interrupted by the waiter.

While Aaron is reeling off his order I glance back towards the building, but the man has gone.

3

JEANETTE

Sunday, 13 October 2019

Eamonn hovers at the gate. He looks handsome and sun-kissed in his pale blue artist's smock, with a streak of red paint on the edge of his sleeve. Their group have had a good session today trying to capture the sorbet colours of the sunset on their canvases, but as much as she enjoys his company, Jeanette wants to be on her own now.

'So, I'll see you tomorrow,' she says, from the other side of the gate.

'Oh, yes, Olivier's dinner party. It should be fun.' He smiles, deep creases fanning out on either side of his sparkly blue eyes. He was widowed a few years ago, like her. That was what first bonded them when they joined the adult art class last spring, as well as both being ex-pats, although Eamonn is from County Cork in Ireland. The others in the group tease her about Eamonn having a crush on her. She likes him, and it's been more than four years since her husband, Jim, died but she's still not ready. She'd been with Jim since she was eighteen years old. She's never even slept with anyone else. The thought of another man seeing her body, all those lumps and bumps that she hates but Jim had loved because he'd

26

loved her, makes her feel queasy. Eamonn is a very good-looking man. She expects he's bedded lots of women in his life. She'd just be a disappointment. Better that he imagines the fantasy rather than have the reality of her.

His face falls when he can see that, yet again, she's not going to invite him in. She never does, although he always walks her home after their art class. He doesn't live far, only in the next village, which isn't even a mile away. And at sixty-five he's still fit and lithe, which he credits to all the walking he's done and still does since moving to France in his late fifties.

'So . . . bye, then.' She gives him a little wave as she backs away, clutching her straw bag, which contains her easel and paint, to her chest, like some kind of barrier, then turns and flees down the path. Once inside she breathes a sigh of relief and stands for a while with her back to her closed front door, heart racing. This is her sanctuary. It's only small, with a rustic kitchen and a living room with a stone fireplace downstairs, a bathroom and two small bedrooms upstairs. She'd managed to sell her house in Chew Norton for a lot more money than she paid for it and, with the proceeds as well as the life-insurance money Jim left, if she's careful, she has enough to live on for many years.

She makes herself a camomile tea then goes through to the living room, settles herself on the sofa and calls Tasha's landline.

'Hello,' says a soft, well-spoken voice that straight away she recognizes as Alice's. There's no trace of the West Country twang that Jeanette and Tasha have.

'Hey, love, it's Mum. What are you doing at Tasha's?'

'I'm babysitting, remember? She's in Venice this week.'

'Oh, I thought it was next Saturday that was happening.'

Alice laughs, but not unkindly. Both of her daughters have teased her for years about scattiness. The trouble is, now that she's retired the days just eat into each other. She wonders what Tasha will make of Venice. She was always the home bird whereas, to Alice, the world was her oyster. Her daughters might look alike but they are so different in personality. She wonders what Holly would have been like, if she was here.

'Is everything okay, Mum?'

Jeanette pushes aside thoughts of Holly, not wanting to disappear down a dark tunnel of what-ifs. Even after all these years this train of thought can derail her. Holly is always in her thoughts but even more so lately with the anniversary coming up. She balances her cup on the gingham cushion on her lap with one hand. 'Yes, everything is great.' She tries to keep her voice bright, she doesn't want to worry Alice. Moving here was her decision after all, but she misses her daughters, her grandchildren and Jim, of course. Her life, which had once been so busy, so full of purpose, has been reduced to this. Sitting alone in a stone cottage in a foreign village at least a thousand miles away. It had been out of character for her to up sticks and move. Jeanette Harper, former legal secretary and a one-time member of the WI and the knitting bee, who had lived all her life in the West Country with one man, wasn't the type to do anything rash. She was sensible. Reliable. Jeanette is the type of person who always thinks things through a million times, summing up every possible outcome before making a decision. 'I was just ringing Tasha for a catch-up. It's been a while since we spoke.' They have a WhatsApp group, the three of them, but they only speak on the phone, or on FaceTime, every few weeks. 'I wanted to catch her before she went away.'

'She'll be fine, Mum. It's good for her. They need a break and to have time for themselves.'

Jeanette instantly feels guilty. She should be there to help. Tasha hadn't been pregnant when she left the UK four years ago, and if she had been, Jeanette would never have gone. Moving to France had been a knee-jerk reaction after Jim died, as it had been their dream. She'd gone ahead with it because she didn't want her daughters to have to feel responsible for her. They needed to live their own lives without worrying about her. She'd had to get away, to be anonymous for a while. Yet now she wonders if she'd made a huge mistake.

'So, how's it going? How are Elsie and Flossie? Is Kyle coping okay playing dad?'

'They're adorable.' Alice's voice softens. 'Kyle loves it. He'd make a great father . . .' She sounds wistful and Jeanette wonders if she might change her mind about having a baby. She wonders what Kyle thinks of it. She moved to France not long after Alice met Kyle and, as a result, doesn't know him that well. Alice told her they'd agreed to no children before they got married but, still, Jeanette doesn't understand it. Alice was always so maternal, a great sister to Tasha and then Holly before . . .

She blinks and tries to concentrate on what Alice is saying. She's talking about how they took the girls to see the ducks and how she'd forgotten what a pretty place Chew Norton is. She hasn't lived there since she went to Oxford at eighteen. Jeanette would love it if Alice one day moved back but she knows she won't. The village isn't big enough to contain Alice, who has always wanted to conquer the world. And, anyway, Jeanette isn't there any longer either – things have changed, people move on. She has to accept that.

'The girls are in bed now,' Alice is saying. 'Otherwise I'd FaceTime you to talk to them.'

'What are you having for your tea?'

'Kyle's just popped out to get a takeaway.' Alice hesitates. 'I keep hearing creaks upstairs and think it's the twins getting up, but it's not. Just the unfamiliar sounds of a different house, I suppose.'

'Yes. It's an old house.'

'Our house in London is old too. But we're surrounded by neighbours. I've forgotten how remote it is here.'

'It's not that remote. Not like where I live now.'

Alice chuckles. 'Well, true. I couldn't live where you do, Mum. No offence.'

'None taken. It's not for everyone.' Sometimes Jeanette can't remember why she'd craved such a rural way of life away from everyone she loves.

'I like the hustle and bustle of London. The pond out the back is quite creepy. Isn't that where Fred Watson drowned when we were teenagers?'

Fred Watson had been the local farmer. She and Jim

had only known him to say hello to but his death had shocked the village. 'Yes. He was half cut by all accounts.' The pond behind Tasha and Aaron's rear garden will be misty at this time of year and desolate with the trees losing their leaves, the ground hardened by frost. Tasha has never been creeped out by it, though. She's always been drawn to anything bleak and Gothic. Jeanette remembers her fascination with the churchyard when she was a child, and she always made a big deal of Halloween, even before she had the twins. And Jeanette doesn't even want to think about some of the dirges that used to blare out of Tasha's bedroom when she was a teenager, usually after a row with Aaron.

'I'm probably being silly,' says Alice, surprising Jeanette, 'but a few times now I've looked out the window of the girls' bedroom and . . . No, it *is* silly.'

Jeanette hears the troubled note in her daughter's voice. 'What is it?'

'It's just . . . I don't know. It's like I've got the sense of being watched.'

'You've seen someone lurking around outside?'

'No. I've not seen anyone. It's just this feeling . . . Like I said, it's silly.'

'You've just forgotten what Chew Norton's like, I expect,' Jeanette replies. She leans forward to place her cup on the coffee-table. The room is in semi-darkness now: she needs to close the curtains and turn on the lamps. 'Trees everywhere. It's a very safe village. And you live in London. Crime Central!'

'I know, but London is busy. There are always people

about.' She pauses, and Jeanette senses there is more she wants to say. Alice isn't given to flights of fancy – that's more Tasha's domain. 'Anyway, Kyle's just come in with our fish and chips so I'd better go. Love you.'

'Okay. Enjoy your takeaway. Love you too,' Jeanette says, ending the call. Then she sits where she is, in the half-dark, and instinctively touches the locket around her neck that contains one of only a few photos she has of all three of her children.

4

TASHA

Sunday, 13 October 2019

'So which outfit of Alice's are you going to choose tonight?'

From the full-length mirror I can see Aaron behind me. He's bare-chested, his half-dozen tattoos on full display. He has Elsie and Flossie's names wound around the top of his left arm. Above his right pectoral muscle there are two love birds that he'd had done on his stag do when he was drunk, a rose on the other side and a snake by his shoulder. On his back he has a few more. My mum has never approved, even of the ones of her granddaughters' names, but I've always liked a man with tattoos. I've even got one myself, an outline of a cat on my hip that I've never told my mum or Alice about.

I'm standing in my underwear holding up dresses in front of me, deciding what suits me best. In theory they all should but some are too girly for me.

'Maybe this one?' I hold up a black full-length strappy dress and matching bolero jacket. Smart enough for dinner at a nice restaurant but not too fancy. Some of these in Alice's wardrobe would definitely be classed as gowns.

'Very nice.' Aaron comes closer and encircles my waist. 'Do we have time . . . ?'

'No!' I push him away. 'I've just had a shower and you've booked that restaurant for eight.'

He shrugs good-naturedly and retreats from the bedroom saying he's going to get one of Kyle's lagers from his endless stash. He's opened the French windows and I imagine him sitting on the balcony in just his jeans, drinking lager and soaking up the view.

It's been a good day and we even managed to get in a gondola trip (despite Aaron moaning about how expensive it was). We spent a good couple of hours perusing the shops on the Rialto Bridge and exclaiming over how much everything cost, considering which extravagant piece of jewellery we would buy if we won the lottery. A stranger kindly took a photo of me and Aaron with the Bridge of Sighs behind us, and afterwards we wandered around the streets stopping every now and again in little pavement cafés. Even though I was missing the girls, it felt lovely to be able to sit and enjoy a cappuccino without having to worry about how to occupy them, or lugging around a bagful of colouring books, crayons and snacks.

Earlier, as we rested our aching feet in a café, Alice FaceTimed us. All four of them popped up on the screen and my heart had lurched at the sight of my daughters, but they all looked happy. Flossie was chatting excitedly about how they'd been to the park and the pond to feed the ducks. It's exactly the kind of Sunday-afternoon family time I love the best.

'So, how is it?' Alice had asked, after the girls blew me kisses and then disappeared from view.

'It's amazing. Your apartment is stunning.'

'We were speechless last night, weren't we, Tash?' Aaron said, over my shoulder, too loudly. Alice had grinned and Kyle gave us the thumbs-up. Alice hadn't seemed to notice that I was wearing her clothes.

'We knew you'd like it. Isn't Venice just the most romantic place? We love it, don't we?' Alice turned to Kyle, who nodded.

'It's one of my favourite cities,' he said, his eyes softening as he gazed at Alice. 'It's where I proposed to your sister. You must take a gondola.'

'We already have, mate,' Aaron said, throwing his arm around my shoulders. See? his manner was saying. *I* can be romantic too.

I stand now and assess myself in the mirror. The burnt amber of my hair stands out against the black, the jacket sitting just on my waist. I eye the dress I wore earlier, discarded on the bed. There is a little laundry room just off the kitchen: I'll have to make sure to wash it before hanging it back up. I spilt a drizzle of coffee down it earlier, so small it's hardly noticeable, but now I worry it might stain. The dress probably cost a small fortune.

I'm applying a quick lick of make-up in the enormous bathroom when Aaron walks in. 'So, what do you think? Should I wear one of Kyle's shirts?' His eyes flash and I hope he's joking. Explaining to Alice that I've worn some of her clothes is one thing, but I can't see Kyle being so accommodating. It would come across as weird. 'You don't have to look so horrified. I'm teasing!' He laughs and walks out again. When he returns he's wearing his favourite pale blue Fred Perry.

I put down my lip-gloss. Aaron leans over the wash-basin to slap some aftershave on his face and elongates his jaw as he does so. It's so familiar, something he's done every day for years, and I feel a surge of fondness towards him. 'You look nice,' I say, even though he looks like he always does whenever we go out. Dark blue jeans, tick. Fred Perry, tick. If it's cold, maybe a jumper or a jacket, and once in a blue moon, a shirt if it's a really special occasion, but that's as far as he'll deviate.

Even though it's October it's warm as we step outside, and the sky is darkening. We hold hands as we cross St Mark's Square and I'm struck once again by how stunning it is, how bustling. People are sitting drinking wine and eating at the white-clothed tables that line one side of the square. A man is playing a jaunty tune on a cello. Crowds have clustered in front of the basilica. People swarm around, some in groups being led by a tour guide, others just milling about, taking photos or chatting. The air smells warm. I feel a swell of happiness. This is the best anniversary. I'm finally beginning to relax and worry less about leaving the twins.

Earlier, while walking to the Rialto Bridge, Aaron saw a restaurant he liked the look of. He wanted to chance it tonight – Aaron is not a planner – but I told him to book a table and now I'm glad he did as the outside terrace is packed. It's similar to where we had brunch this morning, and is next to the Grand Canal with the dome of the basilica in view. Coloured lanterns hang from an over-head canopy, reflecting pinks, blues and greens in the surface of the water.

'This is romantic,' he says, after we're shown to our table. He reaches over to hold my hand. I think of the text message I'd found on his phone a few weeks ago from the attractive new receptionist at the garage where he works and fold it away in the depths of my mind. I won't think about that today. I don't want anything to ruin this moment. And it meant nothing, just banter, as he said at the time. I'm not worried, *exactly*, more conscious that we haven't made much time for each other since the twins were born.

'Shall we have a bottle of wine?' he's saying now, pushing a lock of golden-brown hair from his forehead.

Rain clouds have gathered in the night sky but it's warm here on the busy terrace with the overhead lanterns. I shrug out of Alice's jacket and hang it on the back of the chair. 'Sure.'

'Excellent.' He scans the drinks menu. 'It's all in Italian,' he laughs, 'but I think this one . . .' he points at the word 'Sangiovese' '. . . this is probably like a Sauvignon Blanc.'

Neither of us is a wine connoisseur. 'Sounds great.'

Aaron orders a bottle and it arrives briskly. 'So,' he says, holding up his glass and clinking it against mine, 'happy anniversary. Can you believe it's been nine years already?'

'No.' *And yes.*

We don't bother with presents, or even cards. Not any more. Maybe it's because we were together for so many years before we got married. Although when we were nineteen we split up for nearly a year. I look at him now, sitting opposite me. Thirty-four years of age, a father, a husband. I know he loves me, loves the kids and the life we've built. We've come a long way. And this trip, it's been good for us. It's what we needed. Alice had been right about that.

I sip my wine and then we order food. A huge plate of creamy carbonara arrives at our table. And we drink too much, and laugh like we haven't for a long time and I remember how funny he is, how dry his sense of humour, how much I enjoy his company.

And we don't talk about the kids once.

As we're getting up to leave, the sky lights up and thunder growls. A sudden wind whips a napkin from the table and upends an empty wine glass. We weave through the tables as it starts to rain heavily and I hold Alice's jacket over my head.

'Quick, this way,' calls Aaron, grabbing my arm as we run down a side-street. A souvenir shop is still open and we dart inside, laughing, already drenched. Alice's dress clings to my legs. A gust of wind blows a bin over and we watch it from the safety of the shop as it takes off and clatters down the narrow street. 'This is exciting.' Aaron exudes energy, his eyes bright. He asks the man behind the counter if he has any umbrellas. We pay an extortionate amount for a large green one with 'Italia' written down the side and venture out again. The rain is still bucketing down and we huddle underneath it. 'Come on then, we'd better head back. I think it's this way.'

'You think?'

'I'm sure.' He smells of wine and his hair is rain-soaked, making it look tousled and sexy, and impulsively I reach up and kiss him. When I pull away he blinks at me in surprise. 'What was that for? Not that I'm complaining.'

'I do love you,' I say, emboldened by the three glasses of wine I'd had at dinner.

'I love you too. Wow, we should come away more often.'

Aaron holds the umbrella over us both and I loop my arm through his, leaning into him as we head down a narrow back-street that runs parallel with a ribbon of canal and the backs of hotels with their boat moorings. With the rain, the dark sky, and no longer being in the thick of things, everything looks drab and unease settles over me.

'Shouldn't we head back to the main thoroughfare?' I ask.

'This is a shortcut. It's fine.'

We turn the corner and the pathway narrows even further with steps leading down to the adjoining street. There isn't room for anyone to pass us, not that anyone else is around. The spokes of the umbrella scrape the wall of the building as we pass and the canal water is black and menacing, the rain making the surface ripple. I grip Aaron's arm harder and shiver.

'Are you okay?'

'I'd rather get back to where it's busy. It's a bit creepy around here.'

'It's fine.'

'I keep thinking about that film . . .'

'Which one?'

'*Don't Look Now*.' I shudder as I remember it: Donald

Sutherland's character's obsession with the red-coated figure he's certain is the ghost of his dead little girl that he keeps glimpsing around gloomy off-season Venetian streets, a bit like this one. Aaron had made me watch it once, not long after we first started going out, and I'd been so freaked out by the ending that I couldn't sleep that night.

'I thought you liked the macabre.'

'Yes. From the safety of my own home.'

He laughs. 'Don't be such a wuss.'

I'm just about to retaliate when I spot a figure hunched by the wall of one of the buildings. At first I think it's someone who has stopped to smoke but when they look up my stomach turns over. It's the man from the restaurant this morning, the one who was staring at us. He narrows his eyes as he sees us approaching. Is he following us or is it just a coincidence he happens to be in our path? Aaron is oblivious, chatting away about a horror film he's been trying to persuade me to watch for ages. By now we're only a few paces from the man so I can't say anything in case he hears us. I tell myself it's just a coincidence. Maybe he lives here. These buildings look like the backs of apartments, with their shutters and tiny balconies. The rain continues to splash down and every now and again lightning flashes, turning the sky a dark green, rolls of thunder following close behind. The air smells of wet pavements and canal water. My heart picks up speed as we go to walk past the man. He's just standing there, smoking, staring right at us. Aaron doesn't notice and I deliberately avert my eyes. As we approach I hear him mutter something to us in Italian.

'*Tu mi devi . . .*'

Aaron slows down and my insides turn over. *No, don't stop, don't stop*, I silently urge. But of course he stops. Aaron's not confrontational, as such, but his height coupled with his innate confidence means he's always been secure of his place in the world. As he often tells me, he knows how to handle himself.

'Huh?'

'Come on,' I hiss. I don't like the way the man is looking at us. His eyes are cold and his body language hostile.

The man just stares at us. '*Tu mi devi,*' he says again.

'We don't speak Italian,' says Aaron. The rain drums on our umbrella.

And then I notice it, the flash of silver by the man's thigh, and my blood turns cold when I realize what he's holding.

A knife.

5

ALICE

Sunday, 13 October 2019

Alice surveys the destruction in the kitchen. Jesus, kids are messy. Half-used poster paints, wet brushes, splodges of Play-Doh and bunched-up sheets of paper are strewn across the table, and the tiled floor is littered with dolls' clothes and pieces of pretend wooden food. A Barbie's legs are poking out of the gap in the sofa's cushions and she's sure she has the spike from a tiara embedded in the sole of her foot.

Kyle wanders in with the traumatized look of a road-traffic-accident survivor. He indicates the wet patches on the knees of his jeans. 'And this was just the result of them cleaning their teeth.'

She laughs. 'I'm fucking exhausted and now we have to tidy up. They're like two whirlwinds.'

'More like tornados,' he says drily, picking up an upturned tub of paint and looking at his smeared hand in dismay. 'This stuff is everywhere.'

'Why don't you clear the table and I'll start on the floor?'

'You're the boss.' He uses some of the balled-up paper to wipe the red paint off his fingers.

They work in companionable silence, Tasha's cat, Princess Sofia, eyeing them from the comfort of the sofa. Alice dumps an armful of dolls and teddies into the wooden chest by the back door, and as she's clearing away the fish-and-chips cartons Kyle comes up behind her and wraps his arms around her waist. 'You know they're just going to get it all back out again tomorrow, don't you?'

She grimaces. 'At least they have nursery tomorrow morning.'

'I need wine.'

They vowed not to drink too much, not while babysitting the twins, but Alice has never been as desperate for alcohol. 'Why don't you open that bottle we brought from home?'

'Okay,' he says, resting his cheek against her back. 'I'm too exhausted to move.'

She laughs. 'Why did we sign up for this?' She's joking, really. She adores her nieces.

'God knows.'

Their reflection plays out on the opaque glass of the patio doors in front of them: her in soft grey cashmere loungewear and him with his chin resting gently on her shoulder, their bodies the shape of two inverted commas. And then she remembers the state of his hands and pulls away. 'You'd better not get paint on my jumper.'

He spreads his fingers to show her his palms. There's something childlike about his gesture. 'It's dried now. Right, where's that bottle?'

She indicates the cupboard above her head and watches

as he pours them both a glass. She just wants to veg out on the sofa and not move or speak for hours.

Kyle kisses her temple. 'You go up and make sure the twins are asleep and I'll take these into the living room. I'll get the film ready.'

She heaves her body up the stairs. How can being with two children all day make her feel like she's competed in a triathlon? She's used to working hard. Her hours are long and mentally arduous yet this is like nothing else.

'Aunty Alice,' they chorus, when she walks into their bedroom. They're tucked up in bed, looking angelic. Flossie has her thumb in her mouth and Elsie proffers a book to her.

'Why aren't you asleep?'

'Please,' Elsie begs, her eyes wide.

'Just one quick story,' she says, taking the book, *Angelina Ballerina*, and sitting on the edge of Flossie's bed. She read this to them last night. As well as three others. And she'd read *Tabby McTat* when she'd put them to bed more than half an hour ago.

After she's been cajoled into reading two more stories, she's back downstairs where she slumps onto the sofa next to Kyle and he hands her the glass of wine. 'I can't speak.'

'You're great with them.'

'They're taking advantage of me.' She laughs.

Kyle shifts on the sofa, his earlier affability replaced with a nervous kind of energy. He's lit the gas fire and the small room is hot and soporific. James Stewart's face is paused on the TV screen.

44

'What's wrong?' she asks.

'I had a phone call while you were upstairs.'

She inhales sharply. 'Right?'

'It was Noel at the lab. He's still having issues with the design.'

Her heart sinks. Not this again.

In the four years since they've been together she's come to understand that Kyle is like a kid prodigy whose brilliance needs to be carefully nurtured, moulded, and her role in his life is to reassure and bolster him. He lost his parents in a car accident when he was in his early twenties and she's sure this is where some of his need comes from. They'd met in a bar while out with different groups of friends and he'd been fascinated as soon as she'd told him she was a biochemist. She knows that one of the things he finds most attractive about her is her intelligence.

She switches into her usual patter about how these are just teething problems and the product will revolutionize the health industry, just like she has done a million times before.

He downs the rest of his wine and refills his glass. 'I'm worried.'

'I know, but we've overcome other hurdles, haven't we? And we can overcome this as well.'

'You don't understand technology. And the science is so . . .' He knocks back more Chablis.

There has been an endless litany of problems with the product. The concept is brilliant in theory – an electronic toothbrush that can detect heart disease, diabetes and multiple cancers from a person's saliva with instant data downloaded onto a mobile app. They'd been so excited when they'd come up with the idea two years ago. Ever since they'd met, back in 2015, they'd wanted to combine their superpowers and this was something that had fuelled their passions – her biochemistry knowledge and his technical background. And Alice was happy to be the silent partner and adviser. She's always made clear that this is Kyle's project, that she can't put her name to it because it would then be the property of her employer. If it works it will make him even richer than he already is. He's always been fuelled by money even though that isn't what motivates her. It seems the more money he has the more he wants.

'I was thinking of approaching Stan Swanson at Philips.'

She hesitates. 'Okay. Good idea. As long as he understands it's far from ready. But let's not think about work for tonight.' She reaches up and kisses him. He tastes of wine. 'Let's have a nice evening in front of the fire and finish watching *Vertigo* before I start to fall asleep.' It's a standing joke between them that she can never stay awake long enough to finish a film.

She's relieved when he reaches for the TV remote.

Alice checks on the twins before they turn in for the night. She stands at their bedroom door and watches them for ages, snuggled up with the bunnies she'd bought them, and her heart melts. She couldn't love them more if they were her own. Flossie has her thumb in her mouth,

46

her mop of blonde curls covering her eyes, and Elsie's face is pressed almost to the wall. Tasha has decorated their bedroom tastefully with soft pinks and warm whites. 'Love you both,' she whispers. She'd only shared a room with Tasha for a brief period when they were little and Holly had had her own room. She still remembers her baby sister's bedroom, the cot with the colourful elephant mobile, and how she'd lie on her back, her chubby starfish hand reaching for it as she gurgled happily. She was only in their lives for four short months, and now when Alice thinks of Holly it's like remembering a dream just after you've woken up: the more you pore over it the less clear the details.

She hasn't told Tasha but she's started a savings account for the twins. She's not sure how her sister will feel about it as she can be so weird about money. But Alice has plenty, thanks, in part, to Kyle, and she wants to provide for them. Is that so bad? She knows she'll never have kids of her own so why not save it for them? Tasha and Aaron struggle financially – that was why she'd offered them the Venice apartment. Why have nice things in life if you can't share them with the people you love? That's always been her motto. Tasha is one of the most important people in her life and Aaron is like the brother she never had. In the world she inhabits day to day, usually full of either rich or eminent people in biochemistry, being around Tasha and Aaron and their lack of pretensions is like breathing fresh air. Despite where she lives, how she dresses and the money she has, she'll never forget her roots.

Alice closes the door quietly behind her and makes her way to the spare room where she and Kyle are sleeping. It's a small double with a window overlooking the lovely little garden with the apple trees and the slide Aaron had installed for the twins, and, beyond that, the pond. Alice is ashamed to admit she finds the pond creepy. She used to tease Tasha about her interest in the supernatural or the spiritual, her logical scientific brain refusing to consider the possibility of it. But the view of the pond, especially at night, with the mist floating above it, like a gossamer cloth, and the reeds bending and stretching in the wind is right out of a Charles Dickens novel.

She closes the curtains forcefully and turns back to the bed, where Kyle is already asleep. She stands and watches the rise and fall of his chest, his lips slightly parted, the smell of alcohol seeping out of his pores. He'd drunk a lot more than her tonight. She gets in beside him and he adjusts his position so that his arm drapes over her. She curls into him and tries to sleep but, thanks to nodding off in front of the TV, she's now annoyingly wide awake.

Alice must eventually fall asleep because when she opens her eyes with a start, some hours later, she's covered with sweat and her heart is beating fast. She lies there for a few seconds, listening, trying to calm her breathing.

She nudges Kyle. He opens his eyes. 'Wh-what's going on?' he says groggily, as he shifts his weight onto his elbows. 'What's wrong?'

'I don't know ... but I'm sure I heard something. Downstairs.'

Kyle sits bolt upright and throws back the duvet. He

steps onto the carpet and grabs his phone from the bed-side table. He's only wearing his boxer shorts and he seems a bit unsteady on his feet. 'I'm sure it's nothing but I'll just go and check.'

She clutches the duvet to her chin, her heart still racing. 'I can't remember locking the back door ... The girls were in the garden earlier.'

'Stay here.' The moonlight casts a veil-like shadow over his bare shoulders.

'Okay,' she whispers, her heart hammering.

He disappears out of the bedroom door and she waits.

6

TASHA

Sunday, 13 October 2019

I'm frozen to the spot for a few seconds and I feel Aaron's body stiffen beside me. He's seen the knife too.

Without another word he yanks my arm and we continue down the narrow street, picking up our pace. I glance up at the umbrella above our heads, wondering if we could use it as a weapon if it came to it.

'What the fuck?' he mutters, under his breath, without looking at me.

'Keep walking,' I urge, but my heart is pounding so much I can feel the vibrations in my throat. By now we are almost running, our arms still interlinked.

Despite the rain I can hear footsteps behind us and know, without needing to turn, that the man is following us.

'What does he want?' asks Aaron. I can hear the panic in his voice.

'I don't know.' I look down at Alice's designer bag. Maybe he wants to mug us.

Still holding the umbrella we unlink arms and break into a sprint. Aaron reaches for my hand and I take it as we round the corner. Behind us the footsteps also pick up speed. We have no idea where we're going and the streets are a maze. We run up some steps and I pray that it leads us to an area where there are people. The main thoroughfares are always so busy. Trust us to end up in these lonely lanes. Fear propels me – I've never run so fast in my life. Should I just toss him the bag if that's what he wants? It's not worth dying for.

And then, thankfully, we come out onto a main street. It's heaving and Aaron clutches my hand as we melt into the crowd.

'Turn right,' he urges, his breath catching. 'St Mark's Square's this way.' We slow down and zigzag in and out of the people. Aaron's palm is damp.

'Is – he – still behind us?' I can barely get the words out I'm so breathless.

'I don't know. But keep walking. We need to get back to the apartment.'

'He can't see where we're staying . . .'

'He won't. We'll lose him first. Trust me.' Aaron practically drags me through the square, in and out of the crowds. The sea of umbrellas is hopefully obscuring our pursuer's view. I'm so grateful we're surrounded by people that the desperate fear of earlier begins to dissipate. Aaron looks over his shoulder. 'I think we've lost him.'

I stop and put a hand to my chest.

'Keep moving. We can't afford to stop.' Aaron tugs at my hand and I quicken my pace. His mouth is set in determination and my heart starts racing again. As we leave St Mark's Square we sprint around the corner, through the gates and to the front door of our apartment building, as though we expect the man to be lurking in the bushes. It's not until we're standing in the atrium, the front door firmly locked behind us, that we allow ourselves to take deep breaths of relief.

'I'm sorry, Tash,' he says, his shoulders sagging, finally taking down the umbrella where it drips onto the marble floor. 'I should never have led us off the beaten track.' He glances at my outfit. 'You shouldn't dress in Alice's fancy clothes any more. You're a walking target.' He trudges up the stairs and I follow, my heart heavy, my legs weak.

Wordlessly, Aaron goes into the kitchen and takes a can of lager from the fridge, opening it and downing it in a few large gulps. His hand trembles.

It's not until we're getting ready for bed that I tell him. 'It was the same man I saw at brunch. The man who mouthed something at us.' I hang Alice's damp dress over the bath.

Aaron looks up from the washbasin where he's brushing his teeth. 'What? Are you sure?'

'Yes.' I never forget a face. Aaron is the opposite and, while not exactly face blind, he isn't great at remembering people. 'Do you think he was following us?'

Aaron straightens up and wipes his face with a fluffy hand towel. 'I doubt it. Just luck on his part, I suppose. He couldn't possibly have known we were going to walk that way.' But he looks worried and sadness washes over me that our perfect anniversary has been tainted by this.

'He had a fucking knife,' he says, as we climb into bed. 'What was he doing walking around with a knife?'

My legs are shaking with delayed shock and Aaron folds me into his arms so that I'm lying on his chest. 'It was so scary,' I begin. I let him comfort me for a few minutes and then I move away so that I'm resting on my elbow. 'What did he say to us? It was in Italian but can you remember?'

Aaron frowns and reaches for his phone on the bedside table. He brings up Google translate. 'Something about tui . . . tuey me?'

'*Tu mi devi,*' I say. 'That was it. What does it mean?'

He taps it into his phone, the screen lighting up the concentration on his face. '*You . . .*' he says, and pauses, turning to look at me. '*You owe me.*'

You owe me. What did he mean? 'Owe him for what?'

'Maybe it's not literal. Like, it's a way of saying that we needed to give him money? I think he was just an opportunist. Maybe that's what he does. Mugs tourists who end up along dark, lonely streets. It was stupid of me. Venice is still a city. I wouldn't do it in Bristol so why would I take that risk just because it's a beautiful place?' He puts his phone back on the table. 'I'm sorry,' he says again.

I turn off the light and snuggle into him. 'Stop saying sorry,' I mumble. 'We just know not to do that again.'

We lie there, unable to sleep. I know he's reliving it too. What if something had happened to us? Who would look after the twins? We haven't even made a will. I vow to do that as soon as we return home.

After a while Aaron reaches for me, pulling me to him, and begins kissing my neck and I let him although I'm no longer in the mood, knowing it's a distraction, for both of us.

*

A high-pitched noise wakes me. I blink into the darkness, disoriented, until I realize it's a phone ringing. I notice a chink of light is pressing in on either side of the shutters.

'Aaron.' I prod him. 'Your phone's going off.'

'Wh-what?' He sits up and reaches for it. I'm wide awake now, my body breaking out into a cold sweat. It's six a.m. Why would someone be ringing us this early? 'It's my mum.' He turns to me, his eyes panicked, and I feel sick. It would be five a.m. in the UK right now. Something bad must have happened. 'Mum?' he says, into the phone. 'Everything okay?'

I can't hear what she's saying but Aaron's face pales and my stomach turns over. *Something's wrong.* 'The twins? Are they okay?' He barks into the phone, then turns to me, his eyes wide. 'Okay, okay, Mum, slow down . . .'

My body flashes hot and then cold. 'What is it? What's happened? Are the girls okay?' I feel as if my lungs are being compressed.

He moves the phone away from his ear. 'They're fine. They're with my mum. There's been – there's been some kind of incident.' He holds up his hand to stop me speaking. 'Go on, Mum.'

He nods while he listens. I can hear Viv's panicked voice, although I can't make out what she's saying. 'Shit. Okay. We're coming straight home. I'll ring you once we know flight details . . . Yes . . . Okay, I'll tell her.' He glances at me, his face grave. Then he ends the call.

'What's happened?'

'It sounds like . . .' He swallows, his eyes not leaving

mine. 'It sounds like there's been a break-in at our house. The twins thankfully slept through it all and are with my mum, but . . . Alice and Kyle, they were attacked.'

'Oh, my God!' My hand flies to my mouth in horror, heat whooshing to my face. 'Are they okay?'

I'm horrified to see his eyes filling with tears. The last time he cried was when the girls were born. He shakes his head. 'I'm afraid not . . . ' He hesitates, a shadow passing over his face. 'Alice is in hospital. A head injury. And Kyle. Fuck, I don't know how to say this. I'm so sorry, Tash. But Kyle. He's dead.'

7

TASHA

Monday, 14 October 2019

We travel home in a daze, my mind swimming.

'I can't believe that this has happened,' I say, over and over again, on the plane. We had to wait around at the airport for hours for the next available flight to Bristol. I'd felt like a caged animal and I couldn't settle so forced Aaron to walk circuits of the lounge with me.

Aaron is sitting in the aisle seat, his long legs cramped in front of him and he's unable to keep his feet still. 'I've texted Mum our flight number and she's going to pick us up at the airport. She's got the girls with her.'

I'd spoken to Viv briefly while waiting to board and she assured me that Alice was apparently in a stable condition in hospital and the twins were safe. I'm so desperate to see them that I want to scream. Patience, unfortunately, has never been my strong point at the best of times but now I feel as taut as a piece of wire. The thought that my daughters could have been hurt, or worse, makes my blood run cold. I just want to gather them into my arms and never let them go. 'Who found them?' I scratch at my wrist. My eczema flared up as soon as it began to sink in that Kyle is dead.

'I don't know.' Aaron is flicking through an in-flight

magazine but I can see he's not taking any of it in. 'They're safe. That's all that matters.' Without looking at me he reaches over and takes my hand. We sit in silence after that, weighed down by our own dark thoughts. Tears keep streaming down my face and I'm thankful I'm sitting by the window, partially hidden by Aaron. I keep thinking of Alice in the hospital with a head injury. The worry is making me queasy. I feel helpless and impotent trapped here on the aeroplane, unable to call anyone or find out any information.

Were Alice and Kyle attacked in a burglary? Is that what happened? If so, I bet it was that car, that stupid expensive car. Just like Alice's Gucci bag could have been a target for the man last night.

I can't believe Kyle's dead. Every time I think about it the back of my throat burns. Alice's Greek god of a husband. Affable, intelligent, kind. If Alice died too I couldn't bear it. And then I think of my mum, *my poor mum*. She's already lost one child . . .

'Alice will be okay. She's a fighter,' says Aaron, as though reading my mind. We've landed now and I'm so desperate to get off the plane I feel like rugby-tackling all the people in front of me. I need to see for myself that Elsie and Flossie are unharmed. I need to go to the hospital and see Alice.

'I'm so worried about Alice,' I say, brushing at my eyes as the woman in the row next to ours keeps flicking concerned glances my way. 'Has anyone told my mum?'

'I don't think so, not yet. Unless your mum is Alice's next of kin, which is doubtful . . .'

'Someone should tell her. She'd want to know.'

'Okay, okay. Let's get off the plane first. Why is it taking so fucking long?' Aaron very rarely loses his temper but I can see he's barely suppressing his rage. We're at the back and have only shuffled a handful of steps. A young guy with a blond hipster beard a few people in front of us seems to be taking ages to retrieve his bag from the overhead compartment and is blocking the aisle. Aaron looks wretched, as though someone has punched him in the stomach. His face is so pale it's almost grey. I must look the same. We've already had a few concerned stares from the other passengers, others averting their eyes, our abject misery making them uncomfortable. I grab Aaron's hand, bring it up to my lips and feel him relax.

Eventually Hipster Beard unplugs the way for the rest of us. It doesn't take long to get through baggage claim and finally, *finally*, we're outside the airport and being reunited with our little girls. I cling to them so tightly that Elsie lets out a small cry before I reluctantly let them go so they can hug Aaron.

'Sorry we couldn't come inside,' says Viv indicating her grey French bulldog, Freddie Mercury (named because he has a slick of darker fur under his nose that looks like a moustache). He sits at her feet, his head cocked, his too-large ears drooped forwards. Viv has already explained to Aaron that she hasn't told the girls yet. I'm not sure what she has told them but, knowing her, it will have been the right thing. She has a magic touch with her granddaughters, just like she had with Aaron and his two younger brothers over the years. Her short white hair stands up at the back, as if she hasn't had time to brush it and she's in a checked shirt, jeans and no coat, despite the chill in the air. She never wears make-up. ('Oh, I can't be bothered with all that,' she'd often say, whenever she saw me applying my mascara.) She's a tough cookie, from a working-class background in the East Midlands, who moved to the Chew Valley with her husband, Ray, when she was pregnant with Aaron. Ray died when Aaron was only fourteen and Viv never remarried, devoting her life first to her sons, then her four grandkids and now Freddie Mercury.

Because this isn't the right time to ask about Alice or talk about what happened to Kyle, our conversation in the car on the way home is a strained attempt at jovial as Viv drives us the six miles to our village. I sit in the back of her Astra, which smells of the dog, who is in a crate in the boot. The girls are either side of me and their babble – about *Peppa Pig* and going to see the ducks yesterday with Aunty Alice and Uncle Kyle – is a good distraction. Even so, I have to concentrate on not crying. Flossie, the more sensitive of my daughters, has already asked why my eyes look all 'small and puffy' and I had to pretend it was my allergies playing up.

'What's happened to Princess Sofia?' I ask Viv, in a sudden panic. She's a house cat and doesn't like to go outside.

'She's fine,' says Viv, her warm brown eyes meeting mine in the rear-view mirror. 'She's at my house and, don't worry, she gets along fine with Freddie Mercury. The police say you'll need to stay with me for a few days, just until . . .'

'I understand.' My voice comes out husky and I clear my throat. I turn back to the girls, letting their innocent chatter soothe me.

Half an hour later we've pulled up outside Viv's pebble-dashed semi just around the corner from us, where Aaron grew up. The house is so familiar to me and has hardly changed since I started going out with him, although the bedroom he shared with his younger brother, Jason, has been turned into a guestroom, and the one that used to house Stuart now has bunk beds for when the grandchildren stay – mostly Jason's kids when they visit from Manchester.

Viv ushers us all into the house and the girls run straight upstairs, with me shouting after them to make sure they hold the banister.

'I need to call the hospital for an update on Alice,' I say, upending my bag on Viv's pine kitchen table. 'Where the fuck is my phone?'

I feel Aaron's hand on my shoulder. 'It's here, Tash,' he says, picking it up from the detritus and handing it to me. He meets my eyes, his expression full of sympathy.

Viv passes me a number she's written down on a piece of paper. 'Southmead Hospital. I'll make you a cup of tea while you call them.'

'Thanks,' I say, taking it and rushing into the dining room next door, which has been set up as a kind of den with a large doll's house, a PlayStation for Jason and Lauren's kids, who are eight and ten, and a cupboard full of plastic toys. I plonk myself down on a pink and white spotty beanbag and call the hospital.

'Am I able to come and see her?' I ask after the nurse has given me an update on Alice's condition to say she's no longer in ICU.

'Yes, of course. Visiting hours are until eight p.m.'

'So . . .' I swallow my emotions '. . . she's going to be okay?'

'Yes. There is no swelling or bleeding to the brain. She's been very lucky.'

I think of Kyle, the love of Alice's life and, no, she hasn't been lucky at all. But I thank the nurse and end the call, a surge of relief spreading through me nevertheless. My sister is going to be okay. Thank God, thank God.

I go back into the kitchen to tell Aaron and Viv the good news.

'That's brilliant,' says Aaron, jumping up from the table to hug me.

'I'm going to see her.' My heart plummets again as I remember that Kyle didn't make it, acknowledging this rollercoaster feeling of elation and heartbreak. 'I'll call my mum on the way.'

Viv rustles in the kitchen drawer and retrieves a set of car keys I recognize as mine. 'Here,' she says, dropping them into my palm. 'The police gave them to me, knowing you wouldn't be able to access your house for a few days.' It's a Honda that is nearly sixteen years old, and Aaron's is a clapped-out banger he's always 'doing up' yet it spends most of the time sitting in our garage. 'I noticed both your cars were safe when I went to pick the kids up from Maureen's in the early hours of this morning,' she says.

Maureen and Arthur are our next-door neighbours. She's in her late seventies, a bit of a busybody but kind enough. Arthur spends most of the time in his shed, tinkering with his model railway. Maureen called the police last night and kept an eye on the twins when Alice and Kyle were taken to hospital.

Suddenly Viv looks exhausted and sinks onto a nearby chair, as though her legs are no longer capable of supporting her. She must have been up for hours. I dread to think what time she received the phone call this morning.

'Thanks, Viv,' I say, bending to kiss her cheek, and she pats my shoulder affectionately. 'I'd better be off.' It's only a five-minute walk to our house. I hand my cup to Aaron.

'Do you want me to come with you to see Alice?' he asks.

'No. You stay with the girls.'

He looks disappointed. 'At least let me walk with you?'

'Okay. Come on then, or I'm going to hit all the traffic.'

We pass Viv's car on the way out. The suitcases are still in the boot and Aaron promises to bring them in when he gets back. I think of all the clothes unworn, the dress of Alice's that I never got the chance to wash and that is still hanging in their Venice bathroom. My eyes fill again at the thought of their apartment and that Kyle will never go back.

'Do you think the girls heard anything?' I ask, as we walk briskly to our house.

'I don't think so,' he says, taking my hand. 'Mum said a policewoman had to wake them up. God,' he shakes his head, 'I dread to think what could have happened.'

62

The thought makes me feel sick.

When we turn into our road (named Blackberry Lane although there aren't any berries in sight) I'm shocked to see crime-scene tape around our small front garden. But, of course, it *is* a crime scene. Kyle was *murdered*. I swallow a lump in my throat. I still can't believe this has happened. We stand and watch in silence as a man in police uniform walks with purpose from our front door to a parked van. I imagine the forensics team in our living room, combing every inch of our house, violating it. The home we've lived in for more than ten years, the house that's always been my sanctuary, the place that after a stressful day at work I can't wait to retreat to, where we brought our twins home in matching car seats, my stomach still sore from the planned C-section, still in shock that we had two small babies.

Up ahead, outside our house, we see the bright orange McLaren, like a flashing beacon to attract thieves and degenerates.

Aaron's silence is loaded and I wonder what is going through his mind. Is he thinking what a shame it is that we were on the verge of reconnecting, of falling in love all over again, that for once we actually had time for ourselves, for sex, for intimacy, and it was cut short? He would never say it, he can't, because in the grand scheme of things it would sound selfish and heartless, and I would resent him for it, even if I might be thinking the same. I push away the guilt. My emotions are all over the place.

'This is our fault,' I say eventually, breaking the silence. 'If they hadn't stayed here, if we hadn't done that stupid life-swap thing . . .'

'. . . then it could have been us.' He runs a hand through his unkempt hair. He's wearing last night's Fred Perry, dark patches under the arms despite the grey skies, and I realize he must have got them running away from the man with a knife.

I freeze, thinking about what Aaron's just said.

'Last night . . . that man . . .' I begin. What an awful coincidence that not long after we were running for our lives Alice and Kyle had been fighting for theirs.

He lets out a long, troubled sigh. 'Don't think about that now. Go and see your sister. Make sure she's okay. I'll see you back at Mum's later.' He brushes my cheek with his lips and then I get behind the wheel of my Honda.

This whole thing has rocked my small, secure world. How am I ever going to feel safe in our house again? In any house? But crime happens in this village, of course. After all, look at what happened to Holly.

It's nearly six by the time I pull up in a multi-storey car park near the hospital. It's a good five- to ten-minute walk from there so I ring Mum on the way. It would be seven p.m. in France right now. The reception isn't always great in the place she's renting, somewhere in a little village in the middle of nowhere. I've only ever visited her once, although she's lived there for nearly four years, and I was pregnant at the time, but it's been trickier since the twins were born. At least, that's what I've always told myself. I understand why my mum would want to move to a place like that, some-where she can be anonymous, but I'm also hurt that she moved so far away, especially now she has grandchildren.

When there is no answer I leave her a message to call me back urgently.

I wonder what she's doing and why she can't answer the phone to her daughter on a Monday night at seven o'clock. Maybe she's out with friends. Or a man? And then I realize. Today is 14 October. Tomorrow is the anniversary of when we lost Holly. I say 'lost', but that implies it was our fault, as if we misplaced her somehow, like you would a pen, or an earring, when in reality someone took her from us.

Thirty years ago tomorrow my baby sister was abducted.

8

Alice is sitting up in bed when I arrive. She's been moved to a ward. I can see her from the open doorway but I pause before I go into the room. What the hell am I going to say to her? This is the first time in my life when I feel I don't know how to speak to my own sister. She has a bandage wrapped around her head and she's resting against the pillow, her eyes closed. Her face is so pale it's almost the same colour as the pillowcase, and with her red hair spread around her, like a halo, she reminds me of a woman in a Rossetti painting. The ward is quite small, with four beds, three of which are occupied by women of various ages.

I'm still standing by the doorway when a young nurse walks out of the room. She smiles when she sees me. 'Are you here to see Alice?'

'Yes. I'm her sister.'

'She's doing very well, considering. Don't be too alarmed by the black eye. That's been caused by the blood from the head trauma seeping into the soft tissue.'

I feel as if my heart is being squeezed. 'Thanks,' I say, touched that she's taken the time to reassure me. I must look as nervous as I feel.

I take a deep breath and walk into the room, taking a seat in the uncomfortable blue chair next to Alice's bed.

Another woman, younger than me, is in the opposite bed, an older man sitting beside her and reading a Stephen King novel while she sleeps. I'm assuming – hoping – someone has broken the news to Alice about Kyle. I don't want to be the one to do it. And then I inwardly berate myself for being selfish. Maybe it would be better coming from me. Maybe . . .

Alice's eyes flutter open. 'Hey, the Tashatron is in the house . . .' She tries to smile but I notice tears on her cheeks. Her voice sounds raspy and sore.

'How are you doing?' I ask, swallowing the lump in my throat. There is a purple bruise that blooms over one of her eyes, the lid puffy. 'It's a stupid question, I know.'

'I feel . . .' Her voice cracks and she lifts her head off the pillow.

'No, don't try to move.'

She flops back down. 'I – I can't believe he's gone . . .'

I blink back my tears. 'God, I'm so sorry, Alice. I'm so, so sorry . . .'

'It hasn't properly hit me yet.'

I take her hand. I notice the other one is hooked up to a drip. 'I'm not surprised. It's the shock of it all.' The thought that someone has done this to my sister, that someone has hurt her, killed Kyle, makes me by turns furious and devastated. She looks so vulnerable in the hospital bed with her bandages and her drip that I long to wrap my arms around her, something I've not felt before.

'The twins,' she yelps, her face contorted with fear. 'Are they okay? Oh, God, please tell me they're okay.'

'Ssh, they're fine. They slept through it all.'

67

'Thank God.' She visibly relaxes, although her anguish and grief are still written all over her face. 'I wish I could remember more about it.' Her voice is slightly slurred and I suspect she's been given a sedative. 'All I can remember is that we were in bed and there was this noise . . . this noise coming from downstairs . . . and Kyle, he . . . he . . .' Her face crumples.

I gently squeeze her hand. 'You don't need to talk about it.'

'. . . he went down to see what was going on. And when he never came back up I got out of bed and went down too. But he was . . . he was just lying there, on the carpet . . . Oh, God . . .' She starts sobbing and I get up from the chair to hug her to me, careful not to dislodge the drip.

'Oh, Alice,' I say. I'm crying too now. I can't bear to see her in so much pain. She sobs on my shoulder for a while and I stroke her hair, just like I do with Elsie and Flossie when they're upset. She smells of hospitals and something sharp and medicinal, the fabric of her bandage rough against my cheek. Eventually her sobs subside and she moves away from me. 'You don't have a tissue, do you?'

'Always.' I take a packet from my bag and hand her one.

She blows her nose and composes herself, propping herself so that she's sitting more upright in the bed. 'Well prepared, huh? Now you're a mum.' She tries to smile but I can see it's an effort. 'I'm on so many fucking painkillers.' Her hand hovers above her bruised eye but she doesn't touch it. My sister is usually so strong, so stoic and capable. I've rarely seen her vulnerable. Even when we were kids. Although, once, not long after she'd graduated from Oxford with her PhD and had her first proper job in biochemistry, she'd rung me in tears, saying she felt like she was out of her depth surrounded by all these 'male chauvinist pigs', who talked down to her and didn't listen to her. 'It's such a male-oriented field,' she'd said at the time. 'I don't know if this is for me.' And then something must have clicked because suddenly she was flying, winning awards and promotions. Later, she told me she'd had to harden herself, almost put on an act as it was the only way to get through it. I'd admired her for that. She hadn't let fear faze her. And now she's going to have to learn to be strong all over again.

'So what happened after you found Kyle?' I ask carefully, sensing she needs to talk about it.

'It was . . . it was all so quick. When I saw Kyle lying there I didn't have time to react before I felt a blow to the back of my head and then I felt someone push me hard and I remember this searing pain and then . . . nothing . . .' She reaches around her head and flinches before moving her hand back to her lap. 'It was all so quick,' she says again, her voice sounding small, her fingers playing with the edge of the blanket. My stomach turns as I think again about the girls being in the house at the same time as an attacker. 'I didn't have time to think. Neither of us did. And we'd been drinking, Tash, Kyle more than me, but I wonder if – if that had dulled his senses.'

How much had Alice been drinking? I swallow my

disapproval that she was drinking while in charge of the girls. I like a drink as much as the next person, but Alice and Kyle weren't used to being in charge of two young children.

'The police will find whoever did this,' I say, sounding more convincing than I actually feel. It must have been a burglary gone wrong and, for the first time since I found out about it, thoughts briefly enter my head about what they might have stolen. We have nothing of real value in the house, apart from the electrical equipment, but that's insured. No, the only things of real value are my children, who are now safe at Viv's, and my sister sitting in this hospital bed. And Kyle . . .

Alice's eyes change from sad to furious. 'I want to kill whoever fucking did this to Kyle. To the love of my life. Oh, God, Tash. How am I ever going to live without him?' Fresh tears slide down her cheeks and I don't know what to say. What can I say? Nothing will make this better. We're silent for a few moments as we sit there holding hands, and then she says, 'Does Mum know?'

'I've tried to call her but there was no answer. I've left her a message asking her to call me back urgently.'

'You don't happen to have my phone or handbag with you, do you?'

I shake my head. 'I'm sorry, I don't. Maybe they're back at the house. The police are there at the moment.'

She looks as if she wants to tell me something but then closes her eyes, a flash of pain in her face. 'I feel dreadful,' she murmurs. 'This headache is like nothing I've ever felt before.'

70

'Do you want me to fetch someone?'

'No.' Her nose is red from all the crying and her eye is purpling by the minute, but the rest of her face is unnaturally pallid. 'Stay with me,' she murmurs, without opening her eyes, and my heart breaks just that little bit more when she adds, 'I feel safer with you here.'

I try ringing Mum again on the way back from the hospital but it goes straight through to voicemail. The first seed of worry takes root. We usually catch up on the phone at least once a week and she often forwards me and Alice funny memes on our Three Musketeers WhatsApp group. We've been in touch even more frequently since Dad died. I know his death compounded the grief that Mum's always felt about Holly, and for a while afterwards, I did worry about her mental health, but she came over to visit in May and she seemed back to normal: happier, more vibrant and admitting she loves her new life in France. She's planning to come in November for the twins' third birthday.

By the time I get back to Viv's house it's nearly eight o'clock. My mother-in-law is in the kitchen washing up mugs when I walk in.

'Hi, duck,' she says, looking up from the sink. 'Aaron's just upstairs with the girls. Flossie got a little bit tearful at bathtime. I think they're overtired.'

I race upstairs to Viv's tiny box room. An IKEA flower wall light casts a pink glow over the room and I see Aaron lying on the bottom bunk, his eyes closed, Flossie and Elsie cuddled up either side of him, fast asleep in the

71

crook of his arm. My heart aches and I creep forward, kneeling beside them. Aaron immediately opens his eyes.

'Is everything okay?' I whisper.

He grimaces. 'They were asking about Aunty Alice and Uncle Kyle. I had to tell them about Kyle, Tash. I'm sorry. I know we planned to do it together but I couldn't keep it from them.'

I feel a thud of disappointment. 'What did you say?'

He moves carefully from underneath Flossie and she wriggles away in her sleep so that she's resting next to her sister. He inclines his head towards the door and, after kissing both twins on their warm, soft cheeks, I follow him into the spare room where we'll be sleeping tonight.

He takes my hand and I sit next to him on the bed. 'I just said there'd been an accident and that both Kyle and Alice had to go to hospital. I then told them Kyle died. They asked me about Heaven. I said he was with the angels.'

I start crying again. I believe in life after death but Aaron doesn't. 'Thank you for saying that.' I squeeze his fingers and he wraps an arm around me.

'I didn't mention an attacker, or a break-in. Or any of it. I don't want them to know that. I want them to feel safe in their home.'

'I agree.' I sniff, wiping my eyes with the back of my hand. Princess Sofia saunters in and I gather her up in my arms, feeling the comforting brush of her whiskers against my chin. 'There you are,' I say, into her fur, relieved that she's okay. 'I hope Freddie Mercury is being nice to you.'

We head back downstairs, the cat in my arms. When

Viv sees us she instructs us bossily to sit at the table and eat her lasagne. Princess Sofia wriggles out of my arms and scoots off. The dog, who is lying spread-eagled under the table, barely raises his head. 'You need to look after your-selves,' insists Viv, as she dishes out huge dollops onto our plates.

'Viv, you shouldn't have.' I don't know when she would have found the time or energy to make this.

'I just defrosted one I'd made ages ago. It was no bother.' Once she's finished dishing up she sits down and tucks in. I feel my stomach turn over. I usually love any type of pasta dish – only last night we were in a little Ven-etian restaurant eating carbonara – but I have no appetite. I think of Alice in the hospital, heartbroken and injured. I think of Mum in her little cottage in the depths of France and wonder why she hasn't called me back. I think of Holly and how, this time thirty years ago, this was the last evening we'd get to spend with her. But I don't want to hurt Viv's feelings so I make an effort to force down a mouthful.

'How's your sister?' Viv asks, spearing a piece of carrot with her fork.

I try to push away the image of Alice sobbing on my shoulder. 'Physically not too bad, although she's got one hell of a bruise on her eye and her head was in bandages. But it could have been so much worse. Emotionally, though . . .'

Viv coos sympathetically. 'Of course. Such a terrible thing to happen.'

'Mum said two policemen came here when you and I

were walking to the car,' says Aaron, grinding salt onto his food.

I sit up straighter. Authority figures always make me break out into a nervous sweat, even though I know they only want to speak to us to help. I was arrested once, when I was nineteen, for being drunk and disorderly in Bristol and actually thrown into a prison cell to 'sober up'. I'd been young and going through a bit of a rebellious phase. Aaron and I had briefly broken up and Alice was living her best life at Oxford University and I had felt I was a disappointment to everyone. It had been a self-fulfilling prophecy until I'd managed to wade out of my self-pity pool and sort my head out.

'Oh, okay. It's bad timing that we missed them. What did they say, Viv?'

She swallows before answering. 'Not much. They said they'll come over in the morning. I'm assuming you won't be going back to work this week?'

We'd both taken a week of our annual leave to go to Venice and, as far as our employers are aware, we're still there.

Aaron takes a sip of water. 'I'll probably go back on Thursday. What?' he says, when he notices my expression. 'There's no point wasting leave, is there?'

I can't plan that far ahead. 'Alice will need me,' I say. 'So I'm not sure what I'll do yet.'

'Tim knows I'm back anyway.' Tim is Aaron's boss.

I frown. 'How?'

'I popped into the garage on my way here earlier. I know how short-staffed they are since Alec left.'

I'm about to reply when I hear a noise by the doorway. I turn to see Flossie standing there, clutching the cloth bunny that Alice and Kyle had given her just a few days earlier.

'Darling.' I jump out of my seat and go to her. Her cheeks are red and it looks like she's been crying. 'What is it?'

She leans into me, wrapping her pudgy arms around my neck. 'I was scared.'

My heart sinks. 'It's okay,' I soothe. 'We're all here.'

'I was worried you hadn't come back.'

I exchange a concerned glance with Aaron. 'Come on,' I say, lifting her onto my hip. 'Let's go back to bed. You can sleep with me tonight if you want.'

Aaron puts down his knife and fork and goes to get up but I shake my head at him. 'Finish your supper. It's okay. I'll stay with her.'

When I've settled her next to me in the double bed she turns to me, her eyes heavy. 'I heard a big bang last night. A big, big bang . . .'

I go cold.

'It woke me up. And then . . .' her lip quivers '. . . and then I was scared and it was dark and I didn't want to get out of bed and make Uncle Kyle cross.'

'Uncle Kyle wouldn't have been cross, sweetheart.'

'He got cross because Elsie splashed him.'

I know how rambunctious they can be at bathtime. 'He wouldn't have meant it.'

'I'm sad about Uncle Kyle.'

'I know. Me too.' I cuddle up next to her. 'Try to get some sleep.'

'Why was there a big bang? Is that how Uncle Kyle died? Because of the big bang?'

Had she heard Kyle getting attacked? 'I think it probably sounded like a much louder noise because it was in the middle of the night,' I say. She wriggles further into me and before long I can feel her body relax and her breathing change. But I don't go back downstairs. I lie there, looking up at the ceiling, my daughter's little body curled into mine, and inwardly berate myself for leaving them. It had gone against my instincts but Alice and Aaron had persuaded me and now look what's happened.

What else had my daughters heard last night?

9

TASHA

Tuesday, 15 October 2019

When I wake up in the morning the bed is empty and Princess Sofia is curled up on Aaron's pillow. Last night Elsie, realizing her twin sister was missing, snuck into bed with us too.

I head downstairs in my dressing-gown to see Aaron at the kitchen table with Viv and the girls, eating a bacon sandwich that was no doubt made by his mum, his hair wet from the shower.

'Do you want some bacon, duck? There's some still left in the pan.' Viv hovers over her seat.

I shake my head. 'Thanks, but I'm happy with cereal.' I pull the packet of Rice Krispies towards me.

'Mummy,' cries Flossie, noticing me for the first time. She jumps down from her chair to run over to me. She climbs onto my lap and I give her a big hug. She's wearing her Winnie the Pooh nightdress and her blonde curls spiral over her shoulders. I breathe in her familiar smell of biscuits and strawberry shampoo, as it hits me again how thankful I am that they weren't hurt. She rests her head against me, sucking her thumb. Viv is helping Elsie cut up her toast, but my headstrong daughter is determined to do it herself, even though she's only succeeding in tearing it. Freddie Mercury sits beneath the chair hoping for scraps.

'What time are the police coming over?' Aaron asks, between mouthfuls of bacon butty.

'They said sometime before noon,' replies Viv, giving up trying to help Elsie. She starts clearing away the breakfast bowls.

'Sit down, Viv. I'll do that,' I say, feeling guilty, but she tells me not to be silly and continues clearing up.

'Come on, girls, let's get you dressed,' she says. Flossie jumps down from my lap, her thumb still firmly in her mouth. Elsie follows, dragging a stuffed bear by its arm, and the dog trots after them.

'She likes doing things for the girls,' says Aaron, when Viv and the twins have left the room.

'I know but I don't want us putting on her.' I pour milk onto my cereal.

'We're not.' He finishes off his butty and gets up to take his plate to the sink.

'Did the twins say anything more about Kyle or Alice this morning?' I'd told him what Flossie had said to me when he came up to bed last night.

'Flossie asked if she could see Alice in the hospital but I told her she should be coming out soon.'

'I'm not sure when she'll be discharged,' I say, swallowing a mouthful of cereal. 'I'm worried about the girls. I'm not sure I want them seeing Alice in the hospital.'

'Tash,' he says gently, 'it's important you don't make it into an even bigger thing than it is.'

He thinks I'm over-protective anyway, and I know I am after what happened to Holly. I wasn't that much older than the twins when it happened, but I know I'd be a different person if my sister had never been stolen from us.

'I won't. But I just worry about how this will affect them psychologically. Who knows what they heard that night? I can't bear the thought that Flossie was too scared to move after hearing a noise . . .'

He leans back against the worktop and folds his arms across his chest. He's wearing an old Primal Scream T-shirt he must have found among the things he left behind when we moved in together in our early twenties – I haven't seen it since we were teenagers. I'm amazed it still fits. 'I think they slept through most of it. Flossie might have heard Maureen or the police gaining access, not the actual attack.' He moves towards me so that he's standing behind my chair, then leans over and kisses the top of my head. 'I know today is always difficult,' he says, his tone sympathetic. Aaron isn't the type to dwell on the bad things in life and he won't make a thing about this being the anniversary of Holly's disappearance, but I appreciate him letting me know he hasn't forgotten.

'I'm going to try Mum again,' I say, getting up and handing him my half-empty bowl. 'And I'd better get dressed before the police show up.'

When the police arrive an hour later, Viv takes the girls and Freddie Mercury to the playground. I'm already on edge because I still can't get hold of my mum. The female detective introduces herself as Detective Constable Chloë Jones. She's around my age with a short dark bob and is

79

wearing a long wool overcoat and a brightly striped scarf. Her colleague is mid-twenties, with a round, freckled face. I've already forgotten his name.

'First,' says DC Jones, as they take a seat opposite us and she unwinds her scarf from her neck, 'I want to say how sorry we are about your brother-in-law.'

I murmur a thank-you as I sit stiffly next to Aaron, reminding myself that I am no longer that awkward and unhappy nineteen-year-old who got arrested. Still, there is something about being in such close proximity to the police that puts me on edge. 'I'm your family liaison officer,' she explains, in her soft Welsh lilt, 'so I'll be your first point of contact.'

The male detective adds, 'There has been a spate of burglaries in Chew Norton and the surrounding villages, and at the moment one of our theories is that this could be an attempted burglary gone wrong but we, of course, will be doing a thorough and detailed investigation and looking at all avenues of enquiry.'

'Have you found the murder weapon?' asks Aaron.

The murder weapon. A chill comes over me when I think about how Elsie and Flossie were in the house when their uncle was murdered. I try not to picture Kyle's last moments or Alice's horror at finding him.

'Not yet,' says DC Jones. 'Their injuries suggest they were both hit from behind with a blunt object. We will do everything we can to recover that object and we will be checking CCTV and Ringcams along your lane and surrounding roads. Unfortunately there is no CCTV behind your house or around the pond.'

'Do you know how they gained access?' I ask. 'Is there any sign of a break-in?'

The male detective shakes his head. He has a kind face and pale brown eyes that crinkle at the edges even when he's not smiling.

'There are no signs of a break-in and all your windows were closed and secured. Unfortunately your patio doors were unlocked.'

Alice and Kyle left them unlocked? For fuck's sake. Why weren't they more careful? I doubt they'd have done that in London. Did they feel a false sense of security because they were in a village?

DC Jones leans forward. 'Do you know if either Kyle or Alice had any enemies?'

I reel. *Enemies?* It's not a word I associate with my sister, who has always been well liked, making friends easily, unlike me. I take longer to trust people. 'No. Not that I know of. Alice has always been popular and sociable. I can't speak for Kyle because I haven't known him that long.'

'How long?' asks DC Jones.

'Well, we first met him about four years ago, but only saw him a few times a year. Also,' I glance at Aaron, then back at the detectives, 'when we were in Venice a man followed us with a knife. We thought it might have been random but Alice and I have the same red hair and build and . . .' I can't bring myself to say I was wearing her clothes '. . . maybe he thought we were them.'

DC Jones frowns as she writes this down.

'Kyle was a good guy,' interjects Aaron. 'You probably

81

already know he ran a successful tech company and was very well off. He talked a lot about this new revolutionary product he was developing. Some health-app thing. But it sounds like he was having some trouble with investors.'

I shoot a look at Aaron. He didn't mention this to me.

The male detective scribbles in his notebook. 'What kind of trouble?'

'Oh, something about funding it. It was just a throw-away comment he made on Saturday while he was showing me his new car. I asked him how it was going and he mentioned an investor had pulled out.'

'Did he mention this investor's name?'

Aaron shakes his head. 'No, sorry.'

Alice has never told me any of this, but then we never talk about money or work. I don't even really understand what either of them does, apart from knowing Kyle is techy and Alice is a biochemist. Beyond that I have no clue.

'We'd like to take a quick statement from you,' says DC Jones. 'About your movements at the time of the attack.'

'Why?' Aaron's body language is instantly defensive. 'We weren't even in the country.'

'It's just procedure.' She smiles at us reassuringly. 'We need details of your flights and hotels. That kind of thing.'

Aaron nods curtly and turns to me with an inclination of his head, signalling that it's my turn to speak. *After all, it was your sister's idea*, I know he's thinking.

I tell them about our arrangement. 'My sister called it a life swap, but we weren't really swapping lives. She just wanted to give us a taste of her lifestyle and help out with the kids. She's always been generous like that and she adores her nieces.'

DC Jones smiles sympathetically. 'She sounds like a lovely sister.'

'She is. She was only trying to do a nice thing for us and now . . .' I swallow. I can't cry in front of these detectives. I blink and concentrate on pulling myself together.

Between us we tell the detectives about the phone call from Aaron's mum while we were in Venice and how we flew back early.

'Okay.' DC Jones closes her notebook and hands us her card. 'If you remember anything else, please call. Obviously we're still in the early stages of the investigation but any little thing could prove vital at this point. There's also something else we need to ask. With Alice in hospital and Kyle's friends and colleagues in London, we'd wondered if you'd be willing to formally identify Kyle.'

Nausea washes over me and I turn to Aaron in wide-eyed panic. I already know I can't do it.

'I'm happy to do it,' he says, and I want to hug him.

DC Jones looks relieved. 'We'll arrange for this to be done today, if that's okay?'

'It's fine,' says Aaron.

'And we'll need to take DNA samples from you both, too.'

'Why?' Aaron asks, and I glance at him. His body language has reverted to defensive.

'Just to rule the family out of forensic testing on the

83

crime scene. We will need your mother-in-law's too and anyone else who has stayed in your home over the last few weeks.'

'My mum came over in May,' I say.

'We'll take hers too, just to be on the safe side.'

'She lives in France but I'm trying to get hold of her.' I pick up my mobile phone to illustrate this point. 'She hasn't returned my calls yet but I know when she hears what's happened she'll fly straight here.'

DC Jones explains that someone will be over later to take the DNA swabs.

They stand up and we follow suit. 'You should be able to move back in tomorrow afternoon,' says the male detective. 'Someone will give you a call when you're free to do so. And you'll have to do a full inventory to see if anything has been stolen.'

As we're leaving the kitchen my eye goes to one of Flossie's drawings that Viv has pinned to the fridge with alphabet magnets. It's of a house drawn in blue crayon and something about it sparks a memory. I pause before running to catch up with the detectives in the hallway.

Aaron has opened the front door to let them out and they're crossing the threshold when I say breathlessly, 'Actually, there is something . . .'

They both turn to me expectantly and DC Jones pulls at her scarf.

'It's probably nothing. But when we left our house on Saturday I noticed something on the pavement in the corner of one of the paving slabs. It could have been made by kids, I don't know, but . . .'

'What was it?' presses DC Jones.

'An asterisk drawn in blue chalk and – and it didn't click at the time but I heard once that sometimes drawings or markings outside your house can mean it's been ear-marked by burglars.'

If this sounds familiar to them, they don't show it. 'Anything else you can remember about it?' the male detective asks.

'No. I don't think so. It was quite small. I don't even know if it's still there or been washed away by the rain.'

'Okay, thank you,' says DC Jones. 'We'll be in touch.'

Aaron closes the door on them and we return to the kitchen. I put the kettle on, feeling a bit shaky.

'Why didn't you mention the asterisk before?' says Aaron, coming over to me.

'I didn't think it was important. I was too busy saying goodbye to the twins and mentally preparing myself to be away from them for a week.'

Aaron blows air out of the side of his mouth, which instantly riles me: it's his way of not saying what he really thinks and always makes me feel judged.

'What? It was the first time we'd been away from them, Aaron . . .'

'It's not that.' He rubs a hand across his chin, his fringe dancing on his forehead. What is he not telling me?

'What, then? Do you think the asterisk does mean something?'

'I dunno. It's just something I heard about a while back, in the pub. You know the Knight brothers? Johnno and Shane?'

I remember Shane. He was in our year at school and a hoodlum even then. 'From the Old Dean Estate?'

He nods, his mouth set in a grim line. 'They're part of this gang who do break-ins, petty crime, stuff like that, but some of them are right thugs. I heard they leave a mark on the pavement. I'm not sure what, exactly. It might not be an asterisk.'

I've seen both brothers and their cronies around the village and wouldn't want to mess with any of that lot. Now I'm scared we're on their radar. What if it was them who broke into our house and they come back to finish the job? Maybe they saw Kyle's posh car and thought we'd somehow won the lottery.

'Fuck,' I say, feeling sick. 'Would Shane do that to you, though? You and he used to be mates.'

He shrugs and I can tell he wants to play it down. 'We weren't exactly mates. And it's just pub rumours. Shane has always been fine with me, though. We've sort of had a mutual understanding over the years. I've helped him out a couple of times . . .'

I stand up, my throat dry. 'In what way?'

'Oh, nothing illegal. Just got him a good deal on a car.' But he can't meet my eyes as he says it and leaves the room before I can challenge him further.

10

JEANETTE

Tuesday, 15 October 2019

Jeanette wakes early, the sunlight curling around the slats of the wooden shutters. She reaches for her mobile on the bedside table. Two missed calls from Tasha last night and one this morning. She replaces the phone. She can't face speaking to anyone, even her precious daughter. She just wants to hide away, to bury herself under her duvet and sink into oblivion. The two bottles of wine last night hadn't helped. Eamonn had convinced her to go to Olivier's dinner party, which had been difficult enough as everyone around her was speaking French, and even though she has a good grasp of the language, the more the alcohol flowed the faster they spoke and the less she understood. She'd ended up sitting there, most of the night, drowning her sorrows, and now she has a thumping migraine and a hollow feeling in her heart. She's never been able to handle her drink at the best of times, and now, at nearly sixty-two, she's officially a lightweight.

She can't even remember getting home, although she knows Eamonn must have called her a taxi. She half expected to wake up and find him lying beside her and is thankful that he isn't. She peers under the covers to see that she's still in the short-sleeved silk blouse she wore last night, but her skirt has been removed. She wonders if she took it off or if Eamonn did. A picture of him swims in her mind: his pale blue eyes, his dark beard with only flashes of grey, his springy hair and tanned, weather-beaten skin. She blinks away the image and it's replaced by Holly, a snapshot from the last day she ever saw her, wearing her white Babygro with little pink penguins dotted all over it. It had been one of Jeanette's favourites, bought by her mother.

Every year this day is hard. But really, on reflection, every day was hard. It wasn't just anniversaries when she thought about Holly. She was in Jeanette's every waking thought, her every decision.

What would she look like now, her baby daughter? *If she's still alive.* But she knows, deep in her heart, that she is. She can feel it. Somewhere, out there, her daughter is living a life without her.

She often thinks about that day, 15 October 1989. The day Holly was taken. It had been a Sunday. A bright sunny morning, an Indian summer, the weather forecasters had called it. Holly was a happy gurgling baby, just five months old, but already Jeanette loved her fiercely. Their 'accident' baby, not planned but very much wanted.

Most of the village shops had been closed that day, except for the greengrocer on the corner. Mr Fergal opened up for a brief window on a Sunday morning and Jeanette had been desperate for some cabbage leaves, which Mildred, a retired midwife from across the road, had told her were good for mastitis. It wasn't a serious bout, but enough to make her feel sore and uncomfortable. If only she hadn't taken Holly with her. If only she'd left her with Jim, Alice and Tasha, safe in the house. If only she hadn't been desperate for a home remedy for an inflamed breast. If only, if only, if only.

The greengrocer had been busy when she arrived. The shop was small, with most of the produce piled enticingly in baskets out at the front, but the cabbages had been inside, right at the back, where the shop was the coolest.

The problem with living in a village like Chew Norton was that it gave you a false sense of security and she'd thought nothing of leaving the pram outside when she'd gone in. She'd only be a few minutes, she had reasoned. In and out.

But when she came out the pram was empty and her precious happy, gurgly baby had vanished.

Moving to France had been a mistake. She can't outrun grief. She should have realized that by now. When Jim had died unexpectedly four years ago at the age of sixty, she hadn't known how she was going to live the rest of her life without him. She was only fifty-eight and the prospect of her remaining years stretched out in front of her, dark and lonely, like a motorway late at night. The one thing she did know was that she had to get out of Chew Norton. It had been a spur-of-the-moment decision, one she now regretted.

She knows how precious life is and she's missed the last two years and eleven months of Elsie and Flossie's.

Instead Vivian Pritchard was at the helm, the one Tasha ran to for babysitting duties. Ironic, really, that it had been Aaron Pritchard Tasha had fallen in love with, had married. Viv had been there that day, thirty years ago. She'd been the one Jeanette had run to when she realized, with a sickening horror, that Holly wasn't in her pram. When Jeanette had arrived, Viv had been standing outside, handling the oranges, her youngest, Stuart, in a sling. She'd remembered his pudgy dancing legs dangling in front of his mother's still swollen belly as Jeanette parked Holly next to the entrance, outside the neighbouring shop, an estate agent that's now long gone. Viv had smiled at them and nodded, before following her into the greengrocer's, but they hadn't known each other then, not really, only to say hello to in the park or on the way to nursery or the little village primary school where Alice had just started. Viv had been brilliant that day, rushing to Jeanette as she'd cried out in shock when she'd found the pram empty, dashing back inside the shop to ask if anyone had seen Holly, grabbing people who wandered by and demanding if they had noticed anyone with a baby and then, eventually, when it was beginning to dawn on them that Holly had been stolen, ringing the police to report it. Viv had sat with Jeanette as she crumpled to the pavement, her legs giving way as the truth washed over her, telling her over and over again that it was okay because this was a tight-knit community and Holly would be found. *She would be found.*

Except she never was.

When the police arrived she noticed how Viv cuddled

90

Stuart that little bit tighter, relieved that the nightmare wasn't happening to her, and Jeanette had felt a stab of jealousy so sharp, so pure that she's carried it with her ever since.

There were so many reasons why she'd wanted to get out of Chew Norton. Viv Pritchard was just one of them.

11

TASHA

Wednesday, 16 October 2019

It's a sunny but blowy morning, the handful of crisp golden leaves that dance around our feet heralding the countdown to winter. We stand by the front gate, staring up at our house. From the outside it looks exactly the same, as if no crime has ever taken place: grey stone, black front door, neat Roman blinds at the symmetrical sash windows, yet my palms are damp at the thought of having to go inside. How can I ever feel the same about our home now?

Kyle's flashy sports car is still parked in the same spot near our gate, and I wonder what will happen to it. I want it taken away. We might as well have a neon sign outside signalling for intruders to break into our house.

Aaron interweaves his fingers with mine. We've left the girls with Viv. I didn't want to bring them as I was worried they might pick up my negative vibes. We're trying to keep them as blissfully unaware as possible.

'It's best just to get it over with,' he says, looking straight ahead. I notice a piece of police tape fluttering, like an injured bird, among the long grass of our front lawn. Aaron doesn't move and I don't either. We stand there holding hands for a bit, my heart jumping about in my chest.

I take a deep breath. 'It's still our home.'

'I know.'

I wonder if he's picturing it too? Kyle's dead body prostrate on our living-room floor. He'd been subdued last night after returning home from identifying Kyle. He'd explained he'd had to look at a photograph rather than go into some sterile room, like in the movies. 'He just looked as if he was asleep, really,' he'd said. I still don't know if this was true or if he said that to provide comfort.

He glances down at the pavement now. 'Where was this asterisk you talked about?'

There is no sign of it now.

'It was there.' I point to the upper corner of the paving slab with the toe of my biker boot. A shadow passes over his face but he doesn't say anything further. I'd probed him about it yesterday, after my mum finally called me back apologizing for not answering my earlier calls, but he insisted he knew nothing more than he'd already told me. I don't believe him. I don't know if it's his misguided attempt to protect me – he already knows I'm scared to move back in – or if there's another reason why he's not being honest about it. Or maybe I'm being paranoid. Being pursued by a man with a knife through the streets of Venice was more than enough to shake me up, but coming home to Kyle's murder, to Alice's attack, has shredded my nerves.

Mum had understandably been distraught on the

phone yesterday when I told her about Alice and Kyle, and I could tell she felt terrible about waiting so long to return my calls. She didn't bother ringing me back until early evening. 'I'm getting on the next flight,' she'd said, and I'd convinced her to wait until this morning. She's due to arrive around two o'clock today and I'm picking her up from the airport and taking her straight to the hospital to visit Alice.

'Come on, we can't put it off for ever,' he says, leading me down the path. He takes the key from his pocket and unlocks the front door. He's arranged for a locksmith to come over just to be on the safe side. They're due here within the hour. I won't feel comfortable bringing the twins home until it's been done.

It smells different, I think, as I follow him over the threshold. Something chemical mixed with a metallic scent. Aaron walks down the hallway into the kitchen but I turn right into the living room, remembering how I'd stood at this bay window just four days ago, worrying about what Kyle would think of our modest home, and how frivolous those thoughts were in the light of what's happened since.

The room is tidy but some of our furniture and the books on the shelf have been rearranged. I try not to imagine the police touching our things, dusting for fingerprints and doing whatever other forensic tests they conducted while they were here. The room doesn't feel like ours and I have the sudden urge to clean it.

This is the room Kyle died in.

I feel a surge of emotion so forceful that I bend double.

An unwanted image of my brother-in-law's last moments pushes itself into my mind: hearing a noise and climbing out of bed, probably not even worried at that point, just wanting to investigate, like Aaron has done many times before. A bit unsteady on his feet due to the alcohol they'd consumed. Had Kyle disturbed his attacker? Had they already been in here, about to steal the TV or Aaron's vintage Bang & Olufsen stereo that he'd picked up second-hand and mended? Did they freak out when they saw Kyle and strike? And, if so, with what? Would a burglar come armed? And what about my sister? She'd come down here too and was hit over the head. Had the burglar been hiding behind the door? She'd said she felt someone push her. I shudder and spin around, as though the intruder is still here. I notice our rug has gone, leaving a patch of wood paler than the rest of the floorboards. I feel nauseous when I think that there must have been blood on it. My stomach turns over. I have to stop thinking about it and about Kyle, the soul that was ripped from his body so suddenly that his spirit is probably still in our house. Aaron hates me talking like this – and so does Alice – but I can't help it if I believe in ghosts.

I hear Aaron calling me and I leave the room to join him in the kitchen. It's tidy. There are no dirty plates in the sink or tea rings on the butcher's-block work surface, like there often are. Elsie's pink pig wellies and Flossie's ladybird pair sit side by side next to the French windows, not in an untidy pile like they usually are. My attention goes to Aaron, who's standing in the middle of the room, a look of concentration on his face. He's reading a letter.

He turns. 'This is for you . . . I've opened it.' His expression is troubled as he passes it to me.

I take it. The paper is lined, like it's been torn from a notebook, and folded in two. On the front *Natasha* is scribbled in black ink. Nobody calls me Natasha.

The bottom is sticky and I can see that it had been sealed with tape, which Aaron must have broken. It irks me that he took it upon himself to read it when it's addressed to me.

'It was on the mat when we came through the front door. Someone must've recently shoved it through the letterbox.' His voice sounds strained, serious, and when I read it, I understand why.

It's just six words, written in block capitals.

IT WAS SUPPOSED TO BE YOU.

PART TWO

I'd taken my eye off the ball. I hadn't meant to. I'd been so diligent, watching you. Watching him. Both of you coming and going, following you through the village, him to the garage and you to that depressing dental surgery, with the ugly photos of decaying teeth all over the walls. All summer I've been on your tail and you haven't even noticed, but I've always been good at living in the shadows, on the edge of everyone else's lives. Whenever I could get away I've been there, lurking around your street, following you down country lanes and around the supermarket, watching you scan the aisles for bargains and BOGOFs.

But that Saturday I was too late to see you leave and your sister arrive. Too many distractions in my life when all I'd wanted to do was focus on you.

It was the wrong sister.

It was supposed to be you.

I2

JEANETTE

Wednesday, 16 October 2019

Tasha looks pale and tired, Jeanette thinks, as she eyes her daughter from the passenger seat. Her lovely long red hair, so like her father's, could do with a wash and she's wearing a shabby old band T-shirt with a hole in the hem. She's been quiet on the journey from the airport and Jeanette is worried that she's punishing her somehow, for what she's not yet sure. Maybe for taking so long to return her calls. But she's always felt that way about her middle daughter. She loves Tasha with all her heart, but sometimes finds her difficult, with her hard, prickly edges. She was a sullen teenager, who went off the rails in her late teens, only softening when she had the twins and became a mother herself. She can't blame Tasha. She'd been just four when Holly was taken and had been desperate for love and attention, but Jeanette had been unable to give it, suffering as she was with anxiety and depression in the aftermath.

It had been down to Jim to provide their two remaining daughters with normality, and he'd tried, better than she had, and as a result they had been very close to their dad. But his sudden death had knocked both her girls sideways. And now this. Kyle. Her lovely, charming, handsome son-in-law murdered. He'd cast his golden light on her eldest, already golden child, making her shine that much brighter. Oxford-educated, gifted Alice was Jeanette's success story, proof that she hadn't messed up her children with her parenting skills. And now what? Alice was lying in a hospital bed injured and bereft, her light diminishing, and it was more than Jeanette could bear.

'So,' she begins warily. Tasha's shoulders are up around her ears and her brow is furrowed. 'How are my gorgeous grandchildren?'

It's the right thing to say as Tasha's face brightens and she visibly relaxes at the mention of Elsie and Flossie. Jeanette breathes a sigh of relief.

'They're good. Thankfully, they don't know exactly what happened to Kyle or Alice although we've told them that Kyle has died.'

Jeanette doesn't believe in keeping the children in the dark. She's always told Alice and Tasha the truth, or at least a sanitized version of it. 'Is Alice going to stay with you when she's discharged from hospital? She can't go home . . . not so soon after Kyle. Won't the girls be asking questions when they see her injuries?'

'They're not even three years old,' says Tasha, her voice tight. 'They'll believe what I tell them. I don't want them to know the full truth, Mum. You promise me you won't say anything? I don't want them feeling scared in our house.'

Jeanette bites her lip.

'Mum?' Tasha flashes her a warning look.

'It's not my place,' says Jeanette. She twists her hands in her lap. She doesn't want to antagonize her daughter. She knows Tasha has a tendency to be anxious. Who knows what impact Holly's disappearance has had on both her daughters psychologically?

'Thank you.'

'I understand that you want to protect them,' says Jeanette, sadly. 'That's all we ever want to do. As parents.'

Tasha nods but doesn't say anything. They fall silent and don't speak again until her daughter has pulled into a car park near the hospital. Tasha never has been the most talkative but, even so, she's unusually quiet.

'I'm sorry I took so long to ring you back yesterday,' Jeanette says, as they walk from the car park. Her daughter is striding along so fast that Jeanette has almost to run to keep up with her. She's clutching a tote bag with some clothes and personal items for Alice.

'It's fine.' Tasha pushes a lock of hair away from her eyes. 'I'm not cross with you, Mum. I'm just worried about Alice. I know she's been lucky physically but Kyle was the love of her life. And for his life to end this way, so violently and because of me . . .'

Jeanette reaches out a hand and clasps Tasha's arm. 'Darling, what do you mean? Stop a minute.'

Tasha spins around so that she's facing her mother. Her eyes flash angrily but Jeanette can see the pain too. And something else. Guilt, perhaps?

'This isn't your fault. You can't blame yourself for it.'

Her daughter hesitates, as though about to say

something else. Instead she scratches at the skin on her inner wrist, which looks angry and sore. Tasha has always had flare-ups of eczema, particularly when she's stressed, and as she stands there, a fireball of anger and emotion, Jeanette gets a glimpse of the little girl she used to be, and longs to throw her arms around her: the compulsion to protect her has never gone away. Tasha's always so guarded, as though she believes she'll be judged harshly for saying the wrong thing.

Tasha remains silent, looking down at her chunky burgundy Dr Martens. She still dresses the way she did as a teenager.

Jeanette waits, but her daughter seems to rally herself, drawing on some kind of inner strength, and begins walking again.

'You know,' says Jeanette, when they reach the hospital entrance, 'I called your house on Saturday night because I'd forgotten you were in Venice. I spoke to Alice and she mentioned something that's been worrying me.'

Tasha stops by the door. She has dark circles under her eyes. 'What is it?'

'She just seemed a bit unnerved, that's all. Like she mentioned this strange sense of being watched. And now I feel I should have probed a bit more . . . I'd convinced her it was nothing.' She puts a hand to her chest as guilt washes over her.

Tasha stiffens. 'Alice never mentioned this to me when I saw her yesterday. Did she say anything else?'

'No. Why? Do you know something?'

Tasha shakes her head. 'She's alive, Mum. That's what

we need to focus on. We've been so lucky. It could have been her too.'

Jeanette nods, touching the locket at her neck, then follows Tasha down the corridor to visit her precious, precious daughter.

13

TASHA

Wednesday, 16 October 2019

I can't bring myself to tell my mum about the note. Or Alice. Not yet, anyway. Not until I've spoken to the police. I'd tried ringing DC Jones after I found it but it went straight through to her voicemail, and then I had to leave to pick up Mum so Aaron said he'd make the call.

Mum steps into the ward first and stops, hand theatrically to her chest. I look past her to see the same detective I'd spoken to at Viv's beside Alice's bed.

'Who's that?' Mum turns to me, her blue eyes wide.

'DC Chloë Jones,' I say. 'She interviewed me and Aaron yesterday. She must be taking Alice's statement.'

Mum purses her lips in disapproval. 'Can't it wait? Alice needs to rest.'

'The police are just doing their job, Mum. They need to catch whoever's responsible.'

'I'm just worried it will be too upsetting for Alice to go over it again.'

Before I can say anything else DC Jones stands up and Mum rushes over to Alice's bedside and I watch my strong, brilliant sister collapse into her arms, sobbing against Mum's shoulder while DC Jones looks on awkwardly. She has a phial wrapped in a plastic bag that I recognize from when we had our DNA swabs taken. She must have just done Alice's. My heart aches and the guilt threatens to engulf me. How can I live with this? Someone wanted to hurt me, even though I have no idea who or why, yet Alice and Kyle were the ones who got caught in the crossfire. I think back to what Mum said about Alice feeling she was being watched. That was Sunday evening. The attack happened in the early hours of Monday morning. Whoever was watching the house must have assumed it was me and Aaron inside, not Kyle and Alice.

I picture Aaron that night in Venice when we were caught in the storm. He'd looked so handsome with his damp tousled hair and a smattering of rain on his face, darkening his eyelashes. In that moment it was like we were falling in love all over again. He's not perfect and we have our problems but I do love him. It could so easily have been him who was killed and the guilt hits me again. Guilt layered on top of guilt.

Life is so short. So fucking short.

DC Jones comes over to where I'm still hovering by the door. 'Hi again,' she says, tucking her notebook into the pocket of her wool coat. It's warm in here and she has a colourful scarf draped over her arm. She glances back at where Alice is crying on my mum's shoulder. 'I'm so sorry about Kyle,' she says. 'I just want to remind you that as your family liaison officer I'm here if there's anything that Alice or any of you need. You're bound to get media interest but I would advise that you don't speak to anyone.'

I feel a swell of relief and gratitude. 'Thank you,' I say.

The note from this morning is still at the forefront of my mind and this is the prime opportunity to talk to her about it. 'Would it be possible to have a quick word about something?' I say now to her. 'I just need to give this to Alice.' I hold up a crumpled orange Sainsbury's carrier bag containing a change of clothes and her mobile phone.

She smiles warmly. 'Of course. I'll wait for you in the corridor.'

I give Alice a quick hug and hand over the bag, then leave her and Mum to have some time together. I join DC Jones in the corridor. As we walk towards the hospital's atrium together I tell her about the note. 'I'm not sure if Aaron has spoken to you about it already.'

She shakes her head. 'This is the first I've heard of it. Do you have it on you?' By now we've reached Costa. Her face has become serious and, for the first time, I get the sense that under her ready smile and warm brown eyes she's steely. And tough.

I shake my head. 'I left it with Aaron. I'm . . . I'm scared, if I'm honest. If I was the intended target, what if whoever wrote it returns to the house?'

'You've changed the locks?'

I nod. 'And Aaron bought a Ringcam for the back garden.'

'That's a good idea. There will be a heavy police presence in and around the village anyway as we conduct our interviews and gather information, but if it makes you feel safer we can organize for a car to patrol your street and keep an eye on your house. Or we can arrange for you to stay somewhere else.'

I don't want to uproot the girls and worry them. Mum is staying with us now and Alice is supposed to be coming home tomorrow, all being well. 'A patrol car would be brilliant, if that's all right,' I say.

'Consider it done. And if you have any concerns, any at all, don't hesitate to ring me, okay? And make sure you give us the note.'

I nod. She orders us both a cappuccino, then leaves me to drink mine at the table while she heads off with hers in a takeaway cup saying she'll be in touch. As I watch her leave, clutching her coffee and with her mobile pressed against one ear, I realize that I like her. My nineteen-year-old self would have been shocked.

I sip my coffee, my phone on the table in front of me. The atrium is fairly quiet, just a few people dotted about the tables, either reading or staring at their phones. A cleaner is sliding a mop across the floor nearby. I decide to ring Aaron before I go back up to see Alice. There's no answer so I tap out a quick text: *I bumped into DC Jones at the hospital and told her about the note. She wants to see it so can you drop it in at the station ASAP? xx*

I watch the screen for a couple of minutes, hoping to see the three little dots that signal Aaron is replying. But there is nothing.

It's been so hard hiding my anxiety about the note from Mum. I've never been very good at being fake. Or 'putting on a face', as Mum would call it. Not like Alice. As teenagers we could be in the middle of a raging argument – which wasn't that often, to be fair – but if we were interrupted by another friend, or a passer-by who knew our parents, she would instantly turn on the charm. I'd still be inwardly raging and come across as rude and petulant. I know Mum could tell something was bothering me beyond my worry for Alice, but thankfully she didn't push it. I love my mum, of course I do, but we've never been particularly close. I've always felt she was closer to Alice. They talk about book-club fiction and old films, things I'm not particularly interested in. I'd rather watch a crime documentary or listen to podcasts and, if I read at all, it's more likely to be something non-fiction, particularly autobiographies written by musicians.

I've never really known who I am. I think that's always been my problem, until I had the twins and became a mother, which at least grounded me. Before then I was always floundering, wondering where I fitted into the world. I wasn't intelligent and ambitious like Alice, or well-read and practical like my mother, or vocational like my father. And Aaron has a passion, even if it is something boring like cars.

I've already made up the spare room for when Alice is discharged. She'll have to share the double bed with Mum, unless Mum wants to sleep on the blow-up bed on the floor of the girls' bedroom, which is doubtful. I wish, not for the first time, that we had a bigger house.

I finish the rest of my coffee, then go back up to the ward to see Alice.

Mum looks wistful as we pull up outside my house a few hours later. She doesn't move from the passenger seat, her fingers toying with her necklace – a gold locket my dad gave her for her birthday one year, with a photo of Holly, Alice and myself as kids inside it, which she never takes off. 'This place.' She sighs.

At first I think she's talking about my house until I realize she means Chew Norton as a whole. Before Mum moved to France, my parents had lived here for nearly forty years. They'd grown up in Bristol but when they got married they decided to move to somewhere more rural. I know she's thinking about all the memories, about Dad and probably Holly too. I was too young when she disappeared to remember my baby sister, only snippets, the odd image: the elephant mobile that hung over Holly's cot, her tufty blonde hair and Mum exclaiming that she wasn't a redhead, like me and Alice, her gummy smile, the pink velour dog that held her nappies and always looked like it was grinning. They kept Holly's bedroom exactly the same until one day, when I was about eight, I came home from school to find my dad up a ladder, painting over the pink walls with pale mint and informing me that it was my bedroom now and I no longer had to share with Alice. I longed to tell him that I wanted it in lemon but had sensed it probably wasn't the right time.

Holly's disappearance left a massive chasm in our family, but it wasn't until the twins were born that I realized just how horrific and tragic it must have been for my parents. Having Elsie and Flossie has made me more empathetic as a person and I feel a swell of emotion for my mum. I'm tempted to reach for her hand, or to hug her, but that kind of affection doesn't come naturally to me, apart from with my own children, so I hesitate and then it's too late: she's reaching for the door handle and stepping onto the pavement.

'Whose bright orange sports car is that?' she asks, as I join her.

'Kyle's.' I suppose it's Alice's now but I don't say it.

Nobody in my family, apart from Alice, understands quite how Kyle is so wealthy. Apparently he inherited some money after his parents died ten or fifteen years ago, and recently he's run the small tech firm. I know he's invented some health-related technology that everyone's excited about. Alice had tried to explain it to me and Aaron once over dinner but had given up when we stared blankly at her, my mind already wandering. Alice's job as a scientist is hard enough to understand and I still don't know exactly what she does except that it involves viruses. Or maybe growths. Actually I think it's cells. Whatever, she studied biochemistry at Oxford and has a PhD. And while she has a great career at a prestigious drugs company and earns a high salary, it's Kyle who is the super-rich one. Was. Was, was, was, was, *was*. I'm never going to get used to thinking of him in the past tense.

Mum assesses the car and wrinkles her nose. 'It's too ostentatious,' she says. And then she must remember that her son-in-law is dead because she flushes. 'I mean . . . it's not to my taste but . . .'

'It's okay, Mum. I know what you mean.' Like mine, her idea of an expensive car is a BMW or a Mercedes. A McLaren is enough to blow her mind. I daren't tell her how much it would have cost Kyle, and I only know because Aaron told me. Mum has never been materialistic and she's naturally thrifty without being tight. Ultra-feminine in style, she always looks nice and well put-together, preferring long skirts over jeans, but I know her clothes aren't expensive. She's had most of them for years. Make do and mend is her philosophy. No fast fashion for her. She doesn't drive, but if she did she'd have something old, like my Honda.

Her eyes fill with tears. 'Poor Alice,' she says, clutching her locket, and I nod, a lump in my throat.

When we enter the house the girls come running down the hallway, their little bare feet padding on the floorboards. They're in their nighties, their hair smelling of shampoo. I'm surprised that Aaron has done bathtime without any prompting from me, until I see Viv behind them, a placid smile on her face.

'Nanny!' they cry, barrelling into my mum, and she wraps her arms around them, kissing their damp hair and cuddling them to her. They always call her Nanny or Nanna while Viv is Granny, which is what her other grandchildren call her.

I close the front door behind me but the hallway is too narrow to step around them. I watch as Elsie and Flossie each take one of my mum's hands and almost drag her into the living room.

'Hi, Viv,' my mum calls over her shoulder, and Viv nods back, her smile fixed. It's the first time they've seen each other for a few years but there is no warm hug, or even small-talk. My mum and Viv have never really hit it off, despite living in the same village for most of their adult lives and having me and Aaron in common. But then again they're very different people so it's not that surprising. My mum is sensible and reliable, softly spoken and unfailingly polite and kind to everyone, whether they deserve it or not. Viv, on the other hand, is louder and more the speak-as-you-find type. They both come from working-class families, and even though Mum retired before she moved to France, Viv still does the odd shift as a barmaid at the Packhorse. That's where Aaron jokes he got his love of pubs, having to hang out there every Sunday evening while his mum worked. But I sense underneath there is a competitive edge to their awkwardness around each other, especially since Mum moved to France, and I suspect it's to do with Viv playing a larger part in their granddaughters' lives. And when Mum is here, I think Viv's conscious of not stepping on her toes.

'So, I'll be off then,' says my mother-in-law. She grabs her brown leather jacket from where she'd hung it on the newel post and pulls it on over her checked shirt.

'Thanks, Viv,' I say, and she waves her hand as if it's no bother. 'Where's Aaron?'

'Oh, he had to pop out. I said I'd sort the girls while he was gone . . .'

'You didn't have to do that.'

'Oh, shush, it keeps me young.' She grins and flicks her fringe out of her eyes. 'I'll see you soon, duck.'

'You don't have to rush off. We're planning on getting a takeaway. Why don't you stay?'

She holds up a palm. 'No, I need to get on. I've left Freddie Mercury on his own for too long. But thank you.' She slips on her cross-body bag, blowing me a kiss, and bustling out of the front door. I watch from the front step as she scuttles down the path.

I'm just about to close the door when I see her looking back at the house and there is something about her expression, a hint of hostility, maybe even guilt, that makes my heart race.

And then she turns and almost runs down the street.

14

My mum goes to bed early, not long after the girls, and Aaron still hasn't come home. It's our first night back in the house after Kyle's murder and I'm disappointed that he's decided to go out. He could at least have told me where he was going.

Aaron likes a drink – he's a sociable guy. In that sense he's always been good for me, the extrovert to my introvert. He took on the role that Alice played while we were growing up. And I was aware that being with someone like Aaron came with downsides, like his lads' nights out on a Friday, coming home smashed at three a.m., waking up to find him crashed on the sofa stinking of alcohol. When the girls were born he promised he'd do it less. And he has. But tonight? After the shock we've had? After Kyle's murder and finding the note? I've tried ringing him three more times but it goes straight to voicemail. I leave a message asking him where he is and to call me back.

Despite being annoyed I'm starting to get worried that something might have happened to him. It's only just turned nine, so not exactly late, but I can't shake the fear that whoever hurt Alice and Kyle now knows they've made a mistake. And then what? Will Aaron and I be next?

I go into our bedroom. It's the first time I've set foot in it since we've been back. I've been putting it off, although I can see Aaron has tossed the T-shirt he was wearing today onto the bed. Then I head into the spare room. Kyle has slept here, still evident by the rumpled sheets and the pulled-back duvet. I lower myself onto the edge of the bed wondering if I should change the sheets. Will it be too much for Alice to sleep here after what's happened? The room still smells of Kyle's lemony scent, of good-quality shower gel and posh aftershave. I stand up to open our modest double wardrobe – so different from the walk-in one in Venice – and my heart aches to see some of Kyle's clothes hanging next to Alice's. What an idiot I'd been, thinking I could escape myself by becoming Alice for a few days, as though her glamour would transfer to me, like a fake tattoo. I shut the wardrobe door and leave the room.

I check on the girls again, for the second time this evening. They are both fast asleep, Flossie sucking her thumb and Elsie with her favourite teddy bear tucked under her smooth, plump cheek. Mum is out for the count on the blow-up bed. Their room is at the back of the house, with views over the pond and the countryside beyond. I stand at their window for a while, watching as the moon casts its light over the Mendip Hills in the distance.

It's stuffy in the room but I don't want to open any windows in case someone tries to get in. I know it's paranoia – after all we're two storeys up – but I can't take any chances after what's happened.

As I go to close the curtains I see a flicker of movement

at the edge of the pond below. I look closer. Is that someone standing near the water? It's hard to tell because they're almost hidden by the tall reeds, the mist obscuring their bottom half. I peer closer, my nose almost touching the glass. Yes, someone is definitely down there. From the pond area there is a gate that leads into our garden, although we always lock it. People use the field as a cut-through to the Old Dean Estate from the pub, and I have sometimes noticed the odd person hanging around down there, usually teenagers believing they're obscured by the long grasses.

The figure moves. It's a man.

My heart picks up speed.

Is someone watching the house?

I'm just about to rush for my mobile to call DC Jones, terrified that the intruder is back, when something about the familiar round-shouldered stance and sharp-nosed profile makes me pause. I move as close to the glass as I can get. But, yes, I'm not mistaken. It's my husband. My heart slows and I put down my mobile. Then my initial relief is replaced by suspicion. What's he doing? I see him gesticulating and it hits me that he's not alone. I can just about make out the silhouette of a woman.

I try to get a better look. It seems as though they're just standing there, talking. Or are they arguing? No, it looks like a discussion of some kind. Why is Aaron having secret talks with a woman in the secluded area behind our house?

I thrust the curtains closed, run down to the kitchen and stand at the French windows but it's impossible to see over the fence and the gate from here.

I'm just pulling on my wellies when I hear his key in the front door. He could have walked through the back gate yet he's obviously come to the front because he doesn't want me to know about his secret rendezvous.

He swans into the kitchen with a casual air, whistling to himself, and does a double-take when he spots me sitting at the table in the semi-darkness. I can smell alcohol on him.

'Tash! I didn't see you there.'

'Where have you been?'

He switches on the main light, not quite meeting my eye. 'To the pub.'

'Why? You could have let me know.'

'Sorry. I thought I'd said. It was Tim's fiftieth birthday. He just wanted me to come for a few. I thought I'd be back before now.' He looks contrite and moves to the kettle, clicking it on. 'I thought I'd give you space to talk to your mum.' He reaches up and rubs the back of his neck, something he often does if he feels uncomfortable.

'So who were you talking to?'

'Talking to?'

I stand up. 'Just now. By the pond. It looked like you were talking to a woman.'

'Oh, that's Zoë. From work.'

I freeze. Zoë, the attractive new receptionist. 'What were you doing with her?'

'We were just walking home from the pub together. She lives on the Old Dean Estate. She was a bit scared about walking home alone after . . .' his cheeks redden '. . . after Kyle.'

That's understandable. But I instantly feel jealous. I know nothing about Zoë. I've not even met her properly, just seen her briefly from across the street. She's tall with long blonde hair and an annoying laugh. Oh, and she likes to send my husband the odd semi-flirtatious text wrapped up as 'banter'.

'Right,' I say, swallowing my suspicions. She's just a friend, I remind myself. Aaron has done nothing wrong. He turns his back to me and asks if I want a cup of tea. I say yes and watch as he drops teabags into two mugs. I know I only feel this way because things hadn't been great between us before Venice. But we're okay now. We've recaptured some of our passion, our magic, even if we were away for less than two days.

When he's finished making the tea, leaving the wet, wrung-out teabags on the side, he hands me mine and stands there looking a bit lost, as though he's not sure if I'm about to have a go at him. Instead I walk into the living room, knowing he'll follow. He perches next to me on the sofa.

'So, this Zoë,' I begin. 'Is everything okay between you? Your talk looked heated.'

He laughs. 'Oh, we were arguing over the football. It was all good-natured. She's just a friend.' He looks at me pointedly.

If it was all as innocent with Zoë as he's suggesting, why did he try to hide it from me? 'Why didn't you reply to my messages or my phone call?' I ask instead.

His face falls. 'God, I'm sorry, Tash. I didn't think. I just got swept along. I popped into the garage to talk to the lads and tell them what had happened and they were on their way out and asked me to join them.'

'But you said you popped into the garage on Monday. And that was when you saw Tim.'

'I didn't see the lads then. Only Tim.'

'Did you take the note to the police station at least?'

'Yes. I handed it in, like you told me to in your text. I'm sorry I didn't phone you back.' He's watching my face. 'Do you mind if I put the football on?' He's already reaching for the remote.

'Fine. I'll see you up in bed,' I say, getting up and setting my mug down next to his. I walk out of the room before he can answer.

I'm still awake when Aaron comes up a little later. I'm turned away from him but I can hear the clatter of his belt as his jeans hit the floor, and the bed gives way as he climbs in beside me.

'Are you awake?' he whispers, and I think of us in Venice, just four days ago, and how different things were.

I turn over so that I'm facing him.

'I'm sorry. I should have told you I was going to the pub. It was a last-minute thing. I wasn't expecting to be so long and I thought you'd be okay because your mum's here.'

'Fine. It's just there's a lot going on right now. I'll have a lot on my plate with Alice. I mean, she's lost her husband, for fuck's sake, and . . .' My throat feels tight with emotion. 'I'm scared, Aaron. That note has scared me.'

'I know. I'm sorry.' He pulls me to him and I rest my head on his chest, his arm around me.

'What if we're next?' I say, still talking in hushed tones so as not to wake Mum in the next room.

He stares up at the ceiling. Moonlight seeps around the edges of the curtains, highlighting his angular cheekbones. 'There's a police car outside. I think DC Jones must have sent someone to watch the house.'

'Oh, good.' I instantly relax. I know it's only a short-term solution but I hope they catch Kyle's killer soon.

'You're not worrying about Zoë, are you? She *is* just a mate.'

'I know.'

'Goodnight,' he says, turning onto his side so that he's spooning me.

I lie beside him, unable to sleep, listening to the gentle sounds of his breathing, his hand resting lightly on my thigh. I know Aaron has told me not to worry. I know that he insists Zoë is just a friend. And I know he's a different person now from who he was at nineteen. But how can I forget that the reason we split up all those years ago was because he cheated on me? And even though we got back together and I forgave him, there is the ever-present fear that he might do it again.

15

TASHA

Thursday, 17 October 2019

The next morning I wake up to see Aaron in his overalls, moving around the bedroom like a mime artist, obviously trying not to wake me. I glance at my bedside clock. It's six forty-five a.m.

'So you're going into work?'

He looks at me guiltily. 'Do you mind? I don't want to waste my annual leave and it might be good to give you some space, especially with Alice coming home today. I think the girls should probably go to nursery too, have a bit of normality?'

I feel anxious at the thought of the twins being away from me but I know he's right. The routine will be good for them.

He runs a comb through his hair. 'Me going back to work gives you and your mum the chance to talk to Alice when she gets home. I'll only get in the way.'

I know what he's doing. He's running away from it all. He doesn't want to be around grief. He was similar after my dad died, comforting to me but he avoided my mum, not knowing what to say to her so he said nothing at all. Although he's right: there's no point in him wasting his holiday when there isn't much he can do here. The house will feel full when I bring Alice back.

'Come on,' he says. 'Why don't we have breakfast together before the girls wake up?' I reach for my dressing-gown and pull it on as we head downstairs. I'm about to follow Aaron into the kitchen when I hear voices coming from the living room. I poke my head around the door to see my mum cuddled up with the twins on the sofa drinking warm milk, glued to CBeebies. Mum is knitting: another scarf coiled in her lap in various shades of green. We have an array of them in different hues that she sends from France but, judging by the colours, she's making this one for Alice. Green has always been my sister's favourite.

'Morning, love,' she says softly, looking up at me hovering in the doorway. 'The girls woke up at five thirty. I didn't want them to wake you so I brought them downstairs. Hope that's okay.'

'Of course, thank you,' I say. I'm relieved they slept soundly last night. Flossie hasn't said anything more about a loud noise on the night of the attack and I'm worried about bringing it up with her as I don't want to frighten her.

Elsie pulls her gaze away from the screen and jumps up. 'Can Nanny do my hair today?' she asks, pulling at her long red mane.

'She's remembered,' says Mum, looking pleased. Mum does a great French plait. She's always been good at hair. I, on the other hand, can just about stretch to a ponytail.

'Me too,' says Flossie, from beside Mum, always

wanting what Elsie has, although Flossie's hair is a mass of curls and is much harder to coax into any type of up-do.

'If that's okay with Nanny,' I say, coming further into the room and kissing their warm cheeks. Elsie starts emptying a jigsaw onto the floor but Flossie stays curled up next to Mum, thumb in mouth, her eyes back on the TV.

'I'll take them to nursery today, if you like, so that you can leave early to pick up Alice,' says Mum, pausing from her knitting and looking up at me eagerly.

I realize she can't wait for Alice to get home but every time I think of it my stomach drops. Not that I don't want Alice here, it's just I feel so impotent. I've never been very good with words, always worrying I'm saying the wrong thing. I don't know how I'm going to help her. 'Okay,' I say, pulling my dressing-gown around me. 'If you're sure.' I lower my voice so as not to worry the twins. 'Just . . . be alert, won't you? Don't let them run ahead or anything.'

Mum throws me a hurt look. 'Of course. I won't let them out of my sight.'

I could kick myself. She now thinks I don't trust her because of what happened to Holly.

'I didn't mean . . .' I tail off. I don't know how to explain myself. Because of course it's about Holly. Her spectre follows me everywhere, reminding me of the worst that can happen. But it's also about the note and the attack and the thought that someone, somewhere now wants to harm me.

'I understand,' Mum says, her expression softening.

'Now go and get some breakfast. And I'll have a cuppa if you're making one.'

I smile at her gratefully and close the door behind me. It is lovely having the extra help with the twins, despite the circumstances.

Aaron is sitting at the kitchen table nursing a coffee and scrolling through his phone. 'I've made you some tea.' He gestures towards the mug resting on the worktop by the kettle. I remember when Aaron fitted this kitchen. I'd been pregnant with the twins and we didn't have enough money to replace the one we'd inherited with the house, so we kept the carcasses and Aaron bought new vinyl doors from Homebase and fitted the butcher's-block worktop, which he bought from eBay. It transformed the kitchen and I'd been so grateful that I had a husband who was good at DIY. Some of my friends' other halves can't even put up a picture. I survey him now, his brow furrowed, his golden-brown hair flopping over his forehead as he looks down at the phone in his hands. He'll be reading a Reddit thread about Aston Villa, and I think how petty it is to be annoyed with him because he went out last night. So what if he likes going to the pub now and again? That's who he is. That's who he's always been. It could be worse. Donna from work said she finished with her last boyfriend because he spent most of the night playing Call of Duty, couldn't get up for work in the morning and kept being sacked. My school-friend Leila told me her husband is obsessed with porn and would rather masturbate than have sex with her.

I think of Kyle, who died in this house. Of my sister,

battered and grieving. She'd give anything to have her husband sitting at this kitchen table right now looking at Reddit threads. Even porn. As long as he was alive.

'I'm never going to get over the fact that Kyle died here,' I say, wrapping my fingers around my warm mug and staring out into the garden. It's a dull morning, the sun not yet surfacing, the sky a thick, misty white that blurs the trees in the distance.

Aaron's head shoots up, a horrified look on his face. 'Tash, bloody hell.'

I fix my gaze on him. 'Well, I'm not. Are you?' I don't talk about it much because Aaron hasn't got time for anything supernatural, but I like to think there is life after death, especially after Dad died. I wonder if Kyle's spirit is here, unable to move on after his sudden, violent death, and I glance back towards our garden.

'You can't think about it because we can't afford to move right now.' Aaron's voice interrupts my morbid thoughts. 'We have no choice but to stay here. And, anyway, we'll just have to trust that the police will catch whoever is behind this. Hopefully the note is just a cruel, nasty prank and isn't linked to what happened here.' He stands up and downs the rest of his coffee. 'I'd better go.' He dumps his empty cup on the side and I put my tea down to make one for Mum. He kisses my head. 'I'll see you later. I'll just go and say goodbye to your mum and the girls. Give my love to Alice. I'll grab a bacon butty on the way in.'

And then he's gone.

*

Alice stands on the pavement outside, pain written across her features when she notices Kyle's car. She makes a kind of 'oof' sound and folds her arms across her stomach.

'I'm sorry,' I say, hovering behind her. 'We didn't know what to do with it. We can't find the keys. I think the police still have them. They had to search the car too.' She looks forlorn in the blouse and jeans I'd pulled in a hurry from her side of the wardrobe. She shivers. A wind whips at our ankles and I realize I should have brought her a jacket. Thankfully Mum steps forward, having rushed out of the house as soon as she saw my car pull up, and drapes her navy cardigan around Alice's shoulders.

'He loved that car so much,' she says, a sob in her voice. 'But it's a bloody ugly colour.'

Mum and I exchange a glance over her head.

'Well, yes, it's very bright,' agrees Mum, tactfully. 'Come on now, let's get you in. I'll put the kettle on. Tasha bought you your favourite biscuits.'

Our house looks grey and depressing against the bleached sky. Mum manages to steer her to the front gate but Alice balks, her hands flying to her mouth and her body trembling. 'I don't think I can . . .'

I shoot Mum a look of horror. Perhaps we should have arranged for her to stay in a hotel, after all.

'You don't have to go in,' soothes Mum, her hands still on Alice's shoulders. 'I could see if the Grange has a room.' It's the one and only hotel in Chew Norton.

Alice takes a deep breath and closes her eyes. When I picked her up from hospital earlier the nurse had pressed her medication into my hands with instructions on when she needed to take it. I'd noticed a sedative among the painkillers and she must have taken one this morning – her reactions are slightly delayed and more cumbersome than usual. She grips the front gate, her knuckles white, as though she's going to faint.

Mum narrows her eyes at me as though this is my fault and then turns back to Alice. 'Sweetheart,' she says softly, 'shall we go to the Grange?'

Alice opens her eyes. There are tears on her cheeks and my heart twists. I suddenly hate this house for causing my sister so much pain. She gives a brief shake of her head, then touches the bandage at the temple and winces. 'I can't put it off for ever,' she says. 'I need to do this. I need to face it.'

'You can face it when you feel stronger,' says Mum, peeling Alice's hand from the gate and holding it between both of hers. 'Let's go to the Grange. We can share a room. Just for a few days . . .'

I know it's selfish. I do. But I can't help feeling a little excluded, which I often do when the three of us are together.

Alice pulls away from the gate and lifts her chin in a motion that is instantly familiar. It's something I've seen her do when she's trying to be stoic: her first day at a new school, leaving for university, Dad's funeral.

'I need to face this,' she says. 'I need to be with you all. With my nieces. I want the distraction. What would I do at a hotel? Just lie in bed all day with too much time to think.'

'If you're sure,' says Mum.

'I am.' She takes Mum's arm and I follow them down the front path. I'm impressed with Alice's strength as she steps into the hallway. Her eyes dart to the living room as we pass but Mum guides her to the kitchen where she slumps at the table, as though she has no emotional energy left. Her eyes fill up but she doesn't say anything else and Mum fusses around her, pouring tea and arranging custard creams – Alice's favourite ('Give me a proper dunking biscuit any day, not those fancy jobs,' she's always said) – on a plate.

'Here you are,' Mum says, pushing the plate in front of us but Alice doesn't touch the biscuits. She sits there staring into the distance, her eyes unfocused.

I told Mum about the note earlier but we still haven't had the opportunity to talk about it properly and I don't want to bring it up again now as I'd rather Alice didn't know for the moment.

'Is there anyone we can call?' Mum asks, as she sits down beside her. 'What about any of Kyle's family?'

Alice looks at her hands. Her nails, usually so immaculate, have been bitten down. 'I was his only family. His parents died. I told you . . .'

'I know that, darling. But did he have any brothers or sisters? Extended family?'

'No. He's an only child. And he never mentioned uncles, aunts or cousins. If he had them he never saw them.'

I sit down, too, and sip my tea although it swims uncomfortably in my stomach. I feel utterly helpless, and

I rack my brains for all the practical ways I could help my sister. 'Can I call work for you? Explain what's going on?'

She shakes her head. 'I've already asked my friend Ellen to do that.'

I remember Ellen. She's been friends with Alice since university. Ludicrously bright and driven, she grew up on some country estate with horses. I've always felt a bit intimidated by her and her loud, assured voice.

'Kyle's friends?'

Alice chews one of her nails. 'Ellen's sorted it. She's spoken to Will. He's one of Kyle's closest friends. He said he'll let everybody know. I – I can't face it.'

'Anything else?' asks Mum.

I sense it's too soon to ask her about funeral arrangements or about when Kyle's body will be released so I keep quiet.

'Not right now,' Alice snaps, and then she apologizes for her tone.

Mum pats her hand and tells her not to worry and then, evidently deciding she needs to try to distract Alice rather than bombard her with questions she starts talking about her art classes in France. Alice continues to stare at the table, her fingers knitted together around her mug. She remains silent after Mum has finished her story, and Mum throws me a panicked it's-your-turn-now look over Alice's head.

I dip a biscuit into my tea and prattle on about Elsie and Flossie and their 'lovely and nurturing' nursery, which seems to work as Alice lifts her head, fastens her gaze on me and seems to be engaged. She finally sips her tea, a flicker of interest in her face when I recount a funny story about Elsie and a tin of paint.

'That last night . . .' she says, her voice thick. 'We were clearing up after the twins and Kyle got paint all over his fingers . . .' A smile briefly flickers at the corners of her mouth. 'I felt so close to him in that moment. He was so kind to the girls.' Then her green eyes are on me. 'I'm sorry you had to cut your romantic break short.'

'Oh, Alice, none of this is your fault. If anything it's mine . . .'

Mum flashes me a warning look.

Alice frowns. 'What do you mean?'

'Well, if we hadn't done this life-swap thing –'

'Don't even go there,' says Alice, straightening her shoulders. She sips her tea, her eyes still on mine. 'How was your Venice trip? I hope you managed to recapture some of the magic even if you weren't there long. What did you do on your anniversary?'

I speak without thinking. 'Well, it started off romantic enough.' And then I tell her about the rain and getting lost.

'It can be like that there. Kyle and I have been so many times yet we still don't know our way around.'

Her chin wobbles and I press on. 'Then something scary happened. We were followed by a man with a knife.'

'What?' Mum and Alice say in unison. I'm so relieved that I've succeeded in momentarily distracting my sister that I carry on describing that night, how we felt as he followed us through the crowds and how we managed to lose him.

By the time I've finished Mum looks like she's about to

faint and Alice is staring at me wide-eyed. I've gone too far and I regret it instantly.

'That's dreadful,' Mum says, her hand fluttering around her throat. 'Aaron should never have taken you down back-streets like that.' It's the first time I've ever heard her criticize Aaron. Usually she treats him like the son she never had.

I try to backtrack. 'He wasn't to know and we soon found our way back to the main streets. The man spoke to us in Italian that we reckon translated into something like "You owe me."'

'Wait, what?' Alice asks in alarm. 'Why would he say that?'

'I don't know.' I can't bring myself to tell her Aaron believes we were targeted because I was wearing her fancy clothes and carrying her designer bag.

She's staring at me intently, her eyes narrowed. The bandage is pressing down on her brow, giving her a severe appearance. She puts a hand to her temple. 'I think I'm going to lie down, if that's okay. I've got a splitting head-ache and these painkillers aren't touching it . . .'

I stand up. 'Of course. Mum is in with the girls to give you some peace. I'll come with you.' I know it's going to be hard for her seeing the room where she'd last slept with Kyle.

'No.' She holds up a hand to stop me. 'I want to be on my own for a while. I'll – I'll be fine.'

Mum stands up too. 'Let us know if you need anything.'

And then we watch, as she leaves the room, feeling utterly and completely helpless.

16

TASHA

Friday, 18 October 2019

Donna, the other receptionist, and Lola, a trainee dental nurse, glance up from behind the desk in surprise when they see me walk in the next morning.

'Tasha!' exclaims Donna, standing up. She's a formidable woman at six foot tall, and she peers down at me, her eyes huge behind her thick bifocals. 'We heard what happened. Absolutely dreadful. We can't believe it.'

Of course they would have heard about Kyle's murder. This is a small village where nothing stays quiet for long. I dump my bag beside my chair and fill them in on what happened.

Lola, who must be in her mid to late twenties and gentle, doesn't say anything. Instead she just watches me with her big blue eyes while chewing the end of her pen as Donna stares at me, slack-jawed. Donna is about fifteen years older than me, with an ex-husband and a grown-up son but is always looking for love, usually online, and, as she says herself, always ending up with 'the wrong 'uns'. Her gaze is critical. 'Should you be back at work so soon? If you don't mind me saying, you look exhausted.'

I'm not offended. I've always admired how straight-talking Donna is. At least I know where I stand with her.

From my peripheral vision I see Lola getting up from her chair to go to the coffee machine in the corner. Then she's back proffering a cardboard cup. 'Here. I got you a latte. I'm so sorry about your sister and brother-in-law,' she says shyly, from under her pale blonde fringe, and returns to her seat.

'Thanks, Lola,' I say, her kindness making my eyes well up.

'You shouldn't be here.' Donna is standing over me with a hand on her hip, looking like a matron in the regulation blue scrubs we're all made to wear. She has a clipboard under one freckled arm.

'I've come in to ask for next week off,' I say. 'My sister is staying with me and . . .'

'Oh, my God, of course. Colin would give you compassionate leave.' Colin is one of the partners, the most senior.

Lola, who is leaning against the desk, smiles and nods. 'I agree with Donna. You should be at home with your family. How is your sister?' she asks. Everything about Lola is soft and quiet, even her voice, which is only a little more than a whisper. There is something almost childlike about her, with her fair plaited hair, and her scrubs hang off her small frame. Since she joined two months ago she's become very popular with the patients as she has a calming effect on them, and she's often brought into the dentist's room when Colin is seeing to someone particularly anxious. I've always wondered why she never went into traditional nursing at a hospital as she'd be amazing at it.

'She's not great,' I admit. 'I mean, physically she's been lucky, but emotionally . . .'

Lola's pretty face clouds and she looks distraught at the thought of my sister, whom she's never met, going through any kind of mental anguish and I realize that, no, she probably wouldn't be up for working on a hospital ward because she cares too much. At least as a dental nurse she doesn't have to deal with death or end-of-life care, apart from that one time when old Mr Langley died in the dentist's chair. That, apparently, had nothing to do with Colin and the crown he was just about to give him, but a dodgy heart.

There's a small throb of silence before Lola mutters again how sorry she is and moves away to retrieve the first patient from the waiting room.

Donna opens her mouth to speak when we're interrupted by the tinkle of the bell. A man in his late seventies in a pristine ironed shirt and brown slacks shuffles through the door. It's Arthur, my neighbour. When he notices me his aura changes to one of compassion; it was his wife, Maureen, who came to the girls' rescue that night.

'Hi, Tasha,' he says. 'I'm so sorry about your sister and her husband. What a dreadful business.' He shakes his head so vigorously I'm worried his dentures will fall out.

'Thank you.' I'd knocked for Maureen a few times since we moved back in because I wanted to ask her what she'd heard that night, but there was no answer. 'Now you're both back I'd love to pop over to thank Maureen for what she did for my girls,' I say.

'She'd love to see you. It's not like she sees much of me.' He chuckles. 'As soon as we got back late last night I was in my shed. Although I think she prefers it that way.'

'Oh, I'm sure she doesn't, Mr Medley,' says Donna, as she pushes a clipboard with a form attached across the counter towards him. 'Would you mind filling in this NHS form, please?' She reaches down to retrieve a pen. 'Here you go.'

'Thank you.' He picks up the clipboard and pen and begins writing with a shaky hand.

'Um, I hope you don't mind me asking,' I begin, after he's handed the form back to Donna and is about to head towards the waiting area. 'Did either of you hear anything other than a commotion that night?'

Donna is still hovering behind me, pretending not to listen.

'Why, yes. We were woken up by a loud bang and foot-steps outside – I think in your garden. And then, maybe five minutes or so after, a crashing sound. We always sleep with our window open.'

I think of what Flossie said about a 'loud bang'.

'Did you see anyone?'

He shakes his head. ''Fraid not. Maureen called the police because she knew you'd gone away and she thought it was strange. All these years we've lived next door to you and we've never heard anything like it.'

I think again about the note I received. 'Over the last few days, did you see anybody, other than police, lurking around the house? It's just I had . . .' I lower my voice '. . . a note. It wasn't a very nice note either.'

135

He frowns as he tries to remember. 'No, I don't think so . . .'

Just then Catherine, one of the dental hygienists, walks in. 'Are you ready, Mr Medley?' she asks brightly. She takes the form from Donna and ushers Arthur towards one of the treatment rooms.

When they've gone Donna rounds on me. 'What note? Has somebody been threatening you?' She folds her arms across her large chest. Donna and I have worked together for ten years and she's become a friend as well as a colleague, even though we are polar opposites and she slightly scares me with her no-nonsense attitude. She's the kind who would get up first to do karaoke, sober and to a packed room, or to chat to strangers at bus stops and in supermarket queues. If we're out and I ask her a question she answers it as if she's not just talking to me but to everybody else as well. It makes me shrink with embarrassment but I'm fond of her.

And I trust her with this information.

Donna has such an expressive face that everyone can always tell exactly what she's thinking. Her eyebrows lift in surprise and then horror when I tell her the contents of the note. 'So you think whoever wrote this note attacked Alice by mistake, thinking she was you?'

I rub a hand over my face. I know I must look like shit – I hardly slept last night. 'I don't know. Aaron and I have been back and forth with it. One minute I think so and the next I wonder if it's just someone with a grudge against me.'

I can see the cogs in Donna's brain whirling. 'And that's all it said? "It was supposed to be you"?'

'Yes . . .'

Just then Andrew, one of the dentists, walks in with a concerned smile to offer me his condolences and to tell me that I should definitely take compassionate leave for as long as I need.

It's started to rain when I set off. I don't need to pick up the girls from nursery until later so I go to the supermarket and get some supplies before heading home. I'm walking down the path when the door to the Medleys' house is thrust open and Arthur steps out. 'I'm glad I caught you,' he says, scurrying over to the waist-height hedge that divides our front gardens. He's wearing his slippers and a cardigan, not caring that the rain has started to come down more heavily, spattering his glasses. 'But I was thinking about what you asked me earlier at the dentist's. You know, about seeing someone outside your house over the last few days.'

I stop, my heart beating fast as I approach the hedge. 'Yes?'

'Well, after the police left, I did see a woman hanging around. At first I assumed she was police, but she wasn't smartly dressed or in uniform, and she wasn't wearing any kind of neck thingy. What are they called?' He furrows his already crinkled brow.

'Lanyards.'

'Yes, those.'

'Can you describe this woman?'

'Well, she was around your age, tall with long hair. Blonde.'

I'm disappointed. That description could fit many people. 'What else can you remember about her?'

'I'm afraid not much.'

'Can you remember what she was wearing?'

'Not in detail. Jeans, I think. A leather jacket.'

'And you definitely saw her after the police had gone?'

He takes off his glasses to wipe them with the hem of his cardigan. 'Yes, just after. It was strange. It was as though she was waiting for them to leave.'

I feel sick at the thought. 'And did you see this woman post something through the letterbox?'

'I'm not sure about that . . . she was certainly hovering by your front door.' He puts his glasses back on. 'I hope everything's okay, Tasha. It's very horrifying what happened. It's shocked the whole street. The whole village.'

'Thank you,' I say. 'You've been really helpful.'

'Actually,' he says, as I turn to leave. 'There was something else.' He pinches his septum. 'She had a nose piercing. Right here.'

My stomach turns over. I know someone who fits that description.

17

JEANETTE

Friday, 18 October 2019

After clearing the breakfast things Jeanette sits for a while on the sofa by the patio doors, taking in the quietness of Tasha's house, the soporific thrum of the washing-machine and the gentle vibrations of the dishwasher. She's feeling tired now after getting up so early with the twins, and is tempted to go and lie down, but Alice might need her. She's checked in on her on the hour, every hour. Princess Sofia is curled up next to her, a big cream fluff-ball. She remembers when Tasha had rung her a few months ago to tell her about rescuing the Persian and what her name would be. Jeanette had joked, 'I'm glad I'm not the one who'll be calling her in at night.'

And Tasha had replied tartly, 'Well, she's a house cat, so I won't have to call her in.'

Jeanette had hoped Tasha would work for a vet rather than a dentist. She's always been mad about animals and was forever rescuing them as a child, but she didn't do very well in her GCSEs, which knocked her confidence, so she'd left school at sixteen and gone to a college to do a secretarial course.

Jeanette bends over to stroke the cat as she sips her tea,

gazing out into the garden. The trees have turned russet and gold and look beautiful against the cloud-streaked sky. It's still raining, but every now and again the sun bursts out from behind the trees, bathing the kitchen in a bright dappled light, warming Jeanette's face and high-lighting the smudges on the glass of the patio doors. Jeanette vows to give them a good clean while she's here.

She thinks about the reporter who had turned up at the front door earlier while Tasha was out and the twins at nursery. Thankfully Alice had been asleep upstairs. It had unnerved Jeanette to see the young man standing there, as brazen as they come, wearing an expression that was a mixture of fake sympathy and something akin to excitement. She'd gone against all her polite instincts when she'd shooed him away, before shutting the door in his smug face. All of this reminds her too much of when Holly had gone missing, and it makes her stomach churn to remember the aftermath of her baby's abduction: the false leads, the odd ray of hope that turned into crushing disappointment, the finger-pointing, the gossip, the des-pair at not knowing where she was or even if she was still alive. She remembers how Jim handled it all, never break-ing down, never crying or taking to his bed, refusing to get up, like she had. He was like her human shield, pro-tecting her and giving her the space to grieve while he threw himself into the day-to-day running of their lives, bringing up their two young daughters. But she knows, underneath his stoical composure, that he suffered too. She often suspects his heart attack was caused by all the emotion he suppressed in order to appear strong.

She doesn't want to think of it, that horrendous day back in 1989, but it pushes its way into her mind regardless. The memories strong, even after all this time, but even more so at this time of year.

When she'd walked out of the greengrocer's, there had been a sliver of time, just before she'd realized that Holly had gone, when she'd been happy. Properly happy. She'd looked up at the cloudless azure sky and marvelled at the world, at the trees turning red and orange, at the pretty cobbled street, at this precious gift of a sunny, crisp autumn morning, knowing she was about to go home to her handsome husband and beautiful healthy daughters. Despite the mastitis and the piles and the sheer exhaustion of looking after three kids under five, in that brief moment she'd felt contented.

It was the last time she'd ever feel so light.

When she'd realized Holly was gone, she'd dropped her handbag and her recently purchased cabbage, as emotion after emotion had slammed into her: horror at finding the pram empty, despair when it dawned on her that her baby had been stolen, guilt that she'd left her outside, fear at having to tell Jim and wreck his life. It had been overwhelming. Totally overwhelming. She'd crumpled onto the pavement, Viv suddenly by her shoulder, helping her up, rushing back inside the greengrocer's to call the police and then Jim. The police had been brilliant in the aftermath, closing off the high street and swarming the village, and everyone had come together to search the woods, the pond and the lakes. Known paedophiles in the area were brought in for questioning, and extensive house-to-house searches were made. Jeanette and Jim were even advised to do a television appeal – which Jeanette has never been able to bring herself to watch.

There had been a few leads, back in the weeks and months afterwards: witnesses reported seeing a middle-aged woman wandering around the village in the hours after Holly went missing, in dirty clothes and with unwashed hair, clutching an old teddy bear to her chest, but that line of enquiry went cold when it was established the woman had escaped from a psychiatric hospital after Holly had been taken. Someone else reported seeing a young woman getting into a blue car with a baby in her arms, but they couldn't remember the make or model, or what the woman looked like. The police tried, Jeanette really believes that.

Not once, in all the years afterwards, did Jim blame her for leaving Holly in the pram outside the shop – even though she'll always blame herself. It could have broken their marriage but Jim stood by her. And then he died. Her rock had finally left her, without ever knowing what had happened to their youngest daughter, forcing her to bear the brunt of it alone. And she'd tried to pick up the pieces of her life. To start again.

She thinks about the life she's left behind in France in such a hurry. What will Eamonn think? He was planning on coming over to her today so they could walk to their art session together. She should text him, really. She imagines him standing at the door of her cottage in the little French town that she now calls home, in his smock and sun hat, looking like he's wandered out of a different age, and feels a pang of . . . what? She's not sure yet. Fondness, perhaps. Is she missing him?

She glances at the clock on the wall. It's gone eleven thirty already. She picks up her mobile from the kitchen table and sends him a quick message. *Had to go to England urgently. Not sure when I'll be back.* She deliberates about putting a kiss and eventually decides not to. She's still agonizing over whether or not the text was too abrupt when Alice appears in the doorway. Her eye socket looks even more bruised and swollen today and has turned a yellowy-green, which contrasts starkly with her ashen face. Her red hair hangs down her back and needs a good brush, like she's spent all night tossing and turning. She's wearing a sleek dressing-gown in mink-coloured silk but it does nothing to disguise the anguish she's obviously feeling. Her eyes are red from lack of sleep and tears, and every movement is imbued with grief, from her slightly stooped walk to the fingers that tremble when she touches the bandage on her head.

'Sit yourself down, love. I'll make you a cup of tea,' says Jeanette, getting up from the table, her heart heavy at witnessing the pain in her elder child. 'Have you managed to get any rest?'

Alice pulls out a chair and sinks onto it. 'Not really. The sedatives knocked me out for a bit. DC Jones called me earlier to check in. She told me that Aaron kindly did the formal identification of Kyle and that I can . . . I can go and see him once his body has been released,' she falters.

Jeanette carries two mugs to the table and places one in

143

front of Alice before sitting down next to her. She remembers having to identify Jim after his heart attack. She doesn't wish that on anyone, and especially not Alice after everything she's been through. It was a chance for Jeanette to say goodbye but, even so, it was obvious her Jim had already gone.

Alice wraps her fingers around her mug. 'Someone called Philip Thorne will be the senior investigating officer on the murder investigation. I asked . . . I asked about a funeral. There will be a post-mortem and then the coroner will release his – his body . . .' Her face crumples and she pushes away her mug. 'I want the funeral to be in London, our local church. Not that he went to church, really, but . . . anyway, cremation. That's what I want. Not that we really talked about it.'

Jeanette reaches for her daughter's trembling hands. 'Oh, sweetheart, don't think about that yet. And you've got me to help you, and Tasha.'

Alice nods, swallowing, and Jeanette can almost see her steeling herself. So like her father. 'Where is Tasha by the way?'

Jeanette takes her hands away from Alice's. 'She went in to speak to her colleagues at work about having some time off and then she rang me to say she'd popped to the supermarket. She should be on her way home. What about something to eat? You need to keep your strength up.' Her daughter is wasting away before her very eyes.

'I couldn't possibly, Mum.' She sips her tea and lowers her mug. 'Even this is making me feel sick.' She sighs. 'I want to go home and yet I don't. I can't face it.'

'You don't have to face it yet,' insists Jeanette. She wishes there was a way of taking away her daughter's pain. She remembers all too well that all-consuming feeling of grief and despair. She gets up and pops a slice of bread into the toaster. Hopefully Alice can nibble it even if she's not hungry.

Alice is silent as Jeanette busies herself with buttering the toast, but when she turns back to her daughter tears are cascading down her cheeks. 'Oh, sweetheart,' she says again, rushing to her side of the table and wrapping her arms around her shoulders. She can feel Alice's bones through the thin fabric of her dressing-gown. 'I wish I could do something . . .'

Alice lets herself be hugged for a bit and then she moves away, swiping at her cheeks. 'I'm lucky to have you.' She sniffs as Jeanette fetches the plate of toast still on the worktop. Alice smiles gratefully and, as Jeanette hoped, picks up the toast and starts nibbling the edges. She can tell Alice is trying to put a brave face on things and she wants to tell her it's okay to cry, to show emotion. She doesn't have to be strong all the time. It's better to let it out than for it to fester, like it did with Jim. Even as a little girl Alice rarely cried. When she was told off, which wasn't often, her lip might have quivered betraying her emotions for a couple of seconds, but then a defiant light would shine in her eyes and she'd hold up her head and walk away.

'Mum?'

Jeanette looks up from her mug to see her daughter watching her through her one narrowed eye.

'Can I ask you something?'

'Sure.' She wonders what it will be. Will it be about her life in France, about the possibility of meeting someone new? About how to live with the sudden death of a husband? Oh, how she wishes she knew the answer to that one.

Alice looks a little uncomfortable as she toys with her toast. 'I don't know if it's because of . . . because of Kyle but I keep thinking about Holly.'

Jeanette swallows painfully. They very rarely talk about Holly even if she is in Jeanette's thoughts every day. It had been Jim's suggestion that they didn't because he'd wanted the girls to have a 'normal life' that wasn't in the shadow of their baby sister's abduction. And now, when they do try to talk about her, it feels unnatural and weighed down by their collective underlying grief. There is no grave to visit, no closure to be had, but Jeanette has always told herself that if there is no body there is hope.

'Okay,' says Jeanette, carefully. 'That's understandable.'

'I know it's different circumstances but . . . you must wonder about Holly all the time. I know I do.'

'Well, yes, I think about Holly every day. I just hope that whoever took her gave her a good life and . . .' The back of her throat burns at the thought of the alternative.

Alice wipes at her good eye, suddenly seeming even more exhausted than she did when she came down. 'I'm going back to bed for a bit. When the girls get home will you wake me up? I want to see them.'

'Of course, love.'

As Alice is leaving the kitchen she stops at the doorway. 'Love you, Mum.'

Jeanette's heart swells. 'Love you too.' Her beautiful brave girl.

And then she's gone.

Jeanette is about to dump the half-eaten food in the recycling bin when her other daughter walks through the door with a face like thunder.

'Is everything all right, sweetheart?' she asks, although it's obvious from Tasha's face that everything is definitely not all right. Unlike Alice, Tasha could never hide her emotions.

Tasha shakes her head. She has dark circles under her eyes. 'No. I've just spoken to Arthur next door. He thinks he saw who posted that horrible note. It was a woman, Mum. A woman. Who would do something like that? And the description he gave . . . well, it fits Zoë.'

18

TASHA

Friday, 18 October 2019

I pace the kitchen as I recount my conversation with Arthur. Mum hardly moves as she sits on the chair in her long skirt and white blouse, her legs crossed at the ankles. She's holding a plate of half-eaten toast in her hand, which she eventually places back on the table.

'Zoë? Who's Zoë?'

Nausea sweeps over me. 'She works with Aaron.'

Mum looks concerned. 'Why would Zoë do that? Does she have some grudge against you? Do you really think she could have attacked Kyle and Alice?'

'I . . .' I stop pacing. 'I don't know. I've not even met her properly.' I shake my head. Am I clutching at straws? I can't go around accusing someone based on a loose and ubiquitous description of blonde hair and a leather jacket. But the nose ring. I don't know anyone who has one through their septum except Zoë.

Mum sighs. 'There are lots of weirdos out there. Let the police do their job. It's in their hands now.'

'I suppose,' I say, sinking onto a chair. 'I just wish I knew what was meant by the note.' Pain presses against my temples.

I don't want to admit to her the doubts I've been trying to push away since I saw Aaron and Zoë outside the other night. If Zoë did post the note through my letterbox, the only motive I can see for her doing that would be Aaron. Maybe she wants me out of the way to get to him.

'What is it?' Mum says, eyeing me carefully.

'I . . . It's silly. But before we went to Venice I saw a text message on Aaron's phone. I didn't mean to look – I'm not in the habit of checking his phone or anything like that. But we'd drifted a bit, you know, after the twins were born. Nothing major,' I add, to reassure her, when I notice her face clouding with worry, 'just, you know, not spending enough time together, constantly being wrapped up in looking after the twins or work . . .' I trail off, embarrassed. Mum nods encouragingly. 'Anyway he'd left his phone on the table to go to the loo and it buzzed, the screen lighting up. So I – I looked at it and saw this message from Zoë . . . It was mildly flirty and I asked him about it, about her, and he said they were just friends. That she'd started at the garage in the summer and they'd just hit it off.' I swallow the niggling feeling that I've had ever since I saw that message.

'He's entitled to have female friends, sweetheart,' Mum says gently.

'I know. I know that.'

'He loves you and the girls so much, anyone can see it. Aaron would never do anything to destroy that.'

I fidget. 'Except he has. Once before.'

'What?' Mum sits up straighter. 'When? When has he done this to you before?'

'You remember? When we were nineteen and I found out he was cheating on me with Joanne Parker from the estate.'

'Well . . . yes, but you were kids back then.'

'It still bloody hurt,' I snap.

Mum looks momentarily surprised before her expression softens. 'Sorry, love, I didn't mean to sound dismissive. Of course it must have hurt. I remember how devastated you were.' I'm sure she's remembering the aftermath too, the embarrassment and worry after getting that phone call from the police, and Dad having to pick me up from a jail cell. 'But it doesn't mean Aaron would do something like that now. He's a husband and a father, and he loves you.'

I feel bad for snapping at Mum. Of course things are different now. And after a terrible six months when I drank too much and had a few ill-advised and miserable one-night stands with strangers in nightclub toilets to try to get over him, I pulled myself together. A few months later he admitted he'd made a terrible mistake. We've been fine since then. Happy, mostly, in the way long-term relationships often are, a few ups and downs along the way, but nothing big enough to destroy our love for one another. But since the twins were born and our intimacy has dwindled I'm worried our relationship has changed too much.

I always thought the baby years would be the most challenging, and they were, for so many reasons, like disrupted sleep and getting used to being responsible for keeping a defenceless human being alive – or two in our case – but nobody really talks about the years after that, when the euphoria and novelty of having created a baby together wears off and you're left raising children you love more than anything in the world and who come first. Your relationship with their father gets pushed further down the line. Even Princess Sofia gets more attention than Aaron most of the time. But then I get angry because it's not just *my* responsibility to make our marriage work. It's Aaron's, too, and if he's going to jump into the arms of an attractive woman who gives him a bit of attention every time our relationship gets a bit rough or boring, maybe he's not the man for me.

I sigh. 'Anyway – like you say, it's in the hands of the police now.'

'Exactly,' says Mum. She gets up and squeezes my shoulder as she takes the plate of toast to the sink. 'Oh,' she says, turning back to me. 'Probably best not to mention any of this to Alice yet. She's got enough on her plate and I don't want her worrying about this too. You know how protective she can be over you.'

'I won't. We've already agreed not to tell her about the note yet.'

'Good,' says Mum, turning back to the sink and reaching into the cupboard underneath, taking out a cloth and some window polish. 'I'm going to have a go at that glass.'

I bristle, then remind myself that she's only trying to help and she's not judging me on my messy house.

It's only twelve thirty and I don't need to pick the twins up until one o'clock, but when Mum starts dusting the ceiling lights I know I have to get out of the house. I take the double buggy out of the boot of my car and unfold it on the street. The twins are usually too tired to walk after nursery and without it the ten-minute trip will take more like half an hour. I'm not really concentrating, my head crammed full of Alice and Kyle, the mysterious note and my conversation with Arthur, so when a woman approaches me I don't notice her at first.

'Excuse me,' she says, blocking my path. 'But are you Natasha Harper?'

'Um . . .' I blink up at her. She's tall and slim with long blonde hair gathered into a swishy ponytail. She's wearing ripped jeans, a grey suede biker jacket and pink Converse trainers. My first thought is that she's a journalist. We've had several call the house since Kyle was killed. I stiffen. 'It's Pritchard now. Who wants to know?'

It's then I notice her eyes are red-rimmed, as though she's been crying. 'I'm sorry to ambush you like this. I'm . . .' her elegant fingers find the tassel on her bag '. . . I'm Eve Milligan. I grew up around here, and I've recently moved back with my fiancé.'

'Are you a reporter?' I blurt out.

'What? No, no, nothing like that.' She smiles sadly. She's very beautiful in a Sienna Miller kind of way. 'It's a bit weird but . . .'

Impatience niggles at me. What does she want?

'. . . I knew Kyle. We . . . Well, we used to go out. A long time ago.'

My interest is immediately piqued. 'You were Kyle's girlfriend?' I remember him telling me he went out with someone who came from a nearby town.

She nods, still fiddling with the tassel. 'And I've just heard that he's . . . that he's dead, and it's so awful. I think I'll go mad if I don't speak to someone about it. I can't talk to my fiancé because he's the jealous type and he wouldn't like it if he knew I'd kept in touch with Kyle but . . .' She sniffs and brushes at her eyes. 'So I came to Chew Norton hoping to see you.'

'Wait.' I grip the handles of the buggy tightly. 'Why me?'

'Because I know it happened in your house and I can't talk to Alice about this. Not when she's going through so much.'

A thought occurs to me. 'How did you know where to find me?'

She reddens. 'I'm sorry. I asked around and found out who you were and what you looked like. I promise I'm not some kind of stalker.'

I think of the note. She's tall and blonde but she doesn't have a nose ring. Still, she could have taken it out.

'I just really needed to talk to you.'

'I don't understand. Why?'

She lowers her voice and looks around furtively but, apart from an elderly couple walking arm in arm up ahead, the pavement is empty. 'I saw him the day he died. He called me to meet.'

'Did my sister know about this?'

'He didn't tell Alice. Or anyone. It was all a bit . . . well, a bit weird actually. And now he's dead, murdered, and I feel . . .' She places a hand on her throat. 'I need to talk to someone about it. Can we go somewhere for a coffee?'

'I can't right now, I'm sorry. I'm just on the way to pick up my daughters.'

'Oh, yes, yes, of course.' She looks crestfallen.

This could be important. Why did Kyle meet up with her without telling Alice? Why all the secrecy? Does she know something about Kyle's murder? 'But I could meet you later?' I offer. 'About four?'

Her face brightens with relief. 'Oh, would you? That would be fantastic. Thank you. What about Trudi's Tearoom?'

'Perfect,' I say.

'Great.' She dabs a fingertip gently at a tear in the corner of her eye and moves out of my path. 'I'll see you in a bit, then.'

I nod and continue walking, mulling over our conversation, intrigued to know what she wants to talk about.

After I get back and settle the girls with Mum, I race upstairs to see Alice, wondering if she'll be awake or still sedated.

She's propped up by pillows when I knock and enter her bedroom. She looks terrible, a dark circle under one eye, the other half closed under the yellowish bruise. She's taken the bandage off and I can see where the stitches run behind her parting. She tries to smile at me and my heart breaks. I sit down next to her at the edge of the bed. She shifts her weight. 'I need to get up,' she says. 'I want to see the twins.'

'Do you need any help?'

'Please,' she says. 'Those sedatives are making me feel

woozy and trembly and fuzzy-headed. I need to ... I need to organize my thoughts. There's so much to do, to arrange ...'

'Alice. Stop. You've been through a terrible ordeal and you're still getting better. Mum and I will help with everything.'

'I'm his only family,' she wails. 'It's my responsibility.'

'It can wait.' I try to sound as firm as I can. I don't know how long it takes for a body to be released after a murder but I can't believe it will be quick. 'You have time to organize everything. You need to concentrate on getting well. You were attacked, Alice. Left for dead. You could have been ...' I swallow a wave of emotion at the thought that she could have died too.

She squeezes my fingers, her eyes welling. I can't tell her about Eve. Not yet. Not until I know why she met up with Kyle on the day he died.

I help my sister out of bed and into her silk dressing-gown. She leans on me as we walk down the stairs together, like she's aged forty years.

Elsie comes running over to us as soon as we step into the kitchen. She's holding the cloth rabbit Alice and Kyle bought her. 'Can you help me with this dress, Aunty Alice?' she says, in her little voice, which has a slight lisp. She holds up a pretty dove-grey frock with lace detail and Alice takes it.

'Of course, darling,' she says, going to the shabby two-seater sofa that's next to the patio doors and sitting down. Toys are already strewn over the floor.

Elsie climbs onto her lap and I watch them, Flossie at

their feet, as Alice engages with my daughters. I glance at Mum who raises her eyebrows at me.

I check my watch. I've got a few hours before I need to meet Eve but I have no idea what excuse to give or how I'm going to get away without questions.

19

Eve is already sitting in the window of Trudi's Tearoom nursing a coffee in a tall glass and scrolling through her phone when I arrive. I stand outside for a few moments, watching her, the way she lounges back in her chair, her legs crossed, twirling one Converse-clad foot. She's so composed and confident, despite how upset she seemed over Kyle. Part of me wants to run a mile but the other, bigger, part needs to find out what she wants.

I take a deep breath and walk through the door. She looks up instantly and beams at me. It's like that's her default greeting, though, because her face drops when she sees me. She must remember why she's here and that Kyle is dead.

'Hi,' I say, coming towards her and pulling out the chair opposite. 'Sorry I'm a bit late.' I feel sweaty and out of breath after almost running here. 'Hard getting out of the house.'

'That's okay. What can I get you? My treat.'

'Oh, thanks. A cappuccino would be great.'

'Coming right up.' She hops off her seat and I take off my jacket while she's at the counter. Two minutes later she's back. 'They'll bring it over,' she says, slipping back into her chair.

'Thanks,' I say, feeling awkward suddenly.

'I know it's a bit weird,' she says, 'me asking to meet up.'

Eve is about to say more when we're interrupted by a teenage girl with my cappuccino. The cup is too full and coffee slops into the saucer. 'Thanks,' I say, taking it carefully. The girl looks relieved to have it out of her hands.

When she's gone, Eve says, 'The thing you need to understand about me and Kyle . . .' she blinks back tears '. . . is that we were each other's first and were always special to one another. I think that's why he asked to meet me that day. Someone he trusted from the past, I suppose. We had this bond but . . .' Her expression darkens. 'When we finished university he dumped me. Quite out of the blue. I was absolutely devastated.' She sniffs and reaches into her huge tote bag for a tissue. 'God, I'm all over the place. I'm so upset by his death but have to put on a happy face for Owen. He doesn't even know about Kyle.' She blows her nose loudly. 'Anyway, I didn't see Kyle for about five years, maybe longer. And then one day, while I was living in London, I ran into him again. We met for a drink and had a catch-up. We never started anything back up again, if that's what you're thinking,' she says, as though she's reading my mind. 'We were just mates. I suppose, on some level, I still loved him. I mean, he was gorgeous, right?' She gives a sad laugh. 'But we were just friends. Sometimes years would go by when I wouldn't hear from him. I remember him telling me when he first met your sister. He adored her, you know. I never thought he was the marrying kind but he swept her off her feet. Or should that be the other way around?' She falls silent and sips her latte. Is this the only reason she wanted to meet up? To reminisce over Kyle? I'm sensing not.

'What was the reason he wanted to meet up with you the day he died?' I ask.

She frowns and licks the froth from her lips. 'He said, well . . .' She looks around but the tearoom is practically empty, apart from a group of schoolkids in the corner and the staff behind the counter. She lowers her voice anyway, 'He told me he was scared.'

'What?' I say, louder than I mean to, causing one of the kids to turn to look at me. Why on earth would Kyle be scared?

'He told me not to tell anyone about our meeting. He hadn't told Alice. He wanted to meet by the lakes. I think he was worried someone might see us. Of course I agreed, the sap that I am.' She raises one eyebrow as though challenging me to disagree with her. When I don't she continues, 'When I got there he was in his running gear.'

So that was how he explained his absence to Alice.

'What did he say?'

'Well,' she gives a little cough, 'he told me he'd made some mistakes, got in with some dodgy people, and he was worried he was being followed. He'd been threatened, by the sound of it.'

'Dodgy people? Like who?'

'It sounded like maybe investors. He wasn't making much sense, to be honest. He was talking fast, as though he was worried he'd run out of time. He said Alice had seen someone lurking around the house – your

159

house – and he believed it was these "dodgy people" looking for him. And that he was scared. He said that a few times.' She gulps. 'God, I should have taken it seriously, shouldn't I? I should have told the police.'

'Yes,' I say. 'I think you should let the police know now. Definitely.'

It sounds like Kyle was the intended target, not me after all, and the note was someone's malicious attempt to scare me.

She puts her head into her hands and gives a little groan.

'Did he say anything about Alice? I mean, does she know he was being threatened?'

Eve lifts her head. 'He said Alice didn't know, and he couldn't tell her because he worried about her. He said she puts on a brave face, a tough façade, but that she was vulnerable underneath it all.'

Vulnerable. That doesn't sound like the Alice I know. She's tough, ambitious, dependable. She'd have been the perfect person to confide in. Maybe Kyle was too embarrassed to tell her. 'So Alice didn't know that some dodgy creeps had invested in Kyle's business?' I remember what Aaron had told me about an investor pulling out. Alice must have known about that.

'No. Kyle was adamant that Alice thought his investors were all above board.'

'Right.' My mind is racing. 'What else did he say?'

She plays with her hands, which are resting on the table. 'He said he felt lost, lonely. That he'd made some mistakes. He talked about his brother briefly too.'

160

'His *brother*? Alice said he was an only child.'

'No, he has a brother. Younger, I think. I remember meeting him once, back when Kyle and I were students. He's an addict. He went off the rails in his late teens and they became estranged, after their parents were killed in that crash. His name's Connor. Anyway, Kyle sounded regretful about Connor. And, basically, he was worried so . . . yeah.' She tails off. 'That's it, really. We said good-bye, he hugged me hard, said he hoped to see me again soon, and then he went. Jogged off towards the village. I'd offered him a lift home but he didn't want it. Said running cleared his head. It's hard to believe that later that night he was murdered.' Her eyes fill with tears and she blinks rapidly.

I stare at her in shock, trying to take it all in. Eventually I say, 'You need to tell the police.'

'I know,' she mumbles. 'I've been agonizing over it for days.'

We exchange numbers, then get up and leave. It's nearly five and the staff are packing up the chairs behind us. Aaron should be back now, and Mum and Alice will wonder where I am.

When we're on the street about to part ways, she says, 'Oh, yes, and another thing Kyle said, which I've been pondering. I wish I'd asked him more about it at the time, but it seemed a throwaway comment. The conversation had been so rushed.'

'What was it?'

'Well,' she shifts her weight from one foot to the other, 'when he was talking about Alice and the reasons he didn't want to worry her, he said something along the lines of "Not when she's got all this going on right now with her missing sister."'

I stare at her. 'What did he mean by that?'

'I don't know. I thought your sister was abducted a long time ago, as a baby.'

'Yes. Thirty years ago. So why would he say "right now"?'

She folds her arms across her chest. 'I dunno. It could be nothing but he made it sound like . . . well, like Alice was perhaps . . .' she lowers her voice '. . . looking for her.'

20

When I arrive back at the house Aaron is home. He's playing with the twins in the garden. I can hear their excited cries as he runs after them, catching them around the waist, and the three of them falling onto the damp grass, giggling, legs in the air. I'm so happy to see Aaron playing with his children that I can't be annoyed that the girls will probably be covered with mud when they get in.

Mum is in the kitchen and the smell of cottage pie wafts from the oven. 'There you are,' she says, scraping potato peelings into the recycling bin. 'We were all wondering where you'd got to.'

'Is Alice still in her room?'

Mum nods, looking grave. 'She said she's been speaking with her therapist on the phone.'

'Alice has a therapist?' I say, dumping my bag on the table.

'It would appear she's had one for quite a long time. I'm glad she's talking to a professional about her feelings. I don't want her to bottle it all up . . . like, well, like your father always did.' Mum's face darkens as she says this and she turns away from me to put a pan of mixed vegetables on the hob.

I know Mum always thought Dad didn't express his feelings enough, especially about Holly's disappearance.

He buried his head in his work for the council instead. I was too young to remember the aftermath of Holly's abduction but I do recall never seeing my father cry or even hearing him talk about her. Once, when I was about nine, Alice and I had been to the shops with Dad and when we got back we found Mum in the living room clutching one of Holly's soft toys – a plush brightly coloured dog that we called Rainbow – and sobbing on the sofa. I remember Dad simmering with disapproval and she'd quickly composed herself, magicking away her tears and the toy as if the whole thing hadn't taken place. Throughout the preceding years we'd have an occasional police visit – the same detective, George Benning, who'd investigated Holly's disappearance, whom Mum would usher into the living room along with Dad, leaving Alice and me to eavesdrop at the door. He'd come regularly at first, updating them on any possible sightings, and Alice and I would exchange excited glances, our ears pressed to the door, imagining our long-lost sister returning home and, when she did, which one of us she'd share a bedroom with. Yet these sightings never materialized into a living, breathing Holly and, as the years went on, George Benning's visits became less and less frequent until, five years ago, he retired.

Aaron and the girls burst into the room bringing with them fresh air and the smell of grass. Flossie starts telling me how they'd spotted a family of frogs, her cheeks red, her voice high with excitement, Elsie joining in. And I hug them to me just that little bit harder as they talk over each other to tell me about it.

'Come on, girls,' says Mum, tactfully, knowing I'll want to talk to Aaron. 'Let's get you into the bath.'

She ushers them out of the room. Aaron and I stand awkwardly in the middle of the kitchen. He's still wearing his work overalls. I have so much to tell him, but I don't know where to start.

'Cup of tea?' I ask instead, going towards the kettle.

'Nah, you're all right. You haven't seen my wrench, have you? I was looking for it earlier but it's not in my tool kit.'

'Wrench?'

'Yeah, the wheel-nut wrench. It's where I always keep it.'

I shake my head. I can't even picture what it looks like.

'That's annoying.' He sighs. 'Think I'll jump in the shower. How's Alice?'

'I've hardly seen her today. She's been in her room for most of it and she's hardly eaten, but she's got a therapist apparently, and she's been speaking to him or her on the phone.'

'Oh, right. That's good, isn't it?' He raises an eyebrow in my direction.

'Yes. Of course it is.' He doesn't say it, but I can guess what he's thinking: that Alice inhabits a different world from us. A world with expensive therapists and private health care and members-only clubs.

He frowns and steps towards me. 'Do you think you need to see someone?' His voice is full of concern.

'I don't know. Maybe.' I think of all that's happened to our family. Holly, my dad. So much grief. And how much

I worry about Elsie and Flossie. 'I just feel a bit over-whelmed at times, that's all.'

He pulls me into his arms. 'If you need to see someone we'll find the money,' he says, kissing the top of my head. That's all I needed to hear.

I pull away. 'I do need to talk to you about something.'

'Okay . . . Should I be worried?' He's smiling as he says it but I can see the glimmer of apprehension on his face.

I take his hand, lead him to the table, and then, as quickly as I can before we're interrupted by Mum or the twins, I tell him everything. It's a relief to get it off my chest.

'Jesus,' he says, when I've finished.

'I know.'

'Is Eve going to tell the police what she told you?'

'She said she would. We've exchanged numbers.'

'And Alice knows nothing about this?'

'That's what Eve seems to think.'

He hasn't mentioned Zoë, even when I told him about my conversation with Arthur and his description of a blonde woman with a nose ring being seen near our front door.

'So you think Kyle was deliberately targeted? That someone – maybe someone he owed money to – followed him here to Chew Norton and killed him?'

I nod slowly. 'It's a possibility, isn't it?'

'Yes, it is,' he says, with a sigh. 'And hopefully it means you weren't the intended target.'

I scratch my wrist and Aaron reaches out to stop me. I pull my sleeve over my hand to prevent myself from dragging my nails over it. 'It looks that way. The note must have been from someone who hates me enough to wish me dead.' I laugh drily.

Aaron shakes his head. 'It might not be anyone we know. It could just be a prank. Some horrible troll who likes to mess with people. All this, though,' he throws up his hands, 'it does make me wonder what Kyle was involved in –'

'What do you mean?'

Alice is standing in the doorway.

21

Alice pulls out a chair next to me and sits down. Her bruised eye has opened a bit and looks less swollen but she's still in her nightwear and she smells of unwashed hair and bed sheets.

I exchange a worried glance with Aaron, who is sitting opposite.

'What do you mean?' she asks again, her gaze flickering between us, her expression stony. 'I heard what you were saying about Kyle.' How can I tell her that her husband might have been lying to her? 'Tasha?' Her voice is cold. 'Stop thinking I'm some fragile little thing you have to keep things from. It's fucking annoying. I'm a grown-up. Tell me what you know.'

I look across at Aaron, who nods, and then I carefully fill her in on my meeting with Eve.

Alice's already pale skin goes a shade lighter and she doesn't speak for a moment or two after I've finished.

'Did you know?' I probe. 'About any dodgy investments? Or investors pulling out?'

Her voice sounds thick. 'I knew an investor had pulled out, but I believed it was all legit. I never knew there was anything shady in any of his dealings and I don't believe it. Kyle was an upstanding guy, a fantastic businessman.

There is no way he'd be doing anything illegal or "dodgy", as you put it.'

'He never said anything about being followed or being scared?'

'No. Nothing.' She looks angry and I feel my insides shrink. I wish she hadn't overheard. I should have taken Aaron into the garden to tell him about it. Of course she's not going to want to believe her husband, the love of her life, was involved in anything underhand.

'And you never felt like you were being followed at home in Hampstead or when you and Kyle were in Venice?'

'Never. I don't believe this Eve and, quite frankly, I'm pissed off you met up with her.'

My cheeks grow hot and I catch Aaron's eye. His mouth is set in a straight, disapproving line as though he agrees with Alice. I turn back to my sister, feeling sick at the thought of upsetting her when she's going through so much. 'I'm sorry. I should have told you.'

'It's fine.'

'No, it's not. I'm really sorry.'

'Look,' she sighs, 'Kyle had mentioned Eve to me before. She wouldn't leave him alone, always wanting to meet up, to see him. It's obvious she was still in love with him. In the end he had to give her the cold shoulder to get rid of her. I bet she didn't tell you that. I think she's lying about this. Trying to give herself a bit of limelight and make herself feel important.'

For the first time I begin to doubt Eve's version of events.

'I just don't believe Kyle would say all this to someone he happened to bump into on a jog.' She pulls her dressing-gown further around herself, her jaw set determinedly. I know not to push it.

'Eve said something else.' I haven't even told Aaron this part yet and I'm wondering if I should say it to Alice. What if Eve is lying and I make Alice even more upset and angry?

Alice lifts her chin. 'Go on.'

I falter, knowing this is a big bombshell. 'She . . . she said the reason Kyle didn't tell you was because he didn't want to worry you as you were looking for . . . for Holly.'

The change in the air is infinitesimal but it's there. I can see Aaron's posture has altered: he's more alert, leaning across the table.

'Right.' Alice considers this and a myriad of emotions pass over her face. And then she sits up straighter. 'Well, that's another lie. I've not actively been looking for Holly. I wouldn't know where to start.'

Just then Mum walks in and we all look up at her with guilty expressions. She frowns, first at me and then at Alice, just like she used to do when we were kids and up to no good. 'What's going on?'

'Nothing,' I say, getting up. 'Just chatting.'

'Yep, I need to get the twins to bed,' says Aaron, following my lead. Mum doesn't look convinced but she's interrupted by the twins who come barrelling into the room, fresh from their bath, and straight over to Alice. I watch my sister's face light up at the sight of them. She looked like she was flagging before but she perks up as

Elsie jumps onto her lap and Flossie clambers onto the chair I've just vacated, clutching her floppy cloth bunny.

'Aunty Alice,' asks Elsie, making herself comfortable, 'is Uncle Kyle with the angels?'

I freeze and I sense Mum and Aaron do too. This is the first time either of the twins have brought up Kyle in front of Alice. I hold my breath, glancing at my sister. What will she tell them? Will she be cross with me that I talked to them about angels and Heaven when she's an atheist?

Her chin wobbles but she composes herself to smooth back Elsie's beautiful red hair. 'Yes, my darling. Uncle Kyle is with the angels.'

'I hope they're looking after him,' says Flossie, seriously, her legs in fleecy pyjamas dangling over the chair, much too short to reach the floor.

Alice reaches over and strokes Flossie's plump cheek. 'Yes, they'll be taking good care of him,' she says gently, her eyes shining.

I exhale in relief. I sit and watch her with the twins for a while until Aaron shoos them up to bed. Mum's attention is on the cooking, but as Alice walks past me, she leans in and whispers, 'I need to tell you something. But not yet. Not in front of Mum. Another time, okay?'

And then she leaves before I can ask her what she means.

22

TASHA

'So how are you, really?' asks Donna, passing me a large glass of the house white as she sits down next to me.

We're in the Duck and Toad, the only gastro pub in the village. The other pub, the Packhorse where Aaron and his mates often go and where Viv sometimes works behind the bar, is far less salubrious, with its ugly brown furniture, torn armchairs, sticky carpet and dartboard. We much prefer the rustic open fireplace, the Farrow & Ball-painted tongue-and-groove walls, the scrubbed oak tables and the stone-baked pizzas here. At the Packhorse you'd be lucky to get chicken in a basket.

Our table is next to a mullioned stone window with views over the valley. It's already dark but we can see the twinkly lights of the next village in the distance, like a hundred blinking animals staring back at us.

'I feel guilty about being out tonight,' I say in response, thanking her for the wine.

Alice has been in bed most of the day and she still hasn't told me the thing she can't say in front of Mum. There have been a few times today when she's been about to but then Mum would walk into the room, almost like she knew. Aaron is at the Packhorse with the lads from work, so when Donna invited me out for a drink Mum was insistent that I go. 'You need to get out of the house, love,' she'd said. 'The girls are in bed and I'm happy in front of the TV with my knitting.' Now, as I take a sip of the chilled wine, I feel myself relax for the first time since we arrived back from Venice. 'But I'm okay,' I continue, releasing a deep breath. 'I definitely feel better for getting out.'

'I just can't believe what's happened,' says Donna, grabbing the menus from where they're propped up next to the condiments and handing me one. 'Poor Kyle. And your sister, I can't even imagine what she's going through.'

Every time I think of Alice I get that same swoop of anxiety in my stomach. 'Do you mind if we talk about something else?'

Donna looks up from the menu. 'Sure. But if there's anything I can do, seriously, then please ask. You promise?'

I nod gratefully. I know Donna means what she says. She might be a bit on the mouthy side but she has a heart of gold. She still visits her ex's housebound mother every week and brings her groceries, stays and chats with her. And she can't do enough for her twenty-two-year-old son, Tyler, who is forever popping into the clinic to ask her for money or to borrow her car.

Just then Catherine, our hygienist, walks in, followed by Lola. They're chatting away and I watch, fascinated, when Lola throws back her head and properly laughs. I've only been out with her once or twice in a group and she's usually quite shy, but she seems very relaxed with

Catherine. But Catherine is the type who instantly puts you at ease: she's warm, witty and self-deprecating even though she looks like a cheerleader in an American high school, with perfectly even teeth and clear skin. She's about my age, maybe a few years older, and athletic. She makes Lola look tiny.

Blonde and tall.

I think of Arthur's description of the woman who posted the note through my door as I take in Catherine's leather jacket. Her hair is more of a streaky caramel shade than blonde, and she doesn't have a nose ring.

Donna notices me watching them at the bar. 'Is everything okay? You look very serious.'

I pull my gaze away from them. 'You remember I told you about that note I received? The one that said, "It was supposed to be you"?'

'Yeah.'

I fill her in on what Arthur told me, and when I've finished, she glances at Catherine. 'Surely you don't think . . . ?'

'No.' I shake my head. 'No. Not really. It briefly entered my head but it can't be. Catherine is lovely. But . . . fucking hell, Donna, it's making me paranoid, you know? Every time I see someone matching that description I instantly wonder if it could have been them.'

Donna rolls up the sleeves of her jumper to reveal her freckly arms and she uses the menu to fan herself. She's currently going through the menopause and I can feel the heat radiating off her. 'Well, yes. I'd be the same.' She narrows her eyes as she surveys Catherine, who is in deep conversation with Lola at the bar. 'What do we know about our Cath?' she says too loudly.

'Donna!' I hiss. 'Shut up. You've got a voice like a foghorn.'

She grins. 'All right. Calm down. I'm just saying.'

I mull over what I know about Catherine. She's been with the practice since April, lives a few streets from me with her teacher husband, Thomas. She talks (a lot) about her desire to start a family but is still waiting for 'the right time'. She's often the first to start a collection at work, or to organize a get-together. I've never seen her in a bad mood.

'Lola is blonde too. How much do we know about her?' Donna sips her pint.

'Lola is more of a dirty blonde – light brown,' I say. 'And she's not exactly tall. Plus neither of them has a nose ring.'

'It could have been one of those fake nose rings. Who else do we know who fits the description? This is fun!' She notices my expression because she quickly adds, 'Sorry, hon. I didn't mean it. It must be so scary to receive a note like that. I was getting carried away.'

'It's fine. It's . . .' But I don't finish my sentence because Catherine and Lola have arrived at our table. I stand up to give them a hug, and then I notice that Catherine is holding a pretty floral gift bag. She hands it to me from across the table once we're all seated.

'We had a bit of a whip-round. I hope it's okay, just wanted you to know we're thinking of you,' she says, shrugging off her jacket.

'Thank you,' I say, touched.

175

'Open it,' says Lola, eagerly. I notice she's nursing a lemonade. I've never seen her drink alcohol.

I'm suddenly shy as I delve into the bag and extract a candle in a cyan-blue ceramic pot.

'It was Lola's idea,' says Catherine. 'It's supposed to be calming.'

'It's lovely, thank you.' I put it back into the bag, genuinely moved, and thinking maybe I should give it to my sister. It might help her sleep.

'Right,' says Catherine, taking one of the menus. 'What are we going to order? I'm starving.' Catherine is always starving and usually has chocolate and sweets squirrelled away in her drawer at work. She passes a menu to Lola, who takes out a pair of reading glasses.

'I didn't know you wore glasses,' I say.

'I'm blind as a bat,' she says, smiling shyly. 'I should really wear them all the time but I hate them.'

'That's because they're the wrong shape for your face,' says Donna, matter-of-factly, and I cringe. 'Your face is too small. You need delicate frames, not these ugly things.'

Lola flushes bright red and takes them off.

'Donna. Don't be so rude!' I admonish, even though she's right. Lola has a pretty heart-shaped face and the frames drown her.

'Why don't we go to Maddy's place one day after work?' says Catherine, gently, referring to the optician on the corner. 'Get some that are more suitable.'

'These are my dad's,' she admits, turning them over in her hand. 'They're just reading glasses. But they . . . well, they remind me of him.'

176

'Has he died?' asks Donna, and Lola flinches, blinking rapidly. I want to kick Donna under the table for being so insensitive and nosy.

Before Lola can answer the door swings open and I'm surprised to see Eve walk through, arm in arm with a man who has dark curly hair. I assume he's her fiancé, Owen. I haven't told them about my meeting with her yesterday but when Catherine spots her she lets out a muttered 'For fuck's sake,' under her breath.

'What? Do you know her?' I ask.

'Yes. Unfortunately. Thomas works with her bloke and I've been made to suffer some school charity events with her.'

I've never heard Catherine badmouth anyone and I'm surprised.

'What's wrong with her?' asks Lola, folding her glasses away and taking out her mobile phone instead to snap a photo of the menu.

'She's an attention seeker. Do you know the type? It's always about them. She never asks any questions, always talking about herself and her life and how she was a model in London and all the celebrities she's hung out with, blah blah blah!'

Donna laughs. 'Wow! She's really got up your crack, hasn't she?'

I remember what Alice said about Eve wanting the limelight. 'She used to go out with Kyle,' I say quietly, and they all look at me in surprise.

'What? No way!' exclaims Donna.

I explain about 'bumping' into her yesterday. I don't

mention what she told me about dodgy investors and Kyle being scared. It doesn't seem right to, not after how adamant Alice was that it was all a lie.

Donna elbows me. 'She's tall and blonde,' she says. 'Although I can't imagine her with a nose ring.'

'Tall and blonde?' Catherine raises an eyebrow at me so then, of course, I've got to tell them about the note and the description Arthur gave.

'I wouldn't be surprised if she wrote it,' says Catherine, darkly, after I've finished. 'Not that I think she would've attacked Kyle or Alice or anything like that, or that she has a grudge against you. No, if she wrote it at all it would have been for the drama of it. For the attention.'

I frown, my eyes on Eve and her fiancé who are now, thankfully, making their way to a table at the opposite side of the room with their drinks. I don't think she's noticed me.

'And I think it's weird,' continues Catherine, looking hot and bothered now, 'that she just happened to bump into you on the street.'

'Well, she was looking for me, apparently.'

'Stalking you, more likely.'

'How do you know,' says Donna, 'that she hasn't been stalking Kyle? Is it beyond the realms of possibility that she came into your house, killed Kyle and attacked Alice in some kind of jealous rage?'

Catherine, Lola and I stare at Donna in shock.

'What?' she says. 'You hear about these things. A woman scorned and all that . . .'

'It doesn't explain the note, though, does it? Why

178

would she say, "It was supposed to be you," and address it to me if she was obsessed with Alice and Kyle?'

Donna shrugs. 'I don't know, do I? Who knows what goes on in a psychopath's mind?'

Lola reaches across the table and touches my fingertips lightly with hers, her face concerned. 'You're scaring Tasha,' she says softly.

Donna looks contrite. 'Sorry, hon,' she says, nudging me kindly. 'Let's stop speculating and get some grub.'

'That's right,' says Catherine, kindly. 'I've seen loads of police in the village since Kyle's murder.'

'What's that got to do with anything?' scoffs Donna.

'I just mean there's a lot of police around at the moment. She's safe, is all I'm saying.'

I know Catherine means well, but despite the heat of the fire, a shiver runs down my spine.

23

TASHA

It's turned colder this morning and the weather is crisp with a cerulean sky. I drop the twins at nursery, then walk back slowly, enjoying the time to myself.

When I get home I notice DC Jones on the doorstep with a different male detective, someone older with greying hair and a thin, stern face that immediately makes my palms sweat. It looks like they've just arrived. Mum opens the door as I'm walking down the path.

'Oh, you've all arrived together,' Mum says, as she lets us in. She sounds as if she's expecting them. I kick off my boots by the door. We troop over the threshold and follow Mum down the hallway towards the kitchen. I try not to feel like a guest in my own home. Alice is already seated at the table nursing a glass of water. Mum offers the detectives a drink but they decline and sit down. I shift onto the bench seat next to Alice, and Mum sits at the head of the table. She looks tired and there is sadness behind her eyes. I feel a kick of love for her so strong that I have to swallow the lump in my throat.

Alice was in bed all day yesterday, and every time I

popped my head around the door, either to check on her or to see if she was awake so I could ask her about her cryptic comment on Friday, she appeared to be asleep.

'Alice,' says DC Jones, in a voice that hits the right note, formal but warm, 'this is my colleague, and the senior investigating officer on the case, Detective Inspector Philip Thorne. We wanted to let you know that we've spoken to Eve Milligan, who has told us about her last meeting with your husband on the day he died.'

Alice nods and takes a sip of water.

DC Jones takes a notebook from the inside of her jacket and flips it open. 'You said in your statement that you remember feeling you were being watched,' she reads off her page, squinting slightly. 'Is that correct?'

Alice nods. 'Yes. I was worried someone was watching the house.'

'Did Kyle ever say anything to you about being scared?'

She shakes her head. 'No. Never. He never acted scared either. I . . .' she runs a finger around the rim of her glass '. . . I just don't know if I believe Eve. Kyle told me that she was never able to let go of him. I don't think he would have said this to her. I personally believe she's making it up.'

DC Jones scribbles something in her notebook. 'So Kyle never said anything to you about "dodgy investors"?'

'No. I know exactly who Kyle's investors are. And they're all above board. He has a business manager, Craig Morrison. You can check with him if you need it backed up. But I have been heavily involved with his recent project. It was . . .' She swallows, her chin wobbling. She composes herself. 'It's this amazing product that would have changed everything.' She doesn't elaborate on how or why it would change everything, and she's talking about it in the past tense, but surely someone else could finish what she and Kyle had started.

'Okay, thanks. I'll speak to Craig Morrison,' says DC Jones.

Alice rattles off his phone number and I'm impressed she knows it by heart. But she's always had a photographic memory. I don't know anyone's phone number off the top of my head, even Aaron's.

DI Thorne clears his throat and we turn to look at him. 'This threatening message you received, Natasha,' he says, his stern gaze directed at me. 'Do you have any idea who could have written it?'

Shit. I still haven't told my sister about the note. She rounds on me now, her eyes narrowed. 'Threatening message? What did it say?'

I tell her about the note being delivered the day we moved back into the house and what it said.

'What? Why didn't you tell me?'

'You've got enough on your plate.'

'Tasha . . .'

I meet her frustrated expression and hold up my hands. 'I know, I know, I have to stop treading on eggshells around you . . . I don't know who wrote the note,' I say to the officers. 'Although my next-door neighbour said he saw someone hanging around the house on the morning

I think the note was posted.' I fill them in on what Arthur told me.

DI Thorne leans forward. 'And do you know anyone who fits that description?'

'Well, it fits a lot of people I know. It's not exactly an unusual description, is it? Except the nose ring. There's only one person I know who has a ring through the septum, although I don't really know her, but she works with my husband.' I give him Zoë's name and DC Jones writes it down.

'We've had some results back from the lab,' says DI Thorne. 'As you know, we took DNA samples from all of you, including Kyle, and tested them against the DNA found at the crime scene. The DNA from one source of blood found at the scene doesn't belong to any of you.'

My heart quickens.

'There was a bloodstain on the rug in the living room and a smear on the floor of the kitchen near the patio doors,' adds DC Jones.

Alice pales and I know she's punishing herself for forgetting to lock them.

'But there's more,' continues DI Thorne, and DC Jones throws my mum a look of concern. 'From that sample, what we did find was what we call familial DNA.' He pauses, watching Alice closely. 'This means that, while it doesn't belong to any of you, it has enough similarities to tell us it belongs to a family member.'

'A family member?' says Mum, frowning.

'Yes. Of yours, Mrs Harper,' says DI Thorne.

'But . . .' Mum looks flummoxed '. . . there are no other family members, just the three of us. My parents are long dead and I have no siblings.'

'It's more likely to come from a son or daughter,' explains DI Thorne. 'I won't go into the technicalities, but do you have another child, Mrs Harper?'

PART THREE

So you're still here. Still thriving. I haven't managed to get rid of you yet.

But there's time. I'm working on it.

I suppose you want to know why I have such hatred for you. Well, that's easy. It's because you've got what I want. If you'd grown up in my family you'd realize how lucky you are. But you don't. You take it all for granted.

You take him for granted.

Yours is the life I should have had.

Yours is the life I WILL have.

24

BONNIE

February 2019

Bonnie always knew her family wasn't quite like everyone else's. Her mother, Clarissa, was mostly bed-bound, and had been for the past seventeen years. To Bonnie, when her mother first took to her bed, it had felt like a strange dichotomy because she'd looked perfectly healthy, with her peaches-and-cream complexion, her shiny blonde hair and large china-blue eyes, although she spent her days lying down in a pair of satin pyjamas. Bonnie had been nearly thirteen when she'd returned from school one day to find the bed had been moved to the dining room and her mother was draped across it, like a Disney princess. She asked her father why her mother was so ill suddenly, and he'd muttered something about a recently diagnosed lung condition and hustled her out of the room. Her dad worked on the oil rigs and was away for weeks at a time. When her mother became ill, she wondered if he'd stay to look after her, but he didn't. Instead, after a couple of weeks in which he'd taught Bonnie how to use the microwave to heat her frozen meals, and how to load the washing-machine, he'd skulked back to whatever oil rig in the North Sea he was working on, leaving Bonnie to fend for herself.

They weren't rich, she knew, but they weren't poor either, thanks to the money her dad earned. He was well compensated for his hours away from home, so they could afford a nurse to come in once a day and a cleaner twice a week. And, thankfully, they lived in the town, a nondescript suburb of Birmingham with identical streets of three-bedroom 1950s semis with large gardens, a Spar around the corner and, just a short walk away, the little railway station that took her right into the city centre. But despite the outside help she quickly saw that her mother relied on her, and that, apart from the nurse, the cleaner and her father, who came home once every few months, they saw nobody. She could never invite friends over, apart from her best friend Selma, because she was embarrassed by her languishing mother and their sparsely furnished home, which seemed to lack any joy and was decorated in varying shades of cream and beige. When she went to Selma's house it was like stepping into another world. Selma had a big, bustling extended family and a bunch of brothers, who jostled and teased and filled their terraced house with noise. Returning home afterwards only to be hit by a wall of silence was soul-destroying and made her feel lonelier than ever. Selma always reassured her that every family was different, there was no 'normal', but that didn't make Bonnie feel any better about her own situation.

When she left school she had to watch as her friends went off to university and she was forced to study closer to home so that she could still look after her mother, catching the train every day to Birmingham University, missing nights out and hook-ups, never having the time for a serious boyfriend. How could she have an honest relationship with anyone when she had to hide a large part of her life? Or find the time later when she had a demanding job and was essentially a carer, apart from once every eight weeks when her father came home for a few days. There were never any holidays, and family rarely visited. Each day was the same and sometimes, when she walked through the door to the familiar smell of overripe bins and stale air, and static silence, she had to fight the urge to scream.

Her once beautiful mother aged badly as the years passed, the time stuck inside the house turning her once-soft skin tissue-paper thin, the lack of exercise causing muscle atrophy. By now, at the age of sixty-two, her mother needed an oxygen tank that she was always attached to. On a good day she could just about make it through the French windows of the dining room-bedroom to sit on the patio for fresh air, her face tilted to the sky, her eyes closed. It always made Bonnie feel sad, her mother a wilting flower that was curling up and dying, desperate for a last burst of sunshine, of life.

But even before the illness, and the confinement, Bonnie realized things were different. A sadness had seemed to cloak her mother even before she took to her bed. Back then she'd waft around the house in her loose-fitting dresses that hung off her slim frame, as though she wasn't quite sure what to do with herself. She never worked, or socialized, and hardly left the house, except to do some food shopping or take Bonnie to school. Even before Clarissa became ill she never really lived. At least, not that Bonnie could remember. She was sweet and caring and loved Bonnie, she knew that much. Her mother was in her element when she was teaching Bonnie to draw, or to read, or they were snuggled up on the sofa watching TV together, but she never seemed to have a life of her own. No passions, no interests, no career. She was like a passenger at a station, endlessly waiting for a train that never arrived.

'How did you meet Mum?' she asked her dad, one day, when he was back from the rigs, a few years after her mother had become ill. She was about sixteen then, the notion of boys and romantic love at the forefront of her mind. She couldn't imagine what Jack Fairborn, her strapping, handsome father, with his love of motorbikes, rock music and spicy food had ever seen – she felt bad for thinking it – in her bland mother, apart from, maybe, her beauty. They'd been sitting in the magnolia living room with their bowls of her dad's homemade curry balancing on trays on their laps after Clarissa had refused the food.

His deep brown eyes had lit up at some resurfaced memory and he'd gazed at his daughter. 'She was fantastic, Bonbon,' he said, using his nickname for her, a tinge of sadness in his voice. 'She was an art student, just turned twenty-one, so vibrant, so full of life.'

Bonnie had been shocked. This was the antithesis of the mother she knew. 'She was an art student?'

'Sculptures were her thing.'

What had happened to that person? Bonnie had wondered.

'We were at a party,' he said, putting down his fork and taking a swig of his beer. He smiled to himself and Bonnie imagined that he was picturing it, their first meeting, the way her mother had looked. Had they locked eyes across the room? Her two handsome parents – one tall, dark and striking, the other petite and delicate. 'She was on the dance floor. This would have been, God, summer 1978. She had no inhibitions and she looked just like Debbie Harry.' He stopped talking, sadness filming his eyes. He picked up his fork and continued eating. 'Anyway,' he said eventually, swallowing, 'we had a few good years before . . .' He fell silent.

'Before?' she probed, staring at him intently.

His dark eyebrows knitted together and something she couldn't place flickered in his face, but it was enough to give her a dull feeling of dread. 'Let's just say life hasn't been kind to your mother.'

'Did something happen to her?' she asked, a funny, churning feeling in her stomach. Because that must be it, she reasoned. Why else would her mother go from a fun, vibrant art student who danced with abandon and looked like Debbie Harry to the ghost of the person she'd become?

Her dad shook his head, his face closing. 'Eat your curry before it gets cold,' he said, and she knew the conversation was over.

She supposed on some level it was inevitable and she had been dreading it for years, without even realizing it. And yet, when it finally happened, it hit her full in the face.

She'd had a busy day at work and was running late, missed her train, and by the time she walked through the door she was feeling hot and bothered, just wanting to flop in front of the television. She knew the nurse had been in today – she was coming in more often now that her mother needed the oxygen tanks – so wasn't overly worried about being late. Her mother slept a lot, these days, not even perking up when her dad got back from the rigs. Yet when Bonnie stepped through the door she had a feeling that something wasn't right. The air was even stiller than usual and there was no hum of the oxygen tank. As she wandered through the house she saw that the door to the dining room where her mother slept was closed.

Bonnie pushed open the door, her heart in her throat, not sure what to expect. She took in the scene before her, her stomach dropping when she noticed the oxygen tank wasn't switched on. Her mother was lying back against the pillows, her eyes closed, her face serene, her hair, now white, fanning out around her. She was lying on top of the quilt in her favourite dusky pink satin pyjamas, her hands folded in front of her.

'Mum!' Bonnie said, rushing to the bed. There was an almost blue sheen to her mother's skin. 'Mum?' she said again, almost shouting this time. She touched her mother's cheek, which was cold, and dread lay heavily in her stomach. She glanced down at the floor and saw the tube to the oxygen trailing along the carpet, like an eel, and a sharp, painful feeling spread through her ribs, squeezing her heart. 'Oh, Mum,' she whispered, her hands trembling as she brushed a lock of white hair away from her mother's forehead. She knelt beside the bed, taking one of her mother's hands, holding it in hers and putting it to her lips. 'I wish I'd been with you. Why didn't you wait for me?'

Something fluttered from her mother's lap onto the bed. A piece of paper. Bonnie picked it up, her throat tight, the words swimming on the page.

I love you, Bonnie. I always have. I'm sorry.

25

TASHA

Monday, 21 October 2019

Alice and I sit in shocked silence as Mum shows the detectives out of the door.

'What the actual fuck?' I splutter. 'Are they saying Holly was here? I just – I can't get my head around it.'

Alice has a strange look in her eye.

'What is it?' I ask her. 'What are you not saying?'

She takes a sip of her water, then presses her lips together. 'Nothing. It's . . .' she lowers her voice '. . . like I said the other day, I've got something to tell you. I'm sorry I haven't had the chance before now, but I didn't want to say anything in front of Mum and get her hopes up when . . .'

She stops talking when Mum comes back into the kitchen.

'Well . . .' says Mum, sinking onto a chair and looking flustered. Her hands automatically go to the gold locket at her throat. 'I don't know what to make of all that. Do they really think it could belong to Holly?'

'I think that's what they're assuming,' says Alice, gently.

'So you're saying you believe that Holly has somehow been in my house?' I snap.

'Well, that's what the science is saying. Not me.'

I glance at Mum. She's staring at the table and I can't read her expression. I can't even begin to imagine what she's thinking or feeling. There is evidence that her long-lost child, a daughter she hasn't seen in thirty years, has entered my house. That she's not only alive but that she's come home to us. Yet if this is true why has she not come forward? Asked to meet us? Why would she break into my house?

'Does that mean they suspect Holly of attacking you and killing Kyle?' Mum asks. Her eyes are red-rimmed and something hard seems to be lodged in my windpipe as the implications of all this dawn on me. 'Are they saying Holly is a suspect in a murder case?'

'I – I don't know . . .' Alice falters, picking at a dried-on fleck of poster paint on the kitchen table. 'It doesn't sound like they found any other DNA. But that doesn't mean nobody else was here that night. It just means they could have been careful.' She looks up at Mum. 'But I'm so sorry, Mum . . .' She puts a hand to her head and her eyes flicker from me to Mum. 'I have to tell you both something.'

I take a deep breath. I feel sick and my knees start trembling. I don't think I can take any more revelations today.

'What is it?' Mum asks, in a tight voice.

'I wasn't going to say anything because I thought it was maybe a hoax. But after today, well, now I'm not so sure.'

'Go on,' Mum says, folding her arms across her chest as though to protect herself from Alice's words.

'Back in May I was giving a talk about biochemistry in the health sector at a conference in Liverpool and, afterwards, this woman came up to me. She seemed nice enough and was initially chatting about the talk I'd just given. She seemed intelligent and knowledgeable, but then she started asking me quite personal questions, and it was obvious she knew all about my background, that I went to Oxford, that I come from Chew Norton, that I had a younger sister and a baby sister who was abducted. It was quite a weird conversation.'

'Did she give her name?' I ask.

'No, she didn't. But not long after that meeting I started receiving letters from her.'

My nausea intensifies.

'The letters were always sent to my work address and always typed on a single sheet of A4. They were signed "Holly".'

Mum's mouth falls open. 'What?'

'This woman at the conference was Holly?' I ask, my mind reeling.

'That's what she said in the letters, yes. But I just thought it was a hoax. Mum, you must have been sent letters like this in the past?'

Mum nods grimly. 'A few. Back in the early days.'

'So I just thought it was some nut-job who had maybe googled me. But now . . .'

'Have you got the letters? Can I see them?' I ask.

She shakes her head regretfully. 'They're at my house in London. Although, actually, I did take a photo of the first one because Kyle was away at the time and I wanted to

show it to him. Let me get my phone. It's in my room.'
She stands up and walks out of the door.

I don't know what to say to Mum. She's just sitting in
silence, her whole body rigid, her hands together, like
she's praying, and I wonder what's going through her
mind. This is huge for her.

'Right,' Alice says breathlessly, as she walks back into
the room and sits down again. She scrolls through the
photo roll on her mobile. 'Here it is.' She offers Mum the
phone first but Mum says she hasn't got her reading
glasses so passes it to me and I read it aloud.

Dear Alice,

*I know this is a strange letter to be getting out of the blue, and I
apologize as I know this will be a shock, but I didn't know the best
way to approach you. I couldn't very well blurt it out to you at the
conference, not something like this. Okay, deep breaths! I'm just
going to say it. I think I'm your sister. I think I'm Holly Harper.*
*This isn't some crank letter. This is the truth. At least, I think
it is. I don't have all the evidence yet but I'm trying to find it. I
don't want to come back into your life – into the lives of your
parents (my parents) and Natasha's without being as sure as I
can be that what I think I know to be true is, in fact, true. And
then, I guess, I will have to do a DNA test. But until then I'll
stay away, hidden in the shadows.*
I will be in touch again soon.
Holly xx

I exhale slowly, trying to calm myself.

Mum's face crumples. 'Do you think this is legitimate? What do the other letters say?'

'More of the same. That she's watching us. That she's sure she's Holly. That she'll step out of the shadows soon. She gives nothing away about herself at all.'

'She said *parents*. That means she doesn't know about Dad?' I say, handing her the phone. Without waiting for her to answer, I charge on, 'What did the woman at the conference look like? Did she look like you imagined Holly to look?'

'Well, she had blonde hair and blue eyes like Holly. And she looked around the right age. It's hard to tell exactly but she looked late twenties, early thirties.'

Mum makes a tiny sound, like a baby bird, and Alice gets up and wraps her arms around her. 'I'm sorry, Mum. I'm so sorry. I didn't want to tell you this in case it wasn't true. I didn't want to get your hopes up but, now, with the DNA, it means Holly is still alive.'

And that she might have attacked Alice and Kyle. But I don't say that because I know it's what we're all thinking.

Mum pats Alice's shoulder. 'I think we should tell the police about these letters.'

Alice breaks away from Mum and nods. The colour has gone from her cheeks and I can see that she's flagging. 'I'll give DC Jones a call,' she says. She takes Mum's hand and squeezes it. 'I don't know what all this means, Mum, or why her DNA was found at the scene but there could be a simple explanation.'

Alice doesn't sound very convincing.

'I can't believe that Holly would want to hurt you,' says Mum, tears in her voice.

I exchange a look with Alice.

Holly was just a baby when she was taken. Who knows what kind of person she's become?

26

JEANETTE

Monday, 21 October 2019

Jeanette has spent the last thirty years looking for Holly in the faces of strangers. Each anniversary is marked by a new birthday and a slightly older person to examine. Would she be able to tell, all these years later, if her daughter walked straight past her, a thirty-year-old fully formed being, as though her childhood years had never existed? Jeanette never had the privilege of witnessing Holly's baby face change into that of a toddler, or a little girl, or a teenager. She never got to see her morph into the thirty-year-old woman she'd be now.

And now it seems Holly has been writing to her eldest daughter, had even met her. If those letters are to be believed, that is. The letters might be a hoax but the DNA can't be. They have irrefutable proof that Holly was in Tasha's home on the night Kyle was killed.

On one hand Jeanette is elated that there is evidence, at long last, that Holly is alive. Yet on the other it places her at the scene of a crime. What explanation could there be for her blood on the carpet? Had she attacked Kyle and then hurt herself? But why would she attack Kyle? And, in particular, Alice. Her own sister. It doesn't make any sense to Jeanette yet she can't stop this cycle of thoughts swirling around and around in her mind. She feels as if she's going mad.

Could Holly have had such a terrible life that it turned her into a murderer? She can't bear to think so.

When it was time to pick up the girls from nursery they'd all decided to go. It's the first time since Alice was discharged from hospital that she's left the house, the news of Holly giving her an injection of energy, or purpose, which Jeanette is thankful for.

Jeanette is now sitting in Trudi's Tearoom, dragged in there for a babycino by Elsie and Flossie. Alice and Tasha are still standing at the entrance. From the window she can see them pointing to someone in the distance: a young woman with long blonde hair. Jeanette can just about make out the woman's side profile. She has a confident stride, Jeanette thinks, as she sips her coffee. The woman disappears from sight but Alice and Tasha still stand there. They look like twins from the back with their identical hair and slim build. They always talk fast when they're together, a mass of copper hair and wild gesticulations. She used to joke to Jim that it sounded like they had their own language as nobody else could understand them. She often wonders how their dynamic would have changed had Holly been around. Perhaps they're talking about Holly now.

It's inevitable that they've experienced a different type of grief from Jeanette's. As a mother hers is unrivalled: the one person who could ever truly understand was Jim and he's no longer here. What would he think of the prospect that their daughter has come back to them all these years later? That she could be a criminal? A psychopath? Their little Holly with her chubby cheeks and her toothless smile and her large, innocent blue eyes?

'Nanny want one?'

She turns away from the window to see Flossie proffering a pink marshmallow with a pudgy hand. The twins are sitting opposite her, spooning the froth from their babycinos into their mouths.

'No, thank you, my angel. You have it,' she replies, smiling at her beloved grandchild. Flossie retracts her hand and pops the marshmallow into her mouth, her blue eyes, which remind her of Holly's, wide.

When she was pregnant with Holly she's ashamed to remember she'd hoped for a boy. She recalls viscerally that want. It had vanished, of course, as soon as Holly was born. She fell instantly in love. But now it fills her with remorse. For years after Holly was taken she worried that it was because, for a sliver of time, she hadn't been grateful.

The door of the tearoom is suddenly thrust open, making the little bell tinkle, and she watches her daughters head towards her, their expressions serious.

She remembers all those sightings, in the days, months and years after Holly was first taken, the rollercoaster feeling of elation, of hope, and then of disappointment and despair. Those 'sightings' had never come to anything. It was as though Holly had simply been swallowed into the world.

'Mummy,' says Elsie, her mouth full of marshmallow

as Tasha and Alice come towards the table. Tasha's face brightens as she slips in beside her daughters and they chatter away about their day. Alice squeezes in next to Jeanette and then, as the waitress approaches, orders herself and Tasha a cappuccino each. If Jeanette had ordered for Tasha without asking she knows she'd have got short shrift but her daughter throws Alice a grateful smile over Elsie's head.

'Who were you pointing to?' asks Jeanette, when the waitress has gone. 'That blonde woman.'

'Oh, that was Zoë,' says Alice, 'who Aaron works with.'

Tasha purses her lips, but doesn't say anything, and Alice sighs, looking wretched.

Jeanette can see there is so much her daughter wants to say but doesn't know where to start. She can't imagine what both of her daughters must be feeling: Holly has been in Tasha's home. She could have attacked Alice and killed her husband.

'That night . . .' begins Alice. She stops and takes a deep breath. Jeanette can see she finds it hard to talk about it. She flicks a glance at the twins and lowers her voice almost to a whisper. '. . . I felt someone push me. Kyle was already on the floor and then, just as I was about to bend down to help him, I was shoved really hard into the TV unit. I keep thinking, could Holly really have done that to me?'

She's about to say more but Tasha shakes her head subtly and indicates the twins so Alice changes the subject, telling them she's thinking of going home on Thursday and, after Kyle's funeral on Saturday, back to work next week.

'But you can't,' says Jeanette, shocked. She's always known her daughter's a workaholic but she's grieving, and she still has a colourful bruise over one eye and at one side of her lovely hair there is a patch where her scalp has been stitched after the head injury. The police still haven't found the weapon that killed Kyle but have speculated it might have been some kind of iron pole. They described it as a vicious attack. In every incarnation of Holly that she's thought about over the years, violent and murderous had never even come close.

'I can't stay away for ever, Mum. It's important that I go back. It will be good for me. It will help take my mind off . . .' She trails off. 'I need to face up to things. I can't stay holed up in Tasha's spare room for the rest of my life.'

'There's enough time for all that,' states Jeanette, playing with the handle of her pretty bone-china cup. 'You shouldn't rush things.'

Tasha is deep in conversation with her daughters and doesn't seem to hear them. Jeanette knows Tasha will back her up. It's too soon for Alice to return to her life.

'The funeral is on Saturday at midday. If I go home on Thursday it gives me a bit of time to get the house in order. I was thinking Tasha could come with me on Thursday, if she doesn't mind, and you and Aaron can join us on Friday. You could bring the twins with you, Tash, if you don't want to leave them.'

Jeanette notices the alarm in Tasha's face. 'I'll think about it. I'm not sure I want them to come to the funeral.'

'There's so much to organize for a funeral, sweetheart,'

says Jeanette, gently. 'Have you even made a start on it? Have you done the order of service? Sorted flowers?'

Alice rolls her eyes. 'What do you think I've been doing stuck up in the spare room all this time, unable to sleep?' she says. 'Of course I've made all the arrangements. My friend Ellen has helped me.'

'We offered,' says Jeanette, worried that she hasn't done enough.

'I know, and that was kind but it's easier for Ellen as she's in Hampstead too, and she knows some of Kyle's friends.'

Jeanette stifles a sigh. Alice is thirty-five years old. She's a PhD graduate from Oxford University with an illustrious career as a biochemist. Jeanette can't baby her.

Alice turns back to her coffee and as she lifts the cup to her lips Jeanette notices how her hand trembles and it makes her heart ache for her eldest daughter.

I know you aren't as tough as you try to make out.

27

BONNIE

February 2019

Bonnie couldn't get her mother's note out of her head. It had been all she could think about since her death. Why was she sorry? What did it mean?

Her father couldn't come back straight away, having to wait for a flight from an oil rig on the North Sea, so it was her best friend Selma she called after her mother was taken away. Selma had observed the now empty house with its magnolia walls, mushroom-coloured carpets and sparse furniture, and insisted that Bonnie stay with her family for a few days. There was hardly any space at Selma's house but Bonnie didn't care. Being with Selma's large, boisterous family was like receiving a warm hug. If she ever got married she'd want a home like her best friend's, full of noise and laughter and life.

She thought of her mum often, wondering if she'd unhooked her oxygen on purpose, fed up with living and wanting to end it all. The note suggested that might have been the case, but maybe she was saying sorry for something else. She'd always felt her mother was hiding a secret. A secret so large it ate away at her, making her ill. The funeral was a quiet affair. Hardly anyone came. It was just her father, herself, Selma and the nurse who had cared for her mother standing in the echoey church. There was no wake, no proper send-off. Her mother died as she had lived, and it made Bonnie sad.

'What happened to Mum's parents? And why didn't she keep in touch with her siblings?' Bonnie asked that evening, as she sat in front of the TV with her father, their takeaway fish and chips balanced on trays on their laps. She couldn't recall the last time they had all eaten as a family around a dinner table, like at Selma's house. They were both still dressed in their black clothes, her father's suit straining across his middle and she in the trousers she wore to work. She remembered an aunt and uncle who used to travel from far away to see them occasionally, but that was years ago, before her mother had become sick.

'Your mother was estranged from her family. They never really took to me. I was too . . . rough for them, I suppose. Her parents died a long time ago.'

Bonnie had wondered if she should contact her mother's remaining family to let them know, but decided against it. Her mother had been estranged from them for a reason and she'd feel disloyal if she went against her wishes. 'I wish we could have done more to help Mum,' she said. 'I always felt her illness was just as much mental as it was physical.'

His expression darkened, his eyes downcast. 'I tried over the years, believe me,' he said, pushing his fish around the plate.

'Maybe if you'd been here more,' she snapped, 'if you hadn't been away all the time on those rigs.'

He turned to her. The skin under his eyes was saggy and she could see the red shaving rash on his neck. 'How else was I supposed to keep you both?'

'You could've got a job nearer.'

'The rigs paid better than anything around here. Your mother never worked and the cost of everything . . . this house, the cleaner, the nurse . . .'

'I earn a good wage. I was happy to help out.'

'I didn't want you to do that. Clarissa wasn't your responsibility, Bonbon.'

Bonnie realized then that it was never about the money for her dad. It was about escape. Freedom. She supposed she couldn't blame him for that. Living in a house of sickness took its toll. Bonnie moved her tray off her lap and onto the floor, her food mostly untouched. 'Will we sell the house?' She knew she didn't want to stay there. It had become a prison over the years. It was large enough for a family: big airy rooms and a long, enclosed garden, a perfect place for kids to run about, for a trampoline to stand, for a dog to roam free.

He cleared his throat and speared a chip with his fork, although he didn't eat it. 'I think so. You can use some of the money to buy a flat. A fresh start.'

A fresh start. Selma had talked about a girls' holiday. She'd never been able to go away before, worried about leaving her mum. 'Selma's thinking we could go to Tenerife in April. Somewhere hot.' Before her mother had become ill, holidays were a week in a caravan in Devon. 'I can't believe I've never been abroad. I've never been on an aeroplane even.'

Her father stared down at his plate and she noticed how a muscle throbbed in his jaw. The living room was dark, apart from a lamp in the corner, and shadows flickered along the walls. Bonnie wanted to flee into the bosom of Selma's family. She didn't want to be here eating food that tasted of cardboard, in this house with too many memories of her mother and her illness. Of her father's long absences. It was the right thing to do, to sell it. She imagined another family moving in here, painting over the magnolia walls and ripping out the ugly wooden kitchen. She suddenly wanted that for this house. It deserved better.

'I'm going to fetch a beer. Want one?' Her father put his fork down and stood up, carrying his tray, his fish and chips only half finished. He bent down to pick up hers too.

'No, thanks.' She watched as he moved across the room, balancing the two trays easily, still strong and broad-shouldered at sixty-five. He should be near retiring. It was a sad fact that her mother had aged so much quicker than him, although she had been three years younger.

When he wandered back into the room he was already gulping from the can and Bonnie realized he was nervous. 'What is it?' she asked, as soon as he sat down, the ugly old sofa sagging under his weight. Was this where he would break the news to her about another woman? Maybe even another child? A whole other family?

'The note your mother left. She . . .' He cleared his throat and took another sip of his beer. Bonnie waited.

What was he trying to tell her? 'She was saying sorry because . . . because you're, well . . . There's no easy way to say this, Bonbon, but you're adopted.'

Of all the things Bonnie had thought he was going to say this was never one of them. 'What?'

'Clarissa had fertility problems. She was told, way before I had even met her, that she'd never be able to have children. And it became an obsession, you know?'

Bonnie didn't know. She was nearly thirty and she didn't feel in the least bit broody. She figured there was plenty of time for all that. She studied his face, his strong jaw, his dark eyes, his tanned skin. She looked nothing like him, but then she always thought she'd taken after Clarissa. Jack Fairborn was never particularly paternal, now she thought about it. She knew he loved her, called her Bonbon and was kind to her, but there was always a detachment too. Her mother had been the opposite, smothering her with love until she'd become too ill.

'I think the letter you found, that was what it meant.' His voice was gruff but she was yet to see him cry. Not when she'd called him to tell him the news, or when he'd arrived back from the North Sea a few days later, not when she'd accompanied him to visit her mother's body at the funeral home. He placed one of his large, weathered hands on her forearm. 'I'm sorry we never told you. But you have to know that we couldn't have loved you more if you were our own flesh and blood.'

She felt a lump in her throat. 'Do you . . . do you know why I was put up for adoption? How old was I?'

'You were a baby, that's all I know. We adopted you

when you were a few days old.' He leant forward to put his empty can on the coffee-table. 'I think your parents were too young, that's all. A teen pregnancy.'

Her parents, her *real* parents, were out there somewhere. She could have had a very different life, not that this had been a bad one. She loved Jack and Clarissa and they had done their best for her. It wasn't her mother's fault that she'd been so ill for years. And, anyway, caring for her mother had made her grow up, become more independent and, yes, sometimes she had felt trapped, isolated, encumbered by her mother's illness, but she'd been able to cope with it. And now . . . now all the worries that she might have inherited her mother's strange illness or her father's moroseness dissipated like smoke. Suddenly her life was opening up with all the endless possibilities and different paths it could take.

'I know it's a lot to process. And I'm sorry.' Her father's stolid voice brought her back to the present. 'As far as I'm concerned you're my daughter and always will be.'

She blinked back tears. He'd tried his best and that was all any of them could do. She reached over and hugged him. 'Thank you, Dad,' she said.

Selma couldn't understand why she wasn't angry. 'They kept it from you for nearly thirty years,' she exclaimed, when Bonnie told her. They were in Selma's bedroom, which hadn't changed since they were kids at school. Selma, for all her talk of independence, never seemed in a hurry to move out. She stayed at her boyfriend's a few times a week and that was enough for her. Her job as a junior doctor involved long hours and crap pay, but she always joked that she had no reason to move out because she liked her parents, even though Bonnie suspected it was more to do with the free board and delicious hot meals her mother made. 'Are you going to look for your real parents?'

'I don't know. I've thought about it but it seems too soon after Mum.'

Selma plonked herself next to Bonnie on the bed. 'You could just register with the National Adoption Agency. I was watching a thing about it. Apparently if you ever want to be in touch with your parents you have to register. And then if your birth parents also register to say they're open to being found they can put you in touch.'

'I'm not ready yet.'

'It won't hurt just to register, though, will it?'

Bonnie had thought about it all the way home, and for weeks afterwards. Her father flew back to some desolate rig in the North Sea, the house was on the market and the hospital took back her mother's bed, oxygen tanks and all the other equipment she'd needed over the years. Bonnie was looking around for flats and had asked Selma if she wanted to share. She'd been overjoyed when Selma agreed. 'As long as it's not too far from my folks' house,' she'd said. 'I still need a good home-cooked meal now and again.'

It was the third Saturday after her mother died when she found it.

She was going through the loft, hoping to sort stuff out ready for when the house sold (they already had an offer) when she found a cardboard box with the words NOT TO BE OPENED UNTIL AFTER MY DEATH scribbled in biro on the lid. Bonnie's heart was in her mouth as she peeled back the parcel tape. She felt in a daze, a strange buzzing inside her head as she wondered what was inside. She was surprised to find a stack of newspapers dating from 1989, the year she was born, to 1992, yellow and crunchy around the edges. Maybe this was information about her adoption, she thought, as she reached inside the box to take out one of the newspapers. And then she saw the first headline and recoiled.

'BELOVED' BABY ABDUCTED FROM PRAM. WITNESSES SOUGHT.

As she leafed through every newspaper article, nausea rising with each word she read, everything began to rearrange itself in her head.

She thought again about her mother's note. It was now taking on a whole new meaning.

I love you, Bonnie. I always have. I'm sorry.

28

TASHA

Monday, 21 October 2019

Aaron walks into the bedroom smelling fresh from the shower, his hair wet, wearing a black and red Fred Perry. He slaps some aftershave onto his chin, then seems to notice me sitting on the bed. He appraises me with a smile. 'You look nice,' he says, and I stare down at my grey jeans and my black scoop-neck top. I play with the silver chains at my throat. I don't really want to go out and I'd have work tomorrow if it wasn't for Colin's generosity in letting me have compassionate leave. But when Aaron came home saying that it was Rob from work's birthday (it seems to be someone's birthday every week at that place) and was it okay if he went along to the pub 'for a few pints', Mum had jumped in with the suggestion that I go too.

'How often is it that the two of you can go out together?' she'd said. 'And you need a break and to spend time with one another.' The implication being that I need to talk to him alone about Holly and the DNA. I haven't had the chance to fill him in on it yet as he's been home from work less than an hour. We have so much to talk about. I just wish we were going somewhere by ourselves instead of to Rob's birthday drinks, but I'm hoping we'll get the chance to leave early and maybe go for a bite to eat where we can really talk.

Aaron runs some gel through his hair and I tell him I'm going to say goodnight to the twins. They're still awake. Their beds have been pushed together to make room for Mum's airbed. I wish Mum would share with Alice instead of having to sleep on the floor, but she insisted that my sister needs her own space to grieve. I tell myself it's not for much longer as Alice plans to go home in a few days' time, and it sounds like I'm going with her. The thought of leaving the twins again so soon makes my stomach curdle.

They're both tucked up, their matching fairy duvets pulled up around their armpits. 'Will you read us a story?' they chorus, as soon as I walk in.

'Nanny's read you one.'

'We want one from you,' insists Elsie. Flossie nods and sticks her thumb into her mouth.

I know they're playing me to delay bedtime, but I reach into their bookcase anyway, selecting their favourite, *Tabby McTat*. I've read it so many times I could recite it by heart.

'You look nice, Mummy,' says Flossie, when I've finished reading. I'm standing by the bookcase, inserting *Tabby McTat* behind the bars and I turn to look at her. She's sitting up in bed, her duvet bunched around her, studying me with a frown. 'Are you going out?'

'Yes, with Daddy.'

Her chin wobbles. 'I don't want you to go out.'

My heart sinks and I sit down on her bed. 'Why not?' I ask gently, even though I can guess what she's feeling, even if she's too young to articulate it.

'Bad things happen when you're not here.'

'Are you talking about what happened with Uncle Kyle?' I ask.

She nods.

'How did Uncle Kyle die?' pipes up Elsie, from the next bed.

'He had a baddy head,' I say. We've never told them that someone broke in here and killed him. 'But nothing is going to happen tonight.'

'What if Nanny dies when you're out?' asks Flossie, her cheeks flushing.

'She won't, honey,' I say, taking Flossie's hand and kissing it. 'What happened to Uncle Kyle was very sad but it won't happen to Nanny. And we won't be long, I promise.' I don't leave the room until I'm satisfied I've managed to put their minds at rest. But as soon as I'm back downstairs I tell Aaron to go without me. It's only after he and Mum persuade me, and only once I know the twins are asleep, that I feel able to leave them.

'I'm worried about how this is affecting them,' I say to Aaron, as we walk to the Packhorse, later than planned. 'I hope they haven't heard us talking about Kyle's attack. We have to be really careful what we say when they're in earshot.'

He squeezes my hand. 'We just need to make sure we reassure them as much as possible.'

It's dark now and feels much later than eight o'clock. The air is damp, clinging to my hair and my legs.

'Mum is working at the pub tonight,' says Aaron. I've only seen Viv once since my mum arrived, although I did speak to her on the phone to ask if she could look after Elsie and Flossie when we go to London for Kyle's funeral. I get the sense she's avoiding us because Mum is staying – I've invited Viv over a few times now and each time she's made an excuse not to come.

'It'll be nice to see her. Is ... er ... Zoë going to be there?'

He shrugs. 'Not sure. Why?'

'I'd like to meet her properly,' I say. 'There's something I haven't had the chance to tell you yet.'

'Oh, yeah, what's that?'

I fill him in about Holly.

'Fuck.' He reaches up and cups the back of his head when I've finished. 'This is huge.'

'I know.'

'Why haven't you told me before?'

'I didn't get the chance. But we need to talk about this properly. Do you think we could get away early and grab a bite to eat? Maybe that new Italian?'

He nods and is about to say something else when two guys come charging down the street, leaping onto Aaron's back and getting him in a stranglehold. My heart is in my mouth until I realize Aaron knows them.

'What you doing standing out here in the cold? Get a pint down your neck, lad,' says a burly guy with a baby face, rubbing his knuckles on the top of Aaron's head.

Aaron introduces them as Toby and Wyatt, and we all head into the pub.

I haven't been in here for ages but the place hasn't changed. Aaron and his mates have been coming here since they were old enough to drink and even before that. It smells of spilt beer and male pheromones. It still has the same ugly brown wooden bar as you walk in, the faded patterned carpet, and the mahogany tables with old-fashioned, spindle-backed chairs. A group of lads stand around a dartboard, drinking pints, and when they see us walk in they cheer and chorus things like 'Here's the lad,' and 'You owe me a pint.' My heart sinks. They're nice enough but I want Aaron to myself tonight, the two of us alone over a candle-lit dinner where we can have a proper conversation without the fear that my mum might walk in on us, or we might upset Alice or scare the twins.

Aaron goes over to them and they all clap each other on the back. A stocky guy with spiky hair introduces himself to me as Rob. He's the only one who offers to buy me a drink and I find myself at the bar with him.

'Happy birthday,' I shout to him, over the din the others are making.

'Thanks. So you're Tasha. I've heard all about you.' He grins. His skin is ruddy and I can see he's already had a few. 'We thought he was making you up.'

'No, I'm real,' I say.

'He's a lucky man.'

I find myself blushing. 'Thanks. I hope he knows it.'

'Oh, he does.' He winks at me. Then Viv appears

behind the bar with a slightly harassed air, wearing a short-sleeved checked shirt, carrying empty pint glasses. The two of us are the only women in here.

Her eyes light up when she sees me. 'Tash! This is a rare sight. Here to keep an eye on my son, I hope.' She laughs, and a whoosh of heat travels up my body. I don't want to look like the desperate, clingy wife. I didn't even want to come. Although, deep down, I know why I did. I'm hoping to bump into Zoë. 'What can I get you?' She hangs the glasses up, then rubs her palms on her jeans.

'I'll have a pint of lager, please, Viv, and . . .' Rob turns to me.

'A glass of white wine, please,' I say. 'House is fine.'

'Coming right up.' She smiles at me and chats away to Rob as she pours him his pint. She's so easy with him, with all of them, but she's been working here for years and has the patter down to a T. I look across at Aaron and his mates. There are about fifteen of them, ranging in age from early twenties to late fifties. Surely they can't all work at the garage with him. Some I recognize as mates from school whose wives I like. There's Steve and Lee and Greg – I've been on double dates with them and their other halves. Lee works with Aaron at the garage. I recognize Tim – Aaron's boss, whose fiftieth birthday was last week. The others are a blur, interchangeable in T-shirts and jeans and too much aftershave.

The door opens, letting in a gust of wind, and I shift my body so I can see who is coming in, hoping it's Zoë, but it's just a group of young women who cluster around the bar. Viv moves away from us to serve them.

219

'Is . . . um, Zoë coming tonight?' I ask Rob as we re-join the others.

He nods. 'Should be. She doesn't like to miss a night out, does our Zoë.'

Our Zoë. Just one of the boys. I'm determined to get her on her own tonight. To see if she could be the person Arthur described putting a poison-pen letter through my door.

I have to wait an hour for her to arrive. An hour of my stomach lurching every time the door opens. An hour of going over and over our future conversation in my head, playing out every possibility. By the time she walks through the door I've nearly finished my second glass of wine and I've had numerous imaginary chats with her.

I'm talking to Lee about the time he got a detention at school for setting off a stink bomb in assembly when I hear someone say, 'Here she is!' and a tall blonde is strid-ing towards where Lee and I stand at the bar. She's wearing a black trouser suit, which is low-cut and way too dressy for a Monday night down the pub. Her long hair looks too bright, too artificial in this light, but there is no doubt that she's a very attractive woman with a figure I'd kill for.

She isn't wearing a nose ring. She definitely had one the last time I saw her – which, admittedly, was from across the street. But it was hard to miss.

I glance towards Aaron, who is in the thick of things with his mates. Has he noticed her coming in? He's deep in conversation with Tim.

'Hey,' she says, nudging Lee with her elbow, in a matey

gesture, and then her eyes sweep over me. 'Aaron's wife,' she says, thrusting out a hand. 'We haven't met. I'm Zoë.'

'Tasha,' I say, forcing myself to smile. 'Nice to meet you at last.'

'Likewise,' she replies, then turns back to Lee, chatting to him, and I suddenly feel awkward, standing with them, clutching my wine glass, like the third wheel. I wonder what Alice would think of her. My sister has always been a good judge of character. I can imagine her thinking that Zoë is a man's woman, preferring the company of blokes. And that's fair enough but something tells me – maybe from the way I notice her eyes searching the crowd and landing on my husband – that she might see other women as competition. And then she steps in front of me to order a pint from Viv.

Someone has put an old Bryan Adams song on the jukebox. 'Summer Of 69'. I can feel my heartbeat pounding in my ears. From the corner of my eye I see that Viv has passed Zoë a pint, then moved down to the other end of the bar to serve someone else.

Now that I'm here with her I don't know what to say. I can't very well ask her if she has designs on Aaron. Or if she put the note through my door.

Or if she could be my long-lost sister. She looks around the age Holly would be now.

I'd pointed Zoë out to Alice earlier when we saw her in the street, and asked her if she might have been the woman she met at the conference, but apart from the long blonde hair Alice couldn't really tell. 'She's too far away and I can't see her face properly,' she'd said.

'So, how are you, Zoë?' I begin, moving closer to her.

'I'm . . . good,' she says shortly, picking up her pint. 'I'm . . . um . . . I was sorry to hear about what happened to your sister and her husband.'

'Thank you,' I mumble, into my wine. 'It happened when Aaron and I were having a romantic break in Venice. It was the first time we've been away together since the twins were born . . .' I know I'm babbling.

Her impressive arched brows make a V shape as she taps her orange-painted fingernails against her beer glass. Her gaze flickers towards where Aaron is standing, then back to me. I can sense she'd rather be anywhere else than here, talking to me.

I appraise her, trying to see a family resemblance – if not to me and Alice at least to my mum and dad – but, apart from her colouring being similar to Mum's, I can't see it in her facial features.

I can tell she's about to move away to join the others. Her gaze keeps flickering over to Aaron. I need to keep her talking.

'Didn't you used to have a nose ring?' I blurt out in desperation. She turns her attention back to me again, frowning. 'I remember admiring it . . .' I tail off.

She touches the tip of her nose. 'Oh, yes, I did. I took it out a while back now. Anyway, nice to meet you,' she says, in a monotone.

I open my mouth to say more but she's already weaving her way towards Aaron and his friends.

I turn back to the bar and meet Viv's sympathetic gaze. I blush.

'Don't bother yourself over that one, duck,' she says kindly. 'She's a cold fish.'

'You can say that again.' I laugh to cover up my embarrassment. 'Oh, well, I tried to be friendly. I'm not sure what Aaron sees in her.'

'Here we are, Tasha, love.' Viv pushes a glass of wine across the bar. 'Get that down you. Are you okay?'

'I'm fine,' I lie. I try to pay for the drink but Viv says it's on her. I just want to go home. I take deep breaths, contemplating what to do next. Should I go over to Aaron and demand we leave? But then I'll look like the unreasonable wife in front of his friends. In front of Zoë. Time is ticking on and the intimate dinner I'd envisaged fades away. It's not going to happen tonight. He knows I wanted to talk to him about Holly and the DNA. Holly's been in my house as little as a week ago. She could even be Zoë. I feel a surge of anger towards Aaron.

I grimace at Viv when I hear Zoë's laughter drift towards me. 'I think I'll go home.'

Viv looks crushed. 'You know what he's like when he's with his mates, but that Zoë. She's trouble, I think.'

I'm so grateful she agrees with me that I want to kiss her. 'I think so too.'

'Aaron loves you. You've got nothing to worry about.'

I take a sip of my wine. 'I hope you're right, Viv.'

'I am.' She reaches across the bar to pat my arm reassuringly. 'Go over there and join in,' she says, like I'm some little kid at a birthday party. 'Don't let her think she's won. He's your husband.'

I glance over to them. Zoë is holding court, the men nodding along, clutching their pints like she's some kind of queen. I could go over. I could snake my arm around Aaron's waist, smile at Zoë, and pretend I didn't find her rude and dismissive. But I've never been very good at being fake. If I went over there I'd say something I'd regret. I'd embarrass Aaron and myself.

'No. I think . . . I think it's best I leave now.'

'Get Aaron to walk you home.'

'I'll be fine. It's not even nine thirty. Aaron will be here until closing time I expect.'

She flashes me a sympathetic smile. 'Don't worry, duck. I'll keep an eye on that son of mine for you.'

'Thanks, Viv.'

I'm heading to the door, pulling on my jacket when I feel a hand on my shoulder. I spin around to face Aaron, concern in his eyes. 'Where are you going?'

'Home.'

'I thought we were going for dinner.'

'The moment's passed.'

His face falls in disappointment. 'I'm sorry, Tash. I got carried away drinking and chatting.'

I suppress a sigh. 'It's fine. We can talk about Holly tomorrow.'

'You shouldn't walk back on your own. It's not safe.'

'It's just around the corner, I'll be fine,' I say, turning to leave. He grabs my hand and, in that moment, I will him to come with me. I will him to put down his pint, say goodbye to his mates and walk with me out of the door.

But I can already see he's had a few and isn't in the mood to stop now.

'I love you,' he says, kissing my hand.

I reach up and kiss him full on the lips, knowing that Zoë is probably watching. I pull away. 'I'll see you at home.'

29

TASHA

When I wake up the next morning I notice that Aaron's side of the bed is empty. I sit up slowly, my head spinning as the events of the night before come crashing to the forefront of my mind. I left the pub at nine forty p.m., came home and told Mum all about Zoë. Alice was already in bed when I went up, red-eyed, emotional and tipsy. Did Aaron even come home last night?

I check my phone. It's six a.m. There are no messages or missed calls from him.

I get out of bed carefully, the alcohol sloshing around in my stomach. I only had three glasses of wine, which would have been nothing in my teenage drinking days, but now I'm not used to it and everything aches. I stare at myself in the mirror. My eyes are puffy, my hair is a bird's nest, and I look as if I smell. I pull on my dressing-gown. Once I've had a shower I can face the day, I reason. I try not to imagine Zoë's long legs draped around my husband's waist. Oh, God, I can't face this. I can't face any of it. I slump back onto the bed, my head in my hands, fighting the urge to be sick.

I love Aaron, despite our differences. I always have.

'Wow, still a lightweight, then?'

My head shoots up at the sound of Aaron's voice and I laugh in relief. Of course he didn't spend the night with Zoë. She might fancy him – and after last night I'm sure she does – but it doesn't mean he'd cheat on me with her.

But the relief is short-lived when I think that she could still have written the note and, worst of all, she may be Holly. But that's the worst-case scenario, I tell myself. Even if she did write the note it doesn't mean she was inside the house. It doesn't mean it's her DNA found from the blood on our rug.

I need to find a photo of her to show to Alice. Then Alice can tell me if she was the woman she met at the conference.

Aaron is leaning against the door jamb, fully dressed in his overalls, grinning at me. 'How much *did* you have to drink last night?'

'What time did you get home?'

He shrugs. 'Not that late. Around eleven-ish.' He sits next to me on the bed and takes my hand. 'I'm sorry it wasn't your thing last night. It's a very laddy crowd. I'm sorry we didn't have the chance to go for dinner too. Are you okay?'

'I – I spoke to Zoë. Did she tell you? She didn't seem that interested in chatting to me. Couldn't get away fast enough.'

At the mention of Zoë something dark scoots across his face. 'No, she didn't.'

I bury my face in his chest, the starchy fabric of his overalls rough against my cheek, breathing him in, his musky aftershave and the smell of fabric conditioner. Comforting. Safe.

'Hey,' he kisses the top of my head, 'is everything okay?'

I move my head up to meet his eyes, the irises I love so much, brown and green, like the shell of a tortoise. 'There's so much we need to talk about. So much to say.'

'I know. There is.' His expression becomes more serious. 'Actually, there's something I wanted to tell you,' he begins, but he doesn't get the chance to finish his sentence because Mum rushes into the room, her face pale, her eyes flashing with worry and fear. Instantly I'm on alert, thinking of Elsie and Flossie.

'They're fine. They're downstairs watching telly,' she says, reading my mind. 'It's just . . . I went into their room to open the curtains and make their beds and I . . . Well,' she puts a hand to her head, 'there's something strange. Can you come?'

Aaron and I exchange puzzled glances and follow Mum across the landing to the girls' bedroom. 'My eyesight isn't what it was,' she says, 'so I can't be sure. But look, there . . .' she prods the glass '. . . in the pond. Is there someone in the water?'

I move closer to get a better look, Aaron leaning over my shoulder. The outline of the trees is dark against the milky-white sky, and an early-morning mist is hovering over the pond, but in the water, right next to the bank and tangled in weeds, is what looks like a body.

My hand flies to my mouth.

I feel Aaron tense beside me. 'Fuck. Call an ambulance!'

he cries, and runs from the room. Mum already has her phone out and I follow Aaron as he takes the stairs two at a time, shoving my feet into my wellies and following him out of the back door and across the garden. The early-morning breeze is cold around my knees and I pull my dressing-gown further around my body, conscious I'm still in my nightwear.

'Go back in, Tash,' Aaron barks, over his shoulder, as he unlocks the gate.

'No. Mum's ringing an ambulance. I might be able to help. If it's someone in trouble . . .' But he's already wrenching open the gate, disappearing through it. The ground underfoot is boggy and I almost lose a welly as I squelch after Aaron towards the pond.

Then I stop, frozen to the spot. I don't know what I was expecting to see. Maybe on some level I thought it was a mistake, that it would be just a random piece of clothing that had fallen into the pond. But there is no mistake.

A body lies face down in the water.

I heave and clamp my hand over my mouth.

Hair already tangled in weeds. Black fabric ballooned with water.

I step closer, a buzzing in my ears as everything around me seems to slow down: Aaron, wading into the pond, Arthur from next door standing in his dressing-gown and talking about ambulances, Nick, the neighbour on the other side, late twenties and buff, who also lowers himself into the water to grab hold of the woman.

The hair is blonde and she's wearing the same black

trouser suit as last night. Her feet are bare, her skin mottled and I give a yelp.

I watch, numb with shock, as Nick and Aaron lift her from the water and carry her too-still body onto the muddy grass. Her eyes are closed and there is a mark on her head, maybe a cut or a wound. Did she fall in? Was she drunk? I know this is a shortcut from the pub but why so near to our house? Nick tilts her chin back and blows into her mouth, pumping her chest. Aaron shakes his head, signalling what we already know, what is obvious.

When Nick realizes it's fruitless he sits back on his heels and swears.

Aaron's face has drained of all colour. In the distance we hear the wail of sirens. I turn to see Alice and my mum huddled by the back gate, still in their dressing-gowns, horrified expressions on their faces as I hurry towards them.

'It's Zoë,' I say, as I reach them. 'She's . . . she's dead.'

30

JEANETTE

Tuesday, 22 October 2019

Death. So much death. Jeanette can't bear it. She has to get out of the house, away from the sombre faces and the fug of depression that hangs in the air, like stale cigarette smoke. She makes the excuse that they need more bread and milk and slips out of the front door before they can protest.

She has been unable to think of anything but Holly since the detectives broke the news yesterday. Her mind is scrambled with thoughts and images of her long-lost daughter, sneaking into the house and attacking her sister and brother-in-law. Jeanette doesn't want to believe that this is the sort of person her precious baby has become. The guilt intensifies, sitting on her chest and making it hard for her to breathe.

The back of Tasha and Aaron's house is swarming with police, crime-scene tape already erected around the section of pond and embankment where Zoë was found. Thankfully, Jeanette doesn't spot any police on the street outside the house.

On the way to the supermarket she bumps into two old friends, Lorraine and Denise, who tell her they'd heard she was back and were so sorry to hear about Kyle and Alice. 'If you ever need to talk, we're here,' says Lorraine, placing a hand on Jeanette's arm, and Jeanette feels a tug of guilt that she's lost touch with them since moving to France. She used to work with Lorraine in a typing pool when they were in their early twenties, before Jeanette left to have Alice, and she's known Denise just as long. She pushes them from her mind as she makes her excuses to leave. She hasn't got the headspace for them right now. Her family needs her. She's not come back here to socialize but to look after them.

She keeps her head down in the supermarket, hoping she doesn't bump into anyone else. She's not in the mood for small-talk – how can she pretend to be normal when her nerves feel as stretched and taut as an elastic band? She shoves a loaf of bread, a tub of hummus for the twins and two pints of milk into her basket. Elsie and Flossie drink so much of it even though she can't stand it. She pays for her groceries – she couldn't resist getting some chocolate buttons for the twins – and is just packing them into her tote bag when she spots Viv at the exit. She's smoking furiously, her weird-looking French bulldog at her feet, and she's talking to a woman, in a fluffy white jacket, who also has a dog, some kind of poodle cross. Viv isn't wearing a coat as though she came out in a hurry. She must be cold, thinks Jeanette, idly. She can't hear what they are saying but the other woman moves away when Jeanette walks out, waving goodbye to Viv and pulling at the lead of her dog, a blonde tendril escaping from her hood.

'Cheerio, duck,' calls Viv, to the retreating woman. She turns back to Jeanette, her brows furrowed, as though annoyed at the interruption.

'Sorry, you didn't have to say goodbye to your friend on my account,' says Jeanette, pulling out her umbrella. She tries not to cough at the smoke being exhaled in her vicinity.

'Oh, I hardly know her, just a fellow dog walker.' Viv stubs out her cigarette with the toe of her trainer, then picks it up and pockets it.

'How's things?' Jeanette makes an effort to be polite, as is her way, although she's always sensed that Viv doesn't like her. Even though she had been there the day Holly went missing, and was helpful at the time, in the years since she's felt Viv avoided her. Especially when Aaron and Tasha started dating. She supposes they are polar opposites and Viv wanted to set boundaries early on. Plus Jeanette had Jim, and Viv was on her own, so it's not like they could have become couple-friends.

Viv stares at her now, baggy-eyed, her skin grey. There's an awkward pause between them and Jeanette searches her brain for something to say.

'Bad business about Zoë,' she says eventually.

'Zoë?' Viv looks puzzled.

'You know, the woman who works with Aaron at the garage. She was found dead this morning, drowned in the pond at the back of Tasha and Aaron's house.'

Viv seems to freeze and her face pales. 'What? Are you sure?'

'Yes. I'm definitely sure. I'm sorry,' says Jeanette,

appalled at herself for blurting it out like that. 'Were you close to her?'

Viv shakes her head. 'No,' she mumbles. 'Not really.' She grips the dog lead tightly so that her knuckles turn white. 'She came into the pub a lot. She was – she was there last night. I need to go.' She moves away from Jeanette and hurries in the opposite direction, without saying goodbye, her weird-looking dog trotting by her side trying to keep up.

Jeanette wonders if she should go after her to make sure she's okay. But then decides against it. She doesn't think Viv will appreciate it and doesn't want to make matters worse.

Jeanette had only met Zoë for the first time last night.

31

TASHA

Tuesday, 22 October 2019

Donna and Catherine gawp at me as if I'm not in my right mind, and I look the part with my unbrushed hair, my hurriedly pulled-on clothes and one of Mum's floral rain macs, which I'd grabbed as I was running out of the house. I've just dropped the twins at nursery and have popped in to the dental practice on the way home to pick up some forms.

'Shit, she drowned? How? Did she fall in?'

'I'm not sure. They haven't told us anything yet. A police officer came over and took our statements this morning.' He told us that one of his colleagues would be over later to interview us properly.

What had happened after I left the pub? Did Aaron walk her home like he'd done before?

And then another, more horrific, thought swiftly follows. *Did they argue? Did she admit she was Holly, perhaps, and he pushed her in?*

No, stop. I can't let my mind go there. Aaron would never do something like that and I don't even know yet if a crime has been committed. It might have been a tragic accident. Maybe Zoë had drunk too much and slipped into the pond on her walk home. But then I think of the wound to her head. Maybe she banged it on a rock or something when she fell in.

I wonder if the police will test Zoë's DNA now. If they do we'll find out if she really is Holly. Yet how unfair that would be to Mum if it turned out to be true. Despite the circumstances, for us to find her again only for her to die would be devastating.

'That's just awful,' says Donna. 'I didn't know her, although I'd seen her out and about. She only moved to the village a few months ago, didn't she?'

'I think early summer sometime. It's a dreadful thing to happen.' And it is, even if I didn't like her.

Lola bursts into the room, looking frazzled, her hair wet. 'Sorry I'm late,' she says, sounding out of breath. She unzips her coat and hangs it up on the stand, then turns to us. 'You'll be pleased to know, Donna, that I've got some new glasses.' She grins and then must notice our downcast expressions, because she adds, 'What's going on?'

Donna fills her in and Lola's eyes widen. 'Ponds are so dangerous,' she says softly. 'When I was little we had one in our back garden and my dad took it out because my mum was always so worried I'd fall in and drown.'

'The pond has always worried me,' I admit. 'We always make sure the back gate is locked so the girls can't get out.' It had put me off wanting to move in, but the house was all we could afford at the time and Chew Norton is surrounded by lakes.

'My family dog drowned in a pond,' says Catherine, solemnly. 'She had arthritis and couldn't get back out.'

236

'Bloody hell, this is a cheery conversation first thing on a Tuesday.'

We look up as one of the partners, Colin, walks in looking smart in his pale blue scrubs. 'Why are you all talking about drowning?'

'You haven't heard, Col?' Donna looks up, hugging a clipboard. 'A woman was found dead in the pond out the back of Tasha's house early this morning.'

His pleasant face falls. 'Oh, no, I'm sorry. Did you know her?'

'Not really,' I say. 'Her name was Zoë Gleeson.' I found out her surname earlier when the policeman arrived. 'She was only thirty.'

Colin glances at me and frowns. 'Not that it isn't lovely to see you, but you're supposed to be on compassionate leave, remember? Don't tell me you can't keep away from the place.'

I miss the distraction of working but Alice needs me and so does Mum now we've found this out about Holly. 'Thank you for being so kind about the compassionate leave. I'll definitely be back next week.'

'It's no bother,' says Colin, his eyes softening. 'But you'd better go before I change my mind.'

As I let myself in through the front door I almost bump into Alice in the hallway. She's dressed and looking immaculate in a pair of fern-coloured cords and a balloon-sleeved cream cashmere jumper. She's arranged her hair to try to hide the stitches. I realize she's been waiting for me to get back.

'Where have you been? The detectives are in the kitchen with Aaron.' My heart plummets. Are they talking to him because he found Zoë? Or for another reason? I think again of the empty bed this morning. Had Aaron been truthful when he said he'd come home around eleven-ish?

'Where's Mum?' I ask, swallowing my fears.

'She popped to the shops, said we'd run out of bread and milk.'

That's strange. There was enough milk when I left earlier and if there hadn't been she should have asked me to get some on the way back from nursery. She's probably desperate to return to her life in France. I wonder if she'll go back after Kyle's funeral.

I follow my sister to where Aaron is sitting with DI Thorne and DC Jones at the kitchen table. Both have glasses of water in front of them. Aaron is still in his mechanics overalls, stained from where he'd hauled Zoë from the water. They're all wearing matching grave expressions.

There's something about Thorne that makes me feel particularly nervous. He doesn't smile or make any effort to put us at ease, almost as if he suspects all of us of collectively pushing Zoë into the pond.

I scoot in beside my husband and Alice sits opposite us, next to Thorne. He clears his throat. 'I was just asking your husband here about his movements yesterday evening. It's procedure, but we're talking to everyone who was in the Packhorse with Zoë last night.'

I turn to Aaron. I'm interested to hear what he's got to say.

'So you were saying you left the pub about eleven? And was that alone?'

Aaron nods. 'Yes, it was.'

'And Zoë was still in the bar when you left?'

'That's correct.'

I watch Aaron for any signs he could be lying. His face is ashen and I remember that, for all her faults, Zoë was his friend. I reach under the table and take his hand. He squeezes my fingers in acknowledgement but doesn't look at me.

DI Thorne sits back in his seat and folds his arms across his chest. 'One of the men in the bar with you last night, a Mr . . .' he leans forward to read his notebook left open on the table '. . . Lee Barnsley says you and Zoë had words?'

I feel Aaron stiffen. 'Not words, exactly. But, yes, I was a bit pissed off with her. She – she said something about my wife, something . . . derogatory, and I picked her up on it.'

'What did she say?' asks Thorne, to my relief.

Aaron stares down at his glass of water. 'She said Tasha wasn't a very nice person and didn't deserve me. She – she made it obvious that she had a . . . ahem . . .' he gives a little cough and I squirm in my seat '. . . a crush on me.'

I knew it! I fucking knew I wasn't being paranoid but I don't say anything even though I want to.

Thorne glances at me, his expression stern. Then he

fastens his steely gaze back on Aaron. 'And were her feelings reciprocated?'

'Of course not. I saw Zoë as a mate and nothing more.'

I catch Alice's eyes across the table and she raises her brows.

'And did you tell her this?' Thorne asks Aaron.

'Yes, I did. And she said she understood, but then . . . she tried to kiss me and I pushed her away.'

White-hot anger rises inside me but I swallow it. Aaron's hand is still in mine and I don't move it away even though my palms are sweating.

'Did anyone see this?'

'Yes,' says Aaron, hotly. 'Everyone saw it. I told her she was drunk and that I was going to leave.'

'So she was drunk?'

'Yes. Very drunk, I'd say. It was all just awkward and embarrassing so I left the pub and walked home. I was in the house by eleven thirty at the latest.'

Thorne nods slowly and then looks at me. 'And I understand you were also in the pub last night?'

'Yes, that's right. I left about nine forty.'

'And I was in bed asleep before you ask,' says Alice, curtly. 'All evening. I didn't go to the pub. And my mum was in the living room, knitting.' Thorne makes a note of this. 'Are you saying you think Zoë's death is suspicious?' Alice adds.

'Zoë was found with a head injury. We need to ascertain how she came by it.'

'And has my sister told you that Zoë matched the

description of the woman who posted that horrible note through the door?'

'No, she hasn't.' He looks at me questioningly and I tell him Zoë confirmed to me last night that she used to have a nose ring. I'd tried to find a photo of Zoë online to show Alice so she could confirm if she was the woman she'd met at the conference, but she has no social-media accounts.

'Will you be testing Zoë's DNA to see if she could be Holly?' I ask.

He nods. His voice is crisp as he says, 'Yes, we will.' He clears his throat. 'So you were home before your husband? Can you vouch for him returning at eleven thirty, like he's said?'

My eyes flicker to Aaron who is staring at the table. I feel a whoosh of heat to my throat but I find myself nodding. 'Yes,' I lie. 'I was awake when Aaron got home and I can confirm it was eleven thirty.'

32

BONNIE

February 2019

'You need to talk to your dad about this,' said Selma, surveying the yellowing newspaper cuttings laid out in front of her on the mushroom-coloured carpet in Bonnie's parents' living room. 'I know exactly what you're thinking.'

'How can I not think I'm this missing baby? Why would my mother have kept all these articles about Holly Harper otherwise? And why would she not want that box opened until after her death?' They were both sitting cross-legged in the middle of the floor sharing a bottle of wine. Selma had been the first person Bonnie called after she found the box and Selma had raced straight over.

Selma pulled her long dark ponytail over one shoulder and picked up one of the articles dated October 1989 and started reading it aloud in her strong Brummy accent.

'Witnesses say that a woman was behaving strangely around the town of Chew Norton in the hour before Holly Harper went missing, looking frantic and mumbling to herself, clutching a teddy bear to her chest. Mrs Eileen Heron of Church Road, said: "Both me and my friend Pam saw her eyeing up all the babies. She looked in my pram at my little Ben and I told her to go away. She looked like she might have been on drugs." She has been described as short and slight with long dark hair and an unkempt appearance.'

'That doesn't sound like your mum,' said Selma, replacing the newspaper clipping. 'Your mum was beautiful and blonde, and always looked immaculate even when she was ill. Even as she got older . . .' She trailed off, her expression sad.

Clarissa had been fond of Selma, who would sit for hours after school patiently answering Clarissa's questions about her family. Clarissa was so interested in Selma's parents and grandparents, all her brothers and sisters and cousins. She loved hearing about their quarrels and their lives, however mundane, almost as if she was listening to a soap opera. She would then muse about how she wished she had been blessed with a big family and that it was all she'd ever wanted.

'Ah, this other one, dated a few days later, says the woman had escaped from a nearby hospital,' said Selma, as her eyes scanned the piece. 'So sad. Probably a mental-health patient. Although,' she then turned to another article, 'this other one talks about a young woman with a baby getting into a blue car. I wonder if they ever tracked that car down. I can't see any follow-up to it in these articles. God, this is awful. So many leads, by the look of it, and so many dead ends. Another witness says here that a man was seen lurking in the area at the time Holly went missing. It sounds like a lot of gossip and hearsay to me.

243

The thing is, in the sixties, seventies and eighties a lot of women would think nothing of leaving an unattended pram outside a shop. My mum told me she used to leave me in my pram out in the garden. Can you imagine anyone doing that nowadays?'

'Hmm. True.' Bonnie gently unfolded another article, the paper thin and the ink already smudging. 'Holly Harper went missing in October 1989. She was born the same year as me. In April, on the twenty-seventh according to this . . .' Bonnie stabs the page with her index finger. 'My birthday is . . . well, you know when it is.'

'March the thirty-first. Next month. Have you checked your birth certificate, though?'

'Yes, I have, and it confirms my date of birth. I've seen all the official adoption papers too and my mum and dad are listed as my adoptive parents. I was only two days old when they took me home.'

'Well, then. How can you be Holly? I just can't believe your mum would steal you from a pram outside a shop and tell your dad she'd adopted you when they'd already adopted you by then and you have the paperwork to prove it.' Selma leant back against the leather sofa. 'Adoption is a rigorous process. Even in 1989. Your mum couldn't have done it without your dad. Not if he's listed on all the official paperwork. My second cousin, Kelly, adopted her kids about twenty years ago. I remember her telling my mum how she and Gareth had to jump through hoops and the adoption people wanted to know every little thing about them. It got right up Kelly's nose.'

Bonnie sighed. Something didn't feel right to her. Why

244

else would her mother have kept all these articles about Holly? 'But it would explain her strange behaviour all these years. How she was basically a recluse. She was probably terrified of being discovered. She was obviously obsessed with this Holly Harper case.'

'Maybe she was into true-life crime. A passion, perhaps. Something to occupy her time with your dad away. You and Holly being similar ages. Perhaps it was a case of "There but for the grace of God go I"? And maybe – please don't take this the wrong way as you know I love you,' her voice softened '– but maybe you're obsessing about this to fill the gap that caring for your mother has left.'

Bonnie took a large slug of red wine. She suddenly had the strange urge to throw it over the light-coloured carpet in an act of rebellion. So much had changed in her life in a matter of three short weeks and now she felt at sea, directionless, unsure of who she was, or who her parents were.

'Dad said I was given up for adoption because my parents had been teenagers. I wonder if they're still together or if they're now married to other people, with kids of their own. I could have half-siblings. My adoption certificate doesn't say anything about my birth parents.'

'You look like your mum, though. I was surprised when you told me about the adoption,' Selma mused, assessing her best friend with her intense dark-eyed gaze.

'The colouring is the only thing that's similar.' Bonnie placed her glass carefully on the carpet, her earlier rebellious urge forgotten. That wasn't who she was, who she'd ever been. She was careful, considerate, a geek, shy, caring and loyal, and that was fine with her.

Selma leant forward to peer further into the box. 'Have you dug any deeper? There's more stuff in here . . .'

'I haven't had a chance. As soon as I saw those articles I rang you.'

Selma began to rummage through it. 'There are some baby clothes . . . a lock of hair, and . . . Oh.'

Bonnie's stomach dropped. 'What?'

Selma sat back on her heels, holding an A5 envelope, a puzzled look on her face.

'What is it?' Bonnie frowned, taking the envelope from Selma. On the front in block letters was written 'FINAL RESTING PLACE'. It was her mother's writing. 'What the hell?'

'The envelope is sealed.'

'I can see that,' said Bonnie, turning it over in her hands. 'I'm too scared to open it. What does it mean? Did my mum . . . did she do something to Holly? Is that why she kept all these articles? Will I find a confession in here or something?'

Selma shook her head vigorously. 'No, no, your mother wouldn't have been capable of anything like that.' They both stared down at the envelope in Bonnie's hands. 'You have to open it. You'll always be wondering otherwise . . .'

'I know.' Bonnie drew a deep breath, steeling herself. It was probably less sinister than she was imagining. Before she could change her mind she tore open the envelope.

A photograph fell out onto her lap.

'What is it?' Selma peered over her friend's shoulder.

Bonnie picked up the photo with a shaky hand. 'I don't know.' She peered at the image: tufts of overgrown grass, a stone wall, the overhanging branches of a cherry tree. Bile rose in her throat. 'It looks like the photograph of a garden.' She turned it over but there was nothing written on the back and the rest of the envelope was empty. 'I think it's the bottom of our garden. Look, that's our wall, and the tree . . . the tree . . .' She turned to Selma, horror washing over her. '*Final resting place.* Who the fuck is buried at the bottom of the garden?'

33

JEANETTE

Tuesday, 22 October 2019

Jeanette can't sleep. She can hear Aaron and Tasha arguing in hushed whispers from their bedroom. She's not sure what they are arguing about although she can make an educated guess that it's Zoë. She knows Tasha won't appreciate Aaron keeping that from her and having to hear it for the first time from the detectives. She glances at her phone. It's nearly midnight and they'd all trudged up to bed an hour ago, tired and irritable with each other. Aaron was at home because the garage had closed for the day as a mark of respect, and there was a strange, almost toxic energy in the house when Jeanette returned from the shops, just in time to see Alice showing the detectives out of the front door. She could sense the repressed resentment between Tasha and Aaron that they were trying to hide under polite small-talk.

Jeanette met Zoë for the first time last night, although she hasn't mentioned this to her daughters or Aaron. And she's not proud of herself for keeping this secret from them. But after Tasha had told her that Zoë fitted Arthur's description of the woman seen outside the house on the day she received the note, Jeanette had wanted to see her, to talk to her. And, yes, it's been thirty years since Holly disappeared, and yes, aesthetically she would have changed a lot in that time, but Jeanette was sure that she would just *know*. That something inside her, some kind of mother's instinct, would recognize her daughter if she saw her again.

Jeanette must eventually have dropped off because she's woken with a jolt around four a.m. She looks across at the girls in their matching ivory-framed beds. Flossie has her thumb in her mouth and Elsie has kicked off her duvet, exposing her cute little feet. Jeanette gets up from the airbed. Her back aches. She'd complained about it earlier and Alice had told her they should swap beds but Jeanette had declined. Alice needed her space right now. Somewhere to grieve in peace. She pads over to the twins, tweaks the duvet to cover Elsie's feet, then wanders over to the window, moving aside the curtains, wondering what has woken her. The moon is full, casting its silvery glow over the pond, making the water look like liquid mercury. The crime-scene tape cordons off the area of the embankment where Zoë was found and she tries to erase the memory of the woman tangled in the reeds, her hair floating on the water, like a strange type of algae.

And then she jolts.

Someone is out there. Moving around by the pond. She blinks as they move towards the rear gate and enter Tasha's garden. Is this who killed Kyle and are they back to finish what they started? Her heart picks up speed. Just as she's picking up her mobile to call the police she can see that it's a woman wearing a coat over a calf-length nightdress and wellies. She recognizes the long red hair. She's walking across the lawn towards the house. It's either Tasha or Alice. Jeanette's immediate relief is quickly followed by anxiety. What is one of her daughters doing outside so soon after a woman was found dead?

Jeanette hurries from the bedroom, closing the door quietly behind her, and makes her way to the kitchen just in time to see Alice locking the back door. She's barefoot now but still wearing her coat.

She jumps when she sees Jeanette. 'Mum. What the hell? Are you trying to give me a heart attack?'

'Are you trying to give me one?' hisses Jeanette. 'What are you doing? I saw you out by the pond.'

Alice flushes, looking guilty. 'I'm sorry. I snuck outside for a fag.'

'At four a.m.? You need to be more careful. And I didn't know you smoked.'

'Well, I don't. Not really. Just when I'm stressed.' She turns away from Jeanette to hang the keys on the hook.

'You shouldn't be wandering around at night. It's dangerous.'

Alice wraps her arms around herself. She looks vulnerable and too thin even with the thick coat on. Jeanette wants to fold her into her arms and take away the pain of Kyle's death. 'I know,' Alice says quietly. 'But I figured it was so late that nobody would be around. And I couldn't sleep. I keep thinking about everything. The familial DNA that was found here the night Kyle was killed. The notes – Tasha's and mine. Zoë dying.'

'Zoë isn't Holly,' says Jeanette, firmly, 'if that's what

you're thinking, and we'll know for definite soon enough after the police have tested her DNA.'

Alice looks taken aback. 'I'm thinking that anyone could be Holly right now, Mum. Anyone who is thirty years old. And I'm devastated that all the evidence suggests that my baby sister, whom we've all spent years grieving for, could have done this. Why would . . .' She swallows, and even in the dim light Jeanette can see Alice's eyes are swimming with tears. 'Why would she want to hurt us? Any of us?'

'I don't know, honey. I don't know,' says Jeanette, moving towards Alice and wrapping her arms around her. She feels as if she's fading away. 'It's all I can think about since we found out. And I keep hoping there's a simple explanation for this. That even if Holly had been here that night, it doesn't mean she was responsible for what happened to you and Kyle.'

Alice leans against her shoulder. 'I hope there's another explanation too,' she says sadly, hugging her mother goodnight and going up to bed, leaving Jeanette in the kitchen. She stands at the patio doors for a while, looking out onto the garden washed in a silvery light, her mind full of Holly. 'Where are you?' she whispers, her breath fogging the glass.

Because she knows, with certainty, that Zoë isn't Holly. Her daughter is still out there somewhere.

Zoë's face flashes into her mind. Her hard eyes, her set chin. The sneer on her lips.

No. That creature, the spiteful woman she met last night, couldn't possibly have been her daughter.

34

TASHA

Thursday, 24 October 2019

It feels strange being a passenger in Kyle's car but I'm relieved it will no longer be parked outside our house. I admire the confidence Alice is demonstrating behind the wheel of something so powerful and expensive. The inside looks like a cockpit. I definitely wouldn't want to drive it. But I don't really enjoy driving and I steer clear of motorways if I can help it. We debated taking the train but Alice said she needs to get Kyle's car home.

I feel sick at having to leave the girls again so soon. Especially after a second death so close to our house. I think, in some strange way, I'll feel more relaxed when Aaron takes them to Viv's tomorrow before he and Mum drive up to meet us at Alice's. It's the thought of them all being in the house after everything that's happened. But Aaron had assured me that the police patrol car is still outside, watching the front of our house. I'm trying not to think about who could be watching the back.

It's now two days since Aaron helped pull Zoë's lifeless body from the pond. We were a bit terse with each other when he left, dropping the girls at nursery on his way. Although the space between us will be good for us. Since he revealed that Zoë had tried to kiss him in the pub the night she died we've bickered about it, although I feel like a bad person for bringing it up. Because the truth is that a woman who was vibrant, attractive and full of life drowned. And it doesn't matter how I felt about her, how much I disliked her, because she was young and died in tragic circumstances.

'She was alive and well when I left the pub,' Aaron insisted, when he got home from work yesterday. 'Although you shouldn't have lied to the police, Tash.'

I'd been feeling bad about it ever since and I'm relieved to get out of Chew Norton for a few days, even though I'm dreading Kyle's funeral.

Yesterday Zoë's photo had appeared in the paper and I showed it to Alice, asking if she'd been the woman she'd met at the conference. Alice had scrutinized the black-and-white picture while I'd waited with bated breath, before she turned to me and said, 'I don't think so, but I'm not sure. There is a similarity but I don't think it was the same woman.'

Now, as we drive along the M4, we're listening to some science podcast about genetics, which is so boring I keep nodding off. I'd wanted her to put on one from BBC Sounds about three missing girls who disappeared from a crashed car back in 1998, but Alice dismissed it saying she hates 'true crime'. She seems enraptured with this one, and the only reason I haven't told her to turn it off is because I know it's a distraction for her. The thought of returning to her house in London, without Kyle, must be devastating for her and she'd looked pale and anxious this morning at breakfast, hardly eating a thing.

I must doze off listening to a scientist talking about some genetic mutation because when I wake up we're driving along a pretty, tree-lined street with huge detached houses behind electric gates. I sit up expectantly. This is it. I recognize her road even though I've only been to her house a handful of times. We pull into the driveway of what looks like a quintessential country manor house: red-brick, perfectly symmetrical, with ivy climbing up the walls, sash windows and roof turrets. 'Fuck,' I exclaim, as she stops the car on the expansive drive. 'I'd forgotten how huge this place is, Al. It's a mansion.'

She stares up at the house, clutching the steering wheel, her eyes swimming with tears. 'I'd give it up in an instant just to spend five minutes with Kyle.'

I'm appalled at myself. 'God, I'm so sorry. That was so insensitive of me.'

She smiles sadly. 'Don't be silly. I get it. I thought the same when Kyle first showed me the place.'

I remember her telling me how impressive it was when he asked her to move in with him. There was some talk of buying a house together but that never happened.

'How the hell did he afford this on his own?' I find myself musing.

'I think a large part of it came from the inheritance he received when his parents died.'

I suddenly remember what Eve had told me about a brother. 'Did you ever meet Kyle's brother?'

She swivels to face me. 'He hasn't got a brother.'

'But Eve said . . .'

She tuts. 'Don't listen to that woman. Kyle would've told me if he had a brother.'

'Okay,' I say, reaching for the door handle, remembering what Catherine had told me about Eve being a fantasist.

I'm about to step out of the car, thinking Alice will follow suit, but she continues sitting there staring up at the house. I lay my hand on her arm. 'We can sit here as long as you need,' I say, swallowing the lump in my throat.

She wipes her eyes and takes a deep breath. 'I need to be strong,' she says, almost to herself.

'Alice, you don't need to . . .'

But she gets out of the car before I can finish. I follow her into a large entrance hall with a sweeping staircase that looks like something from *Downton Abbey*. My whole downstairs could fit into the hallway and there would still be space. I take my boots off but Alice walks into the room on the left, which, I remember from when we last stayed here, is the living room. I stand in the doorway, images of one of the last times we were all here playing in my mind, like a home movie: Kyle was at the white baby grand piano at the end of the room playing Beatles songs and we were all singing along, the others merry from his expensive wine. It was when I was pregnant with the twins and I'd not drunk anything. I remembered at first feeling embarrassed at having to sing while stone-cold sober, but then, looking around at Aaron, Alice and Kyle, who were shouting out the lyrics and not caring whether they were in tune (Kyle was the only one out of all of us who could actually sing),

I lost my inhibitions and ended up having a brilliant evening.

'You're remembering the night you and Aaron stayed over, aren't you? When you were pregnant?' Alice is watching me and I nod. 'That was a perfect evening,' she adds.

I swallow. 'It was. Kyle was brilliant on the piano.'

'Kyle was brilliant at everything,' she says. She sinks onto one of the fuchsia pink velvet sofas that face the opulent fireplace. The room looks like it could be out of *Living Etc* with its smoky-hued walls and brightly coloured furnishings. 'God, this house even smells of him.'

I sit beside her. 'Is there any last-minute thing I can help you with for the funeral?'

'No, thanks. Everything is mostly done. I think there will be about ninety people coming back here.'

Ninety people. I doubt I'd get even half that at my funeral, then shake myself out of my macabre thoughts.

'I just need to finalize a few things with the caterers,' she says. 'They're coming to set up on Saturday while we're at the church. They'll be on hand for the rest of the afternoon.' She stands up, goes to the fireplace and picks up a framed photo of her and Kyle on their wedding day in Las Vegas. 'I regret we didn't have a big wedding. It should've been huge. I should've worn a meringue.' She runs her thumb softly over the photo. She'd looked beautiful in a long pale pink dress and Kyle handsome in a powder-blue suit. They're gazing at each other with such adoration. I wonder if Aaron and I have ever looked at each other like that.

'I wish you had. I wish I'd seen you get married,' I say.

She looks at me, her face serious. 'I'm sorry. Were you annoyed about it?'

'No! Not at all. It was up to you, it was your big day. You had to do what worked for you and Kyle. But I'd have liked to see you get married all the same.'

She replaces the frame and moves away from the mantelpiece. 'Anyway, I can't sit here wallowing. I need to get on. Why don't you make us a cup of tea? You know where the kitchen is.' I watch her leave the room, wondering if I've upset her. She's so fragile at the moment, so understandably emotional that I don't want to say anything to make matters worse.

With a sigh I get up and make my way through the entrance hall and down a couple of steps that lead to a huge glass and stone room at the back of the house: the kitchen. It's stunning with wrap-around sliding doors, marble work surfaces and the darkest grey handle-less cabinets. It's immaculate, like the whole house is. There isn't even a layer of dust on anything, although Alice has been away from home for nearly two weeks. She must have had cleaners in.

I make Alice and myself some tea after a few attempts at trying to work the instant hot water tap, opening and closing cabinets until I find the mugs. The stone tiles feel warm under my feet as I head back into the living room carrying the drinks. But she's not there. I try the other rooms downstairs: a snug, a dining room and another reception room but they're all empty. In the basement there is a cinema room but I doubt Alice is down there watching films. 'Alice,' I call, as I walk up the sweeping staircase. I feel a chill to the back of my neck and shudder. As beautiful as this house is, it's too big, too echoey, too old, and I feel a swell of panic at the thought of being stuck here tonight, just the two of us. What if someone broke in to finish the job they hadn't done at mine? 'Alice,' I call again. There is no answer as I step onto the landing. I peer around the first door. It's a study, decorated in a masculine style with a heavy wooden desk, floor-to-ceiling bookshelves and a leather swivel chair. On the desk there is a laptop left open, the screen lit up. I peer at the email that's displayed. It's from the undertakers. This must be Alice's machine.

I'm about to turn around and head out of the door when Alice appears. She's wearing a dressing-gown. 'Thanks, Tash,' she says, taking one of the mugs. 'I can't face replying to the undertakers. Would you mind doing it for me? I want to have a bath. No offence, but yours is tiny.'

'No offence taken.' It's only the girls who use our bath anyway. 'What do you want me to say to them?'

She glances past my shoulder at her laptop. 'Can you just tell them it's all fine? It's about where the flowers need to be delivered . . .' She interlaces her fingers around the mug. 'Thank you,' she says softly, 'for coming back here with me. I can face anything with you by my side.'

My eyes smart. 'Always,' I say.

She wanders across the hall and disappears behind a huge oak door. I turn back to the laptop, making myself comfortable in the big leather chair. I carefully place the mug on a coaster that says I ♡ LONDON and read through the email from the undertakers before replying to them. After it's sent I scroll through her inbox to see if there is anything else I can do to help. But then I freeze when I come to an email with the subject heading 'CONNOR CAMPBELL', dated 18 October, which was just last week. Campbell was Kyle's surname, and Connor is the name Eve gave me for his brother. The brother Alice insisted didn't exist.

I push down my guilt at betraying Alice as I open the email. It's from someone called Bella Laverne.

Dear Alice

Thank you for getting in touch and I've passed on your details to Connor. He says thank you for reaching out but he's still angry with Kyle and isn't ready to forgive him yet, but he knows part of his healing is facing up to his past, including any wrongdoings on his part and on the part of others. It's a work in progress but I assure you I will talk to him and try to convince him to meet up with you both.

Very best wishes,
Bella

I re-read it, my mind racing. At the bottom of the email is a company name and address. A quick Google search reveals Bella Laverne is a counsellor at some kind of rehab facility in Brighton. I lean back in the chair, my mind reeling.

I don't want my sister to see what I'm about to do next

so I get up and go to the door, closing it quietly behind me before sitting down again at the laptop. And then I look through her previous internet searches, scrolling down the list:

- *The Office US ending*
- *Amazon.co.uk*
- *Holly Harper disappearance*
- *Rightmove.co.uk*
- *Hard wood furniture*
- *Venice weather*
- *Chemical genetics in drug discovery*
- *Chimera/genetics*
- *Bella Laverne*
- *Connor Campbell*

I stop when I reach Connor's name. I sit back, breathing out slowly, as I try to understand why Alice would lie to me about Kyle's brother.

35

BONNIE

February 2019

Bonnie could tell her dad was nervous as they sat together at the table in the kitchen with the articles about Holly Harper spread around them. She'd emptied the box to show him everything, and now the old newspaper cuttings, along with the tiny pink Babygro and the lock of silky blonde hair, lay between them, like exhibits from a crime, which was what Bonnie feared they were. He kept swallowing and rubbing his palms along the length of his denim-clad thighs.

Since finding the box last week she'd agreed not to do anything rash until her father returned on his leave from the rigs. Selma had suggested she call the police but she wanted to speak to her dad first. There might be a simple explanation for the photograph. Maybe it was the 'final resting place' of a pet. She couldn't jump to conclusions until she'd spoken to her father, hoping that maybe her mother was just a true-crime fanatic.

She slid the envelope across the table towards him. 'What's going on, Dad?'

He picked up the envelope, a frown on his face, but there was another emotion behind his eyes as he read the words on the front. Fear. 'You have to know that I loved your mother so much. I'd do anything for her.'

His words chilled her. 'Like kidnap a baby?'

He glanced up at her, hurt in his eyes. 'Of course not.'

'Look inside, Dad. What does this mean?'

He opened the envelope, his hand shaking as he held the photo. And then he did something that shocked and alarmed her in equal measure. He started to cry. She'd never seen him cry in her whole life, not even when her mother died.

'Dad, you're scaring me now.'

His shoulders shuddered as he sobbed. He was still wearing his leather jacket as though he wasn't planning to stay and, to Bonnie, it was a strange sight, this big bear of a man in his biker clothing crying like a little boy.

'I'm sorry,' he said eventually, running a hand across his face and placing the photo face down on the table.

It went against Bonnie's nature not to get up to hug him but she couldn't bring herself to move. She was too scared of what he was going to say next. She sat there, rooted to her chair, while her father searched for the right words. He got up and tore a sheet of kitchen roll from where it sat on the worktop to wipe his face before he sat down again. Bonnie couldn't move, dread sitting heavily in her stomach. 'I can't even begin to tell you how obsessed Clarissa was with having a baby,' he began, 'and the adoption process took years because it had to be a new-born baby. She didn't want to take a child that was two, three, four years old. And then when they finally gave us what we wanted she was so happy. God, I'd never seen her so happy, Bonbon. It was like her life was finally complete, you know. When you were six weeks old I took a three-month contract on the rigs.' He twisted the kitchen roll in his hands. 'I know you were young, but Clarissa could cope. She didn't need me around and the contract meant she didn't have to work, she could stay at home, raise you, which is everything she . . .'

'. . . ever wanted,' Bonnie finished for him. 'Yes, you've said. I've seen the adoption certificates and they look legit.'

'Of course they're legit. We didn't fake an adoption if that's what you're thinking.'

'But that still doesn't explain all this.' She indicated the box. 'And where does Holly Harper fit in?'

'When I came back from the rigs you were nearly five months old. But now, looking back in hindsight, that was when I noticed a change in Clarissa. The steady decline of her mental and physical health, though I didn't really piece it all together. Not then. It was only later when I started to suspect . . .'

'Started to suspect what, Dad? Do you think Mum snatched Holly? Why would she when she had me? I don't understand.'

He sighed deeply. 'A few years ago, she had that fever, do you remember?'

Bonnie nodded. Her mother had caught flu and had been really ill. For a few hours they'd worried that they might lose her.

'I was sitting with her, by her bedside, just the two of us. And she reached over and took my hand and started talking about a baby who died . . .'

263

Bonnie froze.

'She kept saying she was sorry, that she'd tried so hard to save her. She then started rambling on about Chew Norton and how she'd gone down to visit her family there . . . and then . . . and then she mentioned Holly Harper and how she'd been out of her mind with grief and hadn't meant to do it but she'd seen her there, in her pram, just left. Just left there. That was what she kept saying, over and over again. And how she hadn't meant to do it.'

Bonnie felt sick. Her father looked at her with red-rimmed eyes. She could see pity in them.

'When I tried to probe her on it,' he continued, 'when I asked her what, *exactly*, she hadn't meant to do, she clammed up, turned away from me and went back to sleep. It was like she was saying it all as part of a feverish dream.'

'Did you ask her again?'

'Yes. The next day,' he said, shredding the kitchen towel between his fingers. 'But she acted like she didn't know what I was talking about. But now, seeing this box, I'm beginning to understand what she was trying to tell me.'

A wave of horror washed over Bonnie.

'Is that what this photo means?' She stabbed it with her finger. 'Final resting place. Did Mum kill Holly? Is she buried at the bottom of our garden?'

He shook his head, his face full of anguish. 'No, Bonbon,' he said sadly, and his next words sent her reeling. 'It's not Holly that's buried at the bottom of the garden. It's Bonnie. The *real* Bonnie.'

36

TASHA

Friday, 25 October 2019

I don't have the chance to talk to Alice about Connor until the next morning. After her bath last night she went straight to bed without eating anything, leaving me to order a takeaway from one of the leaflets I'd found in the drawer. There was no food in the house, apart from some essentials, like milk and bread, which the cleaner or house-keeper or whatever other staff Alice employs must have got in.

I'm relieved that Mum and Aaron are arriving today. I didn't enjoy spending the night in this huge house. I kept hearing noises and would wake up with a start thinking someone was about to break in. I'm assuming Alice has got the place alarmed but she's not in her right mind so I don't even know if she'd set it last night. And the fact she lied about Connor is nagging away at me. Alice isn't a liar: she was always too confident to have to resort to telling untruths. She always said that only cowards lie. So what is she scared of?

I'm sitting at the huge marble kitchen island when she comes downstairs, fully dressed in jeans and a jumper, fresh-faced, her hair tied back. She's holding a black bag and her demeanour is full of purpose and of 'getting things done'.

'What have you got there?' I ask, through a mouthful of toast.

'Some of Kyle's clothes.'

I almost choke on my toast. 'What? Why?'

'They need to go. I can't have them hanging in the wardrobe. Someone could get good use out of them. Kyle loved his designer gear.'

'But, Alice, it's too soon.' Not to mention it's the funeral tomorrow and there is still lots to organize.

Her eyes flash. 'Is it?' She dumps the bag on the floor. 'When am I supposed to do it then, Tash? All this . . . it's just stuff. Material things. It's not him.'

'I know . . . I never meant that. It's just . . .'

'What?' She throws me a challenging stare.

'There's loads of things to organize for tomorrow. Can't it wait?' Wordlessly she picks up the bag and leaves the room. My gut twists with guilt. I'm too sentimental, I know that. Our loft is full of trinkets, old birthday cards, cinema tickets, concert flyers, the soft toys Aaron won for me at the fair when we first met. I've got all the twins' baby clothes, which I can't bring myself to get rid of, and the teddies I had when I was a kid. In contrast Alice gave all her old stuffed toys to the charity shop when she left for university and never keeps anything. This is her way of coping.

I'm putting my plate in the dishwasher when Alice wafts back in. She takes a mug from the cupboard and sits it under some highfalutin coffee machine. It gurgles and grinds, and she stands with her back to it, fiddling with the cuff of her jumper, her face as overcast as the sky outside.

I need to ask her about Connor but she's in such a foul mood I'm scared she'll snap at me for looking through her emails. Instead I say loudly over the coffee machine, 'Mum called earlier to say she and Aaron should be here by midday. They're driving up.'

The coffee machine stops and Alice reaches for the cup. She drinks it black, which I find disgusting. She takes a sip, then says, 'I haven't been honest with you.'

'Okay . . .' I wonder what she's going to say.

'I lied about Kyle having a brother. He does have one. He's four years younger. And he's coming to the funeral tomorrow. I've just had a conversation with him on the phone.'

I'm relieved that she's admitted it without me having to tell her I invaded her privacy, while also thinking it strange that she's chosen to do so just after I've looked at her search history. It's almost like she knew. 'Why did you lie about it?'

'I didn't want you to think badly of Kyle.'

'But why would I have?'

'Because they had a big falling-out years ago, before their parents died. Connor is an addict. Heroin.'

'Shit.'

'Kyle had no choice but to cut him out of his life. Connor was a nightmare, apparently. He stole from Kyle to get money for drugs. I mean, I can't even imagine. I only found out about Connor a few months ago. Kyle lied to me about him too. When he eventually told me I thought it was sad they didn't have any contact so I tried to find him. When I saw he was in rehab I told Kyle about it. Kyle was tentative about them reuniting but I reasoned that if Connor had cleaned himself up they could have some kind of relationship again.'

'But why lie to me about it?'

'Because it was Kyle's business. Kyle had washed his hands of him. As far as he was concerned he no longer had a brother.' She narrows her eyes. 'I suppose you're judging Kyle now, aren't you? Thinking he wasn't very charitable, disowning his brother and all that. But you don't know the half of it and neither do I. But Kyle was the loveliest man. He wouldn't have done it if he hadn't had a reason.' She sets her chin determinedly. She looks so sad that my heart twists.

'Alice, I'd never judge Kyle. Families are complicated.'

'Good,' she says, lowering her gaze. 'I'd hate you to have a bad impression of him.'

'That would never happen,' I say softly. 'We all loved Kyle.'

'Good,' she says again. And her voice catches as she adds, 'Because Kyle was a very special man. And I don't want anything tarnishing his memory.'

By the time Mum and Aaron arrive at lunchtime we've packed all of Kyle's clothes into bin bags and now they line one side of the hall. Alice asked me if Aaron would want any of them but I'd declined, slightly appalled at the thought of him walking around in her dead husband's clothes. I think back to Venice and wearing Alice's clothes. And about the man who followed us. With everything that's been going on, I haven't thought about it much, but now it seems to fit with Eve's talk of dodgy investors. Was that man one of them? Or, at least, working for one of them? Did he mistake us for Alice and Kyle? It's not the right time to ask Alice now, especially as she's so adamant that Eve made the whole thing up about Kyle being scared.

Mum looks smart in a navy waterfall cardigan and beige trousers. She tries to hide how in awe of the house she is as she steps into the hall. But I remember how much she'd gone on about it after the first time she'd seen it.

Aaron raises his eyebrows at me as he carries two hold-alls over the threshold and I'm touched that he's carrying Mum's for her.

'I'll show you where to put the bags,' I say, leading him up the stairs. I want him to myself for a few minutes. Alice and Mum head into the kitchen and I can hear her voice floating up to us about how she's 'gasping for a cuppa'.

'How did it go last night?' Aaron asks, as I show him into the spare room where I've been sleeping. It's huge, with windows that overlook their garden, which even by non-London standards is large. He perches on the edge of the king-size bed. When I left yesterday we were barely talking, but having a night away from each other and being here with Alice, witnessing how distraught she is without Kyle, has given me time to reflect on our marriage and appreciate what I have.

I sit next to him and lean over to hug him, taking in the familiar smell of his clothes and his aftershave, grateful that he's here. 'I missed you,' I say, in a rush. 'I'm sorry we've not been getting on. And I'm sorry about Zoë.'

He wraps his arms around me and kisses the top of my head. 'I'm sorry too. I was naïve, with Zoë. And I suppose, on some level, flattered. You shouldn't have lied to the police about me, though, Tash. I wouldn't want you getting into trouble.'

I move away a fraction to look into his face. 'You definitely left the pub before she did? You promise me you're not lying about that?'

'I promise you. I would never hurt Zoë. Or anyone. I honestly don't know how she got the head injury or if someone pushed her into the pond. I promise I never saw her again after leaving the pub.'

I assess him for signs that he's lying. I believe him. 'I know you wouldn't hurt her,' I say. 'But did you fancy her? Be honest, Aaron. I promise I won't get cross.'

He looks doubtful. 'Really?'

'I think we need to start being more honest with each other. Long-term relationships are hard . . . and we've, well, we've not always made time for our marriage, have we?'

He nods. 'I love you. I didn't have any feelings for Zoë, apart from friendship. I did think she was attractive but, more than anything else, I suppose I liked the attention. It made me feel young again. I'm sorry, it was stupid. But I love you. I really love you, Tash. I don't want to lose you.'

I'm alarmed to hear the sadness in his voice. 'You're not going to lose me, you big softy,' I say, wrapping my arms around him again.

'Good,' he says, into my hair, gripping me tightly. When we eventually break apart I tell him about Connor.

'So Eve was telling the truth about Kyle having a brother,' I finish. 'But Alice is adamant that Kyle wasn't involved in anything shady. Yet . . . that man in Venice. I keep thinking about it and why he was following us.'

'Me too,' he says solemnly. 'I think, when the funeral is over, you need to have a proper heart-to-heart with Alice. I have to say I believe what Eve told you about Kyle being scared and these investors. It fits with us being followed in Venice – and remember, he told me that one of his investors had pulled out. Maybe he got desperate.'

I frown. Something about it doesn't add up. 'We were followed the same night Kyle was killed. I know he was attacked a few hours later but . . . it couldn't have been the same man.'

'He might have been some heavy sent by whoever Kyle owed money to. They might have sent a few to scout for him in different locations. Places they knew Kyle might be. I don't know.'

It's all so removed from our everyday life and feels more like the plot of a movie, but it does sound like Kyle was involved with the wrong people. 'What I still don't understand,' I say, 'is where Holly fits into all this. Why was her blood found on our rug the night Kyle died?'

37

JEANETTE

Friday, 25 October 2019

Jeanette is just settling herself at Alice's humongous kitchen island with a cup of tea when there's a knock at the front door.

Alice turns to her with wide eyes. 'I'm not sure who that could be,' she says, getting off the bar stool. 'I'll be back in a minute, Mum.' She pads across the stone tiles to answer it, and Jeanette can hear the soft baritone of a male voice.

She turns back to her tea, thinking it must be a neighbour or a friend wishing to give their commiserations on Kyle's death ahead of the funeral tomorrow.

Tasha has disappeared upstairs with Aaron. She hopes they can work through their problems. They're good for each other – they balance one another.

Alice reappears, followed by a tall, very slim man in faded black baggy jeans and a grey hoody. His head is shaved, he has an earring through his nose, and is the sort Jeanette would shrink from if she saw him on the street.

'Come in and sit down,' Alice is saying to the young man. Up close he's older than Jeanette first thought. It's his clothes that give the impression of someone younger. In reality he's probably early thirties.

Alice looks unusually flustered as she offers him a coffee.

'Water is fine, thanks,' he says, as he slips onto the stool next to Jeanette. He's well-spoken and, despite his under-nourished appearance and the hardware decorating his nose and ears, he smells of shower gel and freshly laundered clothes.

'Connor, this is my mum. Mum, this is Kyle's brother, Connor.'

Jeanette starts. *Brother?* She's sure Alice said Kyle was an only child, but she smiles politely at Connor and shakes his hand. She can see the family resemblance in the straight nose and the deep blue eyes, and despite his thuggish appearance, he's handsome like Kyle.

Connor is gazing around the huge kitchen with hungry eyes and Jeanette swallows her feelings of discomfort at him being here.

'I know these are horrible circumstances to be meeting in for the first time,' says Alice, placing a glass of water in front of Kyle's brother, then standing by the bi-fold doors. She cranks them open to let in the fresh, cool air.

Connor runs his finger down the glass. 'I should have got in touch with him earlier. And now it's too late.' He hangs his head and Jeanette can't work out if he's genuinely sad. 'All those things we left unsaid . . .' He hunches forwards and Jeanette can see the nodules in the curve of his spine through the thin fabric of his hoody.

'I'm sorry I took so long to find you,' says Alice. 'Kyle only mentioned you to me a few months ago. I didn't even know he had a brother until then.'

Jeanette is surprised at this. What kind of husband doesn't tell his wife that he has a brother? And what else has he lied about?

She's never completely trusted Kyle. Not that he was ever anything but lovely to her. But the way he'd swooped into Alice's life with his flash car and all his money, whisking her off to get married in Las Vegas when they'd only been dating six or seven months, depriving Jeanette of watching her daughter tie the knot, of being the mother of the bride, had made her wary of him. Jim had died early in Alice and Kyle's relationship. The first time she'd met her future-son-in-law was when they came to Chew Norton for the funeral. She often wonders if Alice married so soon to fill the void her father had left behind.

And then she feels a stab of guilt for thinking such thoughts. Especially now Kyle is dead.

'That's not surprising,' Connor is saying, his mouth twisting into something resembling a smile. 'We've had our ups and downs over the years.'

'Kyle told me about the drugs,' Alice says, closing the bi-fold doors when a cold blast of air sweeps in, bringing with it the smell of wood-smoke and damp soil. Jeanette rubs her arms, wishing she'd put on a warmer cardigan.

'Well, yes. I was a nightmare teenager and using heroin even before my parents died. But their deaths really sent me over the edge.'

Jeanette feels a rush of sympathy towards him, quickly replaced by suspicion at what he might want from Alice. 'How long have you been clean?' she asks.

He swivels around to face her. 'Two years. I now work at the rehab centre and I feel like I'm giving something back.' His appearance is at odds with the soft, considered way he talks. There is no aggression, as far as Jeanette can see. She wonders what made him get into drugs in the first place when he grew up so privileged with a family who obviously cared about him. It makes Jeanette thankful that both her daughters have turned out well. There was a time when Tasha went off the rails in her late teens, but it didn't last long and she soon sorted herself out.

And then she thinks of Holly and how she might have turned out if she'd never been abducted that fateful day, instead of a possible killer. Zoë's face flashes into her mind and she folds it away with all the other things she tries not to think about.

Connor jumps down from his stool, asking to use the bathroom.

'Oh, sure, it's just down –' begins Alice but Connor interrupts her.

'I know where it is,' he says, and leaves the room.

Jeanette resists the urge to follow him.

'How does he know where to go?' whispers Alice. 'As far as I'm aware, he's never been here. Kyle told me he'd only bought the house a year or so before we got together.'

Jeanette lowers her voice as she looks furtively towards

the open doorway. 'Just be careful. You don't know any-thing about him. He could still be on drugs . . .'

'Mum! That's not very charitable.'

'I wouldn't be a mother if I didn't worry,' she says in response. She doesn't want to be too judgemental but she also knows Alice is in a vulnerable place right now and she'd hate to see anyone using that to their advantage.

Alice is making herself a coffee when Connor returns and sits down again. She offers him one and this time he says yes. Jeanette's heart sinks. She was hoping he'd leave soon but she can see that Alice wants to talk to him. She starts asking him questions about his and Kyle's child-hood, if they were close, and Jeanette can see her daughter is understandably trying to grasp new nuggets of infor-mation about her husband, as though she knows the opportunity will be lost because it's inevitable that, with the passage of time, she and Connor will lose touch. She's worried, just as Jeanette had been worried, that the image of Kyle in her head will begin to fade. She wants to tell her it doesn't work that way. She can still picture Jim's face clearly, still hear his voice.

'Kyle always was the entrepreneur,' Connor is saying. Alice has now taken a seat next to him and is looking up at him in wide-eyed wonder, her chin resting in her palm. 'Even at school he had a way of making money. He was great at drawing, mostly caricatures, and he'd sell them to his classmates. He was hugely popular, as you can imagine. Clever, sporty.' He rolls his eyes. 'The whole shebang. Girls loved him. Sorry,' he says, suddenly hear-ing what he's said.

276

But Alice waves away his apology. 'I love hearing this stuff about him.'

Connor's expression darkens. 'But he could be a bit of a bully too.'

'A bully?' Alice sits up straighter, and Jeanette wonders why Connor would say that, even if it's true, especially to his brother's grieving widow.

'Just to lesser beings.' He grins but there is pain behind his eyes. 'He didn't always treat his girlfriends well. He was the type to fall head over heels in love but then get bored after a few months. He was young. He knew his power. We all do stupid things when we're young.' He looks down at his hands. His skin is rough and his fingernails are bitten down.

Just then Tasha walks into the kitchen closely followed by Aaron. She stops in surprise when she sees Connor at the island. Alice jumps down from her stool. 'Connor, this is my sister, Tasha, and her husband, Aaron.'

'Connor! Kyle's brother?' Tasha strides over to him and shakes his hand. 'Oh, my God, you're actually here.'

'Um . . . do I know you?' He looks confused.

'Sorry, no.' Tasha blushes. 'It's just we were only talking about you this morning as Alice told me she'd been trying to find you. I'm so sorry about your brother.'

'Thank you. I haven't seen him in years and now . . .' He draws a deep breath.

'I'm sorry,' Tasha says again.

Aaron steps forward to shake his hand too. Then Alice suggests moving into the living room so they all troop out of the kitchen. Once again Jeanette gets the feeling Connor knows his way around the house. He stands at the French windows looking onto the garden, with a wistful expression. 'We used to play out there,' he says. 'My parents had this amazing tree-house built for us.'

Alice's surprise mirrors her own.

'What do you mean?' asks Alice.

Connor turns to face them, back-lit by the weak October sun. 'This was our family home. Didn't Kyle tell you?'

Jeanette can see this information has knocked Alice for six. 'What? No, that – that can't be right. Kyle bought this a year or so before he met me.'

Connor shakes his head. 'No. He didn't. My parents left it to us in their wills. But then he tricked me out of my share, found a loophole that meant I didn't get any of it. He said it was because of my drug habit, but that was just an excuse. I was left with nothing.'

38

TASHA

Saturday, 26 October 2019

After the service I'm helping the caterers peel the cling-film from the plates of cheese-stuffed pastries and smoked salmon when I spot Eve sauntering into the packed kitchen. There is the low-level drone of muted voices and a subdued air, and she looks a little lost as she searches for a familiar or friendly face among the clusters of people. Someone is trying to open the bi-folds with no luck. I haven't seen Alice since we arrived back at the house.

My heart sinks. Does Alice even know she's here? I didn't see Eve at the church, but it had been so rammed that people had had to stand at the back. After the service everyone trooped back here en masse as it's only around the corner. How did Eve know about the funeral? She's never met Alice and I haven't spoken to her since that afternoon we met for coffee. Maybe she heard through mutual friends. I hope she's not here to make trouble.

The sun was up at seven a.m. and hasn't stopped shining since. The kitchen, with its glass roof and wrap-around doors, is like a greenhouse. Everyone is proclaiming it's like June rather than October and I'm already regretting my long-sleeved black shirt and wool trousers, not that I had any other choice. Eve is wearing an elegant shift dress, her blonde hair tied back in a neat bun, and when her eye catches mine her face floods with relief at seeing someone she knows. She pushes through the throng towards me.

'Hi, Tasha, so lovely to see you. I hope it's okay that I came back to the house? Alice said everyone was welcome after the service.'

'Yes, of course. Have you . . . er . . . met Alice?'

'No. Not yet. But I'd like to.'

'Then, who . . .' I search for a way to say it without sounding rude but I can't find one '. . . who invited you?'

Eve's bright smile falters. 'Kyle's friend, Will. He knew that we kept in contact so . . .' She lifts her shoulders. 'Why? Do you think Alice won't like it?'

'I'm sure it's fine if Will invited you,' I lie. Catherine's description of Eve as being self-absorbed filters into my mind. At least we know there is no way she could be Holly. Eve is a good six years older than the age Holly would be now.

After Connor's visit yesterday, and his bombshell about this house once being his family home, Alice is even more on edge. She'd been mortified, offering to sell the house and give him what's rightfully his. Reading between the lines, it had sounded like Kyle and Connor's parents had tied up the house in a trust with Kyle in charge because of Connor's drug problems, but Connor kept talking about being tricked out of what was rightfully his, causing Alice to flinch with every word.

'Anyway . . .' I say now to Eve, balling a sheet of cling-film and pocketing it. I move away from the long table that Alice has pushed back against the wall. It holds all of the food. I grab the key to the bi-folds from where I know it's kept and push my way through a group of people to open them, feeling like I'm releasing a stopper as every-one spills out into the garden, taking deep breaths of the fresh air. When I turn back to the kitchen Eve is right there. I'm not going to get rid of her that easily.

'Where's your fiancé?' I ask her, hoping she'll say he's in the next room. That was the last place I'd spotted Mum and Aaron.

'Oh, I left him at home. I just told him I was going to a friend's funeral. He doesn't need to know he's an ex. So,' she inches closer to me so that there is hardly a gap between us and lowers her voice, 'have you heard any more about Kyle? I keep hearing all sorts of rumours in the village. I told the police about the dodgy investors and what he said to me about being scared and . . .' Her glance skims my shoulder. 'Oh, my God, there's Connor. I haven't seen him in years but he's hardly changed.' She frowns, her eyes flicking back to mine. 'I thought they were estranged.'

'They were but Connor showed up here yesterday. He's clean now and works at a rehab centre.'

'Oh, that's great news. I always liked Connor. I was sad when Kyle told me of Connor's troubles. It hurt him, you know, having to disown his brother. He did it because he was worried that Connor would just waste the money on drugs and end up killing himself.'

'Why don't you go and say hello?' I suggest hopefully.

'It's fine. I'll go over to him in a minute. He's chatting.'

We turn to where he's standing in the corner of the room with some people I don't recognize.

I'm grateful for the air that floats in through the open doors. The kitchen is clearer now, although a line has started forming for the food. I'm about to make my excuses to extract myself from Eve when I see Alice walking towards us with a woman who is vaguely familiar. She's tall with short dark hair and bright blue sparkly eyes. She's smiling at me as she approaches and I remember she's one of Alice's old university mates.

'Hi, Tasha, lovely to see you again. It's Ellen. Ellen Bright. I went to uni with Alice.'

'*Doctor* Ellen Bright now,' says Alice, proudly, even though she has a doctorate herself. 'Ellen is one of the leading geneticists in the country.'

'Ah, well, I don't know about that.' Ellen blushes.

Alice rolls her eyes. 'You're too modest.' To me and Eve she says, 'This woman is brilliant.' I can tell by Alice's demeanour that she has no idea who Eve is and Eve doesn't step forward to introduce herself.

'Talking of brilliant, the app Kyle was designing will revolutionize the health industry,' says Ellen.

Alice dips her chin. 'It would have, but I doubt it'll happen now.'

'Why not?' Ellen asks. 'Can't it still go ahead?'

Alice shakes her head regretfully. 'I don't think so. It was Kyle's baby. He was the brains behind it. I advised him as best I could, of course, but I know nothing about technology. My input was the biochemistry side of things. I've spoken to the investors about next steps, but without Kyle they're getting cold feet and . . . I don't really want any part in it now. It wouldn't feel right without him.'

'That's a shame.' Ellen pats Alice's arm. 'Isn't there another way?'

'I don't know, but I don't think so. Not with me involved anyway.'

There's an awkward pause before I ask, 'What exactly was this health app able to do?'

Alice launches into what sounds like a rehearsed elevator pitch on how the app would be able to detect a variety of different diseases, including some cancers, through a toothbrush that collects your saliva. 'And all within one app so you'd no longer have to go to your GP for all the individual tests,' she finishes.

'Very impressive,' Ellen says, nodding.

'We hadn't come up with a name for it,' says Alice, sadly. 'It was still six months to a year from being finished. There was still so much up in the air but it would have been good. Kyle was a genius.'

'God,' says Ellen, 'I'm so sorry. I still can't believe it. Kyle was so – so *vibrant* and full of life.'

Alice bites her lip. I can see she's trying very hard to be strong and not break down in tears.

'Isn't there a way it could still happen?' I pipe up. 'It sounds like a great idea. Even if it wasn't you taking it over. It seems a shame for all Kyle's hard work to have been for nothing.'

'No.' Alice's eyes blaze. 'I wouldn't want someone to take it over. It was Kyle's.'

'But if it would revolutionize the health industry?'

Alice shakes her head. 'It's too complicated to explain to you now, Tash, but without Kyle . . .' She tails off and I don't want to push it or to sound insensitive but I can't believe only Kyle was clever enough to make it work. There would be other techies out there who could take over, other scientists who could come on board.

It's probably best I change the subject and I'm just about to when Eve steps forward thrusting out a hand. 'I'm Eve, by the way,' she says, in her overly familiar, confident voice.

'Eve?' Alice's eyes widen when it hits her who she is. 'Oh, yes, of course. Kyle's ex-girlfriend.' I can sense the chill behind her smile.

'I hope it's okay that I came. Will invited me.'

Alice looks as if she'd like to throttle Will. 'Of course it's okay,' she says, although I notice her voice has gone up a fraction.

I silently urge Eve not to mention meeting Kyle on the day he died.

'We were childhood sweethearts,' she says, turning to address Ellen. 'I saw him for the last time the afternoon he was killed.'

I want to kick her.

Ellen has obviously picked up on the tension between Eve and Alice because I can see she wants to be anywhere but here having this conversation. 'Oh, right,' she says politely, then takes a sip of her orange juice.

'Yes,' says Eve, twirling the stem of her glass. 'He told me –'

But before she can say anything else Alice cuts in coolly: 'This isn't the time or the place to be talking about that.'

Eve shuts up.

Alice links arms with Ellen, and as she steers her away from us and towards the hallway, she says, 'I'm sorry about that. Eve is a bit of a fantasist, I'm afraid. She was obsessive over Kyle.'

I glance at Eve to see if she's heard, and from the patches of red that have appeared on her cheeks I can tell that she has.

'I'm sorry,' I say, feeling I should apologize even though I think Eve should have kept quiet. 'She's very protective over Kyle and his memory, understandably. I don't think you should go around talking about what he said to you as it makes him look bad.'

Eve goes even redder and looks down at her strappy sandals. 'I didn't think about that,' she mumbles.

'It's okay.'

She glances at me. 'I didn't make up that meeting, you know. Kyle really did ask to see me. We really did meet up and he really did say he was scared.'

'I believe you,' I say. She was right about Connor after all. 'And Alice will too, in time. She's just going through a lot right now.'

Eve smiles uncertainly at me. I hope I've done enough to appease her and to stop her making trouble. 'I thought I was helping. By telling the police.'

'You were. You did the right thing.'

'Then why doesn't it feel that way?'

She moves away from me and I watch as she sidles up to Connor and embraces him. Watching the two of them with their heads bent, chatting, gives me a feeling of unease and I'm not really sure why.

39

BONNIE

May 2019

It was a crisp summer's day in the last week of May when Bonnie finally arrived in Chew Norton. It was as pretty as she'd imagined, with its Cotswold stone buildings and quaint shops. So different from where she lived on the outskirts of Birmingham. She had managed to cobble together a deposit, with her dad's help, to rent a one-bedroom flat in the village but then, as luck would have it, she found a job, dog- and house-sitting for an old couple who were off to New Zealand for six months to spend time with their son and new grandchild. The house was actually an old mill by the lakes in Chew Norton and only a fifteen-minute walk to the centre of the village. And the dog was a five-year-old cockapoo called Biscuit. She fell in love with him instantly. After the six months was up, who knew? She'd probably return to Birmingham and move in with Selma, like they'd always planned.

Back in February, when her dad had admitted he suspected that the baby they'd adopted, the six-week-old he'd left safely with Clarissa while he flew back to work on the rigs, the *real Bonnie*, had somehow died and was buried at the bottom of their garden, everything she thought she'd known about herself, about her parents, changed in an instant.

He'd sat there, in their familiar, blandly furnished kitchen, and told her how the box and its contents confirmed the suspicions he'd held ever since Clarissa's feverish confession, each word shattering her heart.

'She adored the baby and she was a brilliant mother,' he'd said, his eyes red-rimmed, his face pinched. 'I tried to make sense of her ramblings afterwards and now I think it was most probably cot death. But after everything she'd gone through to get a longed-for baby, the grief, the unfairness of it would have sent her out of her mind. I think she went to Chew Norton to be with her family as I was away, then saw an opportunity to steal a baby from a pram outside a shop. To steal you.'

'And when you came back from the rigs and saw me, a different baby, being passed off as Bonnie, didn't you guess?'

He shook his head. 'It was three months later. Babies change a lot during that time. And you had the same colouring as Bonnie. The fair hair and blue eyes, but that's when I first noticed the difference in Clarissa.'

'If Bonnie hadn't been your adopted daughter, I bet you would've realized straight away,' she'd said, unable to keep the bitterness from her voice.

'No, that's not true, but you have to remember, we'd had Bonnie for only six weeks before I went away. It wasn't like I'd had loads of time to bond with her. It was *you* I grew to love. You I taught to ride a bike, to drive . . .' He reached across the table and took her hand. 'And when your mother tried to tell me the truth I was so terrified, so terrified of you being taken away, that I told myself it wasn't true. Do you understand? I didn't want to lose you.'

She withdrew her hand. 'But you lied to me, Dad. First you didn't tell me I was adopted and now this – *this huge thing . . .*'

He hung his head. 'I'm sorry. I'm so sorry. Clarissa never wanted you to know about the adoption, even though I did. We argued about it but it was ultimately her decision. She was the one who would be with you most, so I agreed in the end.'

She was still angry with her dad, but she loved him too. She'd already lost one parent and she didn't want to lose another, so, in the months that followed, they lived in a kind of hiatus.

And then she told him of her plan.

Now here she was. In the village where she was born. The village she was abducted from. She'd read through all the newspaper reports with such forensic scrutiny she almost felt as though she actually remembered it, even though she knew that was impossible.

She was saddened to hear that her birth father had died and that her birth mother had moved to France after his death. Another sister, older, called Alice, lived in London and was some high-flying scientist. But one sister remained in Chew Norton. Natasha.

And Bonnie realized – as she set up home in the Old Mill – that she was scared. Scared to approach these strangers. What if they didn't believe her? Or rejected her? What if they'd somehow got it wrong and she wasn't really Holly Harper, after all? She'd lived her whole life within the confines of her little suburban town and now, suddenly, here she was, about to upend someone's life.

She decided her first course of action would be to watch.

At first Bonnie enjoyed holing up in the Old Mill. It was a beautiful building, quirky, with a winding staircase and irregular stone mullioned windows and big open fire-places. The Holbys, Connie and Reg, had great taste and their house was homely, with family photographs adorn-ing the walls, soft rugs and plush sofas with tartan blankets covered with dog hair.

After a week, though, she knew she had to do more than hide: she began to apply for jobs so she could invei-gle herself into the community.

But first, before all of this, she had to speak to the woman who would have insight into what might have been going through Clarissa Fairborn's mind that Octo-ber day in 1989. Her father had given her the name and phone number of Clarissa's estranged sister. 'I haven't seen her in years,' he'd explained. 'She used to come up and visit when you were a kid – I don't know if you remember – but as you got older and your mother got weaker she distanced herself from her. From everyone. But they'd been very close, once. She might not live in Chew Norton any more. But if she does, this was her last known address and landline.'

She remembered an aunt coming to visit, bringing lemon-flavoured bonbons and a cousin, a boy. There had been a row once, when they visited, but it was a hazy recollection.

Bonnie had taken the slip of paper with these details, knowing she'd have to summon up the courage to call.

And today, she felt, was the day to do it.

She sat in the Holbys' cosy living room with the dog lying at her feet, and the dusty unfamiliar smell of some-one else's home. She picked up her mobile, dialling the number of her mother's sister. After two rings a woman picked up.

'Hello,' she said breezily, unaware that Bonnie was about to throw a hand grenade into her life.

'Oh, hi.' Bonnie's heart thumped so loudly that she wondered if the other woman would be able to hear it down the phone. 'Is that Vivian Pritchard?'

PART FOUR

40

TASHA

Monday, 28 October 2019

I'm relieved to be at home, out of the pressure cooker that is Alice's gorgeous house. I'd missed the twins so much and had made sure to call Viv at least twice a day while I was away to make sure everything was okay. I love Alice but I'm relieved she's decided not to come back with us to Chew Norton. The last two weeks have taken their toll and I just want things to get back to normal, especially for the twins. Well, as normal as they can be with Kyle dead and Zoë's death the talk of the village. The crime-scene tape has thankfully been taken down, but every time I look out at the pond I see Zoë's lifeless body, her long hair floating beneath the murky water like seaweed.

I'd felt a pang in my heart when we left Alice's house last night, waving from the passenger seat as Aaron drove us away. She'd looked so small and lost, standing in the huge doorway, wrapped in a calf-skimming cardigan. She'd insisted on staying behind but Ellen had agreed to move in with her for a week or so. The funeral had gone well – as well as can be expected anyway – and once Eve had left, the rest of the day ran smoothly. I was relieved neither she nor Connor caused any trouble although I am concerned that Connor will be back, guilt-tripping Alice for what he feels he's owed.

I'm thankful I'm not at work until tomorrow, but Aaron has to go in this morning. He's wearing the overalls Mum kindly washed and pressed for him before they'd travelled up to the funeral.

'See if you can find out if there's been any more news about Zoë,' I say, as we eat breakfast in the kitchen with the twins and Mum. She's made scrambled egg on toast and Elsie has squirted tomato sauce all over it and is mixing it in. We've been so busy with Alice and the funeral that we haven't had much chance to talk any more about Zoë.

'I will,' he says, grabbing a piece of toast from my plate and bending to kiss the girls goodbye. 'It's going to seem strange without her . . .' He glances at me as though he's said the wrong thing.

'Of course it'll seem strange,' says Mum, kindly. 'She was your friend.'

I nod and force myself to smile sympathetically. I believe Aaron when he says he turned down her advances. That night at Alice's house I felt we were more honest with each other than we have been for a long time. And just because I didn't like Zoë she was still Aaron's friend and he'll be grieving, possibly even feeling guilty that their last words were in anger.

He leaves for work and the girls get down from the table to play for a bit in the living room. Mum helps me tidy the kitchen, and as I pick up the wellies, I notice that mine are caked with mud. I haven't worn them since the day we found Zoë in the pond and I distinctly remember cleaning them.

'Did you wear my wellies?' I ask, lifting them up and watching a clod of earth thud to the floor.

Mum turns from where she's stacking the dishwasher and frowns. 'No. And if I had I'd have cleaned them.' Her eyes film with some memory and then she adds, 'Actually, the other night, I think Alice wore them.'

'Alice?'

'Yes. The night before you both left for London.' And then she tells me about something waking her and seeing Alice standing by the pond.

'What was she doing?'

'She said she couldn't sleep. That she'd taken to smoking again. Stress of Kyle's death.'

I carry the wellies to the sink. My sister was never particularly tidy. Luckily she has cleaners and staff to do all that for her now.

'Let me,' says Mum, already slipping on a pair of yellow rubber gloves. 'You see to the girls.'

'Thanks, Mum.'

I'm just about to leave the room when Mum says, her back still to me, 'I'm worried about Alice.'

I hesitate by the door. 'I think she'll be fine, Mum. She's a tough cookie.'

'She's not as tough as she tries to make out. I'm worried this will all hit her later, when the fuss of the funeral has died down, when everyone else has gone back to normal. I think I should have stayed with her in London.'

'Mum,' I say softly, 'Alice didn't want that. She was happy for us to leave. She wanted to get back to work, to her life. You don't have anything to feel guilty about. You offered to stay and Alice insisted she was fine. She has her friend with her so she won't be on her own and you can stop worrying.'

'You never stop worrying. You'll realize that as the twins get older. There's just something new to worry about.' She has her back to me as she scrubs at the boots with a brush. I can see the tension in her neck and shoulders.

I go over to her. 'We can always visit her in London again this weekend if you like? Bring the twins this time? You're not planning on going back to France yet, are you?'

'I don't know if I should ever go back.' She scrubs harder.

'Why? I thought you liked it there.'

'I should never have gone.' She stops what she's doing and lets her hands rest against the sink. She turns to me. 'I made a mistake, moving so far from you, Alice and the girls.'

'Well, we'd love it if you moved back, of course.'

'Really?' Her eyes light up.

'We never wanted you to go, Mum. That was your choice.'

Mum presses her lips together and carries on scrubbing. 'I don't understand why Alice lied to us about Kyle having a brother,' she blurts out.

So this is what's been on her mind. It's been on mine

298

too. 'I don't either. Except you know what Alice is like. She wants us all to think everything in her life is sorted. That Kyle is amazing, that they have this wonderful life. Had,' I correct myself.

Mum opens her mouth to defend Alice, like I knew she would, and I hold up a hand. 'I'm not saying this to put Alice down, or to be mean. I'm just stating a fact. That's what Alice is like. Remember when you found out she was being bullied at school? She never told us. We had to hear it from Emily's mum. And when she had that job she hated? She eventually broke down to me about it but that was nearly a year later. And remember her first boyfriend . . .'

'Luke.'

'Yes. And how he constantly lied to her, about everything, and she hid it from us until she could take no more and left him? And when we asked her afterwards why she didn't tell us she said it was because she didn't want us to think badly of him. Or to judge her for staying with him for so long. She wanted to give the illusion that she could cope, that everything in her life was perfect. And with Connor – I've been thinking about this a lot – I reckon she preferred us to think Kyle never had a brother than us judge him in some way because he'd disinherited him.'

Mum looks at me with admiration and despite it all I feel a swell of pride. 'You're a lot cleverer than you give yourself credit for,' she says.

'Well, we can't all have PhDs.' I laugh.

'You have emotional intelligence. And I'm sorry.' Mum bites her lip and I'm surprised to see tears in her eyes.

'What for?'

'If I've ever made you feel . . . less. If you've ever felt in the shadow of Alice. Because I think you're both equally special. I hope you know that. I love you both so much.'

I swallow the lump in my throat. I've spent my life feeling less than Alice but that's not necessarily Mum's fault. 'Where's all this coming from?'

Mum shakes her head, as though trying to dispel the tears. 'I'm being sentimental, I suppose. I've not always got it right.'

'Nobody does,' I say. 'I'm only beginning to grasp how hard it is to be a mother. How difficult it is not to treat one child differently from another, even though I love them both the same, because they're different children with distinct, unique personalities. Sometimes Flossie drives me mad because she can be dreamy and a bit of a space cadet, but she can be so loving and kind. And Elsie has a wicked temper but I love her spirit and how she won't ever suffer fools.'

Mum sniffs and wipes her nose with the underside of her wrist.

'And it's tricky with twins because they do everything at the same time,' I say, smiling when I think of the girls, 'so it's hard not to compare sometimes. Twins must run in the family, come to think of it.'

Mum turns to me with a frown. 'What do you mean? There are no other twins that I know of.'

'Alice told me a year or so ago that when you were pregnant with her it was twins and you miscarried one.'

Mum looks shocked. 'What? When did she tell you this?'

'We were talking about Elsie, Flossie and pregnancy in general, and she said something about how you'd had a vanishing-twin pregnancy with her and how she'd basic-ally eaten her own sibling. Something like that.'

A blush creeps over Mum's skin and she presses her lips together. I've upset her. 'I'm sorry, I shouldn't have said anything.'

'No. It's not that. It's just . . . well, that's not true. I didn't have a vanishing-twin pregnancy, or miscarry a twin. I don't know why Alice would tell you that. Are you sure you heard her correctly?'

'Yes.' I think hard. Now I'm wondering if I'd dreamt it. But, no, I distinctly remember her saying it because it had left me feeling a bit unsettled at how different our lives would have been if Alice had been a twin and whether I would have been left out of things. I can see from my own daughters how close their bond is. Their relationship is special.

Why would Alice lie?

The doorbell rings, preventing me from asking Mum any more questions about it. 'I'd better answer that,' I say, moving towards the hallway. Mum turns back to her task. The doorbell rings again and I mutter under my breath at their lack of patience as I go to answer it.

DI Thorne and DC Jones are standing on the threshold.

'Can we come in?' Thorne says, in his monotone voice. 'We've got some important news.'

41

JEANETTE

Monday, 28 October 2019

Jeanette is peeling off the rubber gloves when Tasha comes back into the room, closely followed by two detectives. Tasha offers them a drink and they decline before taking a seat at the kitchen table.

'They have news,' says Tasha, eagerly, taking a seat opposite them, and Jeanette's heart jumps in her chest. 'Come and sit down, Mum.'

Wordlessly Jeanette slides in next to Tasha on the bench seat. Her mouth has gone dry. Both detectives are wearing grave expressions and Jeanette feels sick, wondering what they are about to reveal.

Detective Thorne gets out his notebook while his eyes flash around the room. 'Where is Alice Campbell?'

'My sister didn't take her husband's surname,' says Tasha, almost proudly. 'She's actually Dr Alice Harper.'

Thorne stares back at her completely expressionless. Everything about him is grey: his suit, his hair, even his skin. He reminds Jeanette of the *Spitting Image* puppet of John Major.

'She's gone home to London,' says Jeanette. 'Why?'

DC Jones leans across the table and smiles. It lights up

her attractive face. She's a welcome contrast to Thorne. 'Well, we have some news. Have you heard of the Knight brothers? Shane and Johnno?'

Jeanette stiffens. She's heard of them. Everyone in Chew Norton has. They're notorious petty criminals who have been in and out of prison for theft over the years.

'All of Chew Norton would've heard of them. They went to my school,' says Tasha. 'Why?'

'They've admitted to targeting your house to burgle it. The blue asterisk that you said was drawn outside, well, that's their calling card. A stupid thing to do because we've picked them up breaking into other houses, and now that asterisk links them to this attempted burglary too. They knew you and Aaron would be away. They didn't realize your sister and brother-in-law were staying. But they deny killing Kyle and attacking Alice. They hadn't planned the burglary until the following evening.'

'And do you believe them?' asks Jeanette.

'There's something else,' says Thorne – smugly, Jeanette thinks – completely ignoring her question. 'We've found some evidence in Zoë's garage that suggests she attacked Alice and killed Kyle.'

Jeanette grips the edge of the table while the kitchen whirls around her, the implications slamming into her, making her feel dizzy.

The blood has drained from Tasha's face. 'So Zoë is my long-lost sister?' Tasha asks, voicing Jeanette's fears.

'We don't know for definite yet,' says DC Jones, gently. 'We're still waiting for her DNA results. But . . . and I'm sorry . . . it's looking that way at the moment.'

Thorne clears his throat. 'Zoë's computer has been searched and a note to you, Natasha, was found, along with a kind of diary where she talks about watching you and wanting to ruin your life. It appears she was obsessed with your husband and she had an unnatural hatred of you.'

'And Alice? Did you find evidence that she wrote to Alice and met her at the conference? I showed Alice a photo of Zoë but she didn't think it was the same woman,' says Tasha.

DC Jones shakes her head. 'Not at the moment, but police are still searching her flat.'

'And what . . . what was it you found in her garage that links her to Kyle's death?' Tasha scratches at her wrist, which already looks red and sore. Jeanette longs to reach out to stop her.

'A tyre wrench,' states Thorne in his monotone voice. 'There was blood and hair on it that we've matched to Kyle.'

'She came to our house with a tyre wrench? Was she planning to attack me?' Tasha shakes her head.

'It's evident she was a very disturbed young woman,' says Thorne, darkly. 'I'm afraid she has form for this kind of behaviour. She stalked her last boyfriend and had an injunction out on her not to contact her ex's current girlfriend.'

'But . . .' Tasha is frowning '. . . she would have known Aaron and I were on holiday.'

'According to a Tim Booth at the garage, she was away the week before. So she might have forgotten Aaron was due leave. Sadly we'll never know exactly what happened that night or what was going through Zoë's mind. But I believe she wanted to hurt you, not Alice or Kyle. You were the intended target. The note she left you – the same note that was on her laptop – is evidence of that, along with the diary we found.'

'Actually,' Tasha sits up straighter, her face paling, 'Aaron told me he was missing a tyre wrench. I've only just thought of it. He kept it in a box in the garden along with some other tools.'

'Right,' DC Jones says. 'We'll speak to him about it. He'll need to identify it.'

'So,' Jeanette begins, her mind racing. 'You think Zoë could have picked up Aaron's tyre wrench from the garden? On the spur of the moment, perhaps?'

'Possibly. Or maybe she knew where he kept his tools,' says DC Jones. 'According to hospital records, your sister's head injury was caused by the edge of your TV cabinet, which knocked her out before the weapon could be used on her.'

Jeanette remembers Alice talking about how she was violently shoved from behind. That fall probably saved her life as it's doubtful she would have survived a blow to the head from a tyre wrench. She feels a whoosh of heat spread up her back and neck. She knows on some level she's still desperately holding on to the hope that the DNA results will prove Zoë isn't Holly. Zoë, with her vengefulness and anger and violence. Zoë, who is now dead. Her hands bunch into fists on her lap. 'Do you know much about Zoë's background? Her parents?' she asks the detectives.

'Her mother has died and we can't get hold of her father. Apparently he's out of the country,' says DC Jones. 'We've done our best to get hold of him but we haven't had any luck so far.'

'Do you think that Zoë was murdered?' Tasha asks, her voice small. 'You said before that there was a head injury. Was that the cause of death or . . .'

'We're still trying to ascertain whether her drowning was accidental and quite when the blow to the head occurred.'

'I saw Zoë in the pub and she didn't have a head injury then,' says Tasha. 'Could she have got it walking back from the pub? Maybe fallen over if she was a bit drunk?'

'It's a possibility,' says Thorne, noncommittally.

Jeanette can't bear to hear any more. She wants them to go. 'Thank you, both,' she says. 'Is that everything?'

Thorne nods. 'We'll let you know when we have Zoë's DNA results back.'

Jeanette stands up. The detectives follow her down the hallway and then she's opening the front door and ushering them out. Just as she's already experiencing the relief at seeing the back of them, Thorne hesitates on the threshold. She feels the urge to push him out of the door. She smiles patiently. 'Was there something else, Detective?'

DC Jones is already at the car but Thorne leans closer to her to ask, 'Did you ever meet Zoë Gleeson?'

Jeanette feels herself blushing. She's never been a good liar. 'No,' she lies.

Thorne's gaze is challenging and his face is so close she

can see the faint scar in the crease of his chin. She holds her breath, waiting to see what he'll say next. To her relief, he takes a step back and pockets his notebook. 'Okay,' he says. 'If you say so.'

She watches his stiff-shouldered walk as he heads to where DC Jones is waiting at the car, wondering if he knows that she met Zoë for the first time on the night she died.

And that they argued.

42

BONNIE

June 2019

A woman was sitting alone at an outside table overlooking the lake when Bonnie arrived at the café. It was early morning, and despite the clear blue sky the air felt cold, as though it hadn't had time to warm up yet. A French bulldog with a dark line of fur under his nose sat at the woman's feet and Bonnie was glad she'd brought Biscuit with her. He pulled on his lead as soon as he spotted the other dog, which was a combination of ugly and cute.

The woman looked up as Bonnie approached. She had short white hair, her lined sun-kissed face devoid of make-up, and she was wearing jeans turned up at the bottom with a short-sleeved checked shirt. Bonnie searched her face for any familiar similarities with Clarissa, but couldn't see anything. Maybe this wasn't Vivian Pritchard after all. She had only a hazy recollection of her.

Bonnie checked her watch. It was five past nine. They'd agreed to meet at nine. Bonnie decided to check inside the café just in case but, apart from an elderly couple digging into cake, it was empty.

'Bonnie?'

She turned back to the woman with the bulldog, who was appraising her expectantly.

'Vivian?'

The woman stood up and tears appeared in her eyes. She surprised Bonnie by pulling her into a fierce hug, then, almost as if she was embarrassed by her burst of affection, released her. 'Wow,' she said, staring at her intently, her eyes searching Bonnie's face. 'It's been so long. So long.' Her voice sounded thick with pent-up emotion. She swallowed. 'Please, call me Viv. What can I get you?'

'A caramel latte would be great if they have it,' she said. 'Thank you.'

'Coming right up. Would you mind keeping an eye on Freddie Mercury for me?'

It took Bonnie a couple of beats to understand that Viv was talking about her dog. 'Oh, yes, sure,' she said. Viv smiled gratefully and disappeared around the side of the café.

Bonnie pulled out one of the plastic chairs and lowered herself into it. It was a bit wet and she could feel water seeping into the back of her jeans. Biscuit sat obediently at her feet and she wrapped his lead around the arm of the chair. The two dogs eyed each other but, thankfully, there was no barking. Bonnie hated seeing dogs fight.

Viv had sounded shocked to hear from her yesterday. After Bonnie had explained she was Clarissa's daughter, Viv had said, her tone sepulchral, 'I've been waiting for this day to come for years.'

Five minutes later she was back carrying two takeaway cups. 'Do you fancy walking around the lake?'

Bonnie nodded and got up again, conscious of the damp patch on her jeans and hoping it didn't look like she'd wet herself.

'I was sad to hear my sister had died,' Viv said, as they fell into step with one another, their dogs trotting ahead. 'We were extremely close once. I did come up and see her a few times, you know. When you were little. Do you remember?'

'Vaguely,' replied Bonnie. 'I remember you both arguing once in the kitchen. When was the last time you saw her?'

Guilt flashed in Viv's face. 'It must have been nineteen, twenty years ago.'

Bonnie's stomach rolled. 'Why did you stop visiting? And why didn't you come to Clarissa's funeral?'

Viv stopped in her tracks and guilt flashed on her face. 'I think we'd better sit down.'

Bonnie felt a burst of outrage that, until now, she'd been trying hard to repress. 'You knew, didn't you? You knew I was really Holly Harper?'

'Please. Please sit down.' Viv indicated a bench by the lake and Bonnie slumped onto it, her legs trembling. Viv sat down next to her, the dogs at their feet. 'I'm so sorry. I didn't realize. Not at first. Maybe I should have.'

'Can you tell me from the beginning what happened?'

Viv took a sip of her coffee and then exhaled heavily. 'Clarissa called me one night. It was two days before she was due to come down and visit. You – no, Bonnie was only six or seven weeks old and I hadn't had the chance to meet her yet. You have to understand that I had three little kiddies of my own. I was up to my eyeballs in nappies. My Stuart was only a few months older than you and I also had Jason and Aaron. But, anyway, that's no excuse, I know. Maybe things would have been different if I'd gone up there to visit her ... maybe ...' she faltered. 'Sorry. I'm digressing. So, anyway, Clarissa was due to come down with Bonnie that Sunday and then, perhaps the Friday, but it might have been the Saturday, I received a phone call. She sounded absolutely distraught. I could barely understand her and she kept talking about a baby being found dead. I asked her if she meant her baby. If she meant Bonnie. But I couldn't get a straight answer from her. Just this sobbing down the phone. It made my blood run cold but then the phone went dead. She'd always been a bit fragile, suffering with anxiety as a child. Our mum had died when we were young and our father was an alcoholic, lots of issues I won't bore you with now. But I was so scared she'd do something stupid. I tried to ring her back but there was no answer, so I called Ray – my late husband – and he got the car and the boys ready to drive up to Birmingham. I told myself if she didn't pick up the phone on the next ring, I'd contact the police and ask them to go and check on her. But she did, thank goodness. And she sounded calmer and told me she'd rung me because she'd had bad news of a friend's baby who'd died of cot death and it had upset her because Bonnie was so small still. That was it. She sounded so calm. Like I was talking to a different person.'

Bonnie tried to imagine her mother's state of mind at that point.

'I asked her if she was still coming to visit on Sunday, and she said yes. She said she couldn't wait for me to meet Bonnie.'

'And you believed her?'

'Of course.' Viv bent down to pat Freddie Mercury's velvety head. 'Clarissa always took on other people's emotions so I could well imagine the news of a friend's dead baby would have sent her into a spin. That was typical of her.'

'It was,' agreed Bonnie, remembering how her mother had mooned around the house for days after Bonnie told her the boy she'd fancied had asked out someone else. Or how angry she got if Bonnie hadn't been invited to a classmate's birthday party (even if Bonnie wasn't that bothered) or if she heard something horrible on the news about a child being abused or a teenager getting stabbed. 'But she never turned up like planned?'

Viv sighed. 'She was supposed to come that Sunday – the day Holly Harper disappeared. She'd told me she'd drive down. She always hated public transport. I popped to the shops to get some vegetables for our Sunday roast. I wasn't expecting her until about midday and this was, oh, about ten thirty. I was standing outside the grocer's. Stuart, my youngest, was in a sling and I saw Jeanette leaving Holly's pram outside the shop. Never gave the pram a second thought. I did it all the time – we all did. Chew Norton felt safe. And then . . .' she angled her body more towards Bonnie, her coffee cup balancing on the bench beside her '. . . and then the weirdest thing happened. I went into the grocer's. It was busy and a queue had formed inside. The till was at the rear of the shop so our backs would have been to the window. I remember turning around – I was right at the end of the queue – and thinking I'd seen Clarissa across the street. Very fleetingly. And then I dismissed it because I thought it must be my mind playing tricks on me. She wouldn't have arrived yet. When I turned back there was no sign of her. I remember poking my head around the door just to double-check and nothing. The pram with Holly inside it was still outside, pushed up next to the estate agent's. I don't remember seeing Holly in it but, then, I didn't look.'

'And when Holly's mum came out you realized the baby had been taken?'

'Yes. Jeanette was in front of me in the queue. She went out first and a few seconds later I heard this frantic cry of "Where's Holly? Where's my baby?"'

Bonnie's blood ran cold. 'What happened after that?'

'Well, we all helped Jeanette. I called the police and stayed with her for a bit until they arrived. And then I left to go home. I had Stuart with me and a dinner to cook but I was obviously very unsettled by it.'

'By the abduction or thinking your sister might have been involved?'

'The abduction initially. I thought – I hoped – that perhaps there had been some mistake. That a friend of Jeanette's had taken Holly. I never allowed myself to believe that something as sinister as kidnapping a baby would happen in Chew Norton. I busied myself with making Sunday lunch but then midday came and went, then one o'clock, two o'clock, and no sign of Clarissa.

That was when I started to worry. I called her at home around three thirty and there was no answer – back in 1989 she didn't have a mobile phone. I tried again a couple of times. I started getting worried she might have had an accident or something but then, eventually, quite a bit later, she picked up. She sounded strange on the phone. Out of breath but also a bit manic. She apologized and said she hadn't had the chance to come down after all because Bonnie had been awake a lot during the night and she'd been too exhausted to drive. I was annoyed that she hadn't bothered to phone to cancel, then disappointed I wouldn't see her and the baby. But then I felt relieved that she was okay. Clarissa always had been a bit flaky so I didn't think too much about it.'

'When did you start to suspect? I'm assuming you did suspect and that was why you stopped visiting and why you didn't come to your sister's funeral.' Bonnie tried to keep her voice even but she could hear anger seeping in.

'At first I didn't think much of it. I was too preoccupied with the kids and with the news that Holly had gone missing. It was an awful time for the village. It was filled with police and reporters and just this horrible, horrible suspicious atmosphere, mingled with grief and shock. And, of course, utter horror and pity for Jeanette. Just terrible. I tried to rearrange with Clarissa. I was desperate to meet my new niece, but she refused to come to the village. She made out it was because she felt paranoid now that a baby had been stolen. She also kept putting off me and Ray from visiting. Looking back, I think she was worried we would recognize baby Holly as her photo was in all the papers. She kept me at arms' length for months and months. I was hurt by it. We'd been close growing up. She was my younger sister and I'd always felt protective of her. I also wanted to respect her wishes so I didn't push it too much. She wouldn't allow us to come up for your first birthday, said she and Jack were going away. I didn't get to see you until you were about eighteen months old.'

'Was that when you realized I was Holly?'

'No. Not then. Not until you were about ten.'

'Ten!' Bonnie cries. 'That long?'

Viv nodded. 'That's probably the time you heard us arguing.'

'How did you guess?'

'I don't know if you remember but I'd come up for the weekend with Stuart. The other two boys were older, twelve and fourteen, so they stayed with Ray. We only came for the day – Clarissa didn't like having overnight visitors, she said. Jack was away, like always. Anyway, I sat with Clarissa, and Stuart ran off to play with you. But an hour or so later you came out to tell us that Stuart was being naughty, going into Clarissa's bedroom. You were frantic about it.'

'Yes, because I knew my mum forbade me to play in there. She was so private.'

'Anyway, Stuart had somehow found a box of newspaper cuttings and upended it on the floor, then ran back out again, not thinking anything of it. But Clarissa had shouted at him, then got down on her hands and knees to put the clippings back inside the box. But not quickly enough. I saw a couple of headlines.'

'About Holly,' Bonnie said. That must have been when her mother had decided to move the box to the loft.

Viv nodded. 'That's right. By then you and Stuart had gone into the garden. I confronted Clarissa, remembering just before you were snatched when she'd rung me crying about a dead baby. And then thinking I'd seen her in Chew Norton the morning of your disappearance in her blue car. Just after you were abducted, a newspaper report mentioned a witness seeing a woman in a blue car with a young baby, but I hadn't thought anything of it at the time. Clarissa denied it all. But she did say, very seriously, as I was leaving, that if anything were to happen to you she'd kill herself. I knew it was a threat. It put me in an impossible position. I didn't know for definite, but I strongly suspected what had happened.' Viv sighed again and picked up her coffee cup. 'You were ten. Clarissa was all you'd ever known. You were happy. You were loved. I knew if I spoke up it would kill Clarissa. And you'd lose the only family you'd ever known. But it wasn't easy. Some days, when I saw Jeanette around the village, I'd decide I was going to do it. I was going to tell the police everything I suspected. But then I thought about my sister, about you. What it would do to you both and I . . .' Her voice caught. 'I just couldn't do it.'

Bonnie closed her eyes. By her feet she felt Biscuit shift and resettle. When she opened them Viv was staring at her with concern.

316

'It was an impossible situation,' Viv said. 'So I told nobody. Not even Ray.'

'Did you see her again? That was the last time I saw you and even that's hazy. It was twenty years ago.'

'I saw her once after that. After Ray died unexpectedly a few months later, she rang me and we met up. She was sympathetic.'

'Not sympathetic enough to Holly's real family, though,' snapped Bonnie.

Viv hung her head in response.

'What did she say to you on that last meeting?'

Viv looked up, her eyes sad. 'She told me she was ill. That she had a lung disease called pulmonary fibrosis. And that she was going to get worse. She didn't want me to visit her, she said. She didn't want me to see her decline. But I think, reading between the lines, she felt it was her punishment for what she'd done. Her illness and enforced imprisonment.'

Bonnie froze. 'So you stayed away again?'

'It suited me to. And I had my own problems, being recently widowed with three boys and Stuart going off the rails. I had told myself that Jeanette had a loving husband, money, two lovely daughters. I knew Clarissa wouldn't cope if they took her child away from her. So I had avoided Jeanette. Until Aaron and Tasha fell in love.'

'Didn't you feel guilty?'

'Of course I did, but I told myself it was only a suspicion. That I didn't know for certain. I convinced myself I was mistaken. I loved Clarissa. I didn't want to destroy her life. There was so much history with me and Clarissa, going back years. She was very fragile. Even though I was only a few years older than her, I took on a maternal role after our mother died,' Viv faltered, rubbing the area of her chest above her heart. 'I always protected her.'

They sat in silence for a few moments while Bonnie digested the information. Eventually Viv asked, 'How did you find out?'

Bonnie explained about discovering the box and questioning her father. She took a sip of her caramel latte, which was now lukewarm, and stared out at the sunshine glinting on the surface of the lake. She swelled with anger and resentment and – she was shocked to recognize it – vengefulness. Her life could have been so different. She could have grown up in a normal, bustling family, the youngest of three daughters. Now, because of Clarissa, because of Viv, she'd never get the chance to meet her real father, to grow up with siblings, to have a big, bustling family like Selma.

Eventually Viv turned to her. 'So what are you planning to do now that you know the truth?'

43

TASHA

Tuesday, 29 October 2019

I'm getting ready to go back to work on Tuesday morning when there is a knock at the door. Aaron, who has just pulled on his overalls, throws me an exasperated who-the-hell-is-that-at-this-time-in-the-morning look.

'I'll answer it,' I say, quickly pulling a comb through my hair and running downstairs, nearly knocked off my feet by Princess Sofia, who wants feeding. It's seven a.m. and Mum is upstairs helping the girls get dressed.

My heart sinks when I open the door and see DI Thorne and DC Jones standing there. A breeze is whipping up the leaves that have started to fall in the front garden.

'May we come in?' DC Jones smiles, but there is an unfamiliar edge to her voice.

'We're just getting ready for work,' I say.

'It's important. We're here to talk to Aaron.'

I take a step back to allow them in, my stomach curdling. I can tell by their grave faces that this is serious. I show them into the kitchen, then run upstairs to get Aaron. He's just coming out of the bathroom and I nearly bump into him on the landing. 'The police are here to speak to you,' I say, in a hushed voice. 'What do they want?'

319

Aaron's face pales. 'Did they say what it's about?'

I shake my head.

He grimaces but doesn't say anything else as I follow him downstairs. Both police officers are standing at the back door when we enter the kitchen. Thorne moves forward first. I notice DC Jones can't meet my eye. 'Aaron, we have some questions about the head injury that Zoë sustained on the night she died and we would like you to accompany us to the station.'

Aaron's whole body stiffens. 'Are you arresting me?'

'No, we're not. We just have a few more questions and would like to formally interview you at the station.'

Aaron turns to me, panic in his eyes, and I wonder why he looks so afraid if he has nothing to hide. A flash of heat descends over my body. Do the police think Aaron hurt Zoë?

'Fine,' he says. To me he adds, 'Can you let Tim know I'll be in late?'

I nod, unable to speak. I feel like I might throw up.

Nobody says a word as the two officers flank Aaron out of the house and to a waiting police car.

I take the twins to nursery, then head in to work, even though I can't concentrate on any of it. The dental surgery is busy and there isn't time to talk, or even to worry. Lola has called in sick, and so has Trevor, one of the dentists.

'Hey, maybe they're off somewhere having an affair,' Donna joked.

'Hardly. Trevor is about thirty years older than Lola. And he's not exactly George Clooney.'

I don't mention to Donna about the police coming over or Aaron 'helping them with their enquiries'. Instead I concentrate on the backlog of work I have owing to my compassionate leave.

As we're leaving work Donna asks me how the funeral went.

I tell her a bit about it, particularly Eve showing up and it all getting a bit awkward. 'Alice has gone back to work now. I spoke to her last night. I think she needs to keep busy.' Which, today of all days, I fully understand. I'd asked her on the phone last night if she'd heard more from Connor and she told me she'd agreed to sell the house and give him half the proceeds.

I ring Aaron's mobile as I'm walking home but there's no answer and I try to quash the unsettled feeling this gives me. When I get home Mum is sitting in the garden with a book, wrapped up in a coat. The sky is bright, despite the cold temperature, and the patio at the back is a sun trap. I'm startled to see Princess Sofia asleep on her lap.

'Mum, Princess Sofia's a house cat,' I say, stepping onto the patio with a cup of tea for each of us. I've got an hour before I need to pick up the twins.

'She's perfectly content on my knee. I won't let her run off. Any news from Aaron?'

'I've tried calling him but there's no answer.'

An emotion I can't read flits across Mum's face. She

crosses her ankles, making sure not to dislodge Princess Sofia. 'I'm sure it's just procedure. Aaron was probably only there for an hour or so, then went straight back to work. He's probably busy underneath some car right now.'

'Hmm.' I sip my tea. I try to imagine what might have happened after I'd left the pub that night, what occurred after Zoë had tried it on with him. He said he'd come straight home but what if he was lying? What if she'd tried it on with him and he'd pushed her away so forcefully that she hit her head? I try to imagine my good-humoured husband lashing out. Not once, not in all the years I've known him, have I seen him lose it to the extent where I've felt threatened. He's not really the arguing kind. I saw him get into fights when he was a teenager but nothing serious, more like scuffles, flexing between mates. I just can't see him pushing Zoë, even by accident.

So why do the police want to talk to him?

And why not in front of me?

44

JEANETTE

Tuesday, 29 October 2019

Jeanette notices another missed call from Eamonn. She has managed to avoid his calls since she's been back in Chew Norton but she knows she has to speak to him soon. He deserves an explanation. After all, he is her friend. And he's been great to her these last eighteen months. She taps out a quick text while sitting alone in the garden. Tasha has left to pick up the girls from nursery. *I'm sorry I can't speak now. So much family stuff going on but I promise I'll call soon for a proper chat.* She deliberates on whether to add kisses to the end of the message and decides on two.

Now that Alice has gone back to London she realizes she should probably return to France. Tasha and Aaron should have their house back. But she can't bring herself to leave. So many things remain up in the air, and her daughters need her right now. She can't run away again, even though part of her wants to.

And there is still the question of Zoë and what happened that night. If she's not Holly – and she still hopes with every fibre of her being that she isn't – then her youngest daughter is still out there somewhere. Maybe still in Chew Norton.

Jeanette closes her eyes, the remnants of the evening sun warm on her face. It's nearly the end of October, the trees beginning to lose their leaves, the evenings drawing in, the smell of bonfires in the air.

Zoë's shocked face from the night she died swims behind Jeanette's closed eyes and she feels another stab of guilt.

Jeanette isn't confrontational. She's like Tasha in that way.

That night, after Aaron and Tasha had left for the pub, she was saying goodnight to the twins, and as she went to close their curtains, she saw Zoë walking near the pond – a shortcut to the Packhorse. She'd recognized the sharp profile, the long blonde hair and the confident walk from where she'd first seen her from the café window earlier that day. Asking Alice to keep an eye on the twins while she popped out, she'd raced through the garden, still wearing her slippers, to the gate at the back, which was unlocked.

'Zoë,' she'd called, as the girl was about to cut down the lane between the cottages further up that led to the high street.

Zoë had stopped, turning, surprise on her face. 'Yes?' She'd inched her bag further up over her shoulder and adjusted her leather jacket. She didn't smile at Jeanette, or look in any way friendly. Her jaw was set and her mouth pursed. Jeanette searched her face in the same way she'd searched the faces of so many women over the years, wondering if they could be Holly, and there was nothing about her that triggered any maternal instinct, any recognition.

Jeanette had acted on impulse, which never used to be her way but was becoming more so since Jim died. Now that Zoë was there, in front of her, she didn't know where to start.

'I'm Jeanette. Jeanette Harper,' she said, talking too quickly in an effort to get her words out. 'I'm the mother of Alice and Tasha.'

'Oh, yes,' Zoë had replied coolly.

'This might sound a bit strange,' she said, walking towards Zoë. 'But do you know that my son-in-law was murdered last week?'

Zoë looked uncomfortable and shifted her weight from one leg to the other. 'I'd heard about that, yes.'

'DNA was found at the scene suggesting someone else had been in the house – maybe that night. Someone who, as it turns out, is a close relation of mine.'

Zoë looked puzzled. 'Right?'

Jeanette was handling this badly, she knew that, but she didn't know how to explain it all. Instead she blurted out, 'Did you put a note through Tasha's front door a few days after Kyle was killed? You were seen by a neighbour.' She knew this was a bit of a lie. Arthur had only described someone tall, blonde and wearing a leather jacket and nose ring. But as Jeanette appraised the woman standing in front of her it was a match, apart from the missing nose ring.

The look Zoë gave her made her shrivel inside. 'What? No,' she said hotly. Defensively, Jeanette thought.

'You were seen, Zoë.'

Zoë had laughed. 'Oh, I see. So that's why the police

325

interviewed me and started asking all these questions about where I was when your son-in-law was murdered. Kyle's death was nothing to do with me. I didn't even know the guy. The only person I'm interested in is –' She stopped as though she had realized she'd said too much.

'Go on,' urged Jeanette. 'The only person you're interested in is? Let me guess. You're interested in Aaron.'

Zoë pulled at the belt of her jacket, but Jeanette noticed how red her face had turned. 'As a friend,' she muttered.

Jeanette wavered, feeling torn. She didn't believe this woman could be Holly. But what if she was wrong? What if she was standing with her long-lost daughter at last? Just because she didn't want to think Holly had turned out like this, it didn't mean that Zoë wasn't her daughter. 'Zoë, I think you did write the note. But did you go inside the house? Did you attack Alice and Kyle?'

Zoë glared at Jeanette. 'Of course not,' she spat. 'Why on earth would I do that?' Her eyes narrowed. 'Who do you actually think I am, Jeanette? Why are you here?'

Jeanette is sitting between her beautiful granddaughters as they watch *Peter Rabbit* on CBeebies. She's busy knitting dresses for their teddies and trying not to think about Zoë, but she can sense Tasha's nervous energy emanating from where she's perched on the armchair in the corner. She knows her daughter is worried about Aaron. She called him earlier and he was at work but told her he'd talk to her properly when he got home.

'Why don't you go and have a bath? Try to relax. Aaron will be home soon,' whispers Jeanette, over Flossie's head.

Tasha nods and stands up, then sits down again.

'Go,' urges Jeanette. Tasha is making her feel on edge.

'Okay,' she says, finally getting up and leaving the room.

Ten minutes later, just as Jeanette is casting off, the wool spooled at her feet, there is a knock at the door. The twins are still riveted to the TV, Flossie resting her head on a cushion and sucking her thumb as Jeanette puts down her knitting and slips out of the room to answer it.

She's surprised to see Viv standing there with a young woman in a long flowery dress. Viv looks nervous and there is a scratch on her cheek that has puckered and scabbed. 'Hi. Can we come in?'

'Um . . . sure. Are you here to see Tasha?'

'Well, both of you. This is Bonnie,' she says, introducing the woman standing with her and Jeanette assesses her properly for the first time.

Bonnie smiles shyly and there is something about her face: her large blue eyes, so like Flossie's, her dimples like Jim's, her fine arched eyebrows like Alice's. So much so that Jeanette lets out a small 'ouf' sound, as though she's been winded, and the hallway seems to shrink.

Because she's one hundred per cent certain that she's looking at Holly.

Before she can react Tasha is pounding down the stairs in a dressing-gown. 'Viv,' she says in surprise, when she reaches them. 'Is everything all right?' And then she stares at the young woman, who hangs her head, blushing slightly. 'Lola! What are you doing here?'

45

TASHA

Tuesday, 29 October 2019

Viv looks stricken and Lola is studying the floor, her cheeks red. Mum looks like she might pass out and is holding on to the wall for support.

Fear grips me. 'What's going on? Is everything okay? Is it Aaron?'

'Aaron is fine,' says Viv. 'But can we please come in?'

Mum springs into action and ushers them down the hallway to the kitchen. I notice she can't stop staring at Lola, who sits next to Viv on the bench seat. Mum is still standing in the middle of the room. She's staring at Lola and, quite frankly, it's a bit embarrassing. Mum's manners are usually impeccable.

There is a weird tension in the room as though the three of them know something I don't.

And then Mum says something that shocks me so much I have to hold on to the table for support. 'Holly?'

Lola dips her chin. 'I think so ... Well, actually I'm sure of it, yes.'

And then Lola stands up and Mum rushes over to her and holds her at arms' length, as though she's a precious exhibit that needs studying, and then she's crying and Lola is crying. Then they hug and cry some more. Viv gets up from the table and comes over to where I'm standing. I think I've gone into shock. 'Come on, duck. I think we should leave them alone for a bit. They've got a lot of catching up to do.' And she steers me out of the room.

I send the twins upstairs to play so I can talk to Viv in private.

'What the hell is going on? Why is Lola saying she's Holly?' I round on her as soon as the girls are out of earshot.

'Please sit down,' says Viv, who has already perched on the edge of the sofa. Reluctantly I sit next to her and she grips my hand. Then she gently explains about a sister she had called Clarissa and a dead baby called Bonnie and a box found in a loft containing old newspaper cuttings and a photograph of a grave and I try to absorb the full horror of it all. 'So Bonnie decided to come to Chew Norton to find out for herself. She's been watching you all, trying to summon up the courage to introduce herself to you. She took a job at your dental practice, using her middle name so that I wouldn't find out who she was, to get to know you better. And then, after she'd been working with you a month or so she approached me. And that was when I found out the truth,' she finishes. 'The whole truth.'

I can't speak for a few seconds. I just stare at her. I've known her since I was seventeen years old and yet, right now, she feels like a stranger. 'So you've known since June and you never told any of us? You never told Mum?' A fresh wave of shock reverberates through me as it hits me

329

that she's known – or at least suspected – her sister snatched Holly a lot longer ago than a few months. No wonder she avoided Mum. I'm surprised she could even look her in the face. I snatch my hand away from hers, fury building as the full implications of this lodge in my brain.

'I'm sorry,' she says, looking down at her hands resting in her lap. 'It was up to Bonnie. It wasn't my place. Bonnie would have come to you earlier but then the whole thing happened with Kyle and Zoë, and Bonnie was worried that, with everything you've had going on, it wasn't the right time. She was worried that your mum would return to France now Alice has gone back to London.'

'So all this time I was working with my sister and I didn't know it?'

Viv nods.

'But has she had a DNA test? Do we know for definite that she's Holly? Shouldn't we do that before Mum starts getting attached? And the blood . . . her blood was found on the rug . . . on my rug . . . the night Kyle was killed. Did she hurt Kyle?' I can't imagine it. Lola – Holly, Bonnie, whatever her bloody name is – always seemed so gentle, so kind. But then she hid this from me for all this time despite working alongside me most days.

'We will do all that, of course, but, Tasha, I really believe she's Holly. I don't know about any blood but the night Kyle was killed Bonnie was staying with me. I haven't known her for long but there isn't a violent bone in her body.'

I stare at Viv, my mouth open, feeling betrayed. I think of her strange reclusive sister, the box full of old articles

330

about Holly's abduction, Mum's reaction when she saw her just now, and I know she's right. Lola is Holly.

But if she's Holly then it can't be Zoë's blood on our rug. It has to be hers. Because Mum doesn't have any more children. Could Holly have been in our house before the attack, cut herself somehow and left blood on our rug?

Just as I'm about to ask more I hear a key in the front door and Aaron's familiar tread. He pushes open the living-room door and peers around it. He's in his work overalls but there are bags under his eyes. He comes into the room, frowning, when he sees me sitting with Viv and the sombre expressions on our faces. 'Is everything okay?'

I don't even know where to start. I jump up. 'First, are you okay? What happened with the police?'

'The police?' Viv asks, surprise in her voice. 'What's this about the police?'

'I was arrested earlier, Mum,' he begins.

'You weren't arrested, Aaron. They just wanted to interview you down at the station,' I say, trying to reassure him and myself.

'They think Zoë was attacked before she fell into the pond. And I know they think it was me.'

'No!' Viv looks appalled. 'They can't really believe that. There's no evidence to suggest you hurt Zoë. Why would you?'

'Because a witness saw us arguing in the pub. But I've got nothing to hide,' he snaps. I know there's something he isn't telling me. It's the way he keeps shifting his weight from one leg to the other and won't look at me directly.

Viv bites her lip and her fingers flutter to her cheek where she has a scab and she absentmindedly picks at it.

'It will be okay,' I say, going over to Aaron. 'If you didn't do it then . . .'

'What do you mean if I didn't do it? Of course I didn't fucking do it. You do believe me, don't you?' His eyes are blazing and I shrink back, shocked. I can see that he's lashing out because he's scared.

'Of course I believe you.'

'God, you're so naïve, Tash. People get arrested and jailed for things they didn't do all the time. They could fit me up for this and there would be nothing I could do about it.'

I exchange a worried look with Viv. She stands up. 'Aaron. You had an alibi. Loads of alibis. A pub full of them. You left before Zoë. We all saw you leave. Zoë was with me right at the end of the night. We had a smoke out the back after I locked up. That was gone midnight.'

'Exactly, and it's not up to you to prove you didn't hurt her,' I say calmly, even though my stomach is in knots as I remember how I lied for him. 'It's up to them to prove you did.'

'That's right,' says Viv.

'I suppose,' he mumbles.

I take his hand and lead him to the sofa. 'There's something else you need to know. My mum. She's currently in the kitchen with – and you'll never believe it – but with Holly.'

The look of pure shock on his face is so comical that, despite the circumstances, I have to suppress a smile.

And then, between us, Viv and I tell him everything.

Afterwards Aaron sits there staring at his mum and I know he's thinking all the things I was thinking when I first heard this dark story. I try to imagine what I would have done if I'd been in Viv's shoes, if I'd suspected my sister of kidnapping a baby. Would I protect her, like Viv protected Clarissa? Or would I run straight to the police?

I like to think I'd run straight to the police but we do stupid things for the people we love. And when Viv justifies her choices to Aaron by saying that my mum already had two children, two beautiful children, whom she cherished, and Clarissa, Viv's poor, unhinged sister, who, she suspects, had lost a longed-for baby, had nothing and would probably throw herself in front of a train if someone had tried to take Holly/Bonnie from her, I feel the fury building in me again.

'So you put Clarissa's needs before ours? You didn't think how this would affect my mum, my dad, me? Alice?'

Viv presses her eyes shut and a tear seeps out of one and rolls down her cheek. 'I couldn't let myself think about any of you at the time. I thought about my sister, the person I loved. Bonnie was already ten when I made the connection. How could I take a ten-year-old girl away from the only family she'd ever known? Ever loved?' She opens her eyes and fixes them on me. 'Your family, Tasha, were strangers to me then. I hardly knew Jeanette, apart from to say hello to. And I love you now like you're my

333

own daughter, but I never knew that was going to happen. I never even imagined back then that one day we'd be sitting here and you would be my daughter-in-law. But you have to believe me when I say that I never really let myself think Clarissa had taken Holly. It was just a suspicion and one I refused to let myself believe. The human mind is a wonderful thing . . . the capacity we have to convince ourselves, delude ourselves, into thinking one thing even though we know, deep down, that the opposite is true.'

She stands up, gathering her bag and coat. 'I think it's best I leave for now. Please tell Jeanette I'm sorry. I really am so sorry.'

Aaron and I exchange a concerned look but we don't say anything else as she leaves the room. A few seconds later we hear the front door close behind her.

'God,' says Aaron, putting his head in his hands. 'This is a lot to take in. I can't even imagine how you're coping with this.'

We stare at each other for a few moments and then he stands up. 'Come here,' he says, and I go to him, burying my face in his chest as he throws his arms around me and kisses the top of my head.

We stand like this for a while and then I move away. 'I'd better check on the twins.'

He nods, his mouth set in a line. 'Before you do,' he says, 'there's something I need to tell you.'

46

I stare at Aaron, dreading what he's about to confess. He shifts his weight from foot to foot.

'What is it?'

'The Knight brothers have been using Gareth at the garage to forge the VIN numbers on cars.' He says this in one long, breathless sentence, then waits for my response.

'What does that mean?'

'It's illegal, is all you need to know. I refused to get involved. But I found out Zoë was in on it and so was another guy, Bruce. Tim knew nothing about it but Zoë told me the night you saw us down by the pond. We were arguing about it. I told her she needed to stop it, that the Knight brothers were trouble.'

'Did you tell the police this?'

'I had to. Someone else saw us at the pond that night as well as you. But now I'm worried about getting Gareth and Bruce into trouble . . .'

'You had to say something. Do they think the Knight brothers could have harmed Zoë?'

'They're not sure. But it's a possibility. As long as they don't think I hurt her in any way.' He rubs his hand over his chin. All the earlier fire has gone out of him and he looks grey and deflated. 'I told her not to get involved with them.' He shakes his head sadly. 'I warned her. I fucking warned her.'

He looks so upset and dejected that I go over to him and wrap him in my arms.

'I'm sorry, I don't know what to call you,' I say, when Mum and Lola eventually come into the living room. I'm sitting on the sofa mulling over what Aaron's just told me. The twins have come downstairs and are now playing with a toy house on the floor. It's started to rain and I can hear it tapping against the windowpanes. Aaron has gone upstairs to have a shower. Mum sits on the armchair opposite. I notice how her eyes never leave Lola, as though she's worried she'll just disappear again.

'Bonnie is fine,' she says, perching on the edge of the sofa. 'Lola doesn't feel like my name, even though I know I've been using it at work. And Holly . . . Holly doesn't feel like me either. I've been Bonnie for the last thirty years. I'm so sorry this is a shock for you and I'm so sorry I haven't told you before. I've been close to coming over a few times. But I've always been too afraid.'

'Are you even a dental nurse?'

'Of course.' She laughs. 'Well, a trainee. I wanted to be a dentist but I couldn't complete my training because of my mum . . . Clarissa . . .' She tails off, her cheeks reddening.

I watch Mum's reaction. She's trying to keep her face impassive but I can see by the blush that blooms up her neck and the tightening of her jaw that she's trying to keep her emotions in check at the thought of Holly calling someone else Mum.

Now that I know the truth I can see the resemblance to Mum in their side profiles. The same fair skin and hair, the same nose.

'I'm so sorry for what happened,' I burst out and I feel suddenly grief-stricken at missing out on so many years with her. A shared childhood. There is something so vulnerable about her, so lovely and caring, that I feel almost maternal towards her. And I have to choke back tears: I finally get to be a big sister. And I try to put myself in Viv's shoes.

Mum tells us she's going to make us a cup of tea and let us catch up on things, then leaves us alone. We stare at each other, both suddenly shy. She tugs at the hem of her coat. She's been here two hours already and hasn't taken it off.

'Your mum told me about the DNA found on your rug,' she says. 'I can promise you it wasn't mine. This is the first time I've ever been in your house. And on the night of the attack I was at Viv's. I would never have hurt Kyle or Alice.'

'We'll need to do DNA tests and everything,' I say. 'To make sure you are Holly.' *And to see if it matches the blood at the crime scene*, I think, but don't say.

'I understand.'

'Viv told me about what you've been through, with your mother . . . with Clarissa. It must have been hard discovering the truth. I can't even imagine it.'

'I've always wanted a big family,' she says, glancing at

337

the twins playing on the floor. 'And now I have sisters and a mother and nieces and a brother-in-law. I can't wait to meet Alice.'

'You haven't met Alice?' I ask, remembering the conference. 'You didn't go up to Liverpool and see her at a conference by any chance?'

Bonnie looks puzzled. 'No. Why?'

'Oh, it's nothing.'

I want to be elated. But I can't let myself. Not yet. Not until the DNA results have come back. There are still so many unanswered questions.

Bonnie stays for dinner, then says she has to get back for Biscuit. Mum walks her to the door and Aaron says, 'She seems lovely. God, I hope the DNA test proves she actually is Holly after all this.'

'I hope so too.'

'You won't tell your mum what I told you about the Knight brothers?'

'Of course not, but you do promise me you're not involved?'

'I promise you.' He grabs both my hands. 'I'd never do anything illegal. You have to believe me. And that includes hurting Zoë. I'd never lay a finger on a woman.'

When Mum walks back into the room she looks at me with pure excitement on her face. 'I can't believe it,' she says. 'I can't believe we've found her.' I half expect her to start ranting about Viv and the part she's played in this but she doesn't. Instead she sinks onto a chair and bursts into tears.

'Oh, Mum,' I say, rushing to her side of the table. It feels the most natural thing, suddenly, to hug her.

'It's okay,' she says, wiping her eyes. 'These are happy tears. I'm so relieved . . . I mean, I'm cross, too, with Viv. Sorry, Aaron, I know she's your mum. But mainly, right now, I'm just so, so relieved.' And then she starts laughing and crying and, despite my vow not to get my hopes up, I find myself joining in.

Alice is stunned when Mum and I FaceTime her later that evening to tell her the news. She sits there, backlit by her glamorous kitchen, pearls of light glistening from the beads of the chandelier above her reflecting on her walls, her expressive eyebrows rising and dipping as the reveals come thick and fast. And finally, when we get to the bit about how Holly turned up on our doorstep with Viv, Alice's eyes are so wide they look like they might pop out of her head.

'I can't believe it,' she breathes, her voice echoey in her large, empty kitchen. 'This is unreal.'

'It's just the happiest day,' cries Mum. 'She's amazing, Alice. You'll love her.'

I glance at Mum. She *is* amazing, what I know of her. And I've been lucky that I've got to spend time with her, even if I hadn't realized she was my sister. But I'm so worried about the potential for Mum being disappointed if the DNA test says otherwise that I want to tell her to wait, to be patient, to have it all confirmed first. Yet I don't want to temper her excitement.

'I asked her about the conference,' I say. 'She said it wasn't her.'

'That's strange,' says Alice.

'I know. So who could it have been if it wasn't Bonnie?'

Alice shrugs. 'I don't know. Perhaps it was just some weirdo. And what about the DNA found at the crime scene?'

'I'm taking Bonnie to see DC Jones tomorrow. She's going to arrange a DNA test. We'll know more after that,' says Mum. 'But Bonnie was with Viv the night Kyle died, love.'

'Well, it seems strange that her DNA was in Tasha's house,' says Alice.

'There must be some other explanation for that,' says Mum.

I throw a worried glance at her. I don't want Alice bursting her bubble. I've got to know Bonnie as Lola over the last few months and I can't believe she'd do something like that to Kyle and Alice. Mum's right. There has to be another explanation for the blood found at the scene.

Unless, of course, there's all been some horrible mistake and Bonnie isn't Holly after all.

'Let's not worry about any of that now,' I say. 'It could just be an anomaly. A contamination.'

Alice frowns and looks as if she wants to contradict me, but she doesn't.

'You must meet her,' Mum says. 'Why don't you come down this weekend?'

'Definitely. I can't believe this.' Alice laughs. 'Two kid sisters. Two that I can boss around.'

'Hey, watch it!' But I'm so happy to see the joy in Alice's

face after everything she's been through, so relieved that she has some wonderful news after Kyle's death that all those negative feelings, the underlying jealousy, the resentment, the not-feeling-good-enough dissipates and is replaced with gratitude that we're all here, alive, happy and well. And that we've found Holly or, rather, Holly found us. At last.

47

TASHA

Friday, 1 November 2019

All week I think about Bonnie. Her three-month contract at the clinic has ended and I feel sad we won't be working together any more. I still haven't told Donna or Catherine about it, not yet. I don't feel I should until the DNA results come back. I really want Bonnie to be Holly but I'm still confused about the DNA found at the house.

And underneath all that, something else is needling me. Something about what Viv said regarding the night of Zoë's death.

I decide to pop over to see her at lunchtime.

It's a crisp, cold day with frost covering the pavements, sparkling on the roofs and crystallizing the tips of the grass. As I drive through the village, Halloween symbols still in windows, I suddenly feel stifled. I wonder what it would be like to move away, to live somewhere completely new, where I didn't know every lane, every road, every shop. And I wonder what I've been scared of for all these years. Was I subconsciously waiting for Holly to come home? Or was it fear that I'd never be able to compete with Alice so I didn't even try? But meeting Bonnie, hearing her story, has made me re-evaluate my own decisions. I've never really known who I am but my life isn't over. I'm only thirty-four. I've still got plenty of time to figure it all out. I don't have to be like Alice and have my career mapped out. Maybe I don't want a career. And that's fine too. Look at Alice, at how quickly her life changed. She never thought she'd be widowed so young, after only four years of marriage. And Bonnie. This time last year she thought she was Bonnie Fairborn, the only daughter of Clarissa and Jack Fairborn, living a lonely life, yearning for a large family, and now she finds out she's Holly Harper.

I pull up outside Viv's house. She answers after one knock and I suspect she saw me coming down the path.

'Tasha, what a lovely surprise.'

'Can I come in?' I say. I feel bad at what I'm about to do but it's the only way of seeing if my suspicions are right.

'Sure.'

I follow her into her pine kitchen and have flashbacks to those hideous few days after we returned from Venice and found out about Kyle's murder.

'Do you want a cuppa?'

'No, I'm fine, thanks. I'm on my lunch break.'

'I can make a sandwich?'

'I'm fine, really . . . Viv . . .' I hesitate and she looks at me expectantly. 'How did you get that scratch? It's quite nasty?'

'I already told you. It was Freddie Mercury. I was giving him a cuddle and –'

'Please don't lie to me,' I say. 'I think Zoë scratched you.'

343

Her eyes widen. 'What makes you say that?'

'You didn't have it that night in the pub. And then you told me and Aaron yesterday that you were the last one with Zoë. That she was with you when you locked up and that it was gone midnight.'

Viv's face flushes. 'Well, yes, she was but –'

'You told me that night that you thought she was trouble. I got the sense you didn't like her. So why did she hang back to talk to you while you were locking up?'

'I . . . well, I was just . . . We were smoking. Out the back . . .'

'Viv, you know the police think Aaron hurt Zoë?' I lie. I don't know if this is the case at all as they've not questioned him again. 'So if something happened between the two of you . . .'

Viv's chin wobbles. 'I saw the way she was, flirting with Aaron all night. I saw how upset you were as a result. She wasn't going to give up and I couldn't let her destroy you and Aaron. Not after everything you've been through. So when everyone left I asked her if we could have a word out the back. She helped me collect glasses – she was a bit tipsy by then, but I could see she wanted to get in with me, being Aaron's mum and all. I just wanted to warn her off Aaron, that's all. I never planned to hurt her. But we argued and she told me she knew Aaron liked her, really, deep down, despite him telling her otherwise. That you weren't good enough for him. She was obsessional, a fantasist. I told her she'd never have what she wanted and then – and then she pushed me. Hard. I hit the back of my head against the wall and I lost my temper. I'm not

344

proud of it, Tash. But she made me see red. Her smug face, the way she was going on about Aaron, so I pushed her back, quite hard. She caught the side of her head, her temple, against the metal edge of the lean-to but she seemed fine. Totally fine. She told me to go fuck myself, and then she stormed off. I promise you that when she left she was alive.'

'Then why haven't you told the police?'

She glances down at Freddie Mercury by her feet. 'I don't know. I'm afraid, I suppose. But I'm fed up with being afraid. I can't let Aaron get the blame for something that's not his fault. I wish I'd been braver with Clarissa. If I had, things would be so different. You believe me, don't you?'

'Of course I do. Do you want me to come with you to the station? We could talk to DC Chloë Jones? She's a nice detective.'

She nods. 'Okay, yes. Let me get my things.' She grabs her handbag and I notice how her hand trembles as she picks up her phone and then, together, her arm linked through mine, we leave the house.

When I arrive home later, DC Jones is in my kitchen, wrapped up in a thick padded coat and her usual stripy scarf, her fingers interlaced around a mug of tea. She's standing at the sink and Mum is seated at the table. Her eyes are misty and she's beaming.

'What is it?' I ask, wondering if it's about Viv. As far as I'm aware she's still at the station. I was hoping she'd be able to talk to DC Jones but she must be with Thorne.

Despite everything I feel a surge of protectiveness towards Viv. I hope Thorne's not giving her a hard time.

'Bonnie's DNA is a familial match,' Mum cries. 'She really is Holly. As soon as I saw her I just knew it.'

I feel a burst of joy. I couldn't let myself believe it until this moment.

'And does it match the DNA on the rug?' I ask.

'No. It doesn't,' says DC Jones. 'And neither does Zoë's.'

I take off my coat and hang it over the back of the chair as this information seeps in.

'Could it be contaminated DNA?' Mum asks, breaking the silence.

'It's a possibility. We still have the murder weapon that was found at Zoë's, but neither her fingerprints nor her DNA are on it. And now we can't place her at the murder scene either. So . . .' she lifts her shoulders '. . . it's a lot trickier but, with the notes she sent to you and her past history, we still believe she's our main suspect. But we'll keep you informed.'

Pushing its way through my joy at having my little sister back is fear. Because how can we truly relax until we know for certain whose blood was found on my rug and what part that person played in Kyle's murder?

PART FIVE

48

JEANETTE

Friday, 13 December 2019

It's a Friday night and Jeanette, Tasha and Bonnie are sitting in Alice's beautiful kitchen. Nearly two months have passed since Bonnie came back into Jeanette's life. Two wonderful months where she got to spend time with her daughter, her wonderful, kind, caring daughter, who is everything Jeanette hoped she would be and more. A lot has happened since Bonnie came knocking at the door.

The remains at the bottom of the garden did belong to Clarissa and Jack's adopted baby, the real Bonnie Fairborn. Jack has subsequently been arrested but no charges were brought against him because the police believed he didn't know.

Then Viv was charged with something called 'unlawful act manslaughter' because the head injury wasn't deemed enough to cause Zoë's death, only to have 'contributed'. Even so, she was given a twelve-month suspended sentence. Jeanette realizes it will take her a long time to be anywhere near close to forgiving Viv for what she did all those years ago. She might have helped Bonnie come back into her life, and for that she's grateful, but she'll never understand how Viv could have kept her suspicions about what Clarissa had done to herself for so long.

She's so happy at how easily Bonnie has slipped into their lives. A few weeks ago Bonnie returned to Birmingham but she keeps in touch and they make sure to meet up regularly. Jeanette has not returned to France and has asked Eamonn to pack up the house and send her stuff back. He said he'll make sure to deliver it personally and Jeanette felt a strange type of thrill about seeing him again. He's arriving next week.

Jeanette has rented a little flat for the meantime but Tasha's been talking about moving away. Aaron has been applying for jobs in Bristol and Tasha is thinking about retraining as a teaching assistant. 'I like being around kids,' she'd said. 'I'd like to work in a primary school. I know I'm not a high flier like Alice . . .' And Jeanette had shushed her and told her to stop comparing herself, that she was equally proud of all her daughters. All three of them.

The only cloud that continues to hang over them all is that nobody has been caught for attacking Kyle and Alice. They've talked extensively about it, bandying around different theories: Alice is convinced the DNA must have been contaminated somehow and that Zoë was responsible even with no concrete evidence. Aaron thinks it might have been the Knight brothers and that they'd lied about their plans to burgle the house the night *after* the attack and that they'd used Zoë as a scapegoat (after admitting to them that Zoë and the Knights were involved in illegal dealings at the garage). Jeanette still isn't sure what to think. She knows Tasha is still bothered about it, though, and she doesn't blame her. She knows that's one of the reasons Tasha wants to move.

'What's happening about Kyle's company?' Jeanette asks now. They have just finished a magnificent lamb tagine that Alice cooked and are polishing off an expensive bottle of wine – Jeanette doesn't know its name but it's definitely superior to anything she's tasted before. This is the first time Bonnie has been to the house and Jeanette is amused to see how she's spent most of the day in wide-eyed wonder. Jeanette still feels that way too. It's a shame the house will be sold, but it's way too big for just Alice.

'The tech side is in the process of being sold. As I suspected the health app never got off the ground without Kyle driving it. He was such a perfectionist.'

'Really?' says Tasha. 'He didn't strike me in that way. That sounds more like you.' She laughs as she says it but there's an edge to her voice, which surprises Jeanette.

Alice seems not to notice. She just laughs sadly. 'Yep. That's another thing we had in common. But our names would have been on this app. Our reputations. *My* reputation. So it would have had to be top notch. And, when Kyle died, there were still too many things wrong with it.'

'Will you get money from the sale?' asks Tasha, her gaze curious, and Jeanette squirms. Why is Tasha being so nosy?

'No. Not really. By the time the investors have been paid off there won't be much left over. Because Kyle isn't around to run it, or to oversee the hand-over, the company has lost a lot of value. The company *was* Kyle.'

'Where will you live when this place is sold?' asks Bonnie, softly, blushing as she speaks. She still seems a bit intimidated by Alice, and Jeanette can understand why. On paper Alice is intimidating.

Alice pours herself another glass of wine and Jeanette admires how strong she's been throughout all of this, although she does worry that her daughter is so busy throwing herself into work and sorting out Kyle's estate, so that Connor gets what's rightfully his, as well as selling Kyle's company, that she hasn't given herself the proper time to grieve. 'I'll go back to my own apartment in Notting Hill where I lived before – before I met Kyle, which I've been renting out ever since.'

'That was a wise move,' says Jeanette. She's sitting beside Alice, at the head of the table, and reaches over to pat her hand. There are no more outward signs of trauma but Jeanette knows from experience that it will take Alice a long time to heal inwardly.

'But . . .' Alice gazes at them, eyes shining '. . . I've won an award at work. For some research I've been doing.'

Jeanette stands up to throw her arms around her. 'That's wonderful, well done, sweetheart,' she says. Tasha and Bonnie get up to congratulate her too.

'The Colworth Medal for my cell research into . . .' She laughs. 'Basically I made some important discoveries in the way we look at certain illnesses, like cancer. I'm beyond thrilled.'

'I'm not going to ask you to explain what you did to win the award,' says Tasha, 'because I doubt we'd understand it.'

Bonnie giggles. 'Very true,' she says, looking at Alice in awe.

'Well, this is definitely a cause for celebration,' says Jeanette, raising her glass. 'To Alice.'

'To Alice,' Tasha and Bonnie chorus.

'And to Bonnie,' says Alice, her glass still raised. 'For coming back into our lives and making our family feel whole again.'

'To Bonnie,' they all cheer, and as Jeanette glances towards the end of the table she wishes Jim was still alive to see this.

49

TASHA

Friday, 13 December 2019

Alice and I are sitting on the magenta sofas in the living room after Mum and Bonnie have gone to bed. The only light is from a small lamp and the fire crackling in the hearth. The atmosphere is cosy, with shadows flickering on the smoke-coloured walls. Alice is sipping the rest of her wine on the sofa at a right angle to me. I tuck my feet underneath me.

Ever since the results have come back stating that the DNA found at the crime scene didn't match Bonnie's I've been obsessing about it. Unless Mum has any other children sequestered away, which she assures me she doesn't, I still can't understand the findings at our house.

'Bonnie's great, isn't she?' Alice says, smiling into her glass. 'We're so lucky she didn't turn out to be some weirdo.'

'Did you ever find out who the woman at the conference was? And who wrote the notes pretending to be from Holly?'

Alice leans forward to put her empty wine glass on the coffee-table. 'No. I think it must have been a hoax. Or maybe it was Zoë, after all. I know the police never found any evidence to suggest she wrote me letters but . . .' She shrugs and sits back against the soft cushions.

'But you've seen a photo of Zoë. You didn't think it was her.'

Irritation crosses Alice's face. 'I don't remember, to be honest, Tash, and I no longer care. We've found Holly so I don't know why you're still going on about it.'

I shift my legs from underneath me and sip my tea. I should go to bed. Alice looks like she's about to get up when I say, 'I've been thinking a lot about that DNA found in our house and I wonder if your friend Ellen would mind if I called her.'

Alice's face is partly in shadow, making her cheekbone look sharper. She raises her eyebrows. 'Why on earth would you need to speak to Ellen?'

'She's a geneticist, isn't she?'

'Yes.'

'Well, she might be able to explain why DNA was found that was similar to ours but wasn't from one of us.'

Alice shuffles, uncrossing her legs. 'Do you really want to rake it all up? Does it matter? It could be cross-contamination. The police have reassured us of this too.'

'I'm just interested, I suppose. I'd like to know who's been in our house. Don't you want to know if we've definitely worked out who attacked you and killed Kyle?'

'It was either the Knight brothers or Zoë. I think it was most likely a burglary gone wrong. The Knights said themselves that they'd planned to break into your house. We'll never know for sure but the police still think it was Zoë and that they just don't have enough evidence to prove it.'

'It doesn't explain the DNA . . .'

Alice waves her hand dismissively. 'It's obviously an anomaly. It can happen.' She folds her arms. 'Why are you so interested all of a sudden?'

'It's not "all of a sudden", Al. I've been thinking about this for a long time. I dunno, I suppose I feel there are questions that haven't been answered and it kind of unnerves me a bit. I can't wait to sell our house. It's got too many unpleasant memories now.'

'Fair enough. That's how I feel about the Venice apartment. I've arranged for that to be sold too. I can't see myself wanting to go back without Kyle.'

I feel a wave of sympathy for her. I know she'd give up all her wealth and career success to have Kyle back. I think of Aaron at home with the twins. Our relationship has improved greatly over the last two months. He doesn't go out drinking as much and wants to spend more time with me and the girls.

'Anyway,' Alice stands up, 'I'm off to bed. It's been a long week and I'm exhausted.'

I stand up to give her a hug. 'I'll just stay here, if that's okay and finish my mint tea,' I say.

'Sure.' She flashes me a smile and leaves the room. I sip my tea, looking into the dying embers of the fire, my mind whirling. Then I pick up my phone and google Dr Ellen Bright. It can't hurt to have a little chat with her, can it?

I have the chance to talk to her the next day. I've popped out early while the others are in bed. I couldn't find her

356

mobile number on Google, only an office one, and because it's Saturday it's doubtful anyone would be there. So I snuck into Alice's study after she'd gone to bed last night and found all her contacts on her laptop.

I stand on the Heath with a view of the city spread out in front of me, like a screensaver. I love Hampstead with its village feel and green spaces, and it seems a shame that Alice won't stay around here, although I can understand why. I sit on a bench. It's still early for a Saturday, not yet nine, and I hope I don't wake Ellen as I dial her number. I wait as it rings, watching the dog walkers and the joggers and the mums with young babies in prams and toddlers in push-chairs, and I think about my own girls, my precious twins, and the twinge of guilt I feel at being here, without them, on a crisp, chilly December morning, but also enjoying the calm and peace.

'Hello.'

I'm so busy thinking about my life and family back in Chew Norton that I start at the sound of Ellen's voice.

'Oh, hi. Ellen? This is Tasha. Alice Harper's sister. We met at Kyle's funeral.'

'Oh, yes.' Her voice brightens. 'So lovely to hear from you. How are you? Are you in London?'

'Yes. In Hampstead, staying with Alice.' I angle myself away from a jogger who decides to rest next to me on the bench. 'I hope it's okay to call you like this, out of the blue, but I have a few questions about DNA, and as you're a geneticist I wondered if I could ask you.'

'Sure. Hold on a sec . . .' I can hear rustling, then her muffled voice asking for a caramel macchiato to go.

'Thanks.' She comes back on the line. 'Sorry, I'm in Star-bucks. What would you like to ask?'

I explain about the DNA found in the house, how it wasn't Bonnie's or Zoë's.

'Right,' Ellen says, digesting the information. The jogger next to me gets up and continues his run.

'So I suppose the question I'm asking is, whose could it be?'

'Oh.' She laughs. 'That's easy. It would be Alice's.'

'What?' I feel a flicker of irritation. I thought Ellen was supposed to be super-intelligent. 'No, it was a close match to Alice's and to mine. The police described it as familial DNA.'

'Sorry, I'm not being clear enough. What I meant to say was that Alice is a chimera.'

Why does that term ring a bell? I rack my brains but I can't think where I've read it before. 'What's a chimera?'

'A chimera is someone who has more than one set of DNA. In layman's terms it usually occurs when a person has shared a womb with another, like in a twin pregnancy, but if one of the embryos dies early in the pregnancy it can be absorbed by the surviving twin, which results in that person having two sets of DNA.'

I think of Alice's talk of Mum's vanishing-twin preg-nancy with her. But when I asked Mum about it she'd denied it. 'Would my mum have known she was carrying twins?'

'Not necessarily,' says Ellen. 'It usually happens very early in a pregnancy, before a scan.'

'So how did Alice know about this?'

'She only found out fairly recently. She was helping me with some research I was doing. I tested her DNA. I ended up having to test it a few times for reasons I won't bore you with, but when I looked at the results I noticed it. It was amazing, really. It's quite rare because most of the time we'd be unaware of it.'

'So Alice knows she has two sets of DNA?' I clarify.

'Yes. Of course. It was all very exciting when we found out.'

'So,' I take a deep breath, trying to quell my nausea that Alice has not said anything about this, given the sample at our house. 'So that's why there was an unfamiliar set of familial DNA found at the crime scene when Kyle and Alice were attacked,' I say, more to myself.

I hear Ellen swallow a sip of her coffee. 'Yes, one set would have been in her blood, for example. And one in her tissue, like her skin or saliva. So if Alice's blood was found at the scene – which it would have been because she was attacked – and they compared that with one taken from her skin or saliva, they wouldn't have matched.'

The blood on the rug was Alice's all along. Yet she would have known this. So why didn't she say?

'Thank you so much,' I say to Ellen. I need to get off the phone. My mind is whirring with so many unanswered questions.

'Glad to help. It's fascinating stuff,' she replies cheerfully. 'If you need to know anything else please give me a ring.'

I end the call, unable to move from my seat. An elderly woman comes and sits down at the other end of the bench and smiles at me, but I can't make my facial muscles move. I feel as frozen as the ice on the nearby lake.

Then I remember exactly where I'd seen the word 'chimera' before.

The night I was staying with Alice and found out she had been lying about Connor. It was in her search history.

So why had she lied?

50

ALICE

Sunday, 13 October 2019

Alice must eventually fall asleep because when she opens her eyes, with a start, some hours later, she's covered with sweat and her heart is beating fast. She lies there for a few seconds, listening, trying to calm her breathing.

She nudges Kyle. He opens his eyes. 'Wh-what's going on?' he says groggily, as he shifts his weight onto his elbows. 'What's wrong?'

'I don't know . . . but I'm sure I heard something. Downstairs.'

Kyle sits bolt upright in bed and throws back the duvet. He steps onto the carpet. He's only wearing his boxer shorts and he seems a bit unsteady on his feet. 'I'm sure it's nothing but I'll just go and check.'

She clutches the duvet to her chin, her heart still racing. 'I can't remember locking the back door – the girls were in the garden earlier.'

'Stay here.' The moonlight casts a veil-like shadow over his bare shoulders.

'Okay,' she whispers, her heart hammering.

He disappears out of the bedroom door and she waits. And waits.

Then she grabs her dressing-gown and makes her way slowly downstairs.

This is it. This is the moment she's been waiting for.

When she gets to the bottom of the stairs she stops and listens. It sounds like Kyle is in the living room. Her heart beats fast. It's now or never. She wasn't planning on doing it here, with the twins sleeping upstairs, but she knows he went to see Eve today. Kyle is a rubbish liar. She checked his phone, saw his desperate text to his ex-girlfriend and their arrangement to meet up. Anger had flared, white-hot and vengeful when she'd read the message.

I need to tell you everything. I've made some stupid mistakes, Eve. And now I'm scared.

He'd promised Alice never to tell anyone and that they would sort it out together. Yet the first chance he gets he decides to blab. He can't keep his mouth shut, that's his problem.

She pulls on a pair of woolly gloves she'd shoved into the bars of the banister before going up to bed, and picks up the wrench propped in the hallway that she'd found in Aaron's toolkit. Her heart is pounding and her mouth is dry. Can she really do this?

But Kyle can't live. He just can't. She'd made that decision as soon as she saw his text message to Eve. He's going to leave a financial mess behind, she's certain of that, but she'll cope with it. She can cope with any of it, but not the loss of her job, her reputation. Nothing is more important to her than that. She's worked too hard

362

for it. It's what defines her. Once he'd spilt the beans to Eve that would be it. The start of a chain of events that would soon spiral out of control. And who else would he confide in?

Because the truth of the matter is, their wonder product, the thing that Kyle hoped would put him on the map, was failing.

She'd known for a while that it wasn't going to work. She'd tried everything to help get it off the ground, but it was flawed. She'd kept it from him as long as she could but it had all come to a head just hours earlier.

She remembers his accusation when she admitted it to him. She wishes now she'd never got involved in the first place. What is it they say? Never mix business with pleasure? Well, she's learnt the hard way about that.

He could be nasty. That's what a lot of people didn't know about Kyle. They were all blinded by his good looks, his charm. Just like she had been when they'd first met.

'You have to make this fucking app work,' he'd spat at her earlier, when the twins were in bed, his face contorted into something ugly. 'Because if you don't your reputation will be over. I doubt you'll be winning any awards at work. You'll be a failure, *sweetheart*, and we all know that word isn't in your vocabulary.'

She'd pacified him, of course. Because that was her role. But she knew the app wouldn't work. They'd tried everything. 'It will be fine,' she'd lied. 'I'll make sure to iron out all the problems.' She'd calmed him down and had felt a whoosh of relief when he didn't go into one of his dark moods. She couldn't risk that, not here with her precious nieces in the house.

But he wasn't stupid. He might not be a scientist but he'd soon see it was never going to work. She's known he's been involved with corrupt businessmen who have ploughed money into their app and who will want a return on it. And if they don't, who knows what would happen? There have been a few too many late-night meetings and recently Kyle's become jittery, always looking over his shoulder when they're out in London as though he's worried someone is following him.

Even the legitimate investors will want a return on their money. Kyle has lied to all of them, leading them to believe the product is way more advanced than it actually is to get them to hand over huge amounts of cash. She's only recently found out about something else, after speaking to one of them, a CEO in a big corporate law firm.

Failure is one thing. But corruption? Her good name dragged through the mud? Because she knows that if Kyle goes down, he'll drag her with him. Or, worse, he'll blame it all on her as the scientist behind the invention. Use her as a scapegoat. She knows he's more than capable.

She grips the wrench tightly in her gloved hand.

It's now or never. She has to surprise him or he'll overpower her. All evening she made sure to top up his wine glass so he'd be less sharp, less agile. She creeps to the door. It's half open and Kyle is standing with his back to her. She's shocked when she hears that he's hissing into his phone. 'I know you've got people following me. Get them to stop. I'm good for it. I told you.'

He ends the call and stands staring down at his phone, the light from the screen washing the otherwise dark room with a ghoulish light.

She has to do it now. While he's unaware. It will be quick. He won't know anything about it. This reassures her as she lifts the wrench and brings it down on the back of his skull as hard as she can. Once, then twice, in quick succession. He falls forwards, crashing to the floor with a gasping motion, dropping his phone onto the wooden floorboards with a clatter.

Alice begins to shake violently and vomit inches up her throat.

She takes a few deep breaths and then the adrenaline hits her. She needs to act. Now.

She creeps forwards, the wrench still in her hands and leans over him. He's on his side. His eyes are fluttering and her stomach rolls when she realizes he's not dead. His eyes meet hers and she sees the confusion in them, then horror. 'I'm sorry,' she whispers, kneeling beside him. 'I had no choice.' He reaches out as though to grab her but his eyes roll back into his head, his arm flopping to the floor.

When she's sure he's dead she takes the wrench and creeps through the house into the garden to hide it. Then she takes off her woolly gloves and mixes them into the basket of hats and scarves under the stairs.

Now for the bit she's been dreading most.

She makes enough noise to alert nosy Maureen next door and for it to look like an attempted burglary, then carefully steps over Kyle's body on the rug, and positions herself next to the sharp edge of the hardwood cabinet, bringing the back of her head down on it, three times, like she'd researched. Enough to make a reasonably superficial wound look worse than it is.

On the third attempt everything goes black.

51

TASHA

I'm still sitting on the bench, staring at my phone in shock when Alice's name flashes up on screen. It's been fifteen minutes since I spoke to Ellen but I can't move. I think of all the conversations I've had with Alice about the DNA. All the times when she could have given me an explanation, yet she never did.

I remember her telling me how she had absorbed her twin. 'I basically ate my twin,' she'd said. I'd been fascinated and repulsed, and relieved that she hadn't been born a twin. And when I'd asked Mum about it she'd had no clue. So Alice had never told her.

She deliberately kept to herself the information that she's a chimera. She pretended to be as confused as the rest of us when the police found the familial DNA, yet she would have known full well why it was there. She made us think it was Holly's when, all along, she knew it wasn't. Why?

I think of the letters from 'Holly', and the woman at the conference who, apparently, spoke to Alice. Was that even true? Or was that just a ruse to make us believe that 'Holly' was out there somewhere? Or to make the police chase a ghost? She's lied about Connor. What else has she lied about?

Why did she want everyone to believe Holly had come back?

I answer Alice's call.

'Hi, Tash. Where are you? We all came down for breakfast and you weren't here.'

'I – I just popped out.'

'Okay.' I sense a steeliness underneath her cheery tone and I wonder if Ellen Bright has rung her already to tell her of our conversation.

'You knew about your DNA?' I manage to say.

A pause. 'Where are you? I'll come and meet you.'

I give her directions and then I stay put. I watch as the old woman gets up, staggering away on her stick, to be replaced by a woman with her toddler. By the time Alice is striding across the Heath towards me, in a bobble hat, a padded designer coat and Burberry wellies, the bench is empty apart from me. My toes are freezing and so is my face but I can't move.

She sits down next to me. She's brought two coffees and I'm so grateful that I forget to be distrustful of her as I take it, using it to warm my hands.

'What's going on, Tash?' She sips her coffee and assesses me with her cool green eyes.

'Why would you lie? Why didn't you just tell the police that the other DNA belonged to you?'

She lets out a deep breath, which fogs in front of her. 'I honestly didn't think about all that when the police said they'd picked up this other DNA. I forgot, I suppose. I mean, I did have other things on my mind.'

I study her. She looks so calm, sitting there. So unruffled. Alice has always maintained she doesn't need to lie.

'I don't buy it, Alice. You wouldn't have forgotten. Why did you want us all to think Holly had come back? You'd have known that the DNA didn't belong to her.'

'My mind's been all over the place. It was ages ago when I found out about all that.' She sips her coffee but it's a feeble excuse and she knows it. 'I was on a lot of meds. I wanted to believe it belonged to Holly.'

She has an answer for everything. That's one thing I remember Mum saying about her. *Your sister has an answer for everything.*

'There's only one reason why someone wouldn't tell the police they were a chimera in that scenario,' I say, 'and that is if they wanted the police to be chasing a ghost. To put someone else at the scene of the crime.'

She doesn't reply. Instead she reaches into her pocket and pulls out a crumpled packet of cigarettes. I watch, surprised, as she lights one in front of me. Her gloved hand trembles slightly. I've not seen her smoke for years. It jogs a memory. 'Mum said she saw you by the pond the night after Zoë's death and you told her you'd gone out to smoke. What had you really been doing?'

'I was just taking a walk. Jesus.'

She has a sip of her coffee and places it next to her while she carries on smoking.

I think of Aaron's tyre wrench, which was suddenly discovered in Zoë's garage. Did Alice plant it there? Is that what she'd been doing that night when Mum saw her? The fields at the back of our house cut through to where Zoë lived.

'So, nothing to do with trying to set up Zoë?'

Her expression changes and she turns to me, her eyes hard. 'What are you trying to say? You do remember that I was attacked as well, don't you?'

'That injury could have been self-inflicted.'

She laughs. 'Seriously? That's doubtful. I don't know how I'd manage to give myself such serious injuries.'

I stare at her, my mind working overtime. She looks so calm. Apart from her shaky hand. She stubs out her cigarette and picks up her coffee, wrapping her fingers around the cup.

And then I think, this is Alice. *My sister.* She loved Kyle. She couldn't have orchestrated all this. She's been devastated by his death. She's not that great an actress. But she wanted us all to believe that the blood on my rug belonged to the intruder. To Holly, in fact. Why would she do that, upset Mum like that and give her false hope? Unless it was to provide her with a false suspect.

She rests her hand on my arm. 'Come on, let's get back to the house. We're going out for lunch.' She stands up. Her cheeks are flushed by the cold, a wisp of her copper hair, so like mine, blown into her face by the icy winds. I don't know what to do. What to think. Why would she want to get rid of Kyle? I remember her talking last night about the health app and her reputation. Was that why? To salvage her reputation? Was the app about to fail because of Kyle's shady dealings? Or because it was flawed? What had she been so scared of?

'This app wasn't as revolutionary as Kyle made out, was it?' I'm still sitting down and Alice is beginning to look impatient. 'Did you know it was fatally flawed?'

'What? Don't be ridiculous. It was as good as Kyle said. It just needed more time, that's all. And if Kyle had lived he'd have got it to work.' She blows on her gloved hands. 'Come on, let's go back to the house. It's cold.'

I ignore her. 'I think he was involved in something dodgy . . .' Alice opens her mouth to object but I charge on, regardless. 'I know you'll never admit it. You'd go to the ends of the earth to make out everything was wonderful. But here's what I think. Kyle had got himself wrapped up in these dubious, perhaps criminal, investors he owed money to. You found out about it. When you realized this health app wasn't going to work, you knew it would all blow up. You had your name – your prestigious, well-regarded name – attached to the project. It would discredit everything you'd achieved so far. So, your only solution to the problem was to get rid of Kyle. You knew you had two sets of DNA and that both would be picked up, making the police believe someone else had been there that night, knowing they would never be caught but casting doubt on the investigation. It was unlucky for you that Bonnie found us because you could no longer make out the DNA was hers. And then when Zoë died you thought you'd try to pin the blame on her. Although that was a bit desperate of you because Zoë's DNA wasn't going to be a match to the blood found at the crime scene.

371

Yet you didn't care about that, did you? Maybe you hoped the police would just put it down to contamination of the scene or something like that.' I stop, breathless, my heart beating fast.

She rolls her eyes but I can see it in her face. I can tell I've hit a nerve. 'Got quite the little story there, haven't you?' she says. 'Of course it's not true. And I'm actually hurt you'd think I'm capable of all that. I'm not a criminal. Or a murderer. Okay, yes, maybe Kyle wasn't as perfect as I've tried to make out. Marry in haste and repent at leisure.' She gives a mirthless laugh. 'Isn't that what they say? I didn't agree with how he treated Connor. I've tried to make amends there. He was single-minded, dishonest and, yes, involved in all sorts that I would do anything to stop getting out. Is that what you want me to say?'

Alice doesn't like to fail at anything. And she certainly wouldn't want to fail at her marriage, her career. To lose face. Sooner Kyle dead than the world know he was a disappointment. I stare at her. The problem is I no longer believe a word she says. I shake my head. 'I always thought we were close. But actually we're not, are we? Because you never let anybody see the real you. You always portray this glossy exterior to everyone, even your family, and you always have. None of us, me, Mum, even Dad when he was alive, really got to know the real you. You never confided in us, never opened up to us . . .'

'What are you talking about? That's rubbish. Look how I opened up to you at the hospital and when I came and stayed with you. The truth is, Tash, you've always been jealous of me. You might not want to admit it to yourself but you have. I saw the way you looked at Kyle. You wanted him so badly it was embarrassing. And you wanted my life. I know you wore my clothes in Venice.'

I stand up, propelled by a burst of anger. 'Stop trying to deflect this onto me. I'm not the one who lied about my DNA. Why would you do that otherwise?'

She takes a deep breath and closes her eyes. When she opens them she's resumed her calm exterior. 'I'm sorry. I shouldn't have said that. We can't fall out, Tasha. We're sisters and we love each other.' She comes closer to me and holds out a hand. There is a tiny hole in the thumb of her red glove. 'We've been through so much together. If Mum knew about any of this it would kill her. She's so happy. We've found Holly – Bonnie – after all these years. Don't ruin it. Please.'

I think of what this would do to our family if I told Mum about my suspicions. It would break her. I can't do it. I can't.

'Okay. But did you do it?' I ask, lowering my voice.

Her next words are spoken so softly I can barely make them out. 'You're right. I'll never admit it.'

I think of Viv covering for Clarissa for all those years by convincing herself she'd got it wrong. Can I go through life doing the same, turning a blind eye? And then I think of Mum and Bonnie, how happy they are, how much they have already been through, have already lost.

We'd do anything for the ones we love. I'm beginning to understand that now more than ever.

I'm faced with an impossible decision.

Alice's hand is still outstretched, waiting for me to take it. Time seems to stand still for a few moments, a kaleidoscope of memories shifting through my mind: us as kids curled up under a blanket dunking ginger nuts and watching *Byker Grove*, Alice buying me presents when she went on school trips, her standing up for me after I was arrested as a teenager, coming to see bands with me even though she didn't like them, sticking up for me if I fell out with friends, or boyfriends. My wingman. Always.

I reach for her hand, clutching it tightly.

Her expression is one of relief and tears appear in her eyes. 'Thank you,' she whispers.

We walk on in silence, crunching over the ice on the Heath, still holding hands, our breath fogging out in front of us.

She's my sister. What choice do I have but to stay quiet?

And if I keep telling myself that, maybe I'll finally start to believe it.

Acknowledgements

The Wrong Sister is my tenth book and I'm so excited that it will be my first hardback! I really enjoyed writing this book, and for that a huge thank you must go to my lovely friend Helen Thorburn. We were chatting about how, every year, her and her sister do a 'life swap' for a week, and it ignited a spark of an idea from which *The Wrong Sister* was born. (Everything else apart from the 'life swap' concept is totally made up, Helen, I promise!)

I also want to thank everyone at Penguin Michael Joseph, who always go above and beyond with every publication. To my wonderful editors Maxine Hitchcock (who shares my love of cake before lunch!) and Clare Bowron, who are insightful, intelligent, creative, kind, supportive, and make my books so much better than they would otherwise be. Also to the rest of the amazing team: Emma Plater, Ellie Morley, Olivia Thomas, Vicky Photiou, Beatrix McIntyre, Christina Ellicott, Sophie Marston, Kelly Mason, Hannah Padgham, and Laura Garrod. To Lee Motley for the beautiful and striking book jackets – I think *The Wrong Sister* jacket is my new fave! To Stella Newing and the audio team who do such a fantastic job on the audiobooks, and to Hazel Orme for her meticulous copy-edits as well as her enthusiasm, kind words and support. I'm so grateful to you all.

To Juliet Mushens, who is the agent of dreams, and who I've been lucky enough to work with now for ten years! I couldn't do this without her and can't thank her enough for changing my life! (A special mention to the cutest new addition, Seth, already showing his mummy's fantastic fashion sense!) I'm also indebted to Liza DeBlock, Kiya Evans, Rachel

Neely, Catriona Fida, Alba Arnau Prado, Emma Dawson, and the rest of the brilliant team at Mushens Entertainment.

To my foreign publishers, in particular to Eva Schubert and Duygu Maus at Penguin Verlag in Germany (*The Couple at No. 9* got to number 1 in Germany in 2023 and I can't thank them enough for all their hard work in making it happen!) Also to Sarah Stein at Harper US for continuing to believe in me and HarperCollins Canada.

To all my lovely friends who have been so supportive over the years and who continue to buy and read my books.

To my West Country author pals, Tim Weaver, Gilly Macmillan, C L Taylor, Chris Ewan and Cate Ray for all the laughs, support, texts, and lunches. And to the lovely LV Matthews for our regular meet-ups, Whatsapps and word races.

To the booksellers and librarians for getting my books into readers' hands, and to book bloggers for the reviews, cover reveals, and support.

To the readers who have bought copies of my books, for the kind messages and reviews. I'm so grateful.

To all the authors who have given their time so generously to read and quote for my books.

To my sister Dr Samantha Holly who is as bright and as brilliant as Alice (but that's as far as any similarities go — apart from the fact we both talk so fast when we are together that nobody else listening can understand us!), for answering any biochemistry questions, for being one of my first readers, for always being so enthusiastic. And for being my wingman. Always.

And, last but by no means least, a huge thank you to my husband, Ty, and my children, Claudia and Isaac, to my mum, dad, sister, nieces, in-laws and step family. I feel very lucky to be surrounded by such a loving and wonderful family and extended family, and this book is for you.

'Her best yet. Gripping, atmospheric and so original'
GILLIAN MCALLISTER

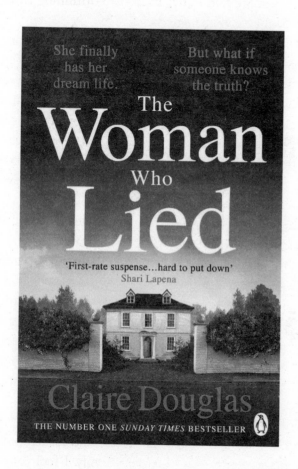

She finally has her dream life.

But what if someone knows the truth?

The
Woman
Who
Lied

'First-rate suspense...hard to put down'
Shari Lapena

Claire Douglas

THE NUMBER ONE *SUNDAY TIMES* BESTSELLER

'Claire Douglas at her very best'
TIM WEAVER

NURTURING WRITERS SINCE 1935

THE NO. 1 *SUNDAY TIMES* BESTSELLER

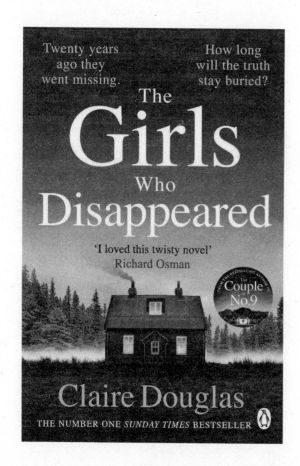

Twenty years ago they went missing.

How long will the truth stay buried?

The
Girls
Who
Disappeared

'I loved this twisty novel'
Richard Osman

FROM THE BESTSELLING AUTHOR OF
The
Couple
at No.9

Claire Douglas

THE NUMBER ONE *SUNDAY TIMES* BESTSELLER

'Clever. Gripping. Terrifically compelling'
SARAH PEARSE

NURTURING WRITERS SINCE 1935

'Twisty, nail-biting and utterly absorbing...you won't be able to put it down'
LOUISE O'NEILL

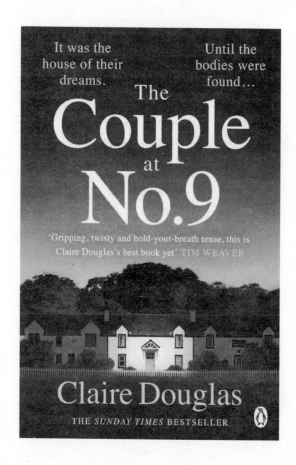

It was the
house of their
dreams.

Until the
bodies were
found...

The
Couple
at
No.9

'Gripping, twisty and hold-your-breath tense, this is
Claire Douglas's best book yet' TIM WEAVER

Claire Douglas

THE *SUNDAY TIMES* BESTSELLER

'Spine-chilling'
SUNDAY TIMES

NURTURING WRITERS SINCE 1935

'An immersive page-turner with a twist I didn't see coming'
SARAH VAUGHAN

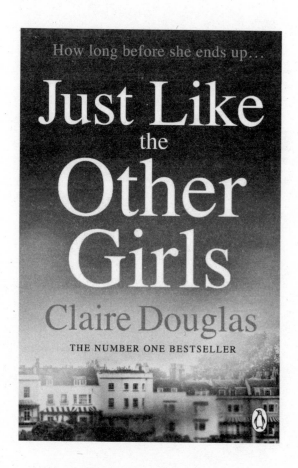

How long before she ends up...

Just Like

the

Other

Girls

Claire Douglas

THE NUMBER ONE BESTSELLER

'Intriguing. Twisty. Surprising'
DOROTHY KOOMSON

NURTURING WRITERS SINCE 1935

'A gripping page-turner'
JANE FALLON

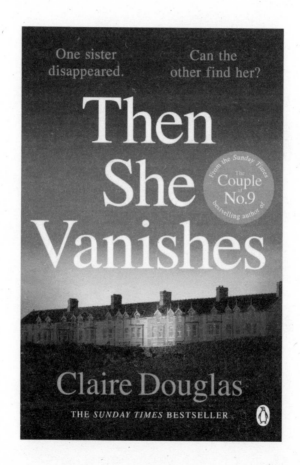

One sister
disappeared.

Can the
other find her?

Then
She
Vanishes

From the Sunday Times
The
Couple
No.9
bestselling author of

Claire Douglas

THE *SUNDAY TIMES* BESTSELLER

'Asks chilling questions about friendship,
loyalty, love and obsession'
GILLY MACMILLAN

NURTURING WRITERS SINCE 1935

'A chilling reminder that sometimes home is where the hurt is'
CARA HUNTER

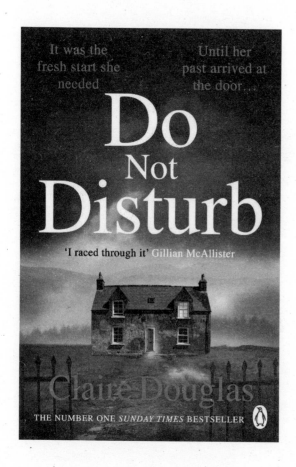

It was the fresh start she needed

Until her past arrived at the door....

Do
Not
Disturb

'I raced through it' Gillian McAllister

Claire Douglas

THE NUMBER ONE *SUNDAY TIMES* BESTSELLER

'Absorbing and chilling'
KAREN PERRY

NURTURING WRITERS SINCE 1935

'Fast-paced and chock full of twists'
PAULA DALY

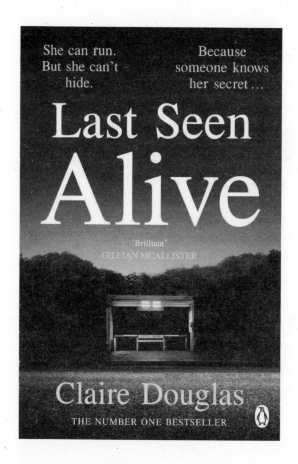

She can run.
But she can't
hide.

Because
someone knows
her secret ...

Last Seen
Alive

'Brilliant'
GILLIAN MCALLISTER

Claire Douglas

THE NUMBER ONE BESTSELLER

'Thrillingly tense and twisty – a great read'
B.A. PARIS

NURTURING WRITERS SINCE 1935